CODE 998
PRISONER

Gail McPartland

Code 998 Prisoner © 2018 by Gail McPartland. All Rights Reserved.

All rights reserved. No part of this book may be reproduced in any form or by any electronic or mechanical means including information storage and retrieval systems, without permission in writing from the author. The only exception is by a reviewer, who may quote short excerpts in a review.

Cover photograph by William Samson featuring actress Lisa Pentland. Cover Design by Andrew Weir.

Although this book is a work of fiction with fictional characters, it is based on actual events.

Gail McPartland
Facebook: gail.mcpartland.5
Twitter: @gail_mcpartland

*Previously published by Yolk Books as Code 998

NOTES FROM OTHER AUTHORS

'Kudos to Gail McPartland- it takes a brave author to tackle such a subject. This is a fascinating read that will be sure to make you think as well as feel.'

Michael J Malone

'The nightmare of the concentration camps should never be forgotten and Gail McPartland has found a new approach. This is moving, but terrifying stuff.'

Douglas Skelton

'A heart-rending story that tackles an often taboo subject with compassion and a depth of understanding. Gail McPartland conjures up the terrifying Zeitgeist of the Nazi concentration camps in her must-read debut novel.'

Barbara Stevenson

Gail McPartland

My sincere thanks to my family, especially my mother and my sister, Anne, and to my loyal friends who encouraged me to keep researching and writing through the many years I was bedbound with the debilitating condition, ME.

I would also like to thank Ayr Writers' Club and the many members who scrutinised my work and provided essential feedback; it truly is, 'A wee gem of a club.'

***

Congratulations!
By purchasing a new copy of this book, you have donated to the NSPCC, giving a child a chance of a decent future.

CHAPTER 1

Berlin, January 1943

'Nadette, it's for you,' Margo held the phone out to me. 'Not acceptable, Nadette. Not tonight.'

'S-sorry, Margo. I'll be as quick as I can.' As soon as Margo's back was turned, I spoke into the phone, 'Hello, Doctor Eichmann speaking.'

An anxious voice whispered back, 'Nadette. It's Ariella.'

I glanced around to ensure no one was paying attention to me. 'Ariella. What're you doing? You shouldn't be phoning.'

'We have to leave tonight.'

'Tonight? Ariella, that's impossible.'

'No choice, girl, we've got to go. There's been a development since I saw you earlier.'

'Oh no, what now?'

'I'll explain later. Get here. Quick as you can.'

Our lounge was packed with Nazis. And Kaarl was nearby, engrossed in conversation with another SS Gruppenführer. Escape was impossible.

'I can't, Ariella, I'm sorry. Can't you wait till morning?'

'No, it's arranged. Ten o'clock tonight.'

Kaarl glanced over. I turned away from him. My throat was tightening but I somehow mustered the strength to encourage Ariella, 'You must stick to the plan, go without me. Please.'

'No. This is your chance. Damn it, Nadette.' I heard a thud as though she had slammed her fist down. There was a pause before she spoke again. A softened voice. 'Ten o'clock tonight, Nadette. We'll wait for you.'

I scanned the room, frantically trying to come up with an escape plan. 'I'll see what I can do. But, Ariella, you must leave without me if I'm not there by ten.'

CHAPTER 2

Kaarl was still talking to his old friend, Otto Schreiner, a powerfully built man in his early thirties whose thin moustache was as sparse as the dark hair on his head. He wore small, round glasses enhancing his beady, grey eyes. The tall men stood impeccably dressed in their grey, SS Gruppenführer uniforms with champagne coupe in hand, sipping the Dom Perignon, continually replenished by the housemaid doing her rounds. Their heads were tilted back, they had that superiority look.

I took a deep breath and walked towards them.

'K-Kaarl, I need... I need to see a patient.'

I felt so petite and fragile against Kaarl; my head was barely in line with his muscular shoulders. Kaarl scowled and tightened his lips. He discarded my dilemma with a backhand flip of his wrist as though he was swatting away an annoying fly. Then with a gentle stroke of his fingers, he swept away a stray blonde curl from his forehead and leaned in closer to Otto to continue his conversation with the man of equal rank.

'K-Kaarl. Please. It's urgent.'

Kaarl's eyes widened. He shot me a look. A tingle ran down my spine. Otto scowled at me as though to remind me I had an inferior position in the world. I cowered down, losing at least two inches from my already average height.

Kaarl's face was drained white. Anger glaring from his eyes.

Otto quickly interrupted, 'Right, time we had a toast.'

Kaarl gave Otto a half smile and tipped his head in agreement with his request.

Otto clinked on his glass to attract the crowd's attention. Nobody seemed to hear the faint tapping. The chatter continued. Kaarl's lips tightened. About twenty SS men and an equal number in women haunted our spacious lounge. The maid glided among them carrying the buffet. The warm, roasted chicken, hot pork and beef presented on silver platters had a floating aroma that could attract the attention from even those with virtually no sense of smell, yet all eyes fell on Otto Schreiner when Kaarl roared, 'Quiet. Otto wishes to make a toast.' The silence was instant as if a babbling radio had just been turned off. Nobody moved an inch.

A clatter behind me disturbed the hush in the room. It was Kaarl's mother. She was only in her fifties but she was so frail. Margo must have stumbled over the Persian rug and knocked over a vase, shattering it to small fragments on the highly polished, marble floor. Her mouth gaped open, terror struck. I reached out and grabbed her arm to steady her. She shrugged me off and insisted on bending to gather up the smashed porcelain. The neatly rolled up, grey chignon, bobbed about her head as she collected the broken pieces. Her stylish, long dress trailed on the floor.

'Mother!'

'Sorry, son, sorry.' Margo's face was ashen. She gripped her walking stick and forced her unsteady body to stand to attention. Despite Margo's imminent death from cancer, the poor woman was still petrified of her son's outbursts.

Kaarl focused his attention back on Otto who stood waiting to commence his speech. Everybody in the room seemed to stand in awe of the leader, as though anticipating an excellent toast.

Otto began his speech, 'Well you all know, Kaarl and I have been friends for years, shoulder to shoulder through the ranks in the SS. Well he's finally done it, he's outranked me.' He paused and reached up and placed his hand on Kaarl's shoulder, 'Thirty three years old and Kaarl's made it to chief in the Gestapo.'

Ha, the Gestapo, I thought. Otto said that like it was something to be proud of. They were the sleazy, Secret State Police who walked into people's lives and arrested them on the spot without question. Every German was terrified of them.

Otto continued to praise Kaarl, 'His dedication to his work and his passion to put an end to homosexuality in Germany has earned Kaarl the promotion.' He turned to his comrade, 'Going to catch them all, Kaarl?'

Kaarl raised his glass. 'Every single one, Otto. No exceptions.'

'Yes, catch those filthy queers, son. If your father was alive today, he would be so proud of you,' Margo shouted over. Her tone was harsh and her fist was clenched. She spoke with such pride for her son.

Kaarl glared at his mother, silencing her. Otto smirked at Kaarl then turned towards the others and raised his glass, 'To Kaarl, new chief in the Gestapo.'

I glanced around the room, watching the puppets, foolishly obeying their master. I refused to toast and edged away from Kaarl. He was too preoccupied, lapping up attention and didn't seem to notice me slipping away.

Kaarl raised his glass again, 'To the Master Race.'

A mumbled response from the crowd. I still refused to toast and moved further towards the door.

A high-pitched, male voice near the door startled me, 'Sir? What about Jewish homosexuals?' he shouted over the crowd.

A creepy silence descended upon the room. The crowd separated like the parting of the Red Sea and exposed the culprit who dared to speak out against Kaarl. A young man, kitted out in full SS dress. He was barely eighteen. His widened eyes and gaping mouth, confirmed he realised his own stupidity.

Kaarl's face drained in colour and fell into a scowl. 'Since when were Jews included in the Master Race?'

Everyone, including myself, froze. Staring. Anticipating another explosion from Kaarl.

Kaarl paused then laughed; a forced laugh.

'Jews. Ha. Good to see the boy has a sense of humour.'

Everybody's shoulders dropped, visible tension released.

'Pointless rehabilitating them, Kaarl, eh?' somebody called out.

'Useless, not worth saving.' They joined in with the laughter and clattered their glasses together and rattled off more derogatory comments about Jews. The red-faced soldier forced a quivering smile and with a shaking hand, he sipped his drink.

Beside the young boy was a short man, not much taller than me. He was more concerned with the buffet than any toast. His tunic lay open at the neck and a button had popped open at his oversized, beer belly; a belly that could've taken his thirty odd years to acquire. The portly SS Gruppenführer swept away a dark wave from his untidy, greasy hair tumbling over his forehead. He stretched his arm over the abundant food table, sinking his heavy stomach into a Wedgwood gravy-boat.

He was the only one at the buffet. I edged towards him to stand closer to the door, planning a sharp exit. He didn't seem to notice me creeping up. I was sure he was pulling faces and mimicking the laughter in the room. He flinched when he realised I had spotted him and stared at me with dark green eyes as wide as a terrorised cat's. I stood, equal height in my heels, holding my breath, eyes as wide as his.

The chubby man gave me the once over. His lips curled to a smile. He threw a chicken leg into the bin and dragged his sleeve across his mouth then smeared his hand over his tunic, wiping away greasy remnants. Still masticating with meat slivers sticking in his teeth, he extended his grimy hand and introduced himself, 'Eric Hagen, Kaarl's...' he paused as though to consider an appropriate title. 'I'm Kaarl Bergmann's friend.'

I made no attempt to shake his grubby hand and cupped my hand over the other, holding on tight to my glass. I merely tipped my head, acknowledging his introduction. 'Nadette Eichmann,' was all I replied. I had no desire to tell him I was Kaarl's fiancée. That was a title I preferred to omit.

'Eric!' It was Kaarl.

A hush fell upon the crowd again. Eric froze. His jaw dropped revealing partially chewed chicken. His eyes stared wide without daring to blink. 'I-I was only-'

'Raise your glass, man,' Kaarl shouted, clearly oblivious to Eric mocking his colleagues. 'And tidy yourself up. You're a disgrace to the German people.'

Eric buttoned up his tunic with trembling hands. I was quite astonished at his swift obedience considering he held the same rank in the SS as Kaarl.

Kaarl's attention had shifted to me. He glowered. I squeezed tight on my glass in an attempt to stop my hands from trembling. Everybody looked in my direction. Not a sound in the room. Kaarl jerked his neck, as if he had just given a last tug on a fishing rod, reeling me over to stand beside him.

I walked across the marble floor, the sound from my stiletto heels pierced through my eardrums with every step. I reached Kaarl's side but stood closer to his mother who was wobbling, uneasy on her feet. Kaarl put his arm around my shoulder, yanked me over and put an end to the awkward silence in the room, 'And another toast, to me and my fiancée, to be married as soon as we've won the war.'

He raised his glass to his attentive audience. Men and women alike replicated his gesture and called out in response, 'To Kaarl and Nadette.'

Then the strangest thing happened. Kaarl turned towards me. For a second I thought he was almost proud to be my fiancé. The blueness in his eyes seemed to sparkle. He took a deep breath and an incongruous, warm smile crossed his face, he had momentarily dropped his façade. But quicker than he could expel his bad breath, his demeanour changed. Barriers re-erected. His face reverted back to its usual harshness. Kaarl resumed control of his emotions. He scowled at me and tipped his head towards my glass. 'Drink. Now.'

I feigned to take a sip.

Kaarl turned back to the crowded room and addressed his captive audience, 'Drink up, everyone, and enjoy the rest of the evening.'

Upon instruction, his entourage gulped down a champagne mouthful then engaged in conversation. Kaarl downed his drink in one. He dropped his arm from my shoulder and touched his palm on my wrist, warning me to stay by his side. He turned back to engage in conversation with his friend, Otto, the man who had just bolstered his ego with his exemplary speech on Kaarl's promotion to chief in the Gestapo.

I was reluctant to interrupt them but my failed attempt to slip away left me with no choice, I had to ask for Kaarl's permission again. I checked my Rolex, a gift from Kaarl to ensure I returned home prompt after my allocated time for my Doctor's rounds. It was after nine already. Ariella and the others would be waiting. I sat my glass down.

'K-Kaarl, can I go now please? My patient sounded quite poorly.'

There was an overpowering waft of perfume. Margo had crept up beside me. 'She can't leave here,' Margo aired her views to her son.

My heart went out to the poor woman. She had been brainwashed and had succumbed to her inferior position as a Nazi housewife and was very much trying to convert me to be the same.

Kaarl stood with fresh glass in hand. Without casting a glance in Margo's direction, Kaarl pursed his lips and breathed heavily through his nose. He casually wiped away a microscopic dust speck from his otherwise perfect uniform. He glowered at me. I shrunk down to a timid posture, wringing my hands together, 'Kaarl. Please. I'm sorry, I'm sorry, I have to see my patient.'

Margo interfered again, 'Your place is here. You need to put an end to this Doctor business.'

Even Otto joined in and had a go at me, 'This is not right.'

Kaarl raised his hand as though to halt squabbling children, 'Enough.' He paused and with an icy tone he tackled Otto, 'So where's Ingrid, Otto? Shouldn't your wife be here for you?'

Otto seemed taken aback and quite flustered. He stammered out an explanation, 'Oh she's, she's not well.' Silenced from then on.

Kaarl slammed his hand on the table, my champagne glass wobbled but steadied itself, determined not to fall over. 'Who is this patient?'

Margo forced a cough and exaggerated her difficulty in breathing. She was determined to keep me there with her son even if that meant emotional blackmail. She was an expert at that. 'It's a disgrace, you should be here. Kaarl needs you. I need you.'

I touched her arm and smiled, 'I know.'

Margo turned to Kaarl, 'If your father was alive today, he would've been disgusted. I waited home for your father every night. Nadette should be home for you,' she dared to shout at Kaarl through her laboured breathing. Kaarl frowned at her, I could read his thoughts, his mother had waited for his father all right, waited every night but Sven seldom showed up.

I touched Kaarl's arm for his attention. My stomach was churning. 'But my patient, Kaarl?'

'Jew?' his voice was quiet and calm.

'Wh-What?'

'German Doctors are not permitted to treat Jews,' he casually reminded me then roared, 'Are you handling Jews?'

A few heads spun around and most people ceased their conversation. Kaarl quivered his hand at them like an eighteenth century king ordering his jokers to continue with their performance. He turned his attention back to me and raised his thick, blonde eye brows waiting for my response.

I dipped my head to make the lie easier, 'No, Kaarl, no, 'course not. I avoid touching anything I despise,' I said and looked up at him.

He pouted his thick lips, looked me up and down and rubbed his forehead with two fingers. 'Go. For now,' and wafted his hand to dismiss me.

I forced a smile and tipped him a grateful nod then scurried towards the door.

In the hall, I grabbed my medicine bag and coat. Before I could don the fur, I heard the door creaking open behind me. Kaarl rushed out from the busy room and lunged towards me. He grabbed me by the throat and pinned me against the wall.

'If I find out it's a Jew you're treating-'

'P-Please, Kaarl, don't.'

The door creaked open again behind Kaarl. Eric Hagen, the slob whom I had the displeasure of almost shaking hands with, strolled out nonchalant, whistling. He reached below his fat belly for his zip.

Kaarl turned round, still grasping my throat and glared at Eric. He froze to the spot, mouth gaping. He glanced past Kaarl and stared at me. I beckoned his help with pleading eyes. Eric's chest rose rapidly up and down. His hands went up in submission. He tipped his head at Kaarl then smoothed back the stray, greasy hair from his face and about turned and pulled the door closed behind him.

Laughter roared from inside the room followed by Otto Schreiner's loud, masculine voice, 'Kaarl. Where the hell are you? Come on man, get in here.'

Kaarl squeezed so tight on my neck I could feel the blood rushing to my face. I was sure I was going to pass out. 'You have one hour.' He swiftly retracted his fingers as though he had recoiled from a prickly rose bush. He straightened up his uniform and dusted it down before pushing the door back open to rowdy laughter and bubbly conversation.

I grasped my throat and sighed with relief. I turned to look in the overhanging, gilt mirror; an artefact left by the Jewish, former owners of the house when Kaarl and his family stole the villa and its contents from them. Ribbon held curtain swags were magnificently carved into the mirror's border, but its centre reflected nothing more than the poor image of a fatigued and crushed twenty-nine year old woman. My pale blue eyes functioned as the windows to a shattered soul. I tilted my head to the side and observed the crimson marks where Kaarl branded me, yet again, in another vicious attack. No emotion reflected from the face I watched in the mirror. I pulled up my silk scarf with trembling hands and concealed Kaarl's brutality.

Without wasting any more time, I snatched my medicine bag and bolted across the marble floor towards the exit and yanked the door open. An icy wind caught my breath.

Kaarl shouted out from the lounge, 'No point in treating Jews anyway, they'll soon be extinct.' Raucous laughter followed from his guests.

I paused before venturing outside. Something wasn't right. I slammed the door shut, still inside. I tiptoed into Margo's bedroom next to the staircase and peered through a gap in the door.

A few seconds later, an SS soldier rushed out from the celebration. It was the young man who had received a severe ticking off from Kaarl after his concern for homosexual Jews. He raced across the hall heading for the door.

I knew Kaarl had let me go too easily.

I waited and listened. The young man didn't return. I tiptoed over and eased the door open but shuddered to a halt. My medicine bag, it was still inside.

Heart racing, I crept back across the floor. The door to the celebration room was ajar. Through the gap, I saw some uniformed men surrounding the buffet table. Eric Hagen, naturally, was nearby. He was about to sink his teeth into another chicken leg when he froze as though sensing my presence. He turned towards me. I was immobilized to the spot like a defenceless animal caught by its predator. Eric cocked his head to the side and frowned at me curiously. He didn't strike me as a man who was concerned about the Nazi movement, or indeed, about any activities of the military partners. Nevertheless, I couldn't take any chances. I daren't move an inch. I stared at him and awaited his reaction.

He twitched his upper lip, shrugged his shoulders and turned his attention back to his food. I reached inside the bedroom door and seized my forgotten medicine bag. Loud laughter bellowed from the celebration room, perfect timing for me to scarper across the hall and escape. Two sentries were up at the other end of the pavement, chatting over a shared cigarette. I slipped out and headed off in the other direction.

CHAPTER 3

I hurried along through the Mitte District, the holding place for many Jews who were still in Berlin. The street was pitch black. The only visible light was from my dimmed torch. It was bright enough to take in my dismal surroundings. Shops and stores, labelled with a yellow Jewish star, abandoned with windows smashed. Boulders lying among the broken glass. The few remaining operational stores, closed for the night. Their window display, Jews will not be served. Even the local library, Jews denied entry.

'C'mon, Nadette,' I urged myself on and pulled the collar up on my fur coat. A feeble attempt to shield myself from the bitterness. The noise from my high heels, echoed through the dark streets. Icy patches slowed my pace. I slipped and almost fell several times. No point causing another casualty. I was almost there anyhow.

Reeking chimney smoke puffed in small clouds above the nearby tenement flats. I shone my torch on the doors, searching. A black Star of David was stuck to each entrance. A compulsory symbol ordered by the Nazis. Easier for round up when selected for deportation. The Jews were like trapped cattle waiting for their turn to be slaughtered.

An army truck skidded round the corner. I fumbled with the torch. It was difficult to find the switch with gloves on. I jumped into the front entrance to a nearby building and hid inside a musty doorway. The truck raced along past me and stopped further down the road.

I edged forward to peer out. My heart pounded. German soldiers rushed into a nearby entrance. A Jewish family, branded by a yellow star, dragged onto the street.

'Where are you taking us?' cried the young mother.

'You will be given accommodation and work,' the soldier said.

'But where? What about my children?'

The toddlers, a boy and a girl, clad in their pyjamas, dragged from their sleep. They yelled and cried for the safety of their mother's arms. A young soldier had gripped them round the waist, one in each arm. Their short legs dangled and kicked. The mother reached out to them. Tiny hands gripped her as she wrapped them in winter coats.

'Board the truck now. Everything will be explained at the Deportation Centre. Move it. Quick.' Another soldier flashed a torch light in her face.

They gathered their herd and caged them into the army vehicle. I so wanted to step out, do something. Do what? My help was limited. I wiped away a tear and stood, head resting against the wall. I closed my eyes and waited until it was safe to move.

At last, the truck engine kicked into gear. The soldiers left the street with the family, guilty, no doubt, for simply being Jewish.

I peered out to check the area was clear. Then scurried down the street searching for the appropriate apartment.

CHAPTER 4

Ariella ran her hands through her hair and paced the floor of the apartment, her trousers trailing the wooden floor in the small room. A room supposed to accommodate her whole family.

Her father, Amit Ish-Shalom, lay on a double bed taking up most of the floor space. A tattered blanket covered him while he slept. His breathing was shallow with a gentle wheeze. Ariella's father was only forty-nine but he looked much older. He had long greying hair, a whitish beard and a face so far drawn, every bone was highly visible. Nazi torment and loss of loved ones, were seriously telling on Ariella's father.

Her attention shifted to her dear friend who nervously poked at the remnants of a pitiful coal fire as though not quite sure what else to do. They were the same age, yet Ester Kolleck looked far from twenty-eight. She had a pretty face with petite features but was so grey and worn she looked closer to a woman in her forties. Her deliberate old-fashioned dress-style didn't help. Her long, brown hair was tied in a knot on the back of her head and she wore an old fashioned, long skirt with a hideous, baggy cardigan. Ariella suspected her phlegm-filled cough had a lot to do with her chosen appearance.

Ariella stopped pacing. 'Where's your luggage, Ester?'

Ester looked at Ariella with a blank stare then resumed her previous surreal stance, prodding with the poker as though hoping to find substance among the ashes.

'Ester, why the hell aren't you packed? Come on. Get your things. She ran at her and spun her round, 'Ester, we have to leave tonight. Come on.'

She jumped with fright and dropped the poker. A clatter on the hearth, Ariella's father stirred and groaned. Ester cowered down and glanced at Ariella through the side of her eyes with a gaze that begged her not to scold her. She stood there rubbing her hands together and mumbled, 'I've got to wait, Ariella. I can't go. I can't. I've got to wait.'

'For Goodness sake, Ester,' Ariella said and paced the room. She ran her hands through her hair again. At last, she was able to put a comforting arm around Ester's shoulder. Her voice was soft and calm yet straight to the point, 'Ester, they're not coming back.' She reached over and picked up a letter from behind the clock on the mantelpiece. 'There's nothing we can do for them now. You know we've got to get out of here tonight.' Ariella held the letter up to her face and reminded her, 'They're coming for my father tomorrow.'

Ester burst into tears, broken. 'No, no. They'll be back. They were only a few minutes late, only a few minutes.'

Ariella took her in her arms and hugged her tight against her chest, 'Ester, come on girl, you know they've gone to camp. Your brothers are strong, young boys. They'll be okay.' She stared over Ester's shoulder and shook her head.

Ester's body physically shook. She bowed her head and started to sob and there commenced another coughing fit. She clenched her shaking hands up over her mouth to silence her bark. It was no use. She spluttered and coughed. It was a sickly cough that rattled and made Ariella grimace and clear her own throat every time. Ariella patted and rubbed her back. Remnants from the last chest infection, she suspected.

'Come on. Sit down,' Ariella said and slipped her arm around her skeletal waist. She guided her to the only seat in their home. They sat on the edge of the worn out sofa, careful not to lean too far back, it might swallow them into its centre. She sobbed into her shoulder.

'They'll come back, Ariella. I know they will.'

'Sshh, calm down.'

Ester's wailing finally woke Ariella's father. He tried to raise his feeble body to sit up. 'Ariella. Ariella what's happening? Where am I?' he said, in between coughs.

'Sshh, Papa. Lie down, get some rest.'

His face was flushed. He was burning up. It's not surprising he was delirious. Ariella looked back and forth between her father and Ester, who still sobbed into her shoulder. She sighed and ran her hand through her hair and held the back of her neck and wondered how the hell she was supposed to get these two out of here before morning.

CHAPTER 5

Ariella and Ester tried to coax Ariella's father to his feet. When he stood up, his legs were so weak and shaky they couldn't hold his feeble weight. Sweat dripped from his forehead from the sheer effort of standing up. His fevered body fell back onto the bed.

'Lie down, Papa. It's no use.'

'No. I can do it, Ariella, I can do it,' he said and grabbed her wrist with his clammy hand. He dragged himself up again. 'I can go, Ariella. I'm dying in no death camp.' Ariella wished she hadn't told him the word going round her underground operation.

He managed a step then stumbled, forced to sit back down. 'We should've left years ago when we had the chance. If I hadn't been so stubborn,' he said and placed his hands over his head.

'Sshh, Papa, No point.' Ariella wrapped her arm around his shoulder. She pulled him closer and stroked his long hair. Her mind drifted off. She remembered exactly how stubborn her father had been. He was determined to stay in his country and refused to be bullied into leaving. But Ariella's mother was the first to pay the price for his stubbornness.

It was April 1941, Ariella's mother had been out shopping with Mrs Kolleck within the Nazi designated shopping hours. When Ester's mother came rushing back home alone, Ariella knew instantly something was wrong.

'She's gone,' Mrs Kolleck said and threw her arms open, like a magician demonstrating a clever vanishing trick. Ariella's heart raced, the adrenalin pumped around her body preparing itself for action.

'Gone? What do you mean gone? Where the hell is my mother?'

'I don't know, I don't know. She was in the baker's. She must've gone over our shopping time,' she rattled out like a rapid barrage of bullets. 'I waited and waited at the corner but no sign. Then I saw a truck pulling away. It was loaded with Jews.' Ester's mother bowed her head and covered her tear-stained face with her shaking hands and wept. Ariella bolted out that door faster than Jesse Owens sprinted for his Olympic Golds. Too late. It was gone. Her mother was gone. No questions asked. No deportation papers issued. Her mother had been swiftly arrested and taken to a concentration camp. And that was the last they had heard.

Ariella had stomped about, bumped her fist against the wall and begged her father to leave Berlin while they still could. He shook his head, convinced the Nazis would bring his wife back. Ariella knew differently. She had witnessed too many arrests and not one single person had returned. Even back then, she knew, it was a matter of time till the Nazis came for them all.

Ester's family had at least tried to get out after the arrest. It was too late. Jewish emigration was officially forbidden in 1941. The Kollecks' were as trapped in Berlin as they were. Until one day, Mr and Mrs Kolleck, two names only had appeared on the deportation papers. Not Ester's. Not her brothers'.

The two young boys had clung to their parents, refusing to let go. Ester's face drained of all colour and tears ran down her cheeks. She yanked her brothers back inside, convinced their mother and father would return. They had watched their parents march away. Escorted to the truck. Destination unknown. And Ester was left to mother two teenage boys. Those poor boys. And where were they now?

Ariella sat in a trance mulling over past and recent events but was swiftly brought back to the moment by two sharp knocks battering on their front door.

Ester jolted. Her body visibly shook. She burst into another coughing fit. 'Sshh,' Ariella ordered. It was foolish to expect her to silence an involuntary, persistent cough. Ariella cast a fleeting look at the clock on the mantelpiece. Quarter to ten. The seconds audibly ticked by as they sat there, listening intently. Two sharp knocks again. She sprang from the bed and rushed towards the door, eased the handle round a fraction and peered out.

'Nadette. You made it. C'mon, get in, quick,' Ariella said. She grabbed her hand and hauled Nadette inside and quickly scanned the hallway for the enemy before she closed the door.

Ariella wrapped her arms around Nadette's neck and hugged her tightly, 'Good girl. How did you manage it? How did you escape from Kaarl?'

'Don't ask,' she said with a worried expression.

Nadette peeled off her fur coat revealing a body-hugging, black, knee-length dress that fitted her slim figure to perfection. Curly waves of blonde hair rippled down her back, like a golden water-fall sparkling in a burst of sunlight. Her make-up was perfectly applied. Her adorable, tiny nose was powdered and rouge was skimmed over her high cheek bones and her autumnal-red lipstick accentuated her fleshy, full lips. Her delicious perfume completed her outfit but unfortunately was probably another fragrance from Coco Chanel, the woman who despised Jews yet had enjoyed the profits from her Jewish-run Perfume Company. Nadette's perfume and attire were no doubt, as per orders of Kaarl Bergmann. Nevertheless her efforts to enhance her appearance as the dutiful, soon to be Nazi housewife were to be applauded. She looked stunning.

'What's happened?' asked Nadette, desperate to find out what the urgency was all about. 'Ariella, if the Nazi's caught you using that phone-'

'It's Ester's brothers,' Ariella interrupted her, 'they were arrested today, late back for curfew.'

'Oh no. Ester, I'm so sorry.'

'Thank you, Nadette,' Ester said. She rose from Ariella's father's side and carefully manoeuvred his weary legs back onto the bed. 'It's okay, we'll all be back together again soon,' Ester said with an unnatural calmness. She picked up one of her brother's shirts that lay on the bottom of the bed. She folded and smoothed out the creases, 'They'll be back, they'll be back,' she mumbled over and over.

Nadette looked astonished at Ester's incredulity. Ariella gave Nadette a look that confirmed she had already tried to explain the severity of the situation.

Ariella slipped her arm around Ester's waist and once again, guided her to sit down. She brushed a few stray hairs from Ester's tired face, tilted her chin up and spoke softly, 'Ester, they're not coming back.' She looked up at Ariella, smiled and patted her arm. To give up hope was not an option for Ester. Her gaze fell on the mantelpiece clock. She rocked back and forth, bit on her fingernails, absorbed in the delusion that her brothers would return.

Ariella bent forward and kissed her gently on the forehead then rose from the seat to talk to Nadette. She tilted slightly to whisper into her ear. 'That's not all,' Ariella said, 'Papa's on the deportation list. They're coming for him tomorrow. I've got to get him away tonight, Nadette, and he's not well. You need to give him something.'

'Ariella, I doubt I'll be able to give him something to get him on his feet that fast. I'm sorry, I'm sorry. I'm just trying to be realistic.'

'He's not going on the transport. You know what will happen?'

'We don't know for sure, Ariella. It's only rumours. Neither of us have seen the inside of a ghetto or a camp.'

'Oh, come on, Nadette. You don't seriously believe they're taking care of invalids and elderly?'

'I-I don't know what to believe.'

'Kaarl's told you what happens.'

'He could just be boasting. I'm not sure, Ariella.'

'Well, what about the resistance? They're confirming everything Kaarl's boasting about. Look, just give him something, will you?'

With shaking hands, Nadette removed a stethoscope from her bag.

CHAPTER 6

I finished examining Ariella's father and popped the black, plastic tubes from each ear.

'Well?' Ariella said, and sprung to her feet.

'I'm sorry, it's Scarlet Fever. He needs to stay in bed.'

'What? We have to-'

I pulled Ariella aside and whispered, 'I'm sorry, he won't make it, who's going to hide him in that state? I'm so sorry.'

Ariella bowed her head, dejected. She touched my arm as though to thank me for trying then wearily sat back down with Ester.

Thoughts were racing through my head, trying to come up with some kind of solution. I stared at the floor, holding the stethoscope still dangling round my neck. I wasn't aware how frantic I must've been chewing on my lip.

'What is it, Nadette? Chewing over a plan there?' Ariella said.

An idea had sprung to mind. I rushed over and crouched down in front of Ariella. 'There is a chance,' I whispered.

'What?' Ariella said, her voice rose at least ten decibels. Optimism returned.

'The Nazis might not pick him up. They don't want sick people in their camps-'

'Is that it? Is that your plan, Nadette?' She jumped to her feet, towering over me. 'What the bloody hell good is that to me? If you must come up with suggestions then suggest something bloody well better than that.' She ran her hand over her hair and paced the room.

I rose from my crouched position and walked towards her. I touched her arm and squeezed it gently. I didn't know if it was my Doctor's touch, a reassuring touch, somehow, I could calm Ariella's rages. I spoke softly, 'The Nazis should give Amit about six weeks grace. I know. I've seen it. They've thrown Jews off their trains because they carried infectious diseases. It's probably to give them false hope, fool them into thinking they really care about their work force.'

'Damn those Nazis!'

'I know, it's awful, Ariella. In this case it works in our favour.'

Ariella breathed in and out through her nose, calming herself down again. 'They could still come for him tomorrow?'

'Yes, afraid so. I know it's a risk,' I stopped abruptly and turned to look at Ariella's father before I continued, 'what's the alternative?'

CHAPTER 7

The notice read, Warning, Scarlet Fever, Do Not Enter. I patted the poster one last time to ensure it was securely stuck to Ariella's front door. 'I hope this works,' I said.

We were inside the hallway that separated the living quarters between three Jewish families. Large flakes of paint fell to the floor each time we rubbed against the wall. We spoke in whispers and crept about, careful not to attract the neighbours' attention. The oak flooring, well past its extravagance after years of alien traffic, creaked with every footstep.

'I hate this place,' Ariella whispered, 'I don't trust these people. They could easily turn you in, Nadette, for treating Jewish patients.'

'They wouldn't do that, surely?'

'Sshh,' Ariella said, with finger over her lips. She guided me along the hall and into Ester's room where her whole family had lived. 'I don't know the neighbours, don't know where they're from or what they're capable of. It's not unheard of for Jews to resort to such spitefulness trying to save their own lives.'

'It must be awful, crammed in here, sharing with complete strangers,' I said.

'If it wasn't for Ester's family, giving us a room, who knows where we would've been shoved when the Nazis stole our home in Kurfürstendamm.'

I turned my head when she mentioned the area where she had lived. I'm sure I was blushing.

'Never mind,' Ariella said, 'the Grosse Hamburger Strasse deportation centre is handy, just along the road,' she added with sarcasm.

'Oh, please don't talk like that, Ariella.'

'What? It's a fact, isn't it, if we don't get out quick.' Ariella slammed her palm against the wall. 'I'm sick of it, Nadette. It's just got worse and worse since Kristallnacht.'

Two double beds occupied most of the floor space in the tiny room. Ariella was pacing the rest.

'I'll get them, some day, those Nazis who smashed up our businesses.'

'Ariella, calm down, please. You're getting yourself all wound up.'

'No wonder. And all because that Nazi, Vom Rath, was shot by his Jewish lover. Let's face it, Nadette, if Hitler hates gays, then why would he bother about Vom Rath, a faggot being shot? Kristallnacht was just another excuse to have a go at us.'

'Sshh, calm down,' I touched Ariella's arm but she was too distressed.

'I couldn't care less if Grynszpan really was his lover or not, I'm just glad he obliterated that Nazi.'

'Oh, Ariella, I wish you wouldn't talk about revenge like that.'

'How can you say that, Nadette?'

Ariella stomped about the room and shivered in the bitter cold. She frantically rubbed her hands over her arms making a rustling sound over her cotton jumper. 'Even after the Nazis held us responsible for the violence and fined us, you don't think I've got a right to be angry, huh? Never again allowed to own another business, huh?' Ariella was frantic, 'Papa owned one of the finest music shops in Berlin and now look at the state of him. He's just not fit for hard labour.'

'I know. Sshh.' I eased my fingers around Ariella's arm and squeezed gently. 'I'm so sorry.'

Ariella ran her hands through her hair and held onto her neck. She breathed deep sighs. Finally she calmed down. Her back was against the wall and her head rested against the flaking paint. 'No, I'm sorry,' she said, 'it's not your fault.'

I touched her arm again.

'We could've been away, Nadette. If only Papa hadn't taken ill.'

'Then we never would've met,' I said and smiled.

I thought back to that rainy night in September last year when I had first appeared on Ariella's doorstep. I was drenched. My raincoat, saturated. Thin strands of hair clung to my face. I held up the soaking, white handkerchief that Ariella had placed on the outside door-handle to ask for help from an Aryan Doctor. She told me she had been dubious about the whole clandestine operation that some Jewish friends had told her about. I looked at her now, pleased that she had made contact. She was seriously malnourished, yet I could not deny the beauty surrounding her bony features. Her eyes were a deep, dark brown and she had a thin, long nose that constantly made me want to pull and stretch my own.

'Do you know you're amazing, Nadette?' Ariella said, snapping me back from my daydream.

'What? I am? Why?'

'Your determination to do your job. Administer a duty of care to all calibre of patients. You know Papa would never have made it if it wasn't for you. If you hadn't brought him medicine and extra food, Papa would be-'

I raised my hand to stop her, 'He's alive. That's all that matters now.'

'I can never thank you enough for everything you've done.'

'No need, Ariella. Besides it wasn't all me, I had help, remember?'

'Are you still working with Doctor Schmidt?' He was the young Doctor involved in setting up the secret system to help Jewish patients.

'He drove me here tonight,' I said.

'Don't you ever worry that Kaarl will catch you? Notice your medicine inventory is low?'

'No,' I said and turned my head to the side and bit on my thumbnail.

My silk scarf must've slid down. Ariella yanked it from my neck. The black contusions must've been glaring at Ariella, the unmistakable evidence from Kaarl's strangulation hold.

'He did that didn't he?'

'No, no it's just a bruise-'

'I'll kill him,' Ariella said and clenched her teeth, fists equally squashed ready for attack.

'Sshh, Ariella,' I whispered and opened the door to check the landing for eavesdropping neighbours. 'Calm down, please, somebody might hear.' I touched her arm in my usual attempt to calm her. It wasn't working this time. Ariella slammed her fist against the concrete wall. She winced. I squeezed her shoulders and gently steered her round towards me. Ariella grimaced and nursed her painful wrist. I checked her bones to confirm nothing was broken. 'You've got to let go of this anger, Ariella, you're going to end up getting really hurt.'

'I know, I know. It's Kaarl, Nadette. The Nazis. I just can't stand it.' She stood with her head dipped and breathed heavily, trying to calm down. She suddenly looked up, 'You can't go back,' she said. 'You've got to stay here with us.'

'No, Ariella, I can't-'

'You're in so much danger.' She ran her fingers over my bruised neck.

'I have to go back to him. I'm sorry.' I tied my scarf to cover the marks.

'You'll never leave him, will you?' Ariella said. Sadness in her eyes. I had seen that look before. Hurt, perhaps even jealousy. Ariella had seen Kaarl before, during one of our secret rendezvous' and had commented on Kaarl's good looks as though that could've been the reason I was still with him.

I gently caressed her face. 'Please don't do this, Ariella, not now. You know I'll leave him, just not tonight.' My hand trembled against Ariella's cheek. 'I have to get back to him.'

'You really that scared of him?' she said, as though finally, my reason for staying with Kaarl had dawned on her.

I fumbled to put my gloves back on and kept my head down.

'Just leave him.'

'I can't. Please, stop.'

Ariella reached for my hands and held them close against her chest. She looked into my eyes. 'I know you're scared, but you can do it.'

'Ariella, please. It's not just me I'm thinking about. He would find me. I'd put you all at risk.'

Ariella squeezed my hands tight and shook her head. She knew as well as I did, Kaarl Bergmann was well known and it wouldn't take long for one of his henchmen to track me down if I disappeared for any longer than my approved time away from him.

She placed her hands on my shoulders and held me at arm's length as though to study my face. 'I'm sorry, I've been so stupid,' she said and leaned over to touch her head against mine. She cupped my face in her hands and tilted my chin upwards and smiled at me affectionately. I choked back tears. 'Don't you give up hope now, girl,' Ariella said. The dam burst. I broke down. Ariella pulled me close against her chest and rested her chin on my head. 'Sshh girl, don't cry,' she whispered and gently stroked my long hair. I wrapped my trembling arms tight around her. Who knew when I would see her again?

'I wish I had your strength, Ariella.'

'You are my strength, Nadette.' She massaged her hands over my back.

I snuggled into her shoulder and rubbed my face against her long, dark hair, smelling her sweetness. My rapid respirations gently slowed down as she held me close. I breathed deep, hanging onto every second of this precious moment. I closed my eyes and felt the warm fire glowing in my heart and visualised a life time of moments like these.

Ariella drew herself away from our magical embrace. She reached round her neck to unfasten her gold, heart necklace.

'Here take this,' she said and fastened the chain around my neck. She tilted my chin to look into my eyes. 'This is a very special necklace, Nadette. It was my grandmother's.'

'Oh, no, please,' I said and tried to remove it. 'I can't take this. It's precious to you.'

Ariella pulled my hands back from my neck and gripped the gold heart. She smiled warmly, and rubbed the necklace, as though feeling its rough texture where the diamonds laced the rim. 'Let me tell you about this necklace.'

I clasped my hands and tilted my head to the side. I was like a curious child waiting for the fairy-tale to begin.

'My grandmother was an amazing woman,' Ariella said, 'she was strong and feisty. She had a real zest for life.'

I nodded and squeezed Ariella's hand, 'I know someone just like her.'

'No, girl, I'm nothing like my grandmother. I wish I was. Nothing got her down. If she had been alive today, she would've smiled through it all, refused to let the Nazis take away her spirit. She believed that everything happened for a reason and that something good would always come from something bad. That's the kind of person she was.'

'She does sound amazing. What happened to her?'

Ariella turned away and stared out of the window at the dark sky illuminated by the light of the full moon. She smiled, as though believing her grandmother was watching over her.

'She had cancer in the womb.'

I clutched my lower abdomen and grimaced with imaginary pain.

'She lay in bed and suffered. She was told she would only last about two months. Two years she hung on. Day after day, she ached in pain. Agony cries at every movement of her withering body. Yet she smiled, thankful for every precious moment she had with my mother.'

'How old was she when she died?'

'Thirty-four. My mother was only six.'

I looked at Ariella curiously. 'I thought you knew her?'

'Oh, I do. Although I never met her, I feel I know her. And I'm sure she's with me all the time. I don't know what it is about her. I know I resemble her. I've seen enough photos. She had the same build, the same dark, wavy hair.'

'And the same personality,' I added. 'It's possible she's looking over you, protecting you.'

'Do you think I'm crazy?'

'No, angel,' I said and caressed Ariella's face. 'I don't think you're mad. I think it's healthy to believe someone's watching over us.' I dipped my head. 'I hope my mother's watching out for me, I just feel so abandoned.'

'C'mon, girl,' Ariella said, 'you're not alone. I'm here, and I'm sure your parents are around you too. And this now,' Ariella squeezed the necklace in her hand, 'this will protect you.'

'But it's a family heirloom.'

'Yes. And it's supposed to carry special powers.' Ariella paused as though to study my reaction. I stared in awe, waiting for her to continue.

'Some great, great grandfather, somewhere way down the line, is supposed to have had bought the necklace for his wife from a handicapped man. Legend has it, because my distant relative paid a substantial amount for the necklace, much more than it was apparently worth, the peddler had said the wearer would always be protected and survive the darkest days - provided the necklace was gifted to them.'

'And your grandmother believed in its power?'

'Yes, she did. And she was grateful to be able to spend two extra precious years with her only daughter. By the time she was ready to go, she passed the necklace to my mother and made her promise to pass it to me.'

'Then you must keep it,' I said, trying once again to remove the necklace.

'No, no, no.' Ariella said. 'I have gifted it to you. To protect you. Please accept it. I know the story behind it is probably nonsense, but just the thought of my grandmother lying there, in agony, believing in the necklace's power, has been enough to give me the strength to carry on. Even when Jews were no longer allowed to keep gold or silver, I protected it and hid it from the Nazis evil paws.'

'No, I can't accept it. Take it back.'

'I want you to have it, Nadette. Please? It's a heart necklace. Let me believe my heart will always be with you, protecting you.'

I smiled a warm smile, closed my eyes and breathed in through my nose and clutched the necklace tight, trying to draw strength from its imaginary power.

'We can survive this, girl. One day we'll be free. Live together,' Ariella said, not convincingly. Nevertheless, we both seemed much more relaxed. Ariella inhaled deeply. A warm smile across her face this time. Her dark, brown eyes seemed to shimmer in the moonlight that dazzled upon us as it cast its silvery beam in through the window where we both stood. Ariella was clearly enjoying the prospect of a joyous future with me as much as I was with her. Ariella slipped her hand under my hair and around my neck. She leaned in and pressed her thick, warm lips against mine and kissed me passionately.

I pulled back from our embrace and quickly opened the door and rushed out to the hallway without looking back.

'I'll come with you. See you get safely home,' Ariella cried.

I stopped abruptly, terror struck, 'No. You'll get us both caught. Go back inside and take care of your father. I'll be back, soon as I can.' I blew her a kiss before I disappeared into the night.

CHAPTER 8

I scurried through the darkness in Kurfürstendamm. My high heels scraped along the pavements. I wished Ariella was with me but it was too dangerous. Not just that. I was much too ashamed to admit to her that we were occupying a grand villa in the area where she used to live.

I stumbled through the dark streets with my miserable guiding torch. I had no idea what was in front of me. Two sets of soldiers' footsteps thumped on the ground, pacing back and forth to protect the SS leaders who gathered inside our home. I shivered and hurried past the marching men and fumbled with my keys to unlock the door to our home.

Loud, raucous laughter still bellowed from the lounge. I tiptoed across the floor, hung up my coat and sneaked upstairs to our bedroom.

To my disappointment, Kaarl was already sprawled out across our bed, naked. His SS Uniform was carefully hung up on a hanger in front of the wardrobe and his grey cap was hooked over the wooden coat-stand.

I reached over and gripped the blanket from the bottom of the bed and eased it up with my fingertips. I turned away in disgust as I covered his nakedness. He stirred.

'Nadette? Is that you?'

'Sshh, go to sleep,' I whispered and clumsily smoothed his hair away from his face.

He grabbed my hand and pulled me over the top of his muscular body. His voice was hoarse and his words were slurred when he spoke, 'Come, woman. Get in here. I need some action.' His breath was vile and reeked of cigarette smoke and various blends of alcohol, probably anything he could get his hands on until he reached this drunken state. My stomach churned. I turned away and wretched.

'Sshh, Kaarl. You're tired,' I said and eased away from him.

'Get in here,' he said. He squeezed my wrist tight and tried to focus his attention on me. His head wobbled and his eyes struggled to stay open in his drunken stupor. 'Or do you want some of this first,' he threatened with his shovel-like hand wobbling in the air.

'Okay, okay,' I said and forced a smile, 'give me a chance to get undressed.' He let go, but kept his eyes on me.

I removed my high heels and slid down my nylons. His eyes widened and a filthy grin crossed his face. He was ogling my bare legs. My hands trembled as I reached around my back and unzipped my dress and dropped it to my shoulders. I swiftly crossed my hands over my chest and held the dress in place, preventing it from exposing me any further. He snarled and swiped his hand like a lion's paw and clawed at my dress. I flinched but quickly composed myself and faked a teasing smile. 'Now, now, patience,' I said. He grinned and fell back against the pillow with his muscular arms up behind his head as though waiting for the show to begin. I smoothed my hand across the blonde hairs on his chest before standing up and dropping my black dress to the floor. I stood there, wearing only a black bra and black pants... and Ariella's necklace. I studied his face for a reaction; lust staring out of him, missing the love.

I flirted and teased, danced around the other end of the bed and discreetly removed the necklace, all the while my stomach was turning. By the time I pulled back the sheets, Kaarl was on his side, he faced me with those piercing blue eyes and breathed his sickening breath all over me. He swiped his powerful arms around me and unfastened my bra, and dragged it down my arms and off; then spun it around his head and tossed it over the far side of the room. It drooped across a full-length, oak mirror. I caught my reflection and cowered, and wrapped my arms around to cover my bare breasts. I turned my head to the side, too ashamed to look at the whore he was turning me into.

He reached up and pulled my arms apart as if he was swishing a pair of curtains open and trying to expose the window to my soul. I shoved my hand against his chest and dropped my naked breasts upon him and pecked his neck with small grudged kisses. He moaned and lay down and wrapped his arms around my bare back. Slowly I moved my tightly puckered lips over his chest and kissed his flesh, like a child forced to lay a kiss on the cheek of an unfriendly relative.

Kaarl moaned. His moaning turned into a grunting snore before I reached his navel. I edged away from him, reached out the bed for my long, cotton nightdress and wrapped myself up protectively. I clasped my necklace. Not really believing the tale, but out of true respect. Hidden away all those years; prohibited from showing its worth, yet against all odds, there was still a sparkle. I closed my eyes and willed myself to dream about Ariella.

CHAPTER 9

The morning breeze surged through the open windows. The maid ventilated the rooms, ridding the filth from the previous night. The fumes from cigarette smoke still lay thick in the air. The maid scurried about, collected empty glasses, dirty plates and popped champagne corks together with their discarded bottles. The celebration must have gone well after I had left. And now the moment had come for me to face Kaarl in his sobriety.

He was standing in full SS dress, glaring down at the young SS man who had been ordered to follow me. Neither of the two seemed to notice me slip into the room with Kaarl's usual morning coffee and the Völkischer Beobachter. I glanced at the Nazi newspaper and scowled at yet another photo of Hitler with a smug look on his face. Kaarl startled me when he roared at the young man.

'Lost her? Lost her? You idiot.'

The red-faced young man stood to attention and mumbled apologies.

'Get out. Now!'

Kaarl watched me, tracked my every step as I walked towards him. His eyes glared wide and his lips slowly tightened, parting just enough to show his clenched teeth. The cup rattled in its saucer as I edged it onto the mahogany table.

'And when did you decide to return last night?' he demanded without raising his voice. He had obviously been too drunk to remember the episode in bed. I had no desire to remind him.

'I-I didn't want to wake you. You had a lot to drink.'

'Well you won't be going out today.'

'Kaarl, my rounds-'

'Silence! You will stay home from now on. The only time you will leave this house is to accompany me. Am I understood?'

His words were like a spike through my heart. My thoughts raced, Ariella, how was I going to see her? How were we going to get away?

'Please Kaarl, my patients. I need to see-'

Kaarl swiped the coffee cup with the back of his hand and spilled the contents over the table. I cowered and squeezed my hands together to stop the trembling.

'You have a cancer patient here at home,' he yelled. Then he lowered his voice. Much more calm. 'Or is there some other need for you to go out?' My heart pounded. A timid shake of my head was all I could manage.

An agonising yell roared out from his mother's bedroom. Kaarl sighed at the interruption to his speech. He tilted his head towards the sound, frowned in annoyance, and listened for further shrieks. He stared at me, poker faced, as though awaiting my reaction to the moan. I tipped my head to acknowledge his request, about turned and scurried across the floor in answer to the call.

CHAPTER 10

Margo sat on the edge of her deluxe bed, dressed in a floral nightdress with matching housecoat. Her head was slumped over her outstretched arm that drooped over a walnut headboard. The greasy aroma lingered in the air from her breakfast tray that lay at her bedside. Only a paltry amount had been consumed from the superfluous plate of varying fried meats and fried eggs served by the housemaid.

Margo's face was screwed up. Her eyes scrunched into tight slits, trying to focus on me. She winced, clearly in pain. This wasn't the same Margo who happily chatted to the guests at last night's celebration. Her cancer seemed to have worsened, she was deteriorating fast.

I rushed over to her bedside and wrapped my arm around her fragile body and guided her legs up onto the springy mattress. I barely touched her waist as I slid her down the bed yet she let out such a yelp. Her whole body seemed to ache. I eased a couple of feather pillows under her wobbling head. She looked right at me. No words. Her eyes pleaded with me to administer some pain relief. I took the morphine syrette from my medicine bag and inserted the hypodermic syringe under Margo's skin and squeezed the drug into her system. Her eyes rolled in relief.

It was awful to see the poor woman in such a state and I would do anything within my power to ease her distress. And although I felt sadness, there was no real heartache at losing her. She had no more love for me than I had for her. I sat on the edge of her bed, watching her drift off to sleep whilst my mind rolled back, remembering our first encounter.

Ten years old, suitcase in hand, on Margo Bergmann's doorstep, I had looked up at her through terrified eyes, not knowing what the future held for me. There didn't seem to be an ounce of compassion in her body. She scowled down at me and snatched an important letter from my hand. It was obvious she didn't want me to be there but I had nowhere else to go. I plonked myself down onto the single bed in the allocated quarters and cursed my mother and father for deserting me, as though it was their fault that their car had gone over a cliff and left me with my one remaining relative, step-aunt Margo.

I realised I was feeling bitter, staring at the dying woman. I got up from the bed and sighed, trying to let it all go. It wasn't easy with Margo's black and white family photos surrounding me. Margo stood with her SS-Obergruppenführer husband,

Sven, and her son, Kaarl. Empowered by his Hitler Youth uniform, Kaarl stood, chest out, with a sycophantic grin on his face, staring up at his dispassionate father. I scanned the walls, looking at Margo's snapshots of her make-believe happy family.

Another photo. Kaarl, twenty years old in his newly acquired black, SS uniform. I ran my finger along the outline of Kaarl's face in the photo and remembered every detail of that night when he came home. As though the new uniform had given him a right to do as he pleased. Margo blamed me. Sven laughed it off. My teeth clenched as my finger ran down Kaarl's image, tracing his figure in that new uniform. 'It's your own fault,' Margo's words echoed through my head. 'You shouldn't have been wearing such a short skirt,' Margo had said. I was sixteen. My skirt was to my knees. I stopped. I didn't want to remember anymore. I prodded my finger hard against the glass, affirming I wouldn't let him get to me. I clenched my fist, breathed deeply and once again, choked down my anger.

The bedroom door was thrown open. Kaarl stood under the arched doorway. 'I have to go to work and you're coming with me. Get your coat,' he said and placed his cap over his thick, blonde curls.

'What about your mother, Kaarl? I've just given her an injection. I'd better, see that she's alright.'

He shot a quick look over to the bed where Margo lay out cold then looked at me from under the rim of his cap. 'Get your coat, I said. She's fine.'

Kaarl's disrespect for his mother was not surprising. Margo had taught him that women were only there to be servants to men, that men were the superior race. Now she was paying the price. She was dying and her son was more interested in his duty to his Führer.

He grabbed my arm and ushered me towards the door. 'We're meeting Otto. He's going Jew hunting. Thought you might want to see that,' he sniggered. 'You despise Jews, remember?'

I pulled back from him. I didn't want to witness Jews being chased down. 'Kaarl, please I should stay here with Margo.'

He grabbed my arm and squeezed it with white knuckle pressure. His eyes glared, 'Get-your-coat. Now.'

I dipped my head, rushed into the hall and donned my fur coat within seconds.

CHAPTER 11

Kaarl dragged me outside to the awaiting Mercedes. Otto was already in the front seat of the open-topped car alongside a young SS chauffeur. We climbed into the back. Kaarl yanked me over beside him and draped his arm masterfully over my shoulder. The air was frosty. The sky was black with imminent precipitation, snow or rain, it was hard to say which, but a swollen cloud hovered above our heads, something was definitely going to burst.

'Headquarters, Kaarl?' Otto asked, leaning his head back to talk.

'No, short outing first. Driver, you know the route.'

'Yes, sir. Should I put the roof up, sir?'

'No leave it down.'

I'm not sure if the open top was to show me off as his trophy, or to make me feel even more uncomfortable in the bitter cold morning as we drove around the streets in Berlin. I didn't know where we were heading, although Kaarl seemed to have a purpose to our long, twisted journey.

We cruised into the Tiergarten district, along past the bare trees that shadowed In den Zelten road. Kaarl pointed up to a grand, three-storey villa at the corner.

'That used to be the Hirschfeld Institute. The idiot owner tried to stand up for homosexuals.' He smirked and continued, his hand wavering in the air, demonstrating his authority, 'Magnus Hirschfeld tried to repeal Paragraph 175 of the German Criminal Code.' He paused to look at me, grinned and glanced over to Otto. 'You know the clause? The one that says homosexuality is a criminal offence?'

I stared at him and nodded. I didn't know much about Magnus Hirschfeld, but I was familiar with the law. Kaarl often boasted about the men he had sent to concentration camps under Paragraph 175.

Kaarl watched Otto in the mirror and smirked at his comrade. 'Remember that day, Otto?'

Otto nodded and sighed. He glanced at his watch.

'The Institute was ransacked. Homosexual books, Jewish books, in fact anything un-German, all taken outside and burned.' Kaarl seemed to find this highly amusing. He chuckled, recalling that shameful day when the Nazis had their book burning bonfire on Opera Square, the evil work of his Führer, that despot, shortly after he came into power.

I stared ahead, and thought about the years of work of Jewish authors and many others. I visualized the bonfire and imagined I could smell the smoke and hear the loud crackle from the books on fire; flames burning bright, then smouldered down till eventually reduced to ashes.

'The Stormtroopers did a good job that day, Otto,' Kaarl said. He sighed. 'Pity they turned out to be full of queers too.' His eyes lingered in the mirror, staring at Otto, as though full of sadness to be betrayed by his comrades. I don't know why, the Stormtroopers were the ones to be betrayed. Hitler used them to get into power and attacked them later because he saw them as a threat. Ernst Röhm, their leader was a known homosexual and so were many of his troops. One of the reasons Hitler wanted them swept aside; the only reason for Kaarl.

I turned away from Kaarl and focused my attention on the district we were now driving through.

The Schöneberg district was an area I had heard Ariella speak about. She said it had once been a popular area for homosexual venues. I felt a slight jealous pang, thinking about her in the night clubs with another woman. I was being ridiculous. Ariella had a teenage fling that never amounted to anything. After all, I thought, it wasn't as if I had never been interested in another woman. I thought back to the time when there was a slight frisson between myself and a young woman. I half smiled, recalling the awakening of my sexual feelings towards the same sex. Nothing happened, of course. Until Ariella. I thought about her soft skin, her warm lips and-'

'Slow down,' Kaarl snapped me back from my daydream. The driver was now cruising down Nollendorfplatz.

'Recognise this area, anybody?' Kaarl was looking at me with a side glance at Otto. Nobody answered Kaarl. He was taking us through the heart of the former gay community and I couldn't understand why.

'Stop. Right here.' The driver hit the brakes. The car screeched to a halt. We were stationed between Motzstrasse and Kalckreuthstrasse. Kaarl smirked again and pointed up to the corner building. 'That was the famous Eldorado Night Club, once full of queers and drag acts.' His lips tightened, 'Marlene Dietrich, she was a performer who seemed to be as equally fond of women as she was of men.' He was looking at me, spitting out his allegation. I wriggled uncomfortably in the seat, not knowing where he was going with this.

'We closed all those joints down, eh, Otto, when our Führer came to power.' Kaarl straightened his shoulders and sat back with proud posture and grinned like a schoolboy who had just won a prize for good behaviour.

I stared at the sorrowful state of the soaring building. It now wore those brutal, Nazi, Swastika flags over every window that interrupted the long, dark walls; another home for Nazi Headquarters.

Kaarl seemed to enjoy demonstrating his knowledge on homosexuals, almost as if to justify his new position as chief in that sub-division in the Gestapo. Otto sat in the front seat, surreptitiously pulled back his sleeve and glanced at his watch. His beady eyes met mine in the mirror. He stared wide without blinking an eyelid. I looked away and observed our latest stopping point on Bülowstrasse, The Café Dorian Gray.

'Another closed homo club,' Kaarl said with disdain then ordered the driver to turn up on to Schwerinstrasse. He sat back, smirked and pointed out the discreet location of the former Topkellar gay bar. It was tucked away through tarnished gates and hidden up a narrow staircase.

Kaarl crouched down to stare into my face. His breath reeked of stale cognac, my early morning coffee almost regurgitated. He lowered his voice, 'Homos can't hide,' he said and glanced over to Otto in the front seat and smirked. I cowered down. I'm sure my face was red. Kaarl's words resonated through my ears. He was definitely on to me.

Otto sighed. He shoved back his sleeve and held his wrist up in front of his face and tutted, 'Okay, Kaarl, you've had your fun. Let's get back. Some kikes are faking illness, avoiding the transports. Let's catch them before somebody warns them.' Otto stared at me in the mirror the whole time he talked to Kaarl. My stomach was in a knot.

'Ah, yes, the Jews,' Kaarl said, his eyes pierced into mine. 'Nadette should enjoy this.'

My stomach churned over.

'No. Keep her with you. I've some matters to attend to first. See you at Headquarters,' Otto said and glared at me.

CHAPTER 12

The Swastika flags drooped over the front of the fierce, four-storey concrete building that prided itself with the structure of an eerie castle. SS soldiers paraded and marched along the street to guard the uniformed men within the Gestapo Headquarters on Prinz-Albrecht-Strasse. Kaarl hauled me out from the Mercedes, firmly holding my trembling arm and forced me to enter the ferocious building.

The place was crawling with men in grey uniforms. My heart was palpitating at the sight of them. I could hear every sound from my footsteps as we marched along the marble floor through the arched corridors. My wobbly legs could barely keep pace with Kaarl. He was well known and met by many higher and lower echelons, greeted by their Heil Hitler salutes.

We entered a rectangular room with walls so high the voices resonated each time the pompous leaders spoke. A blood-red Swastika flag draped across one wall and an overpowering painting of Adolf Hitler dangled across another. The walnut desks with their fancy carvings were cluttered with files and papers. A young SS man, reeking with cheap cologne, the ideal German soldier, blonde locks and blue eyes, came out from behind a desk and saluted Kaarl.

'Heil Hitler, Gruppenführer,' he said and handed Kaarl some sheets of paper.

'What is it?' Kaarl said, his hands remained firmly behind his back. He looked down his nose at the young soldier.

'Suspects, sir,' the teenage boy said proudly and clicked his heels to attention.

'What?' Kaarl said. He looked puzzled.

'Lists of suspects, Herr Bergmann,' the young man rattled out. 'Police handed them in earlier. To be handed directly to you, sir, as new chief in the Gestapo, sir.' He clicked his heels again. He was like an unloved child trying so hard to impress his father, a bit like Kaarl with his own Papa.

Kaarl snatched the sheets from the young man's hand and flicked through them, not really paying attention to the contents. He stopped. His eyes grew wider and his nostrils flared. He focused on a particular page. His top lip seemed to disappear against the protruding clenched white teeth. He raised his head and stared.

I felt the colour drain from my face and a vile, acidy taste rushed up my throat. I bolted out the door.

CHAPTER 13

We didn't waste any time, powering through the streets into the Mitte district and along Grosse Hamburger Strasse. The rain poured down against the houses, the sandstone sopping up the hail. Hard, painful rain bombed the pavements and whirled in pools at the road edge fighting for the drain pipes. The heavens had opened up. I looked up at the sky, there was so much more to come.

Kaarl had ordered the young SS man to drive, no time to adjust the roof. The Mercedes was soaked, the leather seats were ruined. My fur coat was like an otter's after a day on the dam. My hair was clamped to my head and thin, blonde straggly ends clung to my face. The rain bounced off Kaarl's cap and pelted against his leather coat that protected his all-important uniform.

'It's your fault, Nadette. If you hadn't stopped to be sick, we would've got here before the rain,' Kaarl said.

'I'm sorry, I'm sorry.'

'Get out. Now!' He held the car door open, waiting for me to dismount. Not an act of chivalry. He was making sure I followed him into the building. He wanted me there to witness the arrest.

The arresting soldiers followed in a truck behind us. It screeched to a stop. An unnecessary load of armed men jumped onto the street. Kaarl ordered me to stand aside to let the soldiers enter the tenement building first.

My heart was in my mouth. I wanted to run. Where to? And not without Ariella.

'Quiet,' Kaarl ordered the soldiers, 'I want them taken by surprise.'

CHAPTER 14

Ester carried a breakfast tray with black tea and warm toast for Ariella's father.

A thump against the door startled her. She spun around and almost dropped the tray.

'Don't open it,' Ariella whispered and signalled for her to hold still.

'Ariella, it might be Nadette.'

'Not her knock,' she said and shook her head.

Ariella gripped her father's hand and squeezed it tight. His face was all flushed with fever and his chest slowly rose up and down with every wheeze he breathed. Thankfully he was still sound asleep.

Ester rushed over towards Ariella and quietly placed her father's breakfast tray on the wooden table at his bedside. Ariella eased her arm around her shoulder and pulled her in protectively. Ester sat on the edge of the bed and rocked back and forth. A mature woman, acting child, soothed on her thumb. Her whole body trembled.

Ester mumbled, 'It's going to be okay, it's going to be okay.' Her coughing started. Ariella handed her a tissue and turned away while she expectorated into it, imagining similar vile behind the door.

Lightning flashed and thunder cracked across the sky. Bulging clouds had burst. The rain lashed down against their window. It was a bitter cold, thunderstorm outside but inside their poky home reeked of sweat from fear and fever.

Footsteps shuffled along the wooden floor in the hallway. Ariella and Ester gripped each other tightly. Was this it? Ariella thought. The moment they were coming for Papa. Had they seen the Scarlet Fever notice? Did they even care? She expected the door to be burst open any moment and the soldiers to rush in and grab her father and trail him away.

Her entire body was rigid, tense and trembling. Still, her teeth were clenched tight, enraged at the fear those Nazis had instilled in them. They were trapped in that tiny room. She eyed the narrow window and considered making a run for it, until she looked at her ailing father. The rain battered against the glass, intensified each time the thunder roared. Ester cowered in close to Ariella and covered her ears. Ariella held her trembling body tight against her. All they could do was wait to be plucked like hens from a hen house.

CHAPTER 15

Kaarl dragged me into the dark entrance. Paint flaked and crumbled in my hands as I felt my way along the wall.

'Now!' ordered Kaarl.

The soldiers battered on the door, almost as loud as my heartbeat thumping in my ears.

'Open the door.'

No reply.

Louder. 'Open the door. Now.'

The door creaked open. A man peered from the gap. The soldiers shoved the door wide and burst his nose. Blood trickled to his lips. I noticed the SS grey trousers and long black boots when he stepped out from behind the door, holding his bleeding nose.

Otto Schreiner, Kaarl's macho friend, was half-dressed, braces hanging down. His hairy chest bulged out from his shirt that was unbuttoned to the navel.

'What's going on?' he demanded and edged forward. He pulled the door with him.

The soldiers gun-butted the door, forced Otto to let go and knocked the inside handle against the wall. Another man, in his thirties, came out from a nearby bedroom. He was tall and dark like Otto, except he had more hair and was a lot skinnier. His lanky, white legs clashed against his black, silk bathrobe that barely covered his backside. He clasped his hands effeminately against his chest when he spotted the soldiers and darted into the bedroom.

Otto must've been terrified after Kaarl's tour round the gay district and rushed home to warn his lover. And judging by their attire, I would say they were having a farewell frolic.

The respected leader tried to remain in control and grabbed the door and pushed the soldiers back.

'What the hell do you think you're doing?'

The soldiers turned to look at Kaarl, awaiting his orders. Kaarl cleared a path through his subservient troops.

'Kaarl? What's going on? What's this about?' Otto demanded. His shock seemed false.

Kaarl scowled at Otto and skimmed a look of disgust over Otto's half-dressed body, 'You are under arrest,' he said with an extraordinary coolness.

'What? Me?' This time Otto looked genuinely stunned.

Kaarl's eyes were tight, allowed only a slit for him to peek through. They matched the minute gap between his tight lips covering his clenched teeth. With two fingers squeezed together as though he was holding a cigarette, he signalled to the soldiers and ordered them to capture the law-breaking man and his lover.

The soldiers grabbed Otto's arm and dragged him outside.

'I demand to know what this is about.'

Kaarl fixed his cap and tilted his head back to look under its rim, 'You are under arrest under Paragraph 175 of the German Criminal Code. For the crime of homosexuality.'

'Don't be ridiculous,' Otto said.

Kaarl dragged the Lists from inside his coat pocket and flicked through the pages. 'These are the Pink Lists—'

'What? Pink what—?'

'Pink Lists, Otto. Lists of suspected homosexuals. Supplied by the police. Your name is on the list,' he said to Otto with his head tilted to the side and an accusing look on his face. 'I was suspicious of you, Otto. I hoped I was wrong.'

'You *are* wrong, Kaarl.'

'No, no, no. The Lists are correct. You think you can hide in this...' Kaarl wavered his hand around the walls, '...this hovel.'

'Let me see that.' Otto grabbed the papers from Kaarl. He scrutinized the pages. His eyes widened. His hands trembled when he gave the papers back to Kaarl, 'There's been a mistake.'

'No mistake. The police have been tracking you and your...' Kaarl sniffed and drew Otto another look of disgust before he finished his sentence, '...you and your lover.'

Otto looked down the line of soldiers and spotted me edging towards the doorway. I wanted out into the air, I couldn't stand it anymore. Otto looked embarrassed when he saw me, probably because he had such a manly charade in my presence all the time.

His eyes suddenly lit up. He smiled. I turned to see what he was looking at.

Oh my God, Ariella, I thought and covered my hand over my mouth when I saw her rush into the building. We were in the block next door to her apartment. What was she doing in here? She was in some sort of daze with her head bowed. Her long, dark, wavy hair drooped over her face.

'Ingrid,' Otto cried.

The woman looked up. I sighed in relief. She had a round chubby face and wore a masculine suit and trench-coat. If it wasn't for that long hair, she could easily have been mistaken for a man.

'There's my wife, Kaarl. What's got into you? Ingrid, Ingrid, come quick. Tell him,' Otto called out in desperation. Even I could see the marriage was a hoax. It wasn't unheard of, homosexuals to marry for security and avoid concentration camp punishment.

'So this is Ingrid. The one we have never met,' Kaarl said. 'Probably met her in a homo bar before we closed them all down. Your sham marriage will not protect you.'

The woman about turned and rushed towards the door.

'Arrest her,' Kaarl roared.

'What for?' Otto demanded.

Kaarl voice was low and harsh, 'She's a lesbian.'

I covered my mouth, held my breath and watched in disbelief. Kaarl really was arresting homosexual women too. I wanted to speak up. To face Kaarl. To defend her. I opened my mouth but the words wouldn't come out. Otto said it for me.

'That's no crime, Kaarl,' he said, trying to save Ingrid, his phony wife, from punishment.

Kaarl breathed in through his nose. He pouted his lips and rubbed two fingers against his forehead as though trying to come up with an excuse to take her into custody. 'Arrest her for political reasons. She spoke out against the Führer,' Kaarl said.

'What? I did no such thing.' The poor woman was flummoxed. The soldiers wasted no time. They ambushed her and dragged her out to the awaiting truck.

Kaarl summoned another two soldiers and ordered them to take the felonious men to the truck with her.

'Kaarl, you know me. We're friends,' Otto said while the soldiers dragged him out.

I couldn't believe it either, Kaarl arresting a comrade, his lifelong friend. He was determined to fulfil his duty to the Führer, no matter what. He stared at his buddy and reminded him, 'No exceptions, Otto.'

Otto's boyfriend was dragged out behind him by two young soldiers. He was dressed now. He was wearing brown trousers and a Fair Isle patterned jersey and carried a brown overcoat together with Otto's SS jacket. He swung his arm back and threw Otto's jacket to him. The way he flipped his wrist, he smacked a soldier in the face. Whether it was accidental or not, I can't be sure. The soldier flinched and held his cheek. In retaliation, he snatched his gun from his shoulder and thumped Otto's lover across his back with the rifle butt.

Otto couldn't hold himself back. 'Anton!' He shoved the arresting men aside and dropped to his knees on the wet road and held the wounded man in his arms.

Kaarl's eyes widened, watching the SS leader's behaviour. He rushed over, booted Otto in the belly and knocked him over. Otto rolled into a ball, clutched his stomach and gasped for breath. The rain pelted down his face. Kaarl ran at him and kicked repeatedly into his ribs. 'You dirty faggot.'

He dragged his lifelong friend to his feet and shoved him into the arms of the awaiting soldiers.

CHAPTER 16

'Have they gone?' Ester said. 'Do you think it was soldiers?'

Ariella listened at the door. All seemed quiet. She slid the bolt along, eased the door open and checked the hallway.

'Don't go out, Ariella, please,' Ester whispered. She clutched her hands against her ashen face.

'Sshh. It's okay.'

A man ran out from the next room. He wore a black, felt bowler hat and a long, woollen coat and carried a battered suitcase. It was their neighbour.

'Sorry if we disturbed you,' he said and rushed past.

'Where are you going?' Ariella called after him.

'Theresienstadt,' he said. 'We're in luck, got the good one. Must hurry, got to catch up with the others at Grosse Hamburger Strasse.'

'Theresienstadt?'

'Yes the Ghetto in Czechoslovakia,' he said.

'I know that,' she said. 'Don't go.' Ariella reached for his arm.

'What do you mean?' He frowned and glanced at Ariella's hand on his sleeve. She pulled it back.

'It's the good one,' he said. 'A resettlement home for Jewish families, for the elderly, musicians and artists. You might be in luck and get it too.'

'No! It's a lie. A propaganda stunt. The Nazis want the world to believe they're looking after their Jews.'

'What are you talking about? How do you know that?'

The resistance had told her all about it. Confirmed by Nadette. She couldn't tell him that. Kaarl had laughed at the foolishness of the Jews believing it all. Theresienstadt was nothing more than a mini concentration camp with its very own crematorium.

'Just a hunch. Look, just don't go.'

'Don't be ridiculous. I'm not missing a chance like this. Besides, where else is there?' he said and rushed out the door.

Where else, indeed? She closed the door and thought about the hundreds, maybe thousands of Jews gathered at Grosse Hamburger Strasse, waiting to be deported. Nazis were determined to rid Germany of its Jews. She wandered over to the window and drew back the shabby, velvet curtains, shaded in their folds after years of hanging there. She peered through the rain-smeared glass to watch their neighbour run along the road. Her mind was elsewhere though.

She skipped down the street along Kurfürstendamm on a hot summer's day, danced around the leafy trees that lined the boulevard and waved in to her father as he worked in his music shop. Ariella had smiled. Contented. She licked her ice-cream on her way home from school.

The warm sun on her face was wonderful. And she had enjoyed the delicious smell from the flowers in their garden when she arrived home. She ran her hand along the carved, stone columns that complimented their front entrance. And best of all, she had heard her mother's excited cry from their balcony, welcoming her only child home. Ariella skipped inside, across the marble floor, gazed upwards to watch her mother hurry down from the expansive staircase with open arms. She could still smell her perfume, that sweet, delicate fragrance.

Ariella must've been beaming from ear to ear. Esther touched her hand, 'Ariella, are you okay?' Ester frowned in confusion. She must've thought she had lost her mind, standing at the window, facing misery and smiling. She had enjoyed recalling those wonderful times with her family. It was a blow to snap back again. Ariella sighed and frowned at Ester for ruining her daydream, pulling her back to the nightmare.

'What're we going to do, Ariella?' Ester asked. She seemed to expect Ariella to have all the answers. Ariella looked at her father who was asleep on top of the sagging bed. He was still flushed with fever.

What could they do?

'Nothing,' she said. 'We wait.'

CHAPTER 17

The weeks dragged by. Kaarl hadn't taken me out on any more trips. Margo was too poorly. I was ordered to stay by her side. He always appeared as if he didn't care for his mother, yet he seldom left the house. I knew he wanted to keep me under his control, but there was no need for him to station himself at home. He could easily have had me guarded by some sentry to make sure I remained captive. Still, he insisted on conducting most business from the villa. As a result, we had to suffer the blaring telephone and the never-ending ranks of SS men who paraded through our hall into the lounge. I was well and truly imprisoned, and had no way to reach Ariella.

Eric Hagen, the shabby SS Gruppenführer from Kaarl's celebration, rushed into our lounge and removed his cap. Oh no. I wondered if he would he remember me from the last time he saw me when I crept back for my medicine bag?

'K-Kaarl, please. You've got to help me,' Eric said. He twirled his cap in his hands.

Kaarl sat behind a mahogany desk, shuffled through papers and took an occasional sip of his coffee. His pet budgie flew around the room and landed on Kaarl's desk.

'Hello, you,' Kaarl said and put his finger out for it to land on him. He rose to his feet, careful not to frighten it and put the bird back in its cage. 'There you are, safe, my precious one,' he said, closed the cage and gave it some seeds.

'What do you want, Eric?' Kaarl said and moved back behind his desk.

'We go back years, Kaarl. Remember? The Hitler Youth.'

'Mmm,' Kaarl said. He didn't look up.

'We're buddies, right?'

Kaarl raised his head, 'No. What do you want?'

'I'm being sent to Auschwitz. Maintain the records.'

'So?'

'Kaarl, please. I can't go to a concentration camp. Please you've got to help me.'

Kaarl scraped his chair along the marble floor and rose to his feet. 'Can you think of some valid reason why you shouldn't be sent there?'

Eric fed his cap through his hands faster and faster, spinning it in circles. He glanced up at Kaarl through the corner of his eye, his dark, greasy hair swept over his forehead where tiny bubbles of perspiration formed. He bit on his lip as though trying to come up with an excuse.

'You're a weak man, Eric. A useless German. Now get out of here and serve your country.'

Eric's hands trembled, he fixed his cap back on. He rushed towards the door, his eyes met mine. He stopped on his foot, frowned at me as though he had just remembered our last encounter. He rubbed his chubby hand across his mouth, looked back and forth between Kaarl and me. Once again, I was frozen to the spot awaiting his decision. I couldn't stand it anymore and brushed past him to attend to the dying Margo.

CHAPTER 18

'She made a noise, Nadette, check it out,' Kaarl waved me off, ordered me to attend to his mother. He sat on the edge of the bed and sipped his coffee. His mother gasped intermittent breaths into her cancer riddled lungs.

Kaarl had use for me as a Doctor, now. Neither Kaarl nor his parents had any previous interest in my profession and would never have allowed me to study had it not been for my father's money.

When I arrived at their home, I was just a child. Margo made me wait on the doorstep in the pouring rain. My tiny hand quivered and reached up to give her a soaking wet envelope. It was a lawyer's letter to remind her what was expected from the Bergmann's as my guardians. She pulled me indoors, snatched the envelope from me and scowled as she scanned the enclosure and read out the orders to her husband. Sven soared above me in his deathly-black uniform, his wide eyes stared down into mine.

'I don't have time for this nonsense, Margo. You deal with her,' he said and barged between Margo and me. He pushed us aside to storm out the door. 'I've got more important matters than this.' He slammed the door shut and left the bitter woman pining after him.

'It's your fault, Nadette. It's all your fault,' Margo said. It was a phrase I was to become accustomed to.

Margo had reminded me often about the contents of that letter and the reason they took me in. My wealthy father had left his step-sister an unimaginable amount of money, but much to my pleasure, he had insisted that I become a Doctor first before the trust fund fully paid out. His wishes were honoured. The only good thing the Bergmann's ever did for me. And now, any day, Kaarl would decide it was time for me to give up my profession and become his Nazi housewife. In the meantime, he needed me to administer medical assistance to his mother.

'Are you deaf?' Kaarl said.

I sat in the chair in Margo's bedroom, miles away, thinking back to those horrible childhood years.

Kaarl took another sip of his coffee and slammed the cup back in its saucer. 'I said, check her out.'

I jumped from the easy chair where I had been practically stuck to for weeks, watching Margo through those agonisingly long days, my stethoscope and morphine, both ready to hand. I popped the ends of the tubing into each ear and reached over to sound Margo's failing heart.

'Not long now, I'm sorry,' I said and removed the stethoscope from my neck.

Kaarl breathed deeply. He choked back the tears now welling in his eyes. I was quite surprised to even see him at her bedside while I was present let alone show any emotive response to her passing away.

He jumped to his feet, slammed the cup and saucer on Margo's bedside table and let out a roar that made me flinch and grab his mother's hand. If hearing was the last sense to go, then that shout was enough to frighten the remaining life out of the distressed woman.

I felt extremely uncomfortable in the room with Kaarl and his mother, and I was certain he would want a moment alone with her before she died to give him the chance to step out from behind that hard exterior and to perhaps openly show his affection for his mother in private.

I slipped across the tiled floor and eased the bedroom door open. 'I'll leave you alone with her,' I whispered back into the room and leaned on the door handle to draw it quietly over.

Kaarl faced the wall. He spun round towards me. His tears, gone. His face, once again, full of anger. He bolted across the floor and grabbed the door so hard it felt as if he had jerked my arm from its socket. On reflex, I yanked my hand into my chest and grabbed my other hand over my aching shoulder.

'Oh no you don't,' he shouted.

'Kaarl, there's nothing more I can do. Surely you want to spend some time alone with your mother?'

He grabbed my arm away from my chest and threw me across the floor, back into the room. He shoved me so hard I lost my balance, stumbled and fell face down, spread-eagle across Margo's bed.

Margo struggled with her last breaths.

Kaarl stood at the doorway, straightened the collar to his SS Gruppenführer uniform then grabbed the most important feature, his cap. He adjusted the headdress onto his thick, blonde curls and looked down at me under the rim.

'I'm going back out to work. I've had weeks of this bloody misery, watching you, watching her.'

The irritating buzz from the doorbell interrupted him. I thought it was probably another bombardment of uniforms coming into see Kaarl.

'Probably the undertaker,' Kaarl said.

'Undertaker?' I said. Why on earth had he ordered an undertaker when his mother hadn't even died yet, I thought, but dared not to ask.

'Well you said it was imminent. Now stay here and organise the funeral.' He slammed the door shut.

Kaarl's footsteps thumped across the hall. He mumbled to the housemaid to dismiss her. I listened at the door. I could hear his stern voice in the hallway, he was talking to another man. I couldn't make out their conversation though, it was only mumbled chatter.

I glanced over to Margo. She rattled in another crackly breath.

The outside door slammed shut. I flinched and resumed my position with my ear tight against the door. The maid's voice was back, she instructed the man to follow her. I pulled the door slowly towards me, eased it open and peered through the gap. The maid and the visitor entered the lounge. She instructed him to wait. There was no sign of Kaarl.

I had a chance to escape. I glanced back and forth between the door and the bed. I gnawed on my thumb nail, considering what to do. The smell of death in the air was enough to make me want to run for it. I sighed and stared at the dying women. Wearily, I walked back over to sit at Margo's death bed.

CHAPTER 19

The undertaker was a short man and looked grossly undernourished. He didn't look sturdy enough to be a coffin bearer. In fact, he didn't look like an undertaker at all. His long black coat had seen better days and the top hat he carried looked like it was something he'd rescued from a stage act.

I watched him, studied his ashen face as he put the lid on Margo's coffin. He fumbled with the screws as though he wasn't quite sure what he was doing. He looked about fifty but the lines on his brow and under his eyes looked to me as a sign of premature aging. He was probably only around thirty but I guessed he was carrying more weight than a coffin on his shoulders.

He stepped back from the coffin and gave a slight bow that was as false as his outfit. 'Ma'am,' he said to indicate he had completed the task. Margo was ready to take her last journey.

I tipped my head to acknowledge his act, rose from the chair and walked around the bed towards him. There was a distinct shadow on the breast of his coat. As I drew nearer to him, I could see the shadow much clearer. It was a small mark that looked darker than the rest of his coat, as if it had been protected from typical weather conditions, protected perhaps, by a yellow star.

I ran my fingers over the very faint outline on his coat and quizzed him, 'Jew?'

'Wh-What?' He jumped back at least three feet, tugged at his lapel with shaking hands. He swiftly donned his magic hat and hurried past me, ready to make a sharp exit. I grabbed his arm and stopped him in his tracks.

'Please, wait. Don't be afraid,' I said with such calmness as though talking to a distressed patient.

Within a blink, his documents magically appeared from his inside pocket.

'Ma'am. You're mistaken. Here are my papers,' he said and pushed them into my hand. 'See?' he tapped on the pages, forced me to look. I was no master at detecting the authenticity of anybody's papers, but there was no question in my mind that these were forged. The ink looked fairly new yet the papers were coffee stained and crumpled as if to simulate the effect of age. I folded them up and smiled, gave him a 'knowing' look when I handed them back.

'I have Jewish friends trapped,' I said and stared at him to study his face.

He looked at me with a puzzled frown, shrugged his shoulders and displayed helpless hands.

I looked pleadingly into his eyes.

He sighed, long and hard. At last he whispered, 'They're still in Berlin?'

'One of them is too sick to travel,' I blurted out. 'He's got Scarlet Fever and he was already quite poorly. I doubt he'll recover enough to travel anywhere on foot.'

He moved closer to me and placed his warm hand on my shoulder and gave it a sympathetic squeeze. 'They're all being deported to concentration camps now,' he said.

I covered my mouth, horrified at the news. Warm tears bubbled up in my eyes as I stared at him. The sclera of his eyes were clustered with red lines and water flooded there, like a river ready to burst its banks.

He turned away from me. I could hear him take deep breaths, as though to compose himself. After a second or two, he walked back to Margo's coffin.

'Sometimes–' he said.

'Yes? What?' I interrupted and stared at him.

'We can use this.' He tapped on the coffin and looked at me with a serious expression. 'It's not foolproof. Sometimes we can masquerade a funeral and transport Jews to a safe hiding place. It's not pleasant. It means lying in a coffin with mini air vents. If your friend is that sick, it might be his only chance of escape.'

I smiled at the prospect of getting Ariella and the others out. He pulled out a pencil and paper from inside his coat pocket and handed them to me, 'Give me their address,' he said. I stared at the paper without budging. I wanted so much to believe in him and to trust his plan. Yet I was wary I might just be endangering them all.

He seemed to read my mind and squeezed my shoulder again. 'I understand,' he said. 'It's not easy not knowing what's the right thing to do. Making choices and risking people's lives.' He bowed his head, 'My family need my help too,' he said with sadness in his voice.

I felt his pain. 'I'm so sorry, I wish I could help.'

I slipped the pencil and paper from his hands and quickly scribbled Ariella's address.

CHAPTER 20

'What're you doing, Ariella?' Ester said. She peered out of the window while trying to keep an eye on Ariella who was trailing up floorboards. Ariella dug out her Stradivarius she had hidden from the Nazis. She blew the dust off the violin, put it against her shoulder and slid the bow over the steel strings. The sound was truly divine, almost as if the violin was rejoicing, free to express itself after years of oppression.

'What does it look like I'm doing?'

'Stop it, Ariella. You know you shouldn't have that. What if they hear you?'

'Want to have a go?' Ariella teased her. She continued to take great pleasure in sweeping the bow across the strings. Her eyes rolled, she was remembering her days in the Jewish orchestra. She played faster and faster, screeched out aggressive, high pitched chords, and channelled her anger into her forbidden instrument.

'Enough, Ariella.' Her father's voice was calm but his tone was sharp. He was sitting up on the bed, thumbing through an old book. He glanced over the top of his reading glasses to reprimand her. 'I love to hear you both play, Ester is right though. You shouldn't draw attention to us.'

Like a spoiled brat, she obeyed her father's order. 'Sick of those Nazis,' she said and threw her precious violin down so hard it knocked a chip in the neck. She regretted it instantly and reached over and picked it up. She nursed and caressed the nicked maple and held the violin close and smelled its glossy surface. What was the use? What did it matter? She was never going to play again. She was never going to fulfil her dream to become a great musician. Nevertheless, she placed the violin carefully back down, looked over at Ester and held her empty hands out like an insolent child.

'Happy now?'

Ester shook her head and sighed. She turned back to peer out behind the shaded curtains and scan the streets.

'The soldiers are just doing their job, things will be back to normal soon, you'll see.'

Ariella jumped to her feet. 'Wake up Ester. That's just foolish talk. Things will never be the same again. The Nazis are destroying us.'

'Stop, stop,' she cried and covered her ears. 'Everything will be fine. We'll all be back to normal soon, you'll see. My family will be home soon.'

'Will you stop,' Ariella shouted into her face. 'Families are being deported all the time. Do you ever see them coming back, huh?'

Ester started shaking all over. Her coughing started and her head went down. She mumbled into her chest, 'No, no my family will be back, they'll be back.'

Ariella realised she was only getting herself worked up and upsetting Ester. She walked over to her, put her arms around her shoulders and pulled her head in close to her chest. 'I'm sorry, Ester. I shouldn't have yelled. Look you've got us. Haven't I always been here for you, huh? We're your family now. Soon as Papa's well enough and when Nadette gets here, we'll get back to the plan, okay?'

'We should leave now, Ariella,' Papa said and tossed his book aside, 'I've waited too long in the past. Got to get you girls out of here.'

'Papa, you're not fit?'

'If we don't leave soon, I'll be back on the deportation list. If not all of us,' he said and edged himself to try and stand up.

'Papa, you'll never make it on foot. We'll get caught,' Ariella was frantic, 'And, and what about Nadette?'

'Nadette hasn't been here in weeks. She might never come back. We have to go without her. Come on help me, both of you,' Papa said and struggled to his feet.

Ester still had her head poked between the curtains, still scanning the streets, her thumb firmly wedged between her teeth. Ariella slammed her palm against the wall. Ester jumped. 'It's his fault. Kaarl's keeping her there, prisoner. I swear I'll kill him.'

'Enough, Ariella,' her father said. 'You're beginning to sound like one of them. Now, what's the plan?' he said, letting her know who was boss, yet expecting her to manage everything. She paced the floor, thinking, trying to come up with a plan, a plan that included Nadette.

Footsteps scuffed along the pavement, startling them. Ester had momentarily lapsed from her look out post to watch Ariella and her father debate. 'See who it is,' Ariella whispered and gestured for her to edge the curtain back.

Ester slid the curtain folds back in slow motion and slowly tilted her head forward to peer out. Her actions were so painfully drawn out, it seemed like they were waiting an eternity to find out who was approaching their home.

'Ahh,' she said with relief, 'it's Nadette.'

Ariella grinned childishly and hurried over to open the door.

Nadette pushed the door wide, taking Ariella by surprise. She carried a small, stylish suitcase. Her face sparkled, excited, 'I can get us out,' she said.

'Sshh,' I said and grabbed her indoors. 'New neighbours in there. Remember what I told you? They could turn you in for being here.'

'We won't be here much longer,' she said. She smiled and looked really happy. 'I've got a plan.'

CHAPTER 21

My plan seemed to appeal to Ariella but she just wasn't sure. That undertaker, she didn't know if he was trustworthy, neither did I. But they were running out of time and had to get out of Berlin as soon as possible.

Ariella paced the creaky floorboards, stared upwards at the dirty white ceiling as though wondering what to do.

'I don't like it. What if he doesn't get us out? What if he turns us in? How can you trust him, Nadette?'

I sat and fidgeted on the sofa, my backside inches from the floor and my legs slanted to the side. I was doing my best to maintain my femininity and to pretend there was nothing odd about the shapeless seat. Nothing felt comfortable anymore.

I shrugged, 'I'm sorry, Ariella. I didn't know what else to do. He seemed genuine enough.'

'I don't know, Nadette, it's too risky.' She still paced the floor. 'Got to try and get back to the original plan.'

'Oh, Ariella, you don't know if your plan would work,' Ester said. 'You don't know that you could trust your friends to hide us anymore than Nadette can trust this man.' She walked over and sat down on the sofa, forcing me to topple against her. Ester's legs peaked just below mine. She curved them away from me to prevent our knees from banging together. She stretched so far to the side, her long skirt trailed on the ground and dusted the floorboards.

'Look,' Ariella said, 'I've known my friends for years. They've helped loads of Jews into hiding places. They could've hidden us ages ago-'

'If it wasn't for me,' her father said. He lay back down on the bed, exhausted from his slight exertion of trying to stand.

'No, Papa, don't please, I didn't mean-'

'Nadette's right. We have to use the coffin, it's the only way. I'm not well enough for your plan, you said so yourself. I couldn't travel to your friends' hiding place and you know I'm not fit to climb into any attic or to keep moving around from place to place. At least this way,' he paused to look at me, 'with Nadette's plan, the undertaker's plan, he can get us all out, one, maybe two at a time in the hearse. And he's got a good, safe hiding place in a basement in a country farm. I could stay there without worrying about continually having to move.'

Ariella still paced up and down, reluctant to give in. She stopped in front of Ester and me. We were sunken into the sofa. She bent down and reached out to hold my hands. 'Are you sure you want to come with us?'

I looked into Ariella's eyes and said softly, 'My life is with you, Ariella. You're all I've got.'

'We'll be hidden away, probably won't see daylight till the war is over,' Ariella said, 'you'll be giving up your freedom.'

I knew what she meant. The best option for Jews was to hide. But I was an Aryan who should've been free to roam around Berlin as I pleased.

'What freedom?' I said. Kaarl Bergmann had control of my life too. I was as contained as they were, waiting for whatever treatment deemed appropriate.

Ariella stood up, rubbed her hands together and smiled at Ester and me. We both sat timidly staring up at her. 'Okay then. Settled,' she said. 'Let's get some rest before he comes for us.'

CHAPTER 22

I pulled on my cotton nightdress in front of the coal fire in Ester's room. I rubbed my hands together, drawing some heat from the last log that crackled disturbing the silence of the night.

'C'mon hurry up, come in here and get warm,' Ariella said. She patted the sheet beside her and held the blankets back for me to jump in.

I crawled over the bed and snuggled tight into Ariella's arms. She pulled the blankets up and tucked them in cosy round my back and held me in a warm embrace.

'Oh, it's so cold,' I whispered and shivered against Ariella, luring heat from her protective arms. I pulled my knees up into the foetal position and eased my feet between Ariella's legs.

'Ah, your feet are like blocks of ice,' Ariella said.

'Sorry.'

She pulled my head in against her chest. Her flimsy nightdress brushed against my skin. She rubbed warm circles into my back. 'Warmer?' Ariella whispered softly.

'Mmm, much,' I said and smiled.

I lay back on the pillow, and scanned the small room. 'I can't believe Ester's family had to live in here, in this tiny space.' Small puffs of air, visible from my breath when I spoke.

'They didn't have much choice. This was the only space left after they were forced to sublet every other room in their home. Her parents slept in this bed and Ester and her two brothers slept in that one,' she said, indicating the other double bed.

Ariella lay back on the tired pillow, a mere inch off the threadbare sheet and clasped her hands around the back of her neck. She heaved a sigh, 'They've taken everything, our homes, our businesses and even our families,' she said.

I snuggled in. My respirations, rapid. I was trembling again. Tremors, no longer from cold. Ariella turned to face me and pulled my hands towards her. She cupped them under her chin to comfort me. 'Come on, girl. Don't worry,' Ariella said, 'we'll be out of here in a few hours.' I smiled, filled with hope and lay back watching shadows dance in the candlelight on the high ceiling.

Ariella reached down to the small, wooden table that held the flickering candle. She pulled the saucer closer, ready to extinguish the flame. I touched her shoulder. 'No don't,' I said, 'I want to see you. To look at your gorgeous face.'

She leaned over and rubbed her nose playfully against mine, 'I want to look at you too, girl, but we've got to get some rest. Long day ahead of us.'

'We don't know where we're going to be, Ariella. When we'll get a chance to lie like this again.'

Ariella lay back, looked at me through the corner of her vision. 'What are you suggesting, girl?'

'Maybe we should make use of the time we have together?' I whispered seductively. My eyebrows deliberately danced up and down and I gave her an impish grin. I leaned over and dropped a soft kiss on her forehead. She breathed deep through her nose and smiled as though my perfume was already carrying her off. I brushed my lips softly against her cheek and gently kissed the tip of her nose and then down onto her mouth.

'You're teasing me,' Ariella said.

'I am,' I gently parted her lips with the tip of my tongue. I was definitely warming up. A hot tingle shot between my legs, wanting more.

'You're so pretty,' I said.

I smoothed the back of my fingers down over her delicate skin, that skin that was not unlike a peach, both in colour and texture that required gentle handling to preserve its beauty. I covered her peachy cheeks with gentle kisses and nibbled on her skin, like a mother stripping away at her newborn cub's protective layer to unleash the beautiful but terrified creature underneath.

Eventually I spread my mouth across Ariella's. It was a delicious kiss that seemed to last an eternity, a kiss that made me tingle and press my whole body down hard against her.

She placed her hand gently on my shoulder and eased me onto my back. Ariella's eyes glittered with affection. I gazed up at her, waiting for her to touch me, to hold me, to love me.

She reached over and untied the lace on my nightdress and slipped her hand underneath to caress and cup my bare breast. I moaned, stretched my arms up and assisted Ariella to undress me. Within seconds we were both naked. Ariella's skin was warm against mine. Our bodies pushed together, slowly and rhythmically our hips danced in tune.

It seemed like hours before I finally quivered a satiated moan. Ariella kissed the salty tears away from my filling eyes and softly brushed her lips against mine. When she pulled back, her own eyes were filling up. 'You've given me so much hope, Nadette. You've given me back that spark, a reason for me to keep going. I love you, girl.'

I sat up, tears trickled down my face, yet I was smiling. I pulled Ariella close and held her so tight, my own body trembled. I whispered in her ear, 'Ariella, you are my life. I am nothing without you.'

Ariella held me in her arms. We swayed gently back and forth. Locked ourselves together, entwining our limbs securely until we had become one. We lay down, not wanting to let go of each other, our arms still wound together, our lips passionately in motion; one last kiss before sleep.

CHAPTER 23

We rushed about in the morning chill. The fire was dying. The last sturdy log was emitting its final glow.

I paced the floor, flipped my wrist every couple of minutes to check the time. The seconds seemed to creep by. Ariella walked over and put her hand over my watch.

'Stop it, Nadette, he'll be here any minute.'

I grabbed my necklace and squeezed it tight. Ariella pulled my hands back, took the heart of the necklace between her finger tips and kissed it gently. 'Remember, Nadette, my heart will always be with you to protect you.' She clasped her hands around my neck and drew me in close and kissed the top of my forehead.

A car screeched to a halt outside, startled us.

'What was that?' I said.

Ester barged into the room. 'He's here. The hearse is at the door. I'll get Amit,' Ester blurted out and rushed back through to get Ariella's father.

More tyres screeched and stopped outside the building. Heavy footsteps battered onto the ground. It sounded like a whole army. Ariella rushed to the window, stood with her back against the wall and pushed the curtain back a fraction.

'Damn!'

'What is it?'

The sound of more trucks, more screeching brakes and more heavy footsteps running, closing in on us.

Doors were battered, soldiers' voices yelling, up and down the street.

'Open up. Quick,' they shouted.

'What's happening, Ariella?' My two hands were tightly wrapped around my necklace.

'Nazis.'

I couldn't believe it and clasped my hands on my cheeks, 'Oh no, the undertaker, he's been caught.'

A thud and the door barged open. I screamed and ran into Ariella's arms. She held me there with my head close against her chest. Kaarl burst into the room.

'Ha, I knew it,' he said, 'Jew lover.'

More than he knew.

'Get away from her,' he shouted at me.

Ariella hung on tight. 'Leave her alone,' she yelled. He bared his perfect, white teeth at her and swung his arm so fast I don't think Ariella saw it coming. Smack, right in the face. He punched her so hard, she lost her balance and fell against the wall and bumped her head. Ariella looked dazed. She slid down the wall and landed on the floor.

Kaarl grabbed me and pulled me away from Ariella. She looked like she was trying to focus and reached up to grab me. She kept missing, grabbing thin air. She scrambled to her knees, dived at Kaarl and wrapped her arms tight around his legs. 'Let her go,' Ariella shouted.

Kaarl shook his leg furiously, and knocked her off, 'Filthy Jew.'

I signalled to Ariella and mouthed to her to stop. I dreaded to think what he would do to her if she persisted. Kaarl dragged me towards the door.

A young SS soldier shoved the door open and stopped Kaarl in his tracks. He carried a book and Ariella's violin. He clicked his heels to attention. 'The building is empty, sir. And I found these.'

Kaarl grabbed the book. I could just make out the title: *The Homosexuality of Men and Women by Magnus Hirschfeld*. I recognised it. It was one of Ariella's that she had bought years ago.

'Ah, Doctor Hirschfeld,' Kaarl said and smirked, 'that Jewish homo who tried to change the law. This should've been destroyed with the rest years ago. Burn it,' he said and threw the book back to the soldier, 'and that,' he pointed to Ariella's violin.

The soldier threw the book and the precious Stradivarius on the fire.

'No!' Ariella tried to scramble to her feet to stop the soldier. She couldn't. She slumped back down and watched her treasured violin blister in the heat and then go up in flames. Smoke belched up the chimney, strings snapped and the violin pinged its last note.

Kaarl chuckled as though enjoying her pain. 'Let's get out of this shit-hole,' he said and with a tight hold on my arm, he trailed me outside. Ariella made a last dive for Kaarl to stop him. The soldier lunged at her and pulled her back.

CHAPTER 24

By the time the soldier dragged Ariella out onto the street, the other apartments were half emptied. Hundreds of Jews were being hauled out and loaded into trucks.

'You will be given accommodation and work,' the soldiers repeated monotonously. Everybody boarded the trucks without resistance.

A family came out from the building after Ariella; new neighbours, I guessed. The man carried two suitcases and the woman carried a toddler. They barged past Ariella but didn't board the trucks. The man kept cautiously looking back towards her. Ariella looked confused. The couple scurried away along the street as though heading for Grosse Hamburger Strasse. Or were they?

'How could you? Turning in your own kind,' Ariella shouted after them. They disappeared round the corner.

A fat SS Gruppenführer stepped out from a Mercedes and approached Kaarl. It was Eric Hagen.

'Can I go now, Kaarl, please,' Eric said.

'You snake, Eric. You did this,' I said. He must've been too scared after all. Auschwitz too much for him so he'd bargained with Kaarl, turning me in, suspicion of treating Jewish patients.

Eric looked puzzled. He turned back to Kaarl, 'Haven't I seen enough? Please can I go now?'

'Go,' Kaarl said and wafted his hand to chase him away. 'I'll make a man out of you yet,' he shouted after him.

The undertaker stepped out from the hearse, poker faced, walked towards Kaarl. I frowned not quite sure whose side he was on. I didn't know what was going on, couldn't figure out who had turned us in. Kaarl seemed to spot my confusion and proceeded to fill me in.

'I believe you've already met my...' Kaarl paused, rubbed two fingers against his brow, '...my assistant.'

Kaarl gave the short undertaker a manly slap on the back, as if to congratulate him. He tipped his hat.

I was gutted, 'Why?'

The stick insect blushed, embarrassed no doubt. Then bowed his head in shame. Should think so to. Surely he wasn't a Nazi?

He removed his hat like an obedient servant and glanced up to Kaarl, 'My family, sir?'

The smile on Kaarl's face dropped to a scowl.

The undertaker persisted, 'S-Sir, you promised them freedom.'

Oh no, he's no Nazi, I realised.

'Ah, yes,' Kaarl nodded. He slowly unbuttoned his leather coat as though he was going to give the undertaker something, then quickly pulled his pistol and shot the undertaker through the head. 'They're free,' he said calmly, the short Jew dropped dead at his feet, 'and so are you.'

'Alright, alright, there's no need for violence.' It was Ariella's father. Ester reached down to help him into the truck. An SS Gruppenführer shoved him to hurry him. Ariella tried to wriggle free from the soldier who escorted her. It was no use. He had a firm grip of her arm.

'Amit!' I shouted and quickly covered my mouth, realising my mistake.

'One of your patients?' Kaarl said calmly. I shook my head and stared at him. Kaarl marched over and grabbed Ariella's father.

Ariella kicked and shoved the soldier to break free. She knew as well as I did what was going to happen. It was too late. Kaarl reached for his pistol and spun around to face me.

'No, Kaarl, No, please.'

Kaarl pulled the trigger, Ariella's father dropped to the ground, innocent blood spurted from his head. 'They're all going to die anyway,' Kaarl shrugged, hands open and walked back towards me, an arrogant grin on his face.

'Papa!' Ariella bit the soldier's hand, wriggled free and run to her father. The SS Gruppenführer, who had shoved him, stood beside his dead body and blocked Ariella from going any closer. She ran at Kaarl. 'I'll kill you,' she shouted. The Gruppenführer swiped his arm across the back of her neck and knocked her to the ground.

I pushed Kaarl aside, rushed over and dropped to my knees beside her, 'Stop, Ariella. Please, he'll kill you.' Ariella struggled to get on her feet and fell back to the ground. She grabbed me and pulled me close to protect me. I snuggled in against her, wrapped my arms around her back, our bodies were entangled.

'Sshh, it's going to be okay, baby,' Ariella said, she held me tight in her arms and kissed the crown of my head.

Kaarl's smug grin was soon wiped away when he saw us together. It was obvious now, we were more than just friends. The colour drained from his face. His mouth gaped, he looked genuinely hurt.

'What the...' Kaarl said. He looked bewildered, as if he was trying to make sense of the situation. 'N-Nadette?' He looked stunned, blinked several times and shook his head as though trying to wake himself from a nightmare. He stumbled, feeling for the wall behind him. He sat down, both hands on the wall as though to hide the trembling. He tilted his head to the side and stared at me as though I had deeply betrayed him.

A few deep breaths and his hurt expression disappeared. He stood up. Scrunched eyes and tightened his lips. He straightened his tunic and dusted down his leather overcoat.

The SS Gruppenführer walked towards him, 'Kaarl? You alright?'

Kaarl's face twitched, clearly uncomfortable and embarrassed with my behaviour. Probably more so in front of an army of soldiers, particularly another SS leader. His fiancée was down on her knees, held tight in a lovers' embrace, with another woman. And worse still, in the arms of a Jew.

Kaarl laughed. A forced laugh. He pulled a hip flask from inside his army coat pocket and swigged back some courage. He looked to the Gruppenführer as though expecting him to laugh with him. The SS man remained solemn faced, 'Let's go, Kaarl,' he said and tapped his watch. He glanced at Kaarl's pistol and nodded his head towards us.

Kaarl's face changed, looking at us. He didn't look angry, he didn't look sad, in fact, he showed no emotion whatsoever. He simply had a job to do.

Ariella grabbed me tighter and pulled my head in against her chest as though trying to shield my eyes. But I could see. Kaarl walked towards us with his hand on his holster.

He towered above us, pouted his lips and rubbed his forehead with two fingers and stared down. My whole body quivered against Ariella, my knuckles white with grip, clinging to her jersey. Ariella's own arms trembled, squeezing me. She kept my head tucked in, not wanting me to face my executioner. I didn't want to look. But I had to.

Kaarl circled us, hands behind his back. He marched round us in small, deafening steps. What was he thinking? I wished he would just get it over with.

Kaarl dragged his pistol out and fired an angry shot into the air. Ariella tucked her head in against mine and squeezed me even tighter. I thought that was it. Then I heard his evil laugh. I looked up to stare at the monster. He grinned, blew on the pistol and sniffed as traces of gunpowder-smoke filtered into the air. He was deliberately drawing this out.

His pistol was still drawn while he continued to pace round us. All of a sudden, Kaarl swiped his arm around Ariella's neck. He had grabbed her from behind and trailed her to her feet. I clung on to her and screamed. Kaarl rammed the gun into Ariella's temple and warned me, 'Get back.'

Ariella stood with her head to the side, away from the gun and squeezed her hands into fists, refusing to let him frighten her although I suspect her heart was racing.

'Please Kaarl, no. I'm sorry. I'm sorry,' I begged for Ariella's life.

'She means nothing?' He wasn't really asking me.

'You know I belong to you, Kaarl,' I said and shook my head as I spoke.

'Then put her on that truck for Auschwitz-'

'Kaarl, please, no-'

'Do it. Or I'll shoot her right now, limb by limb and you can watch her die slowly.'

'Kaarl, I beg you, I'll come back home with you, just let her go-'

'Now!'

My eyes filled up. I looked at Ariella apologetically and bit on my lip. I didn't know what to say. My hand trembled when I reached out to take Ariella's. I led her towards the truck with Ester in it. Ariella refused to get in. She grabbed my arms and looked into my eyes, 'He'll kill you too,' she whispered.

'He's not finished with me,' I said. The tears were now flowing freely down my face. I lifted Ariella's hands off me and gently pushed her away, 'Go. Please,' I said, trying to save her life yet sending her on a terminal journey to Auschwitz.

Ariella slammed her palm against the tarpaulin on the truck. She glowered at Kaarl as though swearing revenge then boarded the truck alongside Ester.

'I'm sorry, Ariella. I'll find you.' It was a fruitless promise but it was the best I could come up with.

Kaarl's face was contorted. Muscles twitching and lips tightening. I'm surprised he didn't put a bullet in us right there and then, watching us having a last moment together. The fact that he didn't, could only suggest he had something worse in store for us.

I walked back towards him, head down, shoulders hunched. He grabbed my arm and ran me towards another truck.

Kaarl shouted at me, dictating in a monotone voice. He shoved me towards an army vehicle. He still harped on. Yelled into my face. He was in full flow as if he was quoting from a book. I looked up into his face, my mouth gaped; I didn't expect this.

He gave me an almighty shove and forced me to climb in with the other prisoners, my flimsy dress and fur coat restricting my movements.

The truck kicked into gear and drove off at the same time as Ariella's. The heavy vehicles burned down the tar in opposite directions, widening the distance between us.

Kaarl stared at me, rage in his eyes. This was not the last I would see of him.

CHAPTER 25

I sat in that truck, arms squeezed tight around me, head dipped, staring at the floor, going over and over events in my head. Ariella bound for Auschwitz. What had I done? I put my hands over my head. I had to get to her somehow. How was I supposed to do that, now that I had been arrested too?

I thought about Kaarl. How could he do this to me? To us? To Amit and the undertaker? A tear ran down my face, thinking about Amit and how I had failed to save him. Kaarl's face flashed in front of me. He was so cold, no feeling, when he pulled that trigger. He reminded me of the time when we were young kids. I was eleven, Kaarl about fifteen. Sven, Kaarl's father shot a Jewish man through the head, for no reason, other than the fact he was a Jew. Sven Bergmann, impassive, wiped away the man's blood, sprayed over his long, sharp chin. I had managed to hide, but Kaarl was in full view of his father. He timidly turned away and shoved his hands into his pockets as though to hide the shaking.

'Look, boy,' Sven had said to his son. He dragged Kaarl's face back, forcing him to look at the dead man, 'this is how we treat anyone who doesn't belong in our master race.'

When Kaarl pulled that trigger on Ariella's father, his emotionless face resembled Sven Bergmann's.

A mass of gaunt faces surrounded me in that truck. Arrested. Men and women and scrawny children grouped together with the one thing in common, a yellow star stuck to their tattered clothing. I could feel their eyes on me, staring, wondering why I was there with them.

When Kaarl saw me crouched beside Ariella, her loving arms around me, I felt sorry for him. He had never opened up and expressed his love for me but that hurt expression was undeniable. So why couldn't he just let me go? Why did he have to punish me?

His voice echoed through my ears, 'You are a lesbian. And have been with a Jew,' Kaarl had said. 'Lesbians may be excluded from Paragraph 175 of the German Criminal Code. But all German women are required to keep to their traditional duties of marrying and reproducing to perpetuate the pure Aryan race.' It was almost as if he had rehearsed the speech, said it so many times. 'Until you are able to do so, you must be taken into custody and sent for rehabilitation,' he had paused to look into my eyes. 'You will want me by the time I've finished with you,' he said, his voice calm. His face twitching with anger.

I couldn't believe he had actually arrested me. I really believed Kaarl would just take me home and lock me up, away from society. Then again, who knew what Kaarl was capable of? I never had expected him to arrest his closest friend, Otto, either or his pretend wife, Ingrid, who broke no law. They had to find some excuse to imprison lesbians, to punish us until we were ready to be Nazi baby making machines. And just what was that punishment?

CHAPTER 26

I had no idea where we were heading in that bitter, winter morning. It wasn't such a long journey though. A few twisty roads and bumps and then the truck screeched to a halt.

The soldiers jumped onto the road and ordered us to climb down. I felt ridiculous clambering down from that wagon wearing a knee-length dress and my high heels. I pulled up my collar and wrapped up cosy in my warm, mink coat. I felt guilty when other prisoners all around me dismounted in their shabby, winter clothing that looked so worn, I doubt there would be any warmth at all.

There was a damp chill in the air, early morning darkness still surrounding us. We had been dropped inside a large courtyard alongside several truckloads of prisoners. Through the foggy mist, I could barely make out the tall, sinister building. My legs almost buckled under me when I realised where we were - Berlin-Alexanderplatz police prison.

SS soldiers marched us inside. Our footsteps echoed as we walked along the corridors. A soldier struggled and used both hands to pull open a heavy, metal door. It creaked and rattled before he finally managed to wedge it open and order us to march through. The noise of my heels clicking seemed to overpower the gentle tiptoes from my surrounding Jewish compatriots.

We entered a spacious room. A high ceiling and tiny windows high up on the walls with vertical bars ended any notion of trying to escape. The heavy doors swooped closed behind us. A claustrophobic tightness gripped my chest.

The room was packed with prisoners, apprehensive men, women and children, predominantly Jews, wearing a yellow star.

'Queue up and give your details to the clerk. You may find a suitable resting place when all details have been entered.' It was a soldier, he marched up and down the line, repeated the same order over and over.

Everybody moved into the line that formed in the centre of the room. All queuing to give their particulars. Others sat at the side. Weary people lay flat out, exhausted, on mats close to the walls. All waiting for the Nazis next move. The stale smell of sweat, suggested these people had been here for a long, long time.

'Move,' a soldier said, and shoved me on the back. I was forced to join the queue gathering in the centre. I immediately obeyed and glanced up the line to see where they were heading.

A desk was stationed in the middle of the floor and a young SS clerk furiously battered the keys on a typewriter. A pile of papers was stacked by his side. He seemed to be recording every prisoner's details as they arrived.

Poor soul, I thought, what a tedious job he had. He raised his head for a second and rubbed his neck, a quick stretch, then back to the keyboard. That's when I noticed his scar; a long, thick line ran down his neck. My heart skipped a beat. I screwed up my eyes and peered ahead, trying to put a name to his face.

'Next,' the clerk called out. He didn't raise his head.

A young man further up the queue stepped forward. I'm sure he was German. No sign of a yellow star. I wondered what he had done. He bowed his head. His hands and arms trembled.

'P-Please, sir. I've been falsely arrested.' His voice was barely audible.

'Name?' The SS clerk still didn't raise his head.

'You don't understand—'

'No talking,' a soldier nearby said and smacked him on the back with his rifle. He knocked him straight off his feet. The young man's face was screwed up as though he was in considerable pain from the blow. He jumped to his feet and with no further hesitation, he answered the clerk's questions.

I could see the clerk now. I did know him.

In the background the soldiers started wolf-whistling. I spun round to see what was going on. The large, metal doors were wide open and another batch of prisoners filtered through.

'Hey, hey, what've we got here?' the soldiers said, in between their whistles.

'Don't touch what you can't afford, boys,' a woman said and teased the soldiers as she swaggered in.

She was probably about mid-twenties. She had long, curly, reddish-brown hair. Her face was so plastered with make-up she could've played the part as a circus clown.

She staggered up the queue, carrying her fur jacket over her arm, flaunting her flesh in her low cut top and very short skirt. She pushed past everyone else and the soldiers seemed to allow it. They stood back, laughed and whistled, and ogled at her bulging breasts.

The brassy woman filtered in behind me and stood with her hand on her hip, wildly chewing on her gum. She blew bubbles with her gum and looked me up and down.

I gave her a pleasant nod and forced a faint smile then turned to look up the queue. I was desperate to reach the clerk to see if he could help me.

The woman grabbed my shoulder, forced me back round.

'What's your name?' she said, her jaws sweeping open with every bite on her gum. She stood so close I could smell the minty vapours not quite masking the underlying smell of cognac.

'N-Nadette Eichmann,' I forced a smile.

'G-Gabriele Feurst,' she said, mimicking my stutter and then she curtsied, 'Local prostitute,' she said, smiled proudly and stuck her bosom in my face.

Another fake smile, I turned back to check my position in the queue. I felt a hard hand on my shoulder. Gabriele spun me back around. I almost lost my balance with the force. She stuck her face so close into mine I could actually see her freckles despite her attempts to conceal them with dark foundation.

Gabriele stood there with her hands on her hips.

'Hey, don't you judge me. It's my patriotic duty. I provided a good service to the SS and the Gestapo. They only arrested me 'cause I infected one of them.'

'No, no, I'm sorry, I didn't mean...' I touched her arm. My apology was feeble.

'What you here for?'

'I was-'

'Next,' the clerk interrupted before I could explain my reason for internment. The desk clerk faced the typewriter and inserted a fresh form, ready to take my details.

I stepped up to the desk and leaned over the young man and whispered, 'Günther Herman?'

He looked up and frowned at me as if he was trying to place me.

'I'm Doctor Eichmann. You were my patient.' I ran my finger down my neck, 'Remember?'

The desk clerk rubbed the scar on his neck and nodded. I had diagnosed a suspected tumour in his neck and sent him urgently to the hospital to have it removed. He swore to me he would be eternally grateful and would do anything for saving his life.

Today, I thought, my luck had changed. Günther Hermann was going to set me free. Instead he pushed out his bottom lip and turned his palms over. How could he be so apathetic? I faced imprisonment for the pure and simple reason of loving another woman and this man who had once felt indebted to me refused my call for help.

I glanced around the room, checked for nearby soldiers before I leaned over to whisper to him, 'I shouldn't be here. It's a mistake.'

The SS clerk sat back in his chair, folded his arms and looked up at me and sighed.

'It's the truth,' I said.

He shuffled through some papers as if he was pretending to check for me, pretending to look and see if I had been falsely detained. 'Nope. Can't help you,' he said and sat back on the chair. He placed his hands on the typewriter, looked up and waited for my details.

'Günther,' I whispered, 'I saved your life.'

Günther sighed and tilted to the side to look down the queue of people. He frowned and flipped his wrist to check his watch. 'Soldier,' he shouted and jerked his neck to summon him over.

I felt such a whack on my back. I crumpled to a heap and landed on the floor. The soldier stood over me, the butt of his rifle pointed at me, ready to give me another thud.

'No, no, please,' I said and raised my arms in submission. I was now a prisoner of the Alexanderplatz.

CHAPTER 27

An incredibly heavy prison guard with short, spiked hair marched me along the ghostly corridors. She was only young, probably early twenties but nature hadn't been kind to her at all. Her face was scrunched up so tight beneath layers of adipose, her features were barely visible. Her body was so padded, she swaggered from hip to hip, beads of sweat visible on her forehead from the effort of walking.

She puffed and panted with every step, her disgusting, mucous sniffs turned my stomach as we plodded on. She wobbled proudly, full of self-importance in that prison uniform that was so creased it looked like she had slept in it.

The guard reached for her jingling bunch of keys secured to her waist. Carefully she separated the cluster in her grubby, sweaty hands, she seemed to enjoy prolonging the agony of where I was to be detained.

At last she rattled the appropriate key in the lock and clanked the cell door open, the light from the corridor flashed into the dark room.

'In here,' the guard spoke at last. Her voice was deep and harsh.

It was a tiny cell with two bunk beds. A tall man in grey, SS uniform, came out from behind the door. He shielded his eyes as he tried to focus on me. My jaw dropped, Otto Schreiner, Kaarl's best friend had been sent to the Alex to be treated like a common criminal, just like me.

A man's voice, very effeminate, called down from the top bunk. 'What's happening, Otto?' He sat up, and rubbed his eyes as though he had just woken from sleep. He swung his legs over the side and peered forward to nosey down. He wore brown trousers and a Fair-Isle, patterned jersey.

I knew this man. I'd recognise that jersey anywhere. It was... It was... I couldn't put a name to the face and the jersey. Anton. That was it. It was Otto's lover, the man who had been arrested along with him. Why on earth would they put them both in the same cell, was my immediate, jealous thought.

Otto's jacket lay open, exposed his white shirt and braces. The SS man, blinked furiously with the light, his hand still acted as a visor. He peered closer, 'Nadette? What are you doing here? Where's Kaarl? Is he with you? Come to get me out?' He clearly didn't understand the situation.

The guard scrunched her curious face into a mass of wrinkles, frowning between me and Otto, as though wondering how we knew each other. She grabbed my arm and hauled me out of the cell. 'Men only in here. No intimate contact allowed,' she said and slammed the door shut behind us. I bowed to conceal my chuckle.

She gave the same performance with the keys to open the cell next door. The light from the corridor lit up the inside again. It was a much larger cell, not large enough to hold the hundred or so women that were crammed in.

The guard gave me such an almighty shove, I landed on the floor next to a frail woman. She reached her scrawny hand up to grab the guard's skirt.

'Please. Please help me,' she begged the guard.

The guard screwed up her eyes so tight her top lip went up and revealed green, stained teeth. It was as if she was trying to focus without glasses; maybe she thought they would spoil the look of her uniform.

'You again.'

She reached across her waist and pulled out a baton as if she was drawing a sword, and sliced down on the frail woman's fingers. The woman snatched her hand away. The guard ran at her and shoved the baton under the woman's chin. 'I warned you to shut up.' She pushed her back but the woman called after her again.

'Please, don't hit me. I need your help,' she grabbed at the guard again.

The heavy guard booted her so hard in the ribs, she fell back against me. She raised her fat leg again and was about to stamp into her stomach when I put my arms up to stop her. I don't know what I was thinking. I couldn't seem to stop myself from jumping to the frail woman's defence.

The guard jerked back, frowned into her wrinkled face again, puzzled by my actions. I cowered down beside the woman with my arms protectively around her. Timidly we both stared up at the fierce guard. What was she going to do next?

She tightened her lips in annoyance and booted me away from the woman and stamped down on my stomach. I rolled over, gasped for breath. The guard smirked. She marched back out of the cell, pushed the key in the small crevice on the outside of the door and clicked it around until we were locked in. A tightness crossed my chest, I was feeling claustrophobic and gasped for air. Slow deep breaths in and out, I had to get this sorted, quickly.

It took me a few minutes to adjust to the locked cell and to the darkness. A sliver of light seeped in from the small window on the door. The eerie moonlight didn't help; the white crescent skulked between dark clouds and cast an intermittent faint beam through the tiny, barred window on the far side of the cell.

There was an awful stench, I thought I was going to be sick. Where was it coming from? I covered my mouth and looked around to trace the smell. There it was; a toilet in the nearby corner, full of excrement and no flushing mechanism. Over a hundred women were expected to use this facility and it didn't even flush. The tiny window, although open a fraction, had no chance of purifying the room.

The smell didn't just come from the toilet; the air was putrid, stinking with body odour. I scanned the dark room, taking in my new environment. Over a hundred dirty inmates, women and young girls who looked and smelled as if they hadn't seen soap and water for quite some time, were tightly packed into the one cell.

Most prisoners lay sleeping, their grubby bodies exposed to the night air, no blankets to cover them. They huddled together for warmth, each bed heavily occupied. Woman lay back to back or head to toe. The majority however, sprawled on the ground, taking residence in every spare inch of floor space.

The restless women scratched and scraped at their skin as though their bodies were covered in lice. I clawed at my arms, feeling an imaginary itch. The tickle spread to my legs and across my foot. When I reached down to scratch, a dark flicker caught my eye and crossed my shoe. It was a cockroach, I immediately shook it off. But soon noticed there was more than one. The floor was crawling. My flesh tingled, goose bumps all over. I jumped back, let out such a yell and disturbed the sleeping inmates.

Some women were already awake, probably disturbed by the guard's outburst.

'Oh. Scared of little bugs are we?' It was a woman's voice from somewhere in the dark side of the room.

The silhouette approached me through the darkness. She was much taller than me, especially in those high heeled boots, climbing her legs as far as her knees. She had the same provocative dress style as that woman Gabriele whom I had met earlier in the admittance section of the prison. She looked me up and down in the same aggressive way. I bit on my lip and stared.

The cell became noisy. Some more inmates had sat up and moaned, wondered what the rabble was about. Some even rose to their feet and shuffled over to nosey at me. I was surrounded by visible thighs and bulging breasts. The cell may have been eerily dark but it was light enough for me to see I had been imprisoned in a cell full of prostitutes, and I couldn't understand why.

The one with the long boots moved in closer, circled me and pawed at my fur coat. She had a strange, long face with a pointed chin and a heap of blonde, curly hair that sprouted from her head like straw from a burst mattress. Her striking dark eyes were as black as a stormy sky. Massive, black rings circled underneath. She was by far the scariest person I had ever seen.

'What we got here? Rich little German girl?' she said.

'P-Please don't touch me.' I tugged my coat tight around me and edged away from her. She grabbed me by the hair with full force. I could imagine the roots coming away from the follicles. The pain shot through my scalp.

'I'll do what I want with you. Got it?' she said and pushed her fist against my head as she released the bunched hair.

My eyes filled. I grabbed the bars on the cell door, 'Guard. Guard. Please,' I shouted, peered through the teeny space, begging for help.

The frail woman, I had so eagerly tried to defend, scrambled to her feet and pulled me away from the door, 'No. She'll beat you too,' she said.

The rowdy ladies of the night had ganged up on me and were moving closer.

'Guard, there's been a mistake,' I shouted and hammered my fists on the door.

'Shut up in there,' the guard roared.

'Please, get me out of here.' I begged for the aggressive guard to come back. Anything was better than face the crowd of bulldogs who snarled, almost drooled, pining to get their paws on the fresh meat.

'What's going on? Shut up. Trying to sleep here.' The remainder of sleeping dogs stirred and joined in with the attack.

'I said shut up in there.' The guard banged her flabby fist against the metal door.

Tears flooded, a lump in my throat prevented me from coherent speech. 'I-I don't belong here. The words were muffled but clear enough for the attacking inmates.

'Oh. Don't belong here.' The voice came from the instigator, the weird woman with the black eyes and long boots. She mimicked me and laughed, encouraged the others to laugh too. Her voice changed, aggressive again, 'Too good for us, eh?'

'Give her one, Panda, don't let her get away with that,' one of her comrades said.

'Oh, I will, don't you worry,' Panda said, her high heels scuffed the floor, she swaggered towards me.

'No, no, I'm sorry, I didn't mean-'

A tug on my hair again. Panda had grabbed me. She swung me around and threw me into the centre of the room, and like starving dogs, the pouncing women snared me.

The guard's keys clinked in the lock. Hope. She unlocked the door and barged in.

'It's alright guard, we'll take care of her,' the ring leader said and smirked. Her black eyes pierced into mine, confident she could silence my yelps.

'You better shut her up,' the guard said.

'Yes ma'am,' the bullying inmate said and shoved me into the centre of the pack, her eyes glared, her fangs protruded from behind the drawn in top lip. The useless guard rested against the wall and folded her arms as though positioning herself, ready to be entertained by the ring fight. I could hear her laughing over the shouts and screams coming from the bitches as they launched their attack.

My head throbbed and my body ached during that savage assault. My coat was ripped off my back, my Rolex watch, snapped from my wrist. But my necklace, my precious necklace, remained intact, hidden, tucked inside my dress.

A light caught my eye and filtered in through the women's legs surrounding me. It was the cell door being pushed wider. The guard reached out her flabby arm to grab another prisoner and yanked her into the cell. The new arrival was thrown into the fighting arena. 'Another one coming through,' the guard said and laughed, highly entertained by the squabble.

Gabriele Feurst landed face to face, alongside me on the floor. 'What's going on?'

'Help me,' I mouthed the words.

I didn't know this woman. I had only met her hours before but I hoped she would help. She scrambled out through a small gap between the kicking legs. And from the safety of the side-lines, she called out, 'Get up. Get on your feet.'

I couldn't get up. I couldn't get on my feet. Women were piled on top of me.

Gabriele peered in through the gap, 'They'll kill you if you don't get up.'

Her words stung in my ears. Ariella's face flashed in front of me. I wasn't ready to die. I had a life waiting for me. Somehow I curled my fingers into a pathetic fist and landed a punch on the nearest woman and knocked her off me. I surprised myself. I had never hit anyone in my life before and although I hated having to do it now, it felt good. I had succeeded in getting one of those mauling creatures off me. I managed to draw myself onto my knees and before I knew it, I was standing up, facing my attackers. Both my fists were clenched, one arm out straight, the other crossing me. It was a ridiculous stance. I didn't know what else to do.

My eyes were so swollen I could barely see the laughing women. I tried to grit my teeth behind the bloated lips and licked away the blood that trickled into my mouth pretending I had been through all this before. My shaking legs were a bit of a giveaway though.

'Okay, enough,' roared the guard, bored now, her fun was over.

Obediently the pack dispersed, their master had spoken. Within a few minutes they were all back in their corners ready for sleep.

I found myself a space next to the door, slid down the wall and watched the guard close the door behind her and lock us prisoners in for the night.

The frail woman was curled up in a ball, shivering in the corner with only a thin coat to keep the chilly, night air away.

Gabriele had planked herself beside me. She sat with her back against the wall, fur jacket removed and wrapped around her chest. She pulled her knees up, tucked her chin in and closed her eyes ready for sleep.

I massaged my naked arms, trying to warm the blood, and edged ever so slightly against Gabriele for some body heat and a fraction of her warm covering. Every inch of my body ached from the beating. I wanted to cry but my eyes were so badly swollen, the tears would've been too painful. Instead I reached inside my dress, grabbed my necklace and squeezed it tight. Never was there a time so bad that I wanted to believe Ariella's lovely story about the necklace; to believe in its special powers. I knew, it was just a pretty pendant. But it was Ariella's, and that was enough for me.

The cell door screeched open, waking me from my slumber. The corridor light shone in, instantly I covered my eyes and peered through a slat in my fingers to see what the fat guard was up to now. About ten more women were shoved into the already overcrowded cell. I pulled my knees up tighter against my chest and curled my feet in, away from the boisterous new arrivals. It didn't take them long to source a bed, toss sleeping prisoners aside and force them to the floor.

Sleep was impossible for me after that. The air was thick with expelled carbon dioxide, fumes of vile breath. Some women were obviously accustomed to such appalling conditions and slept freely, snoring, grunting and passing thunderous wind. It was going to be a long night.

When the guard returned a few hours later, I gasped, dreading another batch of inmates being tossed in with us. She entered with a clipboard and called out names from her sheet. Inmates, aroused from sleep, shouted out abusive names at her and told her impolitely, to go away. The fat guard scrunched her face, ran at them and trailed the women from their beds onto the floor. There was a mighty thud as their bodies hit the deck. The guard's rubber truncheon rattled against their flesh. The women protested no further. They were marched outside the cell and ordered to form rank ready for transportation to a concentration camp. I pitied them, but have to say, I was glad of the extra breathing space.

New arrivals soon took the place of the despatched. More prostitutes, Jews and even nuns were imprisoned. Within a short while, more disgruntled women were marched out. This coming and going went on all through the night.

I clung tight to my necklace, thinking about Ariella, and wondered if she had already being despatched to the concentration camp.

CHAPTER 28

'Ariella come sit with us,' Ester shouted.

She was sitting alongside another Jewish family, the people who had lived next door to them. They had been on their way to the deportation centre with their call up papers when all the others were arrested. Ariella had apologised, embarrassed for accusing them of being informants.

The exhausted family had already been waiting for hours by the time Ariella and Ester had arrived at Grosse Hamburger Strasse. Ariella thought they were heading straight to Auschwitz, but instead, they had gone on a roundabout tour. The Nazis had stopped several times to pick up more Jews before taking them all to the deportation centre.

Hundreds of despairing people, crammed into the school building that formerly accommodated so many hopeful pupils. Ariella paced up and down, eyes fixated on the tired, hungry faces and withering bodies that lined the walls in the grim detention centre. There was no way out. Soldiers guarded the doors. Bars blocked the windows. Ariella moved closer to look out to the darkness. Guards paraded the grounds. Fatigued travellers arrived by the minute and squeezed into the school or the neighbouring old folks home.

'Come on, Ariella,' Ester called again.

Ariella walked over to join Ester and the family she had befriended.

The toddler was wriggling, his face flushed and skin clammy from the clustered bodies that surrounded him, all tightly packed into that foul smelling waiting station. His clothing was grubby and smeared in food stains, and his nappy was ripe with urine. His mother seemed distraught, trying to calm him through the long, tedious hours.

Ester took over, all smiles, delighted with the child in her arms. She bounced the boy on her knee. Ariella had never seen Ester so happy. They were stuck in the midst of transportation to goodness knows where, yet Ester's strong motherly instincts took over. The boy's needs were all that mattered, rendering her oblivious to the misery surrounding them.

Ester fed him scraps from the hard, crusty bread she had been given for the journey. When that failed to satisfy the restless toddler, she sang to him, pulled faces and tickled the baby boy. Ariella felt sorry for her, knowing she had longed to have her own family, to be a wife and a mother. She looked at her now, dressed in that drab clothing. Ariella was pretty sure if the food hadn't been rationed, Ester would've eaten her way to obesity with her obsessive behaviour to keep a man from becoming too close. She coughed and spluttered, turning her head away from the toddler, as though afraid she would scare him off; the same irrational fear she seemed to have with men.

That troublesome cough had haunted Ester for years, preventing her from fun activities as a child and labelled her as defective, suitable for taunting. Ariella couldn't remember how many boys she had to beat up for teasing her, the same boys who had come back years later hoping for a date. This time, it was Ester who had chased them away.

Ariella watched her now, how happy she seemed with that child. Her joviality with the boy attracted the attention of a middle-aged man, seemingly on his own. He approached Ester and assisted with the calming of the irritable toddler.

The man smiled at Ester, he watched her, his gaze holding longer than necessary. Ariella thought he could see through her cover and spotted the beauty she had underneath. Ester's face flushed. She stammered and mumbled nonsense at Ariella and turned her head away from the man's gaze.

There was a sudden uproar of shouting in the background. The soldiers were rounding everybody up.

Ester jumped to her feet and handed the toddler back to the young mother's arms, 'Come on, Ariella, that's us, time to go,' she said, sounding excited.'

Ariella looked at her curiously. She wasn't sure if she was still trying to be positive, or if she was just relieved to escape the advances of the friendly man. He frowned at her and clambered to his feet then disappeared into the crowd.

Ester's newly adoptive family stood up and huddled together. The mother clutched the child tight and the young father was laden with two heavy suitcases. They filtered into line.

'Where do you think, they'll send us? I've heard such horrible stories,' the young father said.

'Oh, I'm sure they're not true,' Ester said and sauntered in behind him, 'everything will be fine.'

'Everything's not alright, Ester,' Ariella said, the young couple's eyes widened. 'They want rid of us. They hate us.'

'Oh, they do not, Ariella. Don't be so dramatic.'

'Dramatic! They're beating us. Starving us. Taking our families... shooting my father,' Ariella added as a quiet reminder. 'You still think I'm being dramatic? They're evil, every single one of them.'

'I'm really sorry about your papa, Ariella. But I don't think they're all bad. Even that Kaarl, I'm sure he wasn't always like that.'

'They're all evil,' Ariella argued. 'They were born that way.'

'Oh, they were not, Ariella. Nobody's born to be bad. Take a look around. Most of these soldiers are only young boys. They're just doing what they're told.'

'Hmmm, doubt it. It's in their Aryan blood. I'd love to take a gun to any one of them and blow his Nazi brain out.'

'That's horrible. How can you talk like that? And you think they're evil? You've got to stop hating, Ariella. It's destroying your soul.'

'Silence,' a soldier said and pushed Ariella and Ester ahead.

They were led outside. Rows of buses awaited them, their headlights darkened, probably for fear of aircraft bombing.

The restless toddler was in front. He threw a tantrum and broke free from his mother's fierce grip and scarpered across the icy playground.

A soldier ran after him, slipping and sliding on the black ice. 'Halt,' he roared and hauled his gun off his shoulder.

The mother screamed and bolted across the slippery tar. She grabbed the soldier, begged him not to shoot. He swung his rifle around and belted the woman on the face and knocked her over. The young boy turned when he saw his mother on the ground and ran back into her arms.

Ariella glanced up and down the line of bewildered faces. Everybody was facing in one direction, eyes fixed on the incident.

There was so much darkness. All torches shone in the path to the mother and child. Ariella ran her hands through her hair, her mind racing. They could make it round the side of the building. Wait there until the buses pulled away. Slip into the darkness. Cut through the old graveyard at the back and escape.

'Come on, quick, let's go,' Ariella whispered and grabbed Ester's arm, pulled her aside away from the squabble.

'What are you doing?' Ester said and yanked her trembling arm away from her.

'Come on. It's the distraction we need.'

'No, Ariella, it's too dangerous.'

'Come on, Ester, quick. While we've got the chance.'

Ester's body was frozen to the spot. Her trembling thumb wedged between her teeth. 'I can't. You go.'

Time was running out. Ariella stared behind her, thinking how easily she could've disappeared into the darkness.

Ester turned to join the others. Her weary legs, buckling under her carrying her suitcase.

'Damn!' Ariella slammed her fist against the wall and watched Ester struggle. She had no choice but to rush over and carry her baggage.

A gun went off in the background. Two shots fired. Everybody was rigid, heads bowed. Silence among the crowds. Ariella saw the bodies. She couldn't believe it. A child. A mother. The father frozen to the spot. Luggage dropped at his feet. Ester turned away, covered her eyes. No prisoners dared to look at the slaughter. But Ariella did. She glared at the soldiers, waiting for an opportunity to obliterate one of them, just one.

Ester wailed. Her hand was on Ariella's arm jolting her back from her fantasy. 'Stop it, Ariella, please,' Ester said, staring into her face as if she had read her thoughts. Her trembling fingers were up at her mouth again, chewing on her nails.

Ariella looked down into Ester's drawn face and pulled up her collar to shut out the cold. 'Come on, you know I'll take care of you.' She put her arm around her shoulder and walked back with her into the line that was now boarding the buses. The young man was ahead of them, shoved onto the bus, leaving his lifeless family behind. There wasn't another sound in the dead of the night.

CHAPTER 29

The prison cells were dead quiet. No words. No movement. Only the occasional grunt or snore from the inmates rattled across the silence.

I was positioned close to the door, I could hear the slightest movement in the corridor and from the nearby cells.

It was difficult for me to sleep. I was in so much pain. Probably why I seemed to be the only one who heard the masculine voice enter through the prison doors and command attention at the front desk.

'Otto Schreiner? Where is he?' he demanded. It was Kaarl's voice. I could recognise his harsh tone from a mile off.

I scrambled to my feet to peer out past the bars on the small opening on the cell door. I couldn't see a thing, I could only listen.

File drawers screeched open and clattered shut, as if the desk clerk was looking for the prisoner's location.

'Get a move on,' Kaarl roared at the man.

Papers and files still rustled, possibly dropped to the floor. Kaarl probably bullied the clerk into total nervousness, causing him to clumsily drop the files from his fumbling hands.

'What the hell are you doing?' Kaarl's voice again. I was waiting for a bunch of expletives but the desk bell was battered instead.

'Is there anybody in there who knows what they're doing?'

More banging on the bell.

'Get me a competent clerk right now,' Kaarl shouted.

'D-Down the back, along to the right, sir, second door,' the clerk stammered out, file found at last.

'About time too.'

Two sets of heavy footsteps echoed through the corridor and stopped at Otto's cell next door to me. Kaarl with a guard. It wasn't the same female guard who brought us in; she would never have been able to keep up that pace. It was definitely a soldier in heavy boots.

'Hurry up!'

'Yes, sir, almost ready, sir,' the jittery soldier said and fumbled with a bunch of keys.

Before the cell door was opened, another set of footsteps approached. A different voice. A deep voice talking to Kaarl. He must've recognised him. I grabbed the bars and pulled myself up to peer out through the small gap in the door. It was an older man with grey hair. A policeman in green uniform; chief I think. Judging by Kaarl's stance, Kaarl felt inferior to him.

'Kaarl, my man, good to see you,' the police chief said and slapped Kaarl's shoulder. 'Sorry to hear about your father. He was a good man. Bomb blast, wasn't it?'

'Yes, sir, last year.'

'A good man, a good man.' The police chief slapped him on the back again.

A good man? Sven Bergmann? I frowned. Kaarl certainly wouldn't know anything about that. He hardly saw his father when he was growing up. When he did see him, he only saw the badness. Even at home, Sven frequently shouted at Margo, intimidated his mother in front of him.

The police chief patted Kaarl's shoulder, paused to look at the insignia. 'Ah, Gruppenführer. Your father would be proud.'

'Gestapo chief too, sir,' Kaarl said with a childish grin as though seeking approval from his senior; the approval he never did get from his father.

'Excellent, Kaarl. Excellent. What department?'

'Special Office. Tracking homosexuals, sir,' Kaarl boasted.

It was just as well Kaarl couldn't see me through the gap in the cell door; I was scowling, hating him for having me locked up because of my sexuality.

'Oh,' the policeman said, surprised. 'What do you think your father would say about that?'

Sven probably wouldn't have been interested in that either, I thought. It was Margo who pushed him all the way in his career. If Kaarl could track down homosexuals, then he would soar through the ranks, his mother had told him.

'He'd be proud, sir,' Kaarl said with uncertainty.

'Hmm, indeed, indeed,' the policeman replied and rubbed his chin. He probably felt his father would've preferred Kaarl to stay with the police force and progress through their ranks as well as the SS, the same as Sven did, miraculously achieving dual status as General of both.

'And who are you in to see now?' the policeman asked.

'Otto Schreiner, an SS faggot,' Kaarl clenched his teeth. The chief nodded, patted him on the shoulder again and walked off down the corridor.

Kaarl turned to the armed guard and ordered him to open the cell door. The guard had the key in the lock, waiting. A quick click and the door creaked open. I could imagine Kaarl's face when he saw his friend, Otto, imprisoned for the crime of homosexuality, sharing a cell with his male lover. My swollen lips ached as my mouth broke into an uncontrollable grin.

'What idiot put you two together?' Kaarl said. 'Ah, never mind. I've come to get you out,' Kaarl said. 'Because you're a member of the SS, I'm giving you a chance to redeem yourself.'

'I should bloody think so too. Damn clerks. Get me the idiot who made the mistake,' Otto said.

I squeezed my ear through the bars, trying to make out the conversation. There was no way on earth Kaarl had made a mistake with Otto's arrest. I knew he must've had some other plan up his sleeve.

Footsteps shuffled about Otto's cell. I grabbed the bars to the tiny opening and tiptoed to peer out again. There they were, all of them in the corridor. Kaarl was with a soldier, his gun on Otto and his lover. Kaarl pulled his pistol out and pointed it to the ceiling, clicked it, ready to fire. Otto stood in front of his lover, arms out protectively. Anton was crouched in behind him, he hung onto Otto's jacket.

'What're you doing?' Otto demanded.

Kaarl dragged the cowering man out from behind Otto and offered Otto the pistol.

'Shoot this man and you walk free,' Kaarl said bluntly.

I covered my mouth trying to conceal the audible gasp then turned away and glanced inside my own cell. Everybody was still asleep. Nobody seemed to hear the evil that was going on in the corridor.

I couldn't bear to look out, but I couldn't bear not to.

The terrified Anton was crouched in front of Kaarl. His whole body trembled. Otto's face grew hard and tight, 'Put that away this instant,' he roared at Kaarl, pointing to his gun.

Kaarl remained calm. He tilted his head back and looked down his nose from under the rim of his cap, 'You are a homosexual. Shoot him now or you will be sent to camp for rehabilitation.'

'I will not. This is ridiculous.' Otto was outraged and stood with his head up and chest out as if he was determined to let Kaarl know he was proud of who he was.

Anton slowly raised his head, took a deep breath and pushed himself to his feet. He too, stood up with chest out and head held high. He interrupted the conversation, 'Do it, Otto. SS homosexuals don't get to leave concentration camps, you know that,' Anton said. It may have been an effeminate voice but it sounded mighty manly to me.

Kaarl smirked at Anton. 'Quite a man after all.'

Otto paused for a moment, breathing deeply, his lips pulled tight. He shook his head, defeated. He reached out and patted Anton's shoulder, then looked down at the gun still in Kaarl's hand.

My eyes widened. I gripped the bars tighter. A chill ran down my spine. Otto was going to shoot the man he loved. I wanted to turn away, didn't want to witness the murder. My hands were numb, my body rigid, I was frozen to the spot.

Otto switched his gaze from the gun to Kaarl and stared into his eyes, 'Which camp?' Otto asked calmly and buttoned up his jacket.

I heaved a sigh. The tension released from my shoulders.

Kaarl shook his head, disappointment on his face. He calmly turned the pistol round and pulled the trigger on Anton.

Anton's body fell backwards. Dark red blood burst from his head and formed into a puddle at Kaarl's feet. Otto ran to his lover's aid and held his motionless body one last time. Anton's blood saturated through his SS uniform.

'I gave you the chance,' Kaarl said and shrugged. 'Now move it,' he roared. He signalled to the armed guard to drag Otto to his feet.

Everything seemed in slow motion after that. I released my hands from the bars and dropped back down from my tiptoes. The restless inmates had stirred at the gunshot. Their voices seemed to be somewhere in the distance, not registering.

'What's going on? What's happening?' cried one woman after another.

Gabriele was on her feet first. She pushed me aside and tiptoed to nosey out. The others followed, climbed from their slumber and headed towards the cell door. A curious crowd peered through the gap. I stood with my back against the wall, staring, into nothingness.

The raucous women shouted and goaded Kaarl, angry at the dead prisoner lying in the corridor, in a pool of blood. I could hear shouting above the noisy women; it was the voice from the hefty guard. To my surprise, it wasn't the guard who came to the door. Kaarl looked in through the gap. I cowered and slid down the wall, trying to make myself invisible.

'Get away from this door. You bunch of whores,' Kaarl barked at the women who gathered round the steel door and forced even the loudest of the crowd to retreat. I bowed down. I could feel his eyes on me. From the corner of my eye, I watched him, trying to figure out what evil plan he had in store next. He stood blinking, staring at me as if he was astounded to see me in such a beaten state. Did he feel sorry for me? Not for long. His muscles started twitching, his top lip crawled into a sneer. Kaarl had sent me to prison for a purpose and I knew he would make sure that purpose was fulfilled.

He turned to the approaching guard who wheezed in his ear as he crouched to peer in. She seemed to be struggling to catch her breath from her strenuous, lengthy corridor walk.

'Get your stinking breath out of my face,' he snarled at her and shoved her back. 'And lose some weight. How can you handle prisoners in that state?'

The guard seemed to pause then peered in past him. Her face crinkled in annoyance, she gritted her green teeth as though she was going to show him how tough she could be. A raging Kaarl and an antagonised, evil guard, I shuddered to think what was in store next.

Kaarl shoved her aside and looked in again. He closed one eye, pointed two fingers straight at me as though looking down the sights of a gun.

'That one,' he said, pulling the guard over to see where he was pointing. 'Make sure she's on the next transport out.'

The guard screwed up her eyes to focus on his target and gave an affirmative nod. I wrapped my arms tightly around my body, my heart beating faster by the minute.

CHAPTER 30

It was still pitch black when the key rattled in the cell door. I had fallen into a light sleep on the floor beside Gabriele. The guard threw the door open, the bright corridor lights blinded me. I put my hand up to shield my eyes. Some other women sat up and did the same. We focused on the heavy guard who carried a clipboard. She held it so close to her face it was only inches away from her nose. She strained to read from the list attached to its front.

'Krueger, Bader, Eichmann, Gersten, Feurst. Get in line now,' the guard roared. I was so desperate to leave that filthy cell I jumped to my feet. A bewildered Gabriele looked up at me. Her name was on the list too.

'Come on, we're leaving,' I said and extended a friendly hand to pull her to her feet. She was in no hurry to rise and threw her arms wide, stretching and yawning, annoyed at being disturbed from her sleep.

'On your feet.' The guard scowled at her. Her face was scrunched and her teeth were tight.

Gabriele looked up at her, not in the least bit intimidated and waved her off, puffing out an annoyed burst of air. The guard reached for her rubber truncheon and skimmed it across her face.

'Alright, alright, I'm coming,' Gabriele said and crossed her arms in the air defensively. She rose to her feet, her skirt climbing her thighs in the process. She squeezed in behind me and forced the formed line backwards. The women grunted and groaned, half slept. They marched single file out of the cell door behind me. The fat guard pushed us into pairs, proving she was able to handle us.

The corridor was lined with other female prisoners with tired, bewildered faces. All of them, hauled out from their sleep from nearby cells. SS soldiers waited to march us out of the prison.

We stamped on the blood stained corridor where Anton had only hours before been shot; the dead man's blood sticking to the soles of our shoes.

We stumbled to a halt at the prison doors, ordered to stand to attention, eyes front, hands by our sides. One woman in front of us, grunted and slouched, leaning her head on her comrade's shoulder. A flabby arm swiped across her cheek. 'Stand up straight now,' the guard said. The woman jumped to attention.

Nobody made a sound after that. We waited while the guard disappeared into a room. Still silence among the inmates.

The guard was only gone moments before she returned carrying bread baskets with a delicious, hot aroma. She handed us small bread rolls and begrudgingly handed them out.

'Don't eat now. These are to last you for the journey.'

I don't know how long it had been since these women had eaten but they devoured every morsel of that bread within seconds. The guard stared at them, enjoying every bite.

My own stomach grumbled. I realised I hadn't eaten since the day before. But watching these women attack their bread and humiliate themselves in front of the laughing soldiers staved off my hunger. I shoved my bread roll stealthily into my dress pocket and vowed I would never reduce myself to such savage behaviour.

A soldier shouted out orders. We were about turned and marched outside.

It was still dark. I rubbed my arms briskly. The chilly, early morning freshness descended upon my bare arms. I sure missed my fur coat, now securely wrapped around another woman's shoulders who stood in the line behind me.

We piled into the awaiting trucks.

'Come on girls, climb on board,' the soldiers said. They laughed and cheered at the women in their short skirts who clambered into the army vehicles.

'Get lost,' Gabriele said and brushed them away with her hand, too tired to be bothered. She boarded the truck and shuffled along the bench beside me and snuggled her head into my shoulder in preparation for sleep. I was glad of her body heat but she made no attempt to share her fur jacket. The other women huddled together and closed their tired eyes. They didn't seem in the least perturbed at the journey and didn't seem concerned at where they would end up. Perhaps this wasn't their first arrest.

An armed soldier jumped in with us and the truck drove off. I stared out past the tarpaulin that hadn't even been rolled down. The freezing wind whistled in through the moving vehicle. I hoped it would be a short trip.

We arrived at the train station fairly quick. The sky was grey black, early morning light trying to break through. The women moaned, disturbed from their sleep, when the truck jolted to a halt.

'Get down. Now.' The guard dismounted and jerked his neck for us to follow.

We were hurried along, our high heels clicked on the hard surface as we scurried in through the station. Hundreds of women were already lined up on the platform, waiting for the train to arrive. An army of SS soldiers restraining vicious looking Alsatians, marched up and down to guard the prisoners. My whole body trembled.

'You got to toughen up,' Gabriele said.

'I'm fine, I'm fine,' I said and rubbed my trembling hands together, pretending to warm up.

The uniformed men paraded up and down the platform while we waited for the train.

Dawn was breaking by the time our transport arrived. I was apprehensive with no idea where we were going but I was so cold and shivered so much, I didn't care. I just wanted a heat inside the train, crawling into the station.

SS soldiers sat along the roof, hands firmly wrapped around their guns, ready to shoot anyone who failed to comply with orders.

'Move forward. Prepare to board,' the platform soldiers shouted their orders and pushed us ahead. Male faces peered out from some carriages but the others seemed to be reserved for the women.

We climbed on board and entered through a narrow passageway. The train was made up of individual prison cars; grossly overcrowded cells on both sides with female prisoners crammed in. The cell doors had small, barred windows. Deep, grieving eyes and withered faces peered out.

Once again, panic was tightening my throat. Where was I going to be locked in this time? I took deep breaths, my belly rising with each inhalation; a terrific calming effect I had often used on my patients.

I was crammed into a tiny cell alongside Gabriele. Four other women were already squeezed in, all as promiscuously dressed as her. I couldn't believe it; I was jammed in with more aggressive prisoners, prostitutes by the look of them. I looked round the faces, wondering why a lesbian was being locked up with women who had probably slept with a multitude of men.

Gabriele must've seen the look on my face. 'We're all the same now, honey,' she said.

I was actually pleased to be drawing heat, sandwiched among the sweaty, unkempt women who had clearly been travelling for quite some time.

There was no room for us to sit comfortably, we were jammed in tight. Somehow I managed to slither into a corner and squatted down against the wall. Gabriele squeezed herself in beside me. The others stood, staring down and stretched their legs as though they were cramping. Their tired, angry faces glared at the new arrivals as if wondering what we were going to do next. There was nothing to do, except wait. Wait till the journey was over, and wait to see where we were going to be imprisoned.

My stomach grumbled again. Surreptitiously I slipped my hand into my dress pocket and reached for my hidden, bread roll. I curled my fingers to cover the food and discreetly slipped it up to my mouth. The hovering vultures had their eyes on me and watched my every move. Hungry faces, eyes popping out, and mouths salivating. These women looked like they would kill for food. A tall, lanky woman spread her arms out, pushed forward through the fast approaching buzzards, lunged at me and snatched the bread away. It happened so fast I was left with jaw hanging open and an empty hand still lingered in front of my mouth. The other prisoners dived to the floor, attacked the thief and scrambled to steal a precious bite from her mouth.

I cowered in the corner. Gabriele remained beside me. I was surprised she didn't race for the food too. 'You got to stand up for yourself. They're going to keep doing this,' she said.

She had a point. I wasn't going to survive anywhere if these women continued to attack me, especially if they kept stealing my food. I bit down on my swollen lip; it still throbbed from the last fight with the women in the Alexanderplatz. I tried to follow the battle for bread, seeking an opportunity to dive in. Punches were flying and bare buttocks pointed in the air. A tiny piece of bread passed from woman to woman. It was my bread roll. I drew a breath and clenched my trembling hand and worked up the courage to take back what was mine. Slowly I pushed myself up onto my feet. Gabriele raised her leg and shoved her long boot with pointed heel right into my backside. I let out such a roar as I landed among the fighting women.

The bread, my bread roll was in the hands of the lanky woman who stole it from me in the first place. My heart was racing and my stomach was in a knot but I daren't stop now. I sat on her chest and slammed my palm hard against her forehead, pinning her down against the floor and snatched the bread from her. Before I could even tighten my fingers round the precious food, somebody from behind, reached in and swiped it over my head.

I jumped off the lanky lady and followed the sweet smell of dough. A small, hardy woman had escaped into a corner and was about to shove the bread into her mouth when I landed on top of her. My legs were spread across her lap, sitting on her knee. I don't know where the idea came from, but I spread my fingers out and curled the tips like cats claws. I squeezed my teeth together and parted my lips and hissed at her. The woman looked almost as shocked as I was. She tossed the bread up into the cell. Hands and arms scrambled for it. I swiftly rolled off the woman and pounced up into the air like a cat jumping for a bird in mid- flight, and caught my bread roll in my curled paw.

'Victory,' I shouted and crawled into a corner and ripped the roll apart and greedily ate it before anyone else could take it from me. I watched anxiously for approaching predators.

The bread vanished, my lips licked and the taste gone. I sat and looked around the angry women who had retreated and curled into their corners. Within such a short space of time, I had become an animal, fighting for survival and I was only on the train journey. I hadn't even arrived at the place for punishment. How much more of my dignity was I forced to lose in order to survive this ordeal?

CHAPTER 31

The rain battered down across the platform as the train crawled into Fürstenberg. Soldiers armed with rifles lined the platform waiting for the prisoners to descend. Swarms of women scrambled down off the train. There were fewer carriages, perhaps cars carrying men had disappeared.

The soldiers shoved us into line. I stared into the grey face of a young man whose helmet strap looked like it was choking him but he was too afraid to waste time adjusting it. Rain dripped down his cheek. He was merely a boy, probably no more than sixteen. I wondered how a handful of young men could guard about a thousand unruly women but when I looked around the prisoners struggling to walk, stretching their cramping legs, it was obvious no more were necessary.

'What's happening, Nadette? Look and see?' Gabriele said and nudged me forward.

'Looks like they're rounding us up, preparing for a march,' I said, craning my neck to see past the crowd.

Black clouds and a gloomy mist was ruining what little chance we had of day light by the time they eventually rounded us into straggly columns and marched us off. We were taken round Schwedt-See. The heavy rain had darkened the appearance of the stunning lake and caused a disgusting smell from its water.

The rain still poured down, making it even more difficult to march through the slippery mud. Our legs could barely carry us, yet we were forced to continue our march for about a mile round the lake then up a steep hill. I was breathless and struggled with the steep climb. Gabriele paced out ahead of me, 'C'mon Nadette, shift your arse,' she cried, never to offer a hand to pull me up alongside her.

I wheezed and grunted and eventually made it to the top and paused for breath alongside the other women. Our panting rapidly changed to long, drawn gasps. A deathly silence soon crept over the hill.

We stared at the miniature city below with its grey barracks and surrounding concrete walls. And right at its centre, a square, bricked chimney dispersed its remains into the black sky. Darkness was descending upon the concentration camp below.

'Where are we?' I whispered to Gabriele. Before she could answer, a soldier pushed me forward, ordering me to stop talking.

When we arrived at the camp, we were surrounded by SS guards parading the grounds with fierce Alsatian dogs, clearly trained to kill. The dogs bared their sharp incisors as they growled and snarled, smelling the fear from us as we hurried towards the entrance.

The camp was surrounded by high walls with skull and crossbones signs along the top. We entered through the heavy iron gates. The miniature city had now become a vast acreage of gloomy, dull huts, home to the masses of inmates incarcerated inside. Further concrete walls surrounded the barracks. Guard towers rose at intervals, the occupants with their guns ready for any prisoner brave enough to attempt an escape.

'We're in hell,' Gabriele whispered.

'What do you mean?' My speech was fast. Eyes wide, scanning our surroundings.

Gabriele's face was ashen. I checked the other women, their faces also distraught. My heart was racing. What was so bad about this place that even the toughest of women I had ever met were visibly trembling?

'It's Ravensbrück,' Gabriele whispered, still scanning, still taking it all in.

I frowned, no idea what she was talking about.

'The notorious women's extermination camp. Everybody's heard of it, Nadette?'

Not me. Kaarl hadn't mentioned it. The look on Gabriele's face was enough to convince me we were in trouble though. I reached inside my dress and squeezed tight on Ariella's necklace. Silently I prayed for strength from the necklace and hoped it really would see me through the darkest days.

The nightmare was beginning. A squad of women guards in dark blue uniforms ran towards us. The rain pelted down on their soft, felt hats and battered against their capes. They pounded through the mud-filled yard in their heavy boots, splashing the murky water over their navy skirts.

They wasted no time, forming us into a perfect line.

'Two only per row. Move forward to the office,' a guard shouted out.

Gabriele and I were coupled together behind a long queue of women whose quivering bodies stood perfectly to attention. The rain dripped from Gabriele's auburn hair down onto her fur jacket which was already drenched and clamped against her skin. I shivered, shoulders hunched and frantically rubbed at my naked arms to increase the blood flow. How I wished I still had my fur coat.

I looked up the line.

'What's happening?' Gabriele whispered.

'The guard's admitting only two women at a time.'

'Oh, no. We'll be here for ages,' she said and pulled up her soaking, wet collar.

I looked back down the queue. Hundreds of women still poured into the camp. The fierce women in uniform pushed them all into line. Some of the women were so weak they could barely walk and slid and fell in the mud baths formed by the never ending, heavy rain. The guards dragged them to their feet and forced them to plod ahead.

By the time we reached the office, I was completely saturated. There wasn't a single inch on my body that hadn't been soaked by the torrential rain. And yet we remained standing to attention outside that building, waiting in a queue.

I was so focused on the endless line of women entering the camp, I hadn't even realised we were so close to being called.

'Next,' a guard called out behind me.

I flinched at her squawky voice bellowing in my ear. She was standing with her hand on her hip, chewing on something, perhaps tobacco; her breath was foul.

'When you're ready,' she said, breathing her revolting fumes into my face and glared into my eyes as though desperate for an excuse to swipe me with her baton. 'Do you think I've got all day to stand here and wait for you?'

'Sorry, sorry,' I said and stumbled up the stairs. I lost my balance, fell forward and provided the guard with the excuse she had been waiting for.

'Get on your feet.'

A crack came down on my ribs and the pain shot through me. Those rubber batons were solid enough to cause severe inner damage and repeated blows could be fatal. I clutched my necklace for the strength to scramble to my feet and rushed into the office to escape the guard's thrashing.

Inside, another desk clerk clattered on the keys of a typewriter. He puffed and sighed as he typed and even stopped from time to time to rub and twist his neck and blow on his throbbing fingers. I looked at him with pity.

'Next,' he said.

Gabriele swaggered forward. She slouched to the side, leaning her fist on her hip. The clerk looked her over and shook his head, 'Name?' he said and dipped his head, ready to key in her information.

'Again?' Gabriele said.

'Answer him, Gabriele, please,' I said, 'You're no more fed up with this repetitive questioning than I am. Please just hurry up and get it over with.'

The desk clerk raised his head marginally and sighed. If we were tired with continually giving personal details, I wonder how he felt typing them all out. He stared at her with a bored expression, hands to the ready on the keyboard. Gabriele sighed and gave in but decided to add a touch of humour to the monotony. She proceeded to sing out her details.

Her fun was soon interrupted when the same guard who laid into my ribs approached her. She actually looked like she enjoyed whacking Gabriele across her back to force her to comply with the desk clerk's request.

'Okay, okay,' Gabriele said with her palms up in submission.

The women in the next queue were equally unwilling to participate with the guards requests.

'Remove all your jewellery,' the guard ordered them.

An accumulating pile of rings, necklaces, watches and bracelets extended over the length of the table. Tears were in the women's eyes parting with their treasured possessions. Many tried to disobey the order.

'No, you can't take that,' a frail, old woman said as she clung tight to her gold, wedding band. The tears ran down her face. Her hopeless attempt ended when a bombardment of female guards tumbled upon her and swiftly removed the ring from her scrawny finger.

Instinctively I grabbed my necklace. How on earth could I hide it?

'Name?' It was the desk clerk in front of me. Gabriele had moved along to the jewellery queue and it was my turn to enter my personal details as a Ravensbrück prisoner. The guard stared at me, waiting for my name.

'Nadette,' I said. It wasn't an attempt at humour. I was flustered, thoughts all over the place.

The clerk looked up from his tedious task and puffed his cheeks, blowing out a frustrated sigh.

'E-Eichmann. Nadette Eichmann.'

While he battered away on the typewriter, I glanced around to see how Gabriele was coping in the next queue.

'Remove all jewellery,' the guard said to Gabriele in a monotone voice; another one, sick of her tiresome tasks.

'What? Na, this is mine,' Gabriele said and held onto her necklace. 'Hard earned. Know what I mean?' she said, raising her eyebrows at the guard. Her hand was on her hip, she swaggered, demonstrating just exactly how hard earned the necklace was.

The guard reached across and snapped the dangling chain from Gabriele's neck.

'Hey, that's mine,' she said and tried to grab it back.

The bored guard sighed and held her baton up to the side and stared into Gabriele's eyes, awaiting her decision. Gabriele had already experienced swift blows from the torture tool. She backed off, leaving the guard with her necklace and slid all her gold and dress rings from her fingers and thrust them into the growing mound.

While I watched Gabriele, the desk clerk persisted with his robotic questioning. I answered without shifting an eye from the jewellery queue, trying to think of some way to smuggle my necklace past the inspection. There was no way I was giving it up. It was all I had left of Ariella. And special powers or not, the necklace was all that was giving me the strength to survive this incarceration nightmare.

'Move along,' the guard said and shoved me on the back. All questions answered, I was pushed along to the next queue. I reached for my necklace. The tug on my heart was stronger than the mighty snap of the chain. The link to Ariella was broken. It had to be done to pass the next test. I clenched the chain tight in my fist and walked along to meet the jewellery guard.

She wriggled and shuffled from foot to foot as if she was dying to sit down. She was a stout guard with thick, tree-stump legs. Her belly was so big, the buttons on her blouse almost popped open and her tie hung loose around her thick neck.

'Remove your jewellery,' the guard said in a monotone voice. She didn't look up to speak to me. She kept her head down and rubbed her legs. The expression on her face suggested she was in considerable pain. She rubbed her calves. It was cramp, I was sure.

'I said remove your jewellery,' the guard said. She looked up and scowled at me.

My necklace and my engagement ring were the only two items of jewellery I had left. And with great pleasure, I removed the thing that claimed I belonged to Kaarl and held it between my fingers as though it were toxic. I dropped the diamond ring onto the growing pile of stolen jewellery.

'That it?' she sighed. She appeared to be more concerned with her aching limbs.

'Y-Yes.' I was sure I didn't sound at all convincing. The guard paused from her intense leg rubbing. She stared into my eyes, trained to spot the liars. She scanned my body, checking for a wrist-watch, for bracelets, necklaces and even pulled back my hair looking for earrings.

'Pull your sleeves up and hold your hands out, palms up.'

I felt as if my heartbeat was actually visible through my dress, and if it wasn't for the raindrops dripping from my hair, I'm sure she would've noticed the sweat blistering on my forehead. But now was no time for my cowardice. I forced myself to act as brash as Gabriele and snatched my diamond ring back from the escalating pile, 'See this ring,' I said. Hand on hip and egotistically wobbling my head, 'this ring was given to me by an SS Officer. It's worth a fortune, isn't that enough?'

The guard watched my every move with the diamond ring. She failed to notice my other hand wildly rubbing at the necklace to roll it into a ball and wedge it between my fore-finger and thumb. The guard gritted her teeth, snatched the ring from my hand and threw it back on the pile. She looked like she was in so much pain it wouldn't take much to anger her. 'Hands out,' she said again.

I held my hands out straight, palms facing upwards and fingers squeezed tight together. I prayed the necklace wouldn't slip from its hiding place. She stared at me, as though searching my face for clues to the whereabouts of the hidden treasure.

'Cramp?' I blurted out. It was a desperate attempt to distract her.

'What?' she looked puzzled.

'Your legs,' I said and nodded towards her calves. 'Is it cramp in your legs? Have you been standing for a long time?'

She screwed up her face, telling me it was none of my business.

'I'm a Doctor,' I persisted. 'Put half a teaspoonful of salt in a glass of water and drink it quickly. It tastes disgusting but the cramp will disappear instantly.' It was nothing to do with my medical training, it was an old wife's tale I had heard, and strangely enough it had often worked for me after long days on my feet in the hospital wards.

The guard raised her head and rolled out her bottom lip, staring at me as though considering my remedy. She gave a slight whistle and signalled to another guard to approach the table. My outstretched fingers trembled uncontrollably. I was sure I was going to pass out. I took deep breaths trying to remain calm.

The approaching guard gripped her fingers tight around her baton and frowned curiously at the woman with the cramp. Was she called to assist with a body search?

'Take over here,' she said and turned to walk away. I prayed my solution to her cramp problem would work. She looked back and scanned my outstretched palms one last time and tipped her head to the side to wave me on.

My necklace was still in my possession. A secret smile, and a warm glow crept across my heart and calmed its rapid rate.

The joy was short lived. The smile dropped. My mouth gaped, I stared at the next queue. Every single woman was forced to strip completely naked, right there, out in the open, in front of a group of cheering, uniformed SS men. How humiliating. Why did they have to degrade us like that? And those men, those SS men, and us women, naked. What were they going to do with us?

Gabriele was already stripped off. She pranced about in front of the men. She swaggered, taunted and teased them. She looked as if she was enjoying the attention but with a closer look, I could see sadness in her eyes, her charade was nothing more than a smokescreen. I wondered what had happened to this woman to make her behave in such a degrading manner.

She walked through the crowd, passed the scrutinizing eyes of the SS soldiers. Then it was my turn. The SS men clad in grey uniform, lined either side of the queue. They jeered and shouted abuse like a vindictive audience demanding retribution on a captured murderer heading for the gallows. I clasped my hands tight against my chest, squeezing my necklace and covering my nudity. The SS prodded and poked at me as I passed by. One man stepped forward and looked me up and down, enjoying my embarrassment, 'Hiding something?' he said.

My tightened fists were pressed firmly against my chest and my chin was perched on top. I had Ariella's necklace protected in my clenched hand. I kept my head down.

'I said, what're you hiding?'

Without raising my chin, I timidly shook my head, 'N-Nothing, sir.'

He prised my arms away from my chest and stood there ogling my bare breasts. I could feel my face burning. I turned my head to the side and closed my eyes. His hands were tightly wrapped around my wrists. My fingers remained clenched, squeezing so hard I could feel my nails digging into my palms.

At last he released my arms and shoved me along the line of voyeurs. I kept my head down as I was bounced from one uniform to the next. When I reached the end of the line, Gabriele was waiting for me. She grabbed my arm and pulled me into the next line.

'You're never going to believe this,' she said and pushed my head out, forcing me to look down the queue. 'Heard the Jews got this, but not us,' she said. The naked women were being pushed into seats and ambushed from behind. Inmates, who were already clad in prison skirts and dirty white blouses, attacked the heads of the seated prisoners and chopped off their hair. They wasted no time. The scissors clicked incessantly, women were scalped in minutes. Mounds of beautiful curls accumulated on the floor. Tears were welling in my eyes watching the barbaric treatment of these women. They were like sheep, herded along for shearing then dipped in identifiable ink.

The sheep shearers were already bald and branded by a purple inverted triangle on their upper left arm.

'The purple triangles,' Gabriele said and nodded towards their armbands, 'Jehovah's Witnesses. Daft cows. They've only got to renounce their faith and they can get outta here.' She screwed up her eyes and twisted her finger at the side of her forehead. I had to agree, they must be mad not to even pretend they had changed their beliefs. Surely it had to be worth it just to get away from this hell?

I felt a shove on my back. A Jehovah's Witness pushed me into a chair. Gabriele was seated next to me. I closed my eyes and squeezed hard on my necklace, dreading the sound of the scissors slicing through my long, blonde hair.

'Stop!' a familiar voice yelled out.

The scissor clicking ceased. The chatter fizzled out. The room was silent. Only one person I knew could command attention like that. What would he be doing here? I slowly opened my eyes and watched Kaarl stride towards me, hands clasped behind him, head tilted back, looking down his nose under the rim of his cap. His footsteps deliberately smacked against the wooden surface to make his presence felt among the trembling, naked women. My shaking hands fumbled with the necklace. Had he seen it? Was that why he was approaching me? Making sure I gave up the last I had of Ariella. My mind was racing. Why was he in the camp?

He sneered at me, paced around me and scanned my naked body, never to utter a word. I kept my head down and clutched my shaking hands together, securing the necklace within. My knees visibly knocked together. Kaarl sniggered at the tremors.

At last the silence was broken. 'Leave this one,' Kaarl called out to the Jehovah's Witnesses, his hand was on my shoulder, 'and this one, and her, and her,' He pointed out the women who were to be spared the hair shaving ordeal.

About twenty women, including myself and Gabriele were picked out and ordered to stand in a row in front of everyone else. I couldn't understand what was so special about us and why we were allowed to keep our long locks. I scanned the selected women looking for something in common among us. Nothing that I could see.

'Hey, hey. Must be 'cause we're good looking,' Gabriele said. She grinned and ran her fingers through her auburn hair.

'I know, it's great, isn't it,' said another woman.

The other women giggled and wrapped their locks round their fingers. I didn't crack a smile. I wasn't so sure we were the lucky ones.

'Who was that guy?' Gabriele said with interest, as if he was somebody she really wanted to get to know.

'Kaarl Bergmann.' I was scowling at him.

'Didn't you say-' Gabriele said, scrunching her eyebrows together.

'Yes, my fiancé,' I choked over the words, 'he sent me here.'

Kaarl walked towards us and paraded up and down in front of his selected women. He examined our naked bodies as if he was checking for flaws.

We stood to attention, hands by our side. The necklace was still squashed inside my fist. It was hard to control the trembling, especially in the hand that held the treasure. I'm sure Kaarl was suspicious. He lingered around me for much longer than he did with the others, sniffing around my neck. Perhaps he missed the closeness he had demanded from me, or maybe he knew I was hiding something. His breathing intensified, a chilling shiver ran down my spine. I quivered with the sensation and felt slightly giddy. The giddiness gave me an idea. I rolled my eyes as though I was about to pass out and let myself fall against Gabriele. I grabbed Gabriele's hand to steady myself and released the necklace into her safe keeping. Gabriele looked down to see what had just happened. Instantly she snapped her hand closed and snared the necklace within.

The faint was convincing, even to Kaarl. In a reflexive action, he jumped to catch me but quickly snapped his heroic hands back and resumed his aggressive stance.

'Cold showers,' he said with a flip of his wrist, signalling to the gloating SS men. 'That should wake them up.' The SS men snapped to attention and formed us into a line and marched us towards the shower room.

Gabriele curved her wrist backwards and discreetly passed the pendant back to me. I smiled thankfully, pleased that the jewel had once again survived and returned to my protective care. I squeezed it tight again, believing Ariella's necklace truly was giving me the strength to carry on. At the first opportunity, I would repair it with some thread from my clothing.

CHAPTER 32

Ariella and Ester had been in the train for days. Ester was exhausted with all the travelling. She sat with her back to Ariella, her head leaning against her chest. Ariella's knees were bent up and Ester was wedged between them as though they were on a sledge. At least she managed to straighten her legs slightly. Ariella was trying to make the journey as comfortable as possible for Ester but it wasn't easy with about eighty Jews crammed into a cattle car of a freight train. Not even the simplest provision had been made for sanitation, the air was foul. Ariella gagged at the smell and Ester coughed and coughed as they sat there and patiently waited for the journey to end.

Tired, weary faces surrounded them. Husbands, wives, and children squeezed in with luggage, all that was left of their precious possessions, hurled together and compacted into a single suitcase each. Ester guarded their two cases between her legs. They had been packed for quite some time in preparation for going into hiding or for deportation, whichever came first. They didn't have much left to pack, some clothes, photos and a few items of sentimental value. Their last possessions. Ariella wondered how long it would take before the Nazis stole them too.

The train slowed down and the heavy bolts that locked them in were slid back. The door opened a fraction and a bucket of water and a ladle was passed into the carriage to quench the thirst of so many. They were transported like cattle and like cattle they were expected to drink from a trough. The door was dragged shut again and the thirsty passengers scrimmaged for the bucket.

'Look at them. Fools. Playing into their hands,' Ariella said, determined to maintain some pride and to refuse to drink from the bucket.

'Get me some water, Ariella, please. My throat's so dry,' Ester begged over her incessant coughing.

'No, Ester. We can't give in to them. They want us to behave like animals.'

'Ariella, please?' She was so weak.

For her sake, Ariella pushed through the crowd and scrambled to the bucket and scooped a ladleful for her, and although it was against her grain, the temptation was too great, Ariella sipped a drop herself.

The water was soon gone but the crowd was far from satisfied. Ariella looked around the sad faces. Many women were in tears, clutching their young. One woman repeated her baby's name over and over, 'Isaac, Isaac,' she called, gently trying to stir him. He was wrapped in a white blanket, motionless in her arms. There wasn't even a whimper, his face was grey and his lips were purple. Hunger or dehydration possibly killed the infant, or was he crushed to death among the tightly packed torsos that surrounded him? It was a harrowing journey for all.

We continued along those bumpy rail tracks, stopping every so often at stations. Crowds of Jews swarmed the platform and piled into the carriages taking up every inch of space that was left. Breathing became more and more difficult for the passengers.

After several days of a long, tedious journey, the train eventually slowed down, screeching its brakes and crawled forward. Ariella's gut feeling told her they were descending this time.

A thunderous roar, a storm was brewing. Violent rain battered down on the carriage rooftop. 'Oh no,' Ariella mumbled. Typical, she thought, that was all they needed, just as they were about to disembark. What more misery was to come?

Everybody pushed forward to peer out through the barred windows on the cattle-wagon. Ariella managed to struggle onto her feet, grabbed the iron bars and shoved her face through to see where they were. They were approaching a ramp.

At last the train stopped dead. Anxious faces stared towards the doors. The heavy, iron bars were slid back again and the wooden doors were hauled along the rails. Light shone in and almost blinded everybody after such a dark and horrible journey. The early evening breeze that blasted in through the opened door was welcomed by long gasps from the passengers as they filled their lungs with fresh, cool air.

An army of SS waited on the platform. 'Outside. Quickly,' they shouted. 'Step onto the Judenrampe.'

'The Judenrampe?' Ariella mumbled. So many Jews must have passed through here, the Nazis had actually named the ramp after them.

The crowd stormed forward and crawled down from the train. Ester struggled to her feet. She was exhausted and in urgent need of some food. She stood up and stretched her frail body then coughed and coughed as she tried to climb down from the train. Ariella jumped down onto the platform. 'C'mon girl. You can do it,' she said and reached up to help Ester off the freight car.

The train was stretched up and down the length of the platform. Masses of people descended from its carriages. Men and women. Boys and girls. Jews. All shapes and sizes. They piled onto the Judenrampe, like ants emerging from a dark hole after their home had just been trampled. Everybody stretched their aching legs after being seated or forced to stand in the same position for such a long time.

The heavy rain poured down on them, soaked them through to the skin in their threadbare, winter coats. Some people turned to grab their suitcases. A tannoy announced, 'Form two lines. Women and children in one line, men in the other.

Leave your luggage. It will be forwarded to you. Form two lines, Women and children,' it continued to repeat.

Ariella frowned. It sounded a bit strange. She couldn't imagine Nazis carrying their luggage for them, something wasn't right. She persisted and reached inside the car for their cases.

'Leave it,' an SS soldier warned her and grabbed her arm. 'Your luggage will be forwarded to you.'

'Sure thing,' she said, and pushed past him and grabbed their cases.

'Ariella, no,' Ester said, her fingers curled in front of her mouth.

The SS man grabbed her shoulder and pushed Ariella into a forming queue of women.

The soldiers paraded the ramp making sure everyone formed into ranks. Ester coughed and coughed and struggled to stand upright. The soldiers grabbed her, forced her to stand to attention.

Ariella linked her arm through Ester's. They walked forward along the platform.

Families clung together but the guards soon parted them, forced women and children into one line and the men in the other. Ariella and Ester tagged in behind a row of women who shuffled along the platform.

'Leave your luggage,' the tannoy continued to repeat. Ariella wanted to smash it to tiny pieces and stop that irritating, squeaky man's voice from screeching through her ears. Ester seemed to read her face. She firmly grabbed Ariella's arm and pulled her into line.

They slipped in behind a heavy woman who had a padded, broad back and chunky wrestler's arms. Ariella couldn't help but wonder what size she was before their food was rationed. The woman threw her warrior's arms around a man's neck, presumably her husband, who was in the parallel queue. She was determined to hang onto him.

The woman was well built, had a chubby face, broad nose and dimples on her chin. Her husband was leaner than an old carcass after it had been ravaged by vultures. Perhaps his wife had eaten his rations too.

She yanked her husband back from the men's line that formed alongside them.

'Get in line,' screeched a skinny, female guard who was less than five feet in height. She appeared from nowhere, and ran towards the fat woman, her long boots thumped onto the platform.

The guard pulled the man away from her. But the heavy woman was determined to hang onto her husband and pulled him back with her strong, mighty arms. The short guard was equally determined. She ran at the woman, reached up and grabbed and twisted her fair hair round her knuckles.

The guard's face was covered with thick, heavy makeup, failing to mask the evil underneath. She yanked the woman away from her loved one and shoved him into the men's line. 'Women and children only in this line,' the guard shouted into her face.

The heavy woman persisted but her weeping husband eventually guided her back into line.

The prison guard's blue eyes protruded from their sockets and cast an evil stare up at the insubordinate woman. The guard may have looked short and puny but Ariella could tell she was no push over. She was going to be a problem.

She pranced about in a cape and military style visor hat and looked down under its rim to watch her prisoners. There was something about these uniform hats that seemed to increase the wearer's head size. All of a sudden they were somebody important when the hat rested on their head. The guard strutted along that platform, every now and then she raised her short arm to whack both men and women on the back of the neck to force them to move forward.

A stampede of men thumped onto the wooden platform and rushed past them. Their hair was so far shaved down, Ariella could actually see grazes on their heads. They were all dressed the same in a blue and white striped uniform, all Jews with that degrading yellow star on their upper left arm. They stormed the carriages of the train and swiftly passed the luggage off. They weren't porters carrying their luggage to their room that was for sure. Somehow Ariella knew that was the last they would see of their remaining possessions. Her fists clenched at the thought.

Ariella felt a whack on the back of her head and turned to see the miniature guard snarling up at her, 'Eyes front, Jew.'

'Hey, back off,' Ariella said and rubbed her throbbing head.

The guard's eyes squeezed into tight slits. She walked closer and strained onto her tiptoes to go nose to nose with Ariella. She could see why the guard needed such thick make up, her face was all pockmarks and hair sprouted sporadically around her chin. Ugliness oozed from her pores. The guard's hat slid back on her head and knocked the blonde bun out of place. She quickly adjusted the important headdress before she pursued her attack.

'What did you say?' she said and banged her baton repeatedly against her hand.

Ariella clenched her fists and stared down into her bulging eyeballs.

'Leave it, Ariella, please,' Ester said, pulling her away.

'I'm not taking that from a Nazi elf,' she said and pushed back up the line.

'Ariella, please don't do it,' Ester said in between coughs. She was shaking all over.

Ariella sighed, put her arm around Ester and moved back into line, she glared back at the evil guard; she would get her on her own, sometime. She was too busy looking back to notice the line had stopped. She crashed into the women in front. They hovered about some SS Officers who seemed to be performing an inspection.

The officers scanned the bodies as they approached and ordered everybody into new lines. Ariella couldn't understand what was happening at first. Then she realised.

People in crutches, elderly men and women and young children were all selected to form another line on the left-hand side. A slow formation padded forward. The selected group were then assisted into nearby trucks by a smiling SS man.

By now everybody was soaked from the downpour. Hard pellets shot down sideways, sweeping across the ramp, washing it clean as if they were wiping away any evidence that a Jew had ever been here. Children screamed as the violent rain battered against their bare legs. And the Pied Piper led them into the sheltered truck.

An SS Officer pushed Ariella to the right-hand side where another line of prisoners formed. No sick, elderly or children were present. Ariella guessed they were the stronger. For what?

The SS man paced around Ester, inspecting her. He frowned and rubbed his chin. Ariella silently begged her not to cough. He seemed more interested in her walk and forced her to shuffle forward, checking her gait.

'Having difficulty, my dear? Perhaps a lift in one of our trucks?' The SS man said. He smiled and patted Ester's hand.

Ariella's stomach was in a knot. A gut feeling, the trucks weren't safe.

'Oh, well. Thank you, sir,' Ester said, ever so grateful and so bloody trusting. Sometimes Ariella wanted to scream at her for being so naïve. The SS officer carefully slipped his arm under Ester's and grabbed a firm hold, all the while he was smiling into her face. Oh, he was good, Ariella thought and watched how he manipulated her. Together they walked towards the trucks, chatting away like old school friends.

Ariella tingled, anger bursting out of her. She slowly curled her fingers to fists and ran at them. 'Ester, come this way,' she said and grabbed her arm.

'Ariella, no. This kind man is helping me.'

'What do you think you're doing?' the SS man said, his eyes wide, nostrils flaring.

Ariella's heart raced. She took a deep breath, 'She's with me.'

'Get back in line. She can't walk.' He sneered at her.

'She can walk.' She was like an irritating insect that persisted around a heavy pile of shite.

She pulled Ester towards her, yanked her arm away from the SS leader's hand, 'Ester, come with me,' she said, forcing the words passed a very tight throat. She hoped he wouldn't notice her shaking legs.

'Get back in line or you'll go too,' he roared at her and pulled Ester back.

She ran her hand over her hair, trying to come up with a quick solution. Perhaps he would respond to a softer approach. How the hell could she pull that one off? Somehow she managed to plaster a fake smile on her face and walked over to the man who was leading Ester away, 'Please sir, she's just tired from the journey.' She smiled into his face. Her voice was so pathetically convincing, even Ester looked surprised.

The SS man seemed interested. He stopped in his tracks and rubbed at his chin again and looked Ester up and down. Ariella's fake smile, still etched across her face as she stood there, innocently looking up at him, her trembling hands clasped behind her back.

Out of the blue, a stout guard rushed towards them. She wore a navy-blue skirt and a water-proofed cape covered the rest of her uniform. Her long boots squelched into the mud puddles now forming on the ground as she hurried over. Her fat, chunky fingers held tight to her hat to stop it from slipping off her cropped, blonde hair.

'I've got them, sir. I'll make sure she walks,' the guard said with a soft, Austrian accent. She yanked Ariella and Ester by the hair.

The quiet, calm voice didn't match her brutal appearance at all. She had such a firm grasp, their heads sloped to the side as she pulled Ariella and Ester back over to the right-hand line among the stronger prisoners.

He was a high ranking SS officer, a man in his forties being bullied by a woman in her late twenties. He jerked back in amazement and stared at the persuasive guard. The guard stared back, head to the side, urging him to agree on her decision. She was either incredibly brave or incredibly stupid. Whatever, the SS man's flabbergasted face eventually softened into a smile and he nodded his approval. Clever girl. But why was she helping them?

Ariella shoved her arm around Ester's shoulder and pulled her away before the SS leader could change his mind. Ester plodded on, exaggerating a limp, determined to get a lift in one of the trucks.

'Why couldn't I go in the truck?' she asked, like a child who had been refused a treat. Ariella didn't know what to tell her, her gut feeling would never have satisfied her.

'I'll tell you why.' The stout guard was back marching alongside them, apparently ready to answer any questions.

'See that smoke?' she whispered.

They looked up. Black clouds of smoke emitted from the tall, bricked chimneys in the camp ahead. Simultaneously they spun towards each other, frowning and shrugging in confusion.

'Those not fit for work, they gas them, you know,' the guard whispered. Ariella stared at the chimneys. Surely not? Was it imagination, or could she smell the burning corpses?

Ester gasped. She threw her arm around Ariella's waist and promptly straightened herself up. Phoney limp gone.

'This can't be right? Ariella?' she asked as if Ariella should know if the guard was lying. She didn't know. She didn't trust any of them. Why would she say such a thing? Surely they weren't gassing people? Her mind raced along with her heart, she stared at the camp ahead.

The guard looked at Ariella, her sadness looked genuine, with even a convincing sympathetic smile.

'Move on. Quick as you can please. Get you ready for work,' her soft voice called out and marched the prisoners forward into Auschwitz-Birkenau concentration camp.

CHAPTER 33

Rows of brick buildings and dark, wooden barracks seemed to go on for miles inside Auschwitz. There must've been thousands of prisoners locked up inside this creepy camp. The air was foul with ashes dispersing from the chimneys. That stout guard who saved Ester, surely her story was a myth? The thought of all those people, discarded, considered useless to society, murdered then cremated, surely not possible? Ariella shuddered at the thought. Nonetheless, she clung tight to Ester's arm, holding her upright as they paraded through the puddles in the miserable downpour.

A workforce of prisoners rushed past them, hauling their heavy work tools and were pushed forward by aggressive guards. Some prisoners risked whispering over to the new arrivals. Ariella couldn't make out what they were saying, something about showers. They scurried away too fast for answers before the guards caught them speaking.

Jews in a nearby sorting area, sifted through the contents of the luggage whilst guards watched over them.

'Kanada,' whispered a prisoner standing near the entrance. She nodded towards the luggage inside.

'What?'

The prisoner bowed quickly, there was an approaching guard. Ariella didn't know what she meant but the piles of jewellery and ornaments were enough to tell her that their possessions were being stolen. Not that she had much left. The only thing worthwhile was her gold necklace and she had given that to Nadette. Nevertheless, she glared into the sorting area, and whispered under her breath, 'Thieving Nazi-'

'Eyes front. Ha, you again.' It was the short guard with the heavy makeup. 'You gonna be trouble, Jew?' Ariella wished she had knocked her block off earlier when she swiped her with that baton.

'Don't say a word, don't say a word,' Ester said and hurried her past the aggressive guard.

Ariella stamped on, marched in time with the group, but continued to glare back at the elf who whacked as many Jews as she could as they passed her by. Ester grabbed her back. They trod forward, through the water-logged camp, the torrential rain still pouring down on the thousands of Jews arriving in Auschwitz.

They were taken to an admittance section where they were told they had to wait to be accommodated. Needed to make space, they said. Ariella dreaded to think what that meant. In the meantime, they were to be de-loused.

'What? De-loused?' Ariella asked. 'Don't be ridiculous.'

'Orders,' the guard said. 'You stinking, infested Jew,' she said and sneered at Ariella.

'Don't say anything, Ariella. Come on, let's go,' Ester said and dragged her into line.

They filed them into a queue where some inmates attacked their hair with long, sharp scissors. The clickety click of the instruments hacked through wads of hair. Within minutes, Ariella's wavy, brown hair was cropped and lay among the growing pile on the floor. Ester was in tears. Her dark hair, ruffled out from its tidy bun and chopped off with one fine snap of the scissors.

They were then ordered to strip naked and pushed into a nearby shower room. About fifty trembling women, all squeezed into a dank-smelling room where a trickle of water spurted down from a sprinkler to wash over their supposedly infested bodies. Ester stayed close to Ariella, her arms tightly closed against her chest and her legs crossed over in an attempt to cover her nudity. Some women standing next to them, stared upwards, lapping water from the dribbling sprinklers. Their hands clasped against their faces. They smiled as if they were somehow relieved. One of them turned to Ariella; she must've seen her curious look.

'We got real showers. We're lucky,' she whispered.

'Lucky?' Ariella frowned as if the woman had lost her mind. Maybe she had. Or maybe she knew something that Ariella didn't. 'What do you mean?' Ariella asked, but the water stopped trickling and the steel doors clunked open. A female guard ordered them back out. The women swarmed the doors, it was impossible to finish the conversation.

A small, blue towel was handed to them when they stepped outside the shower room. A guard paraded around the naked women and handed out a smock dress in blue and white stripes; the Auschwitz prison uniform. Reluctantly Ariella pulled the dress on which didn't smell fresh at all. Was this once worn by a Jew who was gassed? Ariella dismissed the thought immediately.

At last she was clad in prison clothes and ran her hand over her stubbly head. 'How can they do this to us? Somebody's going to pay.'

'Stop it, Ariella. Come on just do as they say until we get out,' Ester said, tears trickled down her face.

'We're not going to get out.' Ariella tugged at the remaining turfs they had left of her hair. She settled her hand on the nape of her neck and stared up at the wooden ceiling and sighed.

'Don't give up, Ariella. You've still got Nadette-'

'Yeah, sure thing, Ester. Don't you get it? Nadette's probably in a camp as well.' Ariella dropped her hand back down by her side and glared at her friend. 'We'll never be together again. If only I could get my hands on that Kaarl-'

'It's that one there I want.' It was a woman's voice interrupting them. A hard voice. From Frankfurt, Ariella guessed. It was a familiar looking heavy set woman. Ariella struggled to recognise her with her cropped hair and prison uniform. Her muscular arms almost ripped the sleeves of her dress. It was the fat face and dimpled chin that jolted Ariella's memory. It was the same woman who had earlier tried to keep her husband by her side. She was glaring at the short, ugly guard with the heavy make-up who had dragged her husband away from her. 'I'm going to get her, first chance I get,' she said.

'Stop all this revenge nonsense,' Ester said. 'It won't get us anywhere. You beat her, the guards beat you. What's the point of that? Just focus on getting out.'

Ariella was astounded at Ester's outburst. She jerked back, stared at her without blinking an eyelid. Ester Kolleck had left her speechless.

'She's right, you know.' The soft voice called out from behind them. It was the cropped, blonde guard who had helped them earlier. She walked towards them. Ariella ignored her, pretending to fix her dress. She still couldn't figure out why she had prevented Ester from being taken in that truck to be gassed.

The guard tilted her chin up for eye contact. She was about five feet, four. Ariella was only about an inch taller yet she seemed to deliberately look up to her. She was like a man in drag, in a masculine body but with a delicate, feminine face. Her features were small and her blue eyes sparkled like marbles, gazing into Ariella's. She extended her broad hand to introduce herself, 'Jana Bach, one of the good ones,' she said softly.

She seemed friendly enough but Ariella daren't trust any of them. She stared at her outstretched arm, made no attempt to reach out to her.

'Is there such a thing?' Ariella asked her and stared into her eyes.

Jana's lips twitched into a half smile, her face blushed and she curled her fingers back in at Ariella's rejection. Ariella almost felt sorry for her. Her outer façade most certainly did not match the kind person underneath. Or was she trying to fool her?

The ever trusting Ester, smiled up at the woman. She looked pleased that they had found a good guard. She grabbed Jana's recoiling hand and introduced herself.

'Ester Kolleck and,' she put her hand up on Ariella's shoulder, 'this is Ariella Ish-Shalom.' Ester paused and looked towards the stout Jew who had been separated from her husband, 'And you are?' Ester said. The woman scrunched her eyes and stuck her fat face out to scrutinize the guard. She looked as wary as Ariella.

'Sarah,' she said. Nothing more. No last name. No pleasant greeting. She walked away and joined the queue of women forming near the door.

Jana shook her head and sighed as if she was sick of receiving so many rejections from unfriendly Jews. She smiled at Ariella again. Perhaps she thought she was in with a chance for friendship after Ester's pleasant introduction.

'I admire your courage, Ariella. Not many people would try to argue back with the SS,' Jana said.

Ariella didn't think she was brave at all. She saw Ester being taken away from her and had to act fast. After all, she had promised to take care of her and how would she manage that if they were separated? She didn't answer Jana, she turned away from the guard.

Jana clumsily placed her chubby hand on Ariella's arm and guided her back to face her. She was persistent, 'Please, I mean no harm. There are some of us in here doing what we can, you know.'

Her voice was calm and soft, almost likeable. But she was a Nazi. Ariella scowled at her, stared at the fat paw on her arm, waiting for her to remove it. The guard snapped her hand away. Ariella frowned, puzzled. Jana Bach didn't seem to fit the character for an Auschwitz guard at all.

Ester had quite taken to her and was determined that Ariella should befriend her, 'Oh, Ariella, don't be like that,' she said, 'they don't all hate us.' Ariella hadn't been so sure of that up until now. She thought Ester could be right this time. Nevertheless, she was still wary and remained aloof.

Jana seemed comfortable enough to warn them about other guards, 'Be careful,' she said, 'they're mostly like her, you know,' Jana nodded towards the short guard with the thick make-up partially covering her moles and pockmarks. She stood next to the door and ordered women into two lines and allocated them work.

'Eva Dorr,' Jana said. 'Better known as Evil Eva.'

An appropriate title. Summed up Ariella's thoughts of her earlier when she rammed her face into hers. She was right, she was one to watch.

Evil Eva was whacking their new friend, Sarah, across her broad back.

'Why is she hitting her?' Ester asked Jana.

'Does she need a reason?' Jana said. Ariella looked confused.

'Sarah was going to get revenge on that guard for taking her husband away,' Ariella said. 'Maybe she's attacked her. 'Good on you, girl,' Ariella said and shook her fist.

She shifted from side to side, trying to see what was happening at the end of the queue. 'Sarah must've jumped between the two working lines,' Ariella said.

'Get in that line. Go where I tell you, Jew,' Eva roared and beat Sarah again. Sarah fought back and swiped her strong arm across Eva's ugly face. Eva beat her with the baton, 'Useless Jew,' she said and forced her to stagger to the designated work line.

Another guard stood at the door. She also wore a blue skirt, blouse and tie and a pair of those long boots. She handed Sarah a pick that looked heavy to lift even for

Sarah's build. The guard pushed the door open. The rain still battered down. Darkness wasn't far off. Ariella guessed they could still get a few hours of labour out of them yet. Sarah was shoved out alongside other workers carrying similar work tools. How the hell did they expect women to carry out heavy labour?

'And what can you do?' Ariella asked Jana.

'Whatever I can,' Jana mumbled, pulling a helpless face that dragged her lip to the side convincing Ariella that she had no authority and no plan. She was a lone ranger out to fight injustice on her own.

'You two,' It was Evil Eva shouting at Ariella and Ester, 'move it,' she roared with a screechy voice.

'Better do as she says,' Jana whispered, barely moving her lips as if she was afraid that Eva would see her talking to Jews.

'Come on, Ariella, quick, don't antagonise her,' Ester said and reached out a trembling hand to grab Ariella's arm. Her legs were buckling under her. Then her cough started again. Ariella eased her arm around her back and discreetly tucked it in at her waist and pulled Ester towards her to take most of her body weight.

Eva was pushing the women in the queue in front of them into two lines. One line was doomed for heavy labour and the other was allocated, presumably, lighter duties.

'Road construction, Factory,' Eva called out to the women and shoved them into line.

The women bowed and obeyed the short, bumptious guard.

'Roads. Factory,' she continued.

It was their turn to face her. Ester tried to stand upright and smiled at the guard. Eva reciprocated with an evil grin showing off her randomly missing teeth. She cricked her neck to glare at Ariella. Her eyebrows went up in recognition and her eyes slanted into an evil stare. She tilted to see where my arm was leading and padded around Ester's back. She yanked Ariella's arm away from Ester and forced her to stand alone. Ester wobbled and tried to stand upright while Eva thoroughly inspected her.

'Heavy labour, road construction,' Eva said and smirked. She grabbed a heavy pick from the guard at the door and handed it to Ester.

Ester gasped. She said nothing, as ever, not wanting to cause trouble. She reached her hand out ready to take the pick. Ariella put her hand up in front of her and shoved the pick back to Eva. 'No. She can't,' she told her.

'It's okay, Ariella, I'll be fine.'

'She'll go where I say,' Eva spat out the words, determined to show her authority over the inferior Jews.

'She'll never cope.'

'I'm okay, Ariella. Really. Please, leave it.'

Ariella grabbed Ester's sleeve, pulled her back and glared at her, warning her to be quiet while she negotiated a better work task.

'Want to make it harder for her?' Eva said. She had a smarmy look and bumped that rubber baton repeatedly against her hand again.

Ariella took a deep breath to calm herself and tried the softer approach that she had used earlier on the SS leader, 'Please ma'am. She's not fit. I beg you, put her in the factory.'

Eva seemed to enjoy her grovelling and spread her toothless grin across her face again. Her head wobbled about as if it had just been inflated. Ariella thought her charm had worked on her too but then she signalled past her to catch somebody's attention. 'Guard,' she called out, 'that one there,' she said and pointed to Ester, 'make sure she gets no food today.'

'Yes ma'am,' a feeble voice cried back.

Ester's eyes were wide and her face was drained of all colour. She was shaking her head, willing Ariella not to retaliate.

The adrenalin was flowing. Ariella lunged on the troll. She pounded her fists into her ugly face.

Eva reached for her baton and laid into her back with it. Ester scrambled between them, trying to pull Ariella off. She wouldn't stop.

All of a sudden, Ariella was surrounded by guards. They trailed her away from Evil Eva. The guard scrambled to her feet, hands frantically covering her face, as if she was afraid her ugliness was now visible after a disturbance in her make-up.

The other guards had a hold of Ariella, both arms outstretched and held back. She was expecting a punch in the guts from Eva. Instead she called out orders, 'Put her in the factory line, away from the other one.'

Ariella tried to wriggle free to get to Eva. It was no use. The guards had a firm grip. She looked for Jana. She was at the back of the room, shrugging her shoulders, hands out to the side. So much for being in there to help them.

Ester stepped outside the barracks and into the pouring rain. She carried a heavy pick alongside her.

CHAPTER 34

It was almost dark in Ravensbrück by the time we were dressed in a striped prison uniform and marched off. All the women thumped their feet into the ground, keeping perfect time with the guard's footsteps. With every step I took, I could feel the grey, prison knickers slide further down my legs. Convinced they were on full view of the striped army behind me, I discreetly slipped my hand round the back and hauled the cotton pants up and tucked them under the waistband of my striped skirt. A quick skip and I soon picked up the marching pace and swung my arms in time with the others.

Women of all shapes and sizes, all clad in prison uniform, each with an armband on their upper left arm, branded them. A coloured triangle had been issued appropriate to their crime.

I frowned curiously, wondering what each colour represented. I had already met the purple triangle lot, the Jehovah's Witnesses, but the other colours, I hadn't a clue. And as for mine and Gabriele's, a black triangle categorized us as anti-socials, similar criminals. For the life of me, I couldn't work out where the similarity lay.

'Why's ours black?' I asked Gabriele, nodding towards the triangle.

'You're in here for having an affair with another woman, Nadette. They class that as anti-social behaviour. Same as prostitutes,' she said and smiled at me, raising her finger up, owning up to her crime.

'Halt,' the guard cried.

We had arrived at the admittance block. The guard told us we would be kept there for several weeks until we were allocated permanent accommodation. We were crammed into barracks worse than the Alexanderplatz. Hundreds of women piled into the bunks. I couldn't care less about the bug ridden straw mat we had to lie on, I was just so desperate to rest my head and my weary body.

My straw mat caused me great displeasure the next morning though when the siren sounded at four-thirty. We sprang from our beds and everybody spent an incredible amount of time straightening their mats.

'What's the fuss about?' I asked Gabriele. 'What are they all doing?'

'I dunno.'

'Got to get the edges straight,' said an inmate next to her. 'You'll be punished if you don't get it right.' She hurried back to perfect her own straw mat.

I did my best to straighten the mat but they all looked the same to me, I couldn't see what she was talking about. I hoped for the best and hurried along to the washroom alongside the others.

There were nearly three hundred women in the block and only about twenty sinks to accommodate us. Women pushed and shoved to reach the spigots. It was a rabble. Some were pushed to the ground and trod over. Prisoners roared and yelled a string of expletives.

'This is hopeless, Gabriele, we're never going to reach the taps.'

'Oh, no?' Gabriele said, 'watch this.' With a look of determination she pushed among the fighting women and shoved until she got through to the sink. 'Come on, Nadette,' she signalled for me to join her.

I took a deep breath and ran among them, palms out, fiercely pushing the women aside as though I was swimming for the championships. At last I reached the taps and ran my fingers under the running stream and splashed lavish amounts of delightful, clean water over my face. I cupped my hands and lapped up the goodness. Water never tasted so delicious.

Heavy boots thumped across the floor, startled the women and dispersed the thirsty flock from their water troughs. Everybody stood to attention at their bedside awaiting an inspection by a tall guard who had just walked into the barracks.

'What's this?' the guard asked, pointing her whip at my straw mat.

I glanced over to the mat. I couldn't see the flaw. Hands squeezed tight by my side, I stood to attention awaiting the guard's comments.

She stamped her boots into the wooden floor, pacing towards me and stuck her face in against mine, 'That's not straight,' she said. She drew her whip back and lashed it across my bare legs. For such a skinny woman, she certainly had the strength to draw that whip. My legs throbbed from the sting. 'You will see me after work,' she said.

'And you,' she said, swiping Gabriele across the legs, 'your bed is a disgrace.'

'Ow, that hurt,' Gabriele said and clenched her fist ready to take a swing at the lanky woman.

The guard grabbed her by the hair, and pressed her face in against hers, 'Go on, make my day,' she said. Gabriele backed off, hands up.

Inmates entered the barracks carrying pails of coffee, distracting the guard from her evil deeds. She kept her screwed-up eyes firmly on Gabriele as she walked off backwards and edged towards the door.

The women rushed from their bedposts, following the aroma from the arriving coffee. The two Barracks Elders, who were responsible for each half of the block, poured the coffee for their thirsty, irritable comrades.

The coffee tasted vile, yet divine. We were so hungry and so thirsty, even dirty water would have been delicious. We hardly had the chance to gulp it down when the siren roared again. The women scrambled for the door to ensure they were on time for roll call.

All the barracks were emptied and everybody stood outside in rows of ten in the early morning chill. The sky was still dark and overcast. It didn't look like the sun was going to shine today.

The guard began to count heads and called out our allocated numbers. Names were no longer significant. It must have been at least an hour since we stood there and shivered. The wind howled and lightning cracked across the sky. Thunder roared. A heavy downpour soaked our prison uniforms and chilled us to the bone.

'Wish she'd get a move on,' Gabriele whispered.

'Shut up. No talking in ranks,' the guard roared. 'Now look what you've done.' She walked up to Gabriele and smirked. 'You've only gone and put me off my count. Back to the beginning, prisoner number...' the guard called out all the numbers from the sheet again. My body was aching from standing there all that time already, what was it going to be like after another hour?

At last the roll call came to an end and we were marched off to work in the pouring rain. The hardest labour was demanded from all. Women shouldered spades and went digging, some were sent to transport coal and others sent to build roads. Gabriele and I had been assigned the Sisyphean task of rock pulling. Boulders were loaded and piled high onto wooden carts. Frail, skeletal women were then forced to haul these wagons from one end of the camp to the next, for no reason, no purpose whatsoever other than simply punishment.

'I'm shattered, I need to rest,' I said to Gabriele and gasped for breath.

'Don't you dare stop,' cried an inmate. The guards will beat you and still make you work.

'I can't breathe, I'm exhausted.'

'What's going on here?' The guard from our barracks was standing over me. 'Need a rest?' she said with an evil grin. She waved her whip in my face and held the leash to a snarling, German-Shepherd dog. The dog may have had a furry coat and a cuddly appeal, but those great white fangs and its drooling mouth told me this was not a man's best friend.

Gabriele grabbed my arm and forced me to hold onto the cart.

'I'm fine,' I forced the words out.

An elderly woman at the other side of the cart slid on the muddy ground and fell over. The lanky guard raced through the puddles to her side and roared at her to get up. The old woman lay still. The rain battered against her body and her saturated prison uniform clung to her skeleton. A bony ribcage and broad hip bones stuck up from the ground like an abandoned carcass after a hungry pack of wolves had stripped the flesh from its prey.

'Had enough, Jew? You could always take the easy option,' the guard said and pointed to the electrified fence. The frail, old woman scrambled to her feet, grabbed the cart with her blistered hands and plodded on through the muddy camp roads.

The rain dripped from my hair, ran down my face and blended with streaming tears. I stared in awe of the old lady. She must have been in her seventies. What an inspiration she was for me that day.

At lunch time we marched back to the barracks. Inmates scrambled to the tables at the smell of hot food. A fight broke out among them. One woman had thieved a potato from another's plate. They clawed at each other, like wild animals fighting to the death over a scrap of food.

The elderly woman who had fallen earlier, sat alone in the corner. Blood oozed from the open wounds on her hands.

'I'm a Doctor, let me help you,' I said.

The old lady smiled revealing her rotten tooth stubs. She patted my hand. Who was I trying to kid, there was little I could do. There was no medicine and no bandages. I ripped a piece from my dress, cleaned around her wounds and bandaged her hands as best as I could. I offered her my last potato. Her face lit up with pleasure, her wrinkled mouth circled, masticating on my last bite.

The siren wailed again and the inmates rose from their stools, back out to commence the heavy labour until late evening.

After work, we returned to the barracks for a meagre piece of bread. I didn't even get a smell of coffee before we were ordered outside for evening roll call. Then the prisoners were given half an hour free time to stroll along Camp Street and chat with the others. Most, however, were too exhausted and collapsed onto their bed. Gabriele and I, on the other hand, were ordered to remain, standing to attention after the group dispersed.

'Did you think I'd forget?' The lanky guard smirked and walked around in front of us in the pouring rain.

I was trembling and didn't know what was coming. I didn't even know what we had done wrong.

'Your straw mats weren't straight,' she said, as if reading my mind. 'You will stand here until I'm ready to let you back inside.'

I closed my eyes and remembered my feeble attempt to straighten my straw mat before early morning roll call; I swore to myself I would get it right tomorrow.

The guard stood under a doorway and smirked, watching us shiver in the cold, wet night. 'Don't you dare move an inch,' she said then marched off and left us standing there.

It seemed like hours we had been standing there. My legs were cramping. Gabriele was swaying, ready to drop. 'This is awful, Nadette, we're never going to survive this shit-hole.'

'Yes, we will, Gabriele. Look at that old lady in there, not a complaint. If she can do it, so can we.'

'Let's go, Nadette, the guard's gone,' Gabriele said and walked off towards the barracks.

I heard a gun bolt slide along the barrel ready to shoot. A soldier up in one of the towers was taking aim on Gabriele. I had a split second to make a decision. I ran at Gabriele and pulled her back into rank and prayed that it was enough to satisfy the soldier.

Ages later, the guard came back, wiping her greasy face, looking suitably replete after a hearty meal. 'Get inside,' she said. 'No food till tomorrow.'

My stomach grumbled at the thought. My legs were aching from standing in the same position for such a long time. It was an effort to take a simple step.

When we got inside, most women were sleeping, snoring, or groaning in pain. I crept up to the old woman's bed to check her. Her bandaged hand hung over the side, her eyes were closed and her mouth lay open displaying her rotten tooth stubs. I lifted her arm across her chest. She was cold, very cold. She didn't even have the thread of a pulse. I kissed her forehead and pulled the blanket up over her head and said goodbye to my inspiration.

CHAPTER 35

The weeks dragged in, stuck in the admittance block, awaiting permanent accommodation. At last, the day came when we were marched off towards our new home. I hoped it would be brighter and more spacious than our temporary set up.

It was dusk by the time they marched us off. At least it was dry and warm. Our bare feet crunched into the gravel and our arms swung in perfect time. No clogs were allowed between April and October they told us, and many women suffered the crippling effects. Night after night I bathed their swollen, bruise and gashed feet but with no medicine or bandages, their wounds had no chance to heel. Yet the women remained stoical, heads held high, noses in the air, and blood and pus oozed from open, septic cuts in their feet. They marched on, not a grumble about pain. Well, most of them.

'My feet are killing me,' Gabriele moaned. 'Sick of this place and logging that cart about. They better get me a change of duties, Nadette.'

'They're not changing our duties. Weren't you listening?' The guard had already explained it was only our accommodation that was changing.

'Yeah, well at least it better be good barracks. Better than that filthy hole we were in.'

'Doubt it,' I said, not wanting to get my hopes up. Yet silently I prayed for a bed to myself with warm, cosy blankets.

'Halt,' the lanky guard at the front called out. The marching women instantly obeyed the order. Gabriele and I had a delayed reaction to the command forcing us to crash into the prisoners in front.

'Red triangles,' the guard called out, 'political prisoners, in there,' she said and pointed to the nearby barracks. The red triangle brigade fell out of line and walked over to their new accommodation. A woman wearing a green triangle, sleepily followed the others. 'Hoy, dozy,' the guard called after her, 'red triangles only. Jail birds haven't been called yet.' The sleepy woman strolled back into line amongst the roars of laughter from the assembled women. The guard silenced the crowd with a roar then continued to allocate accommodation. 'Black triangles, A-Socials,' she called out our colour. I drew in a deep breath and waited, hoping for a half decent sleeping base. 'Block Two,' she said.

I glanced over to see where she was pointing. Darkness was falling but I could still see the women who were being ordered into the wooden hut by another ferocious guard, a short guard, whose uniform sagged over her body. Her height and build didn't deter her from bullying the aggressive inmates. She swung her truncheon on the backs of the malnourished women until they complied with her orders. I couldn't help wondering if an evil nature was a pre-requisite for the job.

Some women in front of our new barracks had their hair chopped off but some, had their long hair dangling over their shoulders. They were clearly off duty from work.

I turned back to the guard who was allocating accommodation. She stared at me, sniggered and called out, 'In there, prostitutes block.'

Instinctively, I clutched my necklace. 'Oh my God,' I whispered, unable to comprehend why I was once again grouped with those aggressive women. I pulled my necklace up against my nose and imagined I could smell the sweet fragrance of my lover, 'Give me strength, Ariella,' I whispered.

'Are you mad?' Gabriele said.

'I don't care what you think. I believe the necklace is helping me and that's all that matters.'

Gabriele shook her head, 'C'mon,' she grabbed my arm and pulled me towards our new quarters. A few more A-socials fell out from the marching line to join us.

It was quite dark in the barracks. The exhausted inmates sprawled in their beds. Hundreds of women crammed tight into the three-stacked tiers.

We walked through the barracks, passing the sleeping inmates. Our new grumpy guard led the way, seeking a place for us to rest our heads. Every bed was heavily occupied. Women were piled two, sometimes three to a narrow bed and others less fortunate, grabbed a corner on the floor. Some women lay groaning, irritable, trying to sleep whilst others cried out in agony. The women looked malnourished, overworked, exhausted and broken.

'Get out the way, Jew,' the guard said and shoved her boot into a woman who lay curled in a ball nibbling on a salvaged piece of bread.

'Oh, leave me alone, please,' the woman groaned.

I wanted to bend down to see that she was okay but Gabriele grabbed me back and pushed me in behind the guard to follow her. We passed groaning woman and crept towards our own sleeping area.

'You two. Up here. And here.'

The guard had found us two beds, both on the top bunks. Gabriele and I followed her to the appointed beds. We were each instructed to share with two other women who were already asleep.

I climbed up onto the bed but was brutally kicked back down. A disgruntled inmate was refusing to make room for one more. It was understandable; she was already lying top to toe with another woman.

I started trembling again and scanned the floor to search for a spot to lay my exhausted body.

Gabriele seemed to have no problem squeezing in beside her bed-mates. She shot me a look, urging me to get up and fight.

The women would continue to bully me if I didn't stand up for myself, was Gabriele's earlier sound advice. I still wasn't finding it any easier after all these weeks.

I squeezed my necklace again for courage to scramble to my feet and climb into the bed. I reached up and grabbed the woman's leg and shoved it aside, 'Get over. Let me in,' I said in my deepest voice.

'Ah,' she groaned as though I had hurt a painful leg. I was about to apologise when I noticed her legs easing over the bed, making room for me to crawl in.

I lay trembling with a pair of scrawny feet stuck in my face. I pulled my necklace off, wrapped it around my knuckles and smiled down at my treasure.

My thoughts wandered off to my last love-making episode with Ariella. Her gentle touch, her fingertips had glided over my bare skin. A tingling sensation and a missed heartbeat as I imagined our naked bodies pressing together. Her arms wrapped tight around me, protecting me as we slept. There was a lovely, warm feeling in my heart as I blissfully stepped into a safe place away from my grim reality.

It was short lived. The camp searchlight swooped through the barred windows, shone directly on my face and reminded me exactly where I was. I huddled up, grasped the thin blanket, hauled it to my chin and stared straight ahead. My necklace was still tightly wrapped around my fingers. I squeezed it tight and vowed that I would get to Ariella, somehow.

I was really hot during the night and I slipped into a pleasant dream of Ariella. I was miles away, living in a comfortable apartment with her. I dreamt the sun was shining bright and the heat was beaming in through our open windows. It was too hot in fact. The sweat trickled down my back. I turned round to see Ariella, to look into her brown eyes and see her warm smile. Instead I was greeted by a timid grin from a wrinkled woman in her sixties. She lay trembling with an apologetic look on her face. The smell suddenly hit me. I realised, it wasn't perspiration on my back.

'Get up,' roared our new short guard who was at my bedside, staring up at me. 'I have a job for you,' she said, 'and this,' she drew back the blanket and screwed up her nose at the stench, 'this is not acceptable. It will be your job to see this doesn't happen again. Got it?'

I looked between the guard and the bed-wetter and frowned. What kind of job was she talking about?

'On your feet, now,' she roared. 'You are now the Barracks Elder. The last one has been released, served her time.' She threw a green armband at me.

'What? I don't know anything about being a Barracks Elder,' I said and climbed down from the bed.

'You'll soon learn, she'll show you,' she said and nodded to the Barracks Elder for the other half of the block.

'Please, please, I beg you. Choose someone else. These women won't listen to a word I say.'

She stretched up on her toes and rammed her craggy face in against mine. She was about forty with greying, dark hair pulled tight into a bun.

'You'll do as I say,' she said and cracked her whip in mid-air. 'You don't keep this place in order, then its detention for you. Now move. Get to the washroom and get rid of that stink,' she said. 'And as for you,' she turned to the old woman who looked ashamed at her mishap, 'stay behind after roll-call tonight, no food.'

The woman was shaking. She nodded her head in obedience and remained to attention until the guard marched away.

I had no idea what to expect for my duties as Barracks Elder but put the armband on my left arm like the other inmate who had been allocated the same role for her side of the block. 'What am I supposed to do?' I asked her. She had just shouted orders to one of the prisoners.

'Keep these women in line. Stop them fighting. Stop them stealing food from each other. Make sure their beds are straight,' she rattled out the orders. 'The barracks must be scrubbed out from top to bottom. Any mess,' she paused to stare at me, 'and you're to blame,' she said and raised her eyebrows as if I should know the penalty for such a pathetic crime.

My heart was beating faster again, I nodded frantically, trying to take it all in.

'Don't worry, you'll learn,' she said. 'Start by pouring everybody's coffee.' She pointed to the inmates who carried pails of the disgusting, brown liquid that was expected to quench our thirst on that sticky hot, sunny morning.

At least I was relieved of rock hauling duties for a while. Two other worn out inmates were sent to work with me. Their bodies were so frail, the women struggled to stand let alone perform the heavy cleaning tasks expected of them. We scrubbed and cleaned floors, windows, stools and tables. Washrooms and toilets were kept meticulously clean ready for inspection by the guards. By the end of the day, our backs were breaking, our limbs ached and our hands had even more calluses and blisters after the already inflicted injuries from rock pulling duties. Our day was most certainly not any lighter than the laborious outdoor duties.

I waited eagerly for the outdoor workforce to arrive and dreaded having to keep them in line. The aggressive women came into the barracks and trailed mud everywhere. I stiffened my back and took a deep breath ready to bellow at them and force them to clean up the mess. I couldn't do it. I ran over to their feet and eagerly swept up the dirt myself.

Gabriele came in, exhausted from another day on the rock carts. She rushed over. 'What're you doin', Nadette? Get up. You got to make them do it.'

'I can't. They'll beat me up.'

'It's going to be worse if you get detention.'

'I won't. I'll clean it for them.'

'You're mad. They'll just make it harder for you.'

She was right. A tall woman swaggered in, freeing her blonde, curly mane from its tight, elastic band. Her hair sprang up into a spiral frizz. I gasped, recognising the strange hairdo and that long face and deep, black eyes. It was Panda, the woman from the Alexanderplatz. I rubbed my head, feeling an imaginary throb as I re-called that night she twisted my hair around her knuckles and threw me among the pack of wild dogs who savagely attacked me in that police cell.

She noticed my panicky effort to clean up the dirt on the floor and smirked. She paused, furrowing her brow, staring at me. Her eyebrows peaked and her face lit up, recognising me. 'You again,' she said, 'Rich little German girl?' She grinned, deliberately trailed her muddy feet and walked towards me.

'No, please, don't touch me.'

'So, we've got a skivvy in 'ere. Eh girls?' She deliberately raised her voice and attracted the attention of her aggressive comrades.

The other women walked over to see what was going on and fired questions. 'What is it, Panda?'

'Do you know her?'

'Sure do, met her in the police prison. Thinks she's better than us. Well let's see about that,' Panda said, then carefully shook the mud from her feet onto the floor that I had just washed. 'Clean it up, Cinders, she said.'

Gabriele looked at me, eyebrows raised. I took a deep breath and slowly rose to my feet. Panda's aggressive look, together with my recollection of my last encounter with her, told me it wasn't worth the trouble. I crouched back down and swept up the mess. The women in the barracks laughed and joined in, dirtying the floor with whatever rubbish they could find. They had picked up on my weakness and laughed amongst themselves, as though scheming up a plan to make my life harder.

Day after day I put up with the same behaviour from the women. I suffered their taunts and insults and acted as their slave and cleaned up their deliberate mess. Many women were genuinely ill but still did their best to make my life hell. Some had bad stomach pains, probably a reaction to the disgusting food and drink. I watched them crouch over, hug their swollen abdomens then rush to the toilet to vomit all over the place, and leave their foul, smelling mess for me to clean up. I didn't even have the heart to request help from the inmates who were allocated cleaning duties in the barracks. They were so weak and worn and in desperate need of medical attention.

As the weeks went by, my two assistants took to their beds permanently. I nursed them with whatever medicine and bandages I could salvage from the new arrivals who still had some of their belongings. Meantime I soldiered on with the scrupulous cleaning tasks in my half of the barracks which accommodated over a hundred and thirty women. I scrubbed and cleaned every inch to ensure it would pass the guard's inspection.

'Anything to report?' the grumpy guard said, disappointed at having to agree that the barracks was in good order.

'No, nothing ma'am,' I said, breathing heavily, hoping she wouldn't notice my lie once again.

'Block Elder says you haven't reported anything wrong in this side of the barracks for weeks. You sure?' she said and scrunched up her scraggy face and stared into my eyes.

Barracks Elders were supposed to report bad behaviour back to the Block Elder who was in charge of the whole barracks. Everything that went wrong with the women: disobedience, arguments and food thieving, were all to be reported back to the Block Elder who would in turn, report to the guard. Canings were frequent practice in the other half of the block. The Barracks Elder in that side reported everything. She refused to stand for any insolence from the inmates. She told the guards about every squabble and reported anyone who didn't carry out their duties to perfection.

'No, nothing to report, ma'am,' I told the guard.

'Hmmm, if I find out you're lying...'

I stood to attention and focused on a tiny dot on the barracks' wall refusing to make eye contact until she dismissed me and left the block. I sighed with relief at my narrow escape again.

Nobody from my side of the barracks was sent for punishment. I didn't report their squabbles or their fights for food and I cleaned up their mess. It was beginning to show on me though; I couldn't keep up my performance. My body was weakening and so was my spirit. How I longed to be back on the rock pulling duties with Gabriele.

'I told you, you got to stand up for yourself,' Gabriele said and flopped down onto her straw mat after her heavy day's work. She looked pale and weak; hauling the heavy boulders through the camp was taking its toll on Gabriele's health.

'They're going to kill you,' Gabriele said, 'making you skivvy after them all the time. If they don't, the guard will. She'll send you to detention if she finds out what you're up to.'

I was extremely weak and felt giddy with exhaustion and couldn't listen to her naggings anymore. I needed to put my head down and rest, and collapsed onto my straw mat.

'And you got to do something about that Panda,' Gabriele said and sat up to lean on her elbow to talk to me. 'She's thieving bread from those women again.' She pointed her thumb back at the two women who were supposed to be my assistant cleaners.

The two women had a severely swollen abdomen, a high temperature and continuous vomiting. Their foul-smelling, yellowish diarrhoea, all over their beds, was replaced with black, blood-lined faeces. It was typhoid. I was sure of it. They must've drunk contaminated water. It was more than just the digestive system that was riddled with bacteria now, I was sure they were bleeding internally. They needed urgent treatment. There was none. To send them to the hospital in that state would only sign their death certificate. I had heard about inmates who were murdered there if they were unlikely to recover within a few weeks.

As the women's diseased and withering bodies struggled to keep breathing, night after night, the cold-hearted, aggressive Panda thought nothing of it to steal their food. Every time she approached their beds, my adrenaline rushed. I so wanted to run at her, but my body remained rigid, frozen to the spot.

'They're going to die anyway,' Panda said and pulled a face as though to dismiss a trivial matter. 'What you going to do about it, Cinders?' she said and glared at me with those dark, evil eyes.

'Here, take mine,' I said and offered my last morsel of bread to Panda. She snatched it from my hand, sniggered and devoured my precious bite within seconds. Then slowly she pulled out the stolen bread from her apron pocket and held it up in front of my face, I just knew what she was going to do with it. I shook my head and moved closer to the dying inmates and watched them suffer yet another night of starvation.

'You got to tell the guard,' Gabriele said. 'You can't keep giving away your bread to the needy or to that bitch. Apart from that, the guard's going to get suspicious. Nobody in here's been caned the whole time you've been Barracks Elder and that cow next door's got prisoners beat up every other day. The guard's going to know something's going on,' Gabriele ranted on.

'Leave me alone, please,' I said. I couldn't take anymore and crawled back into my bed, pulled up the blanket and began shaking with starvation and exhaustion. I huddled into a ball and grabbed my necklace, ready to wrap it around my knuckles.

My trembling hands dropped it. The clink of the necklace hitting the concrete floor caught Panda's attention.

'Ah ha, what's this, Cinders?' Panda said and raised her eyebrows eagerly.

'It's nothing.' I jumped out of the bed and snatched my necklace back into safety.

'Let me see that,' she demanded and twisted my arm around and opened my fist. I tried to keep my grip but my hand was so weak, she easily prised my fingers apart.

'Please, Panda, I need this.'

'Yeah?' she said and snatched the necklace from my hand. 'I need it more. Could trade this for something better than a measly piece of bread.' She sniggered and headed back to her bed, studying the necklace. I felt the colour drain from my face and unconsciously clenched my fists. A surge of adrenalin pumped through me. I had had enough.

'You,' I shrieked across the room and glared at Panda.

She spun around and stood, hostile, with a hand on hip, 'You talkin' to me?'

'Give me that back.' I roared.

'Fuck off.'

Panda turned to stroll away. I ran at her and grabbed her arm and spun her around, 'Give me that necklace, now.'

'Or what?' she said and shoved my arm away. We had attracted the attention of the others. A crowd was closing in.

'Bitch fight. Come on get her, Panda,' one of them shouted and pushed my antagonist on the back, ploughing her against me.

I lost my balance, stumbled and fell back against Gabriele. Panda sniggered and turned to walk away again.

'Don't back down,' Gabriele whispered.

Although I was shaking all over and my heart was racing, losing my necklace was at stake and I had no intention of backing down. I pulled on my last reserves of energy and curled my fingers into claws and drew in a deep breath before pouncing on Panda. I grabbed her frizzy, mad hair and twisted it around my knuckles, jerked her head back and turned her around to face me. Her dark, evil eyes glared. I glared right back and squeezed my hand into a fist and landed her one on the jaw. She fell on the floor and the necklace flew from her hand and chinked against a steel leg of a nearby chair. I dived on it and snatched it up and tucked it into my dress pocket.

'You bitch,' Panda cried and jumped on me and battered my head against the concrete floor.

Within seconds, we were surrounded by inmates. I expected the others to join in; a repetition of the Alexanderplatz beating. Surprisingly enough, they all kept out of it and stood on the side-lines, laughing, shouting and spurring us on.

Gabriele stood back, air punching with her scrawny fists. 'C'mon, Nadette, kill the bitch,' she roared, but the instant her words were out, she scanned the jibing inmates who frowned at her for cheering on the underdog. 'Eh, I mean, c'mon, Panda, get her.'

I glanced with an evil stare at the traitor then turned my attention back to the mauling animal that was ripping my dress to shreds, searching for the hidden necklace. Her foul smelling body odour was turning my stomach as her arms reached over my head and grappled around the floor for Ariella's necklace that had slid out from its safe place. Her long face and that pointed feature hung above my mouth. Without thinking, I sank my dirty teeth into that witch's chin. She let out a scream as she pushed me off and then cowered in a corner. The astonished inmates stood over me. Nobody dared move an inch towards the avenging animal.

The barracks' door flew open, the guard in the uniform that was too big for her, rushed into the block, 'What the hell's going on in here?' she said and waved her whip in the air.

The inmates scarpered and retreated to their beds. Panda still sat in the corner, licking her paws and wiping healing saliva on her grazed chin.

I looked up innocently at the guard, 'It's alright, ma'am. Everything's taken care of.'

'Get on your feet,' she roared. 'I knew there was something going on in this side of the block. Nobody's been for punishment. You think you can cover it all up? You better start talking now. Who's to blame for this? Who caused the fight?'

I looked over to Panda who sat shivering. If she had a tail, it would've been well tucked between her legs by now. Her hands were cupped over her wounded chin. She timidly stared at me. Then her gaze shifted to something sparkly lying on the floor. My forbidden necklace. Panda's dark eyes lit up. Her hands shifted to her hips. She tilted her head to the side, raised her eyebrows, grinned at me and awaited my decision.

'It was me,' I said to the guard, my eyes still fixed on Panda, 'I caused the fight.'

The guard grabbed my arm and forced me to my feet but not before I swiped the necklace and slipped it into my pocket. She twisted my arm up my back and ran me out of the door.

'Detention for you, Eichmann. And you can kiss goodbye to your privileged duties as Barracks Elder.'

I secretly smiled and hurried to keep pace with the lanky guard.

CHAPTER 36

Early morning and there was already heat in the air, perhaps a bright, spring day ahead.

Jana marched Ariella along towards the construction workers who were heading towards the camp gates. Everybody looked exhausted, weary and ready to drop before the day even began. They were on their way to another day's heavy work on the road further down from the camp. And now, Jana was marching Ariella along to join them.

'Sorry I couldn't get you here sooner, Ariella,' Jana said.

Ariella carried a pick, prepared for heavy, outdoor labour. She had begged Jana repeatedly to find a way to get her on the construction force beside her friend, Ester. The only way Jana could wangle it was to provoke Ariella every day and cause her to retaliate. It was risky and could've meant something more perilous for Ariella. Fortunately the plan worked. Jana was ordered to drag her out from the factory for more appropriate duties.

'The factory work is just as back breaking, you know.'

'Yes, I know,' Ariella said, rolled her eyes and rubbed her lower back. 'I've got to be near Ester. Help her, somehow.'

'She's bad, you know,' Jana said.

'What do you mean?'

'Evil Eva's never off her case.'

'How bad?'

Jana stopped abruptly and glanced over to the construction workers who marched towards the exit. 'See for yourself,' she said and nodded to Ester who was among the workers. She coughed and spluttered and struggled to handle the heavy pick. Ester was nothing more than a skeleton wrapped in a fine layer of warm skin. Ariella's jaw dropped at the sight of her dear friend. She was walking alongside Sarah, the woman they had befriended when they entered the camp.

Eva, the evil guard was still determined to break the workers. She walked alongside the women, cracked her baton across the back of the workers and forced them to march faster. Sarah received a sharp blow. She must have felt the thud from Eva's weapon without her extra padding. She had lost quite a bit of weight, wasn't nearly as stout as she was. Sarah made to dive for Eva but another inmate pulled her back. She was clearly every bit as angry as she was when they first met her and still as determined to throttle the fur-faced but not so cute, guard.

Eva reached over and swiped the baton across Ester's shoulders. She winced but kept her head down.

Ariella's skin was all goose bumps, she seethed with anger. She shoved the pick aside and ran towards the rat who beat up her friend. Jana grabbed her and spun her around with brutal force. Ariella was surprised at how tough the timid guard could be.

'Stop, Ariella, please. You don't want to end up in there, do you?' Jana said, nodding to the punishment cells.

'I can't let her away with that.'

'I'll get you alongside Ester. But, Ariella, you mustn't go for Eva. Even if she hits you or Ester. Agreed?'

Ariella glared at Eva, willing her to look around.

'Do you want to help Ester or not?'

'Of course I do.'

'Then calm yourself down. You'll only make things worse for you, and for Ester.'

Ariella looked away and sighed.

'Okay? Are you up for this?'

Ariella nodded.

'Right, let's go. Sorry about this.' Jana grabbed Ariella by her stubbly hair and ran her over to Eva. 'You've to get this one.'

'Says who? The elf said without turning around.

'Orders, Eva. She won't do a thing she's told in the factory.'

'Is that so?' Eva looked around. Her eyes lit up. She recognised Ariella once again. 'Ah, the troublemaker,' She smirked and slapped her baton against her hand. 'We'll soon sort you out, Jew. Get in line now.' Eva was too pre-occupied with her challenger returning, she missed Ariella squeeze into line alongside her dear friend, Ester.

CHAPTER 37

'Do you think you've got friends now, Nadette?' the guard said. I was marched into the death house in Ravensbrück. Inmates occupied rows of cells inside the detention centre, their loud, terrified screams echoed through my ears when I entered the building.

The guard pulled on a heavy door to one of the cells, the hinges eerily creaked.

'No, no please.' I let out a high-pitched wail, and resisted with everything I had left. She shoved me in, slammed the door shut and slid the bolt along, locking me in the darkness.

'Let's see if you're so smart when you come out of here, Eichmann.'

'You evil bitch,' I shouted and pounded against the steel, 'You know I was only trying to protect the women.' Her footsteps faded as she walked out of the detention building, leaving me alone with my thoughts.

I couldn't see an inch in front of me. No window, no sunlight and not even a flicker of light from the corridor. The heat didn't help. With spring upon us, the air was humid, making breathing more difficult. I reached out, feeling for the security of the brick wall. I edged against it and slid to the floor. I clutched my chest, gasping for air, remembering the last time I was shoved into a similar dark hole; the basement in Kaarl's parents' house.

He had dragged me in and locked the door.

'You're, mine now, Nadette,' Kaarl had said and zipped up his trousers of his first SS uniform. He left me there, curled in a ball in shame, put the light out and locked me in until I was ready to admit to him I had wanted it.

The buried memories had surfaced. I was breathing faster. My wind-pipe was closing and tightness crossed my chest. Air just wouldn't go into my lungs. My fingers were all pins and needles and I lost sensation in my left arm. My immediate thought was a heart attack but my Doctor's training told me it was panic. I knew I was about to pass out unless I got a hold of it.

I began deep belly breathing and focused my mind on pleasant things; Ariella. I imagined her arms around me, comforting me, stroking my hair, nibbling small kisses into my ear. I wondered what Ariella would think of me now? What I had become. Where did that outburst come from with Panda? What was this place doing to me? Was I actually learning their evil behaviour? That thought was scary.

Although I was calming down, my rapid heart-beat still echoed. I grappled around the cell, feeling for some kind of familiarity. The smell of death lingered in the air. Somebody had died there recently, or maybe they were still in there? I bumped into something solid. With trembling hands I reached down to feel for the object. The top was smooth, perhaps a wooden surface. Down underneath, there were the legs of a stool, screwed to the floor.

I crawled around the den and searched for other objects. There was nothing but the seat in there with me. To be locked up in such a small dungeon in complete blackness was enough to drive a person insane.

Time seemed to drag by. I got up and paced the tiny floor, counted each step, counted each second.

Guards came in time and time again to deal with lawbreakers; the flogging table was well used. I could hear the women being hauled out from their cells and strapped to the table.

'Twenty five lashings,' cried the guard, 'You thieving pig.'

'It was only a piece of bread, I'm so hungry.'

'Start counting,' the guard cried. And the sound of a whip cracked across her back. If the suffering inmate had miscounted the blows the guard would go back to the beginning.

It was random guards, male and female, each one as evil as the other. I couldn't help wondering how on earth they could be so wicked and perform such treatment on another human being.

This went on throughout the day, every day. The only way I could tell it was evening was by the lack of guards' visits to the building. I was glad to be in the still of the night, but I couldn't help worrying if it would be my turn tomorrow.

I sat in there with a slice of dry bread and black coffee for nourishment each day. I wasn't too bothered about the lack of food, my appetite had strangely left me. Maybe with the stench inside the cell or maybe my stomach was too far knotted, waiting for my turn to be strapped to the rack and flogged like the others.

The door to the detention centre rattled open. 'Oh no, it's morning,' I shuffled over to listen at the door for the prisoner's name to be called for the beating.

'Eichmann.'

I edged back against the corner of the cell, curled my fingers in front of my mouth and waited for the cell door to be opened. The light from the corridor burst into the cell. I held my hands up as a protective shield from the stabbing light shooting through my eyes.

'Out. Now,' cried the all too familiar guard in the overly large uniform. Her scraggy face, screwed up with an evil stare. 'You must be punished, Eichmann.'

The guard dragged me from the cell and another male guard awaited me outside the door. I was strapped to the punishment rack in no time at all. I took deep, panicky breaths, closed my eyes and waited for the horrific blows. And then the most painful crack I have ever experienced in my entire life thundered down across my protruding vertebrae. 'Aagghh. No more. Please stop.'

'Count. Pig,' cried the man who was belting my back with the leather whip.

'One,' was my agony cry. 'Aagghh. Two.' I cried, forcing myself to pay attention to the blows. The pain shot through my entire body. It was horrendous. I couldn't go through another twenty-five lashes. I had to keep count. 'Three...'

By the time they were finished, so was I. They dragged me to my cell, my legs couldn't carry me. I was almost unconscious when they dumped me into the darkness, I didn't even try to get up. I lay perfectly still on the cold floor. I winced, feeling the pain in my back. It was going to be all over soon. I was sure I was going to die. I wished I was going to die. I closed my eyes and drifted off.

Then from nowhere, a silhouette appeared in the corner. I tried to focus. Was I dreaming or hallucinating? Was there really somebody there? The figure was clearer now, a woman with a surrounding bright light. She was beautiful with long, dark hair and a warm smile. Ariella? Is that you? She shook her head but still smiled. She grasped at her neck, tugging at something and pointed to me as though encouraging me to do the same. I couldn't understand what she meant. I reached for my neck and remembered the hidden necklace, Ariella's family heirloom. That's when I realised, I had to hold on for Ariella. I reached out to touch the guiding light but she smiled and faded away.

I woke up in the morning, aching, with swollen ridges on my back. Was last night real? Did I see someone in my cell? Was it all my imagination? Did it matter? The lumps in my back were real. I needed medical attention, cream, like I had given to so many women who came back from the detention hell. I swapped my bread for whatever medication I could from the new arrivals. I wondered if anyone would do the same for me.

The outside door swung open again. Guards. Another inmate was about to have the last remaining spirit knocked out of her.

'No please. I was hungry, it was only a tiny piece of bread,' she cried.

I recognised that voice.

'Please don't hurt me.'

It took every bit of strength I had left to get up from that stinking floor and crawl over to listen.

The prisoner was being strapped to the table. She howled, begged for her life. 'Aagghh,' she screamed as the whip cracked down on her bony back.

'Hang on, Gabriele,' I shouted, knowing I was risking another beating.

'Nadette. Help me,' she cried.

'Don't let them break your spirit.'

'Aagghh, Nadette, do something.'

'Count, Gabriele, count. You can do it.' I begged her to count the lashings, hoping she wouldn't have to go back to the beginning.

At last, it was all over. She was thrown into a cell next door to me.

I was aching. My back throbbed. My wounds were open and blood oozed from the gashes. I needed to know that Gabriele was going to be okay. 'Hey, Gabriele, we're going to get out of here,' I shouted over to the next dark cell.

'No. I'm never going to make it, Nadette. I can't do this.'

'Sure you can. Come on, we're both going to make it,' I said then collapsed into unconsciousness on the cold floor.

Several days had passed before we got out. Gabriele and I were released at the same time. She looked as if she had recovered from her beating but her fighting spirit had far from returned.

The light stung our eyes as we staggered onto Camp Street. Several inmates came to our aid and shouldered us back to the barracks. I dreaded what awaited me back in Block Two.

Panda stood at the door when I walked inside. Her face had healed from the fight but a minor scar remained where I had sank my teeth into her chin. I bowed, ashamed and shuffled past her.

'Stop,' Panda said.

Oh, no, what now?

'Nadette,' she said and looked into my eyes.

I could barely see her after so many days in darkness.

'Here,' she said and offered me a piece of bread.

I frowned at her, hesitating whether to accept it or not. What had she done to it?

'Take it,' she said. I eased the bread from her hand; I really didn't fancy another fight after what I had just endured in detention. She slapped me on the shoulder, 'You're alright,' she said then strutted off to talk to the new Barracks Elder.

The door swung open behind us. The lanky guard entered with a new inmate in front of her. The prisoner looked so worn and was covered in scabs. Disease reeked from her body. Without further examination, it was hard to tell exactly what was wrong with her.

'In there,' the guard said and pushed her into a corner with the baton, clearly not wanting to catch her disease.

'What's wrong with her?' I whispered to Gabriele. She knew everything from the inmates.

'Probably back from the Sonderbau,' Gabriele said. 'She'll be given a phenol injection later.'

'Phenol?'

'Yeah, death injection. Nazi doctors slam it straight into the heart,' Gabriele said without batting an eyelid. 'Better that way,' she said, 'look at her, she's never going to survive in that state is she?'

I shook my head in sorrow. What horrific ordeal had this dear woman been through to end up in this condition?

'What's the Sonderbau?'

Gabriele looked sad, shook her head as if to tell me I didn't really want to know. 'Get some rest,' she said, 'we're up at four thirty in the morning. We've got heavy labour ahead. Rock pulling duties.'

CHAPTER 38

Summer 1943

The sun was coming up. It was going to be way too hot for heavy labour. Ariella feared for Ester. They marched towards the camp gates. Ester was already weary and struggled to hold the heavy work tool.

A new girl's orchestra played at the entrance while the exhausted labourers headed out of the camp. Although their music was upbeat to encourage a fast trot from the marching crew, their bows glided over the steel strings and produced delightful sounds. The orchestra were as thin as the rest of the prisoners and showed the same fear as they performed to save their lives. The marching lot taunted them, spat and sneered for playing for the Nazis.

Ariella looked around at the ensemble, strumming away on their instruments. And as though she had just been slapped in the face, Ariella had a sudden idea to help her friend. Now, where was Jana?

It took Ariella a few minutes before she finally caught Jana's attention.

'Ester's a violinist,' Ariella whispered.

'Hmmm. Afraid that won't do her any good in here,' Jana said, her eyes on the construction workers.

'Jana, look,' Ariella nodded to the recently formed orchestra.

'Oh, no, Ariella. You don't know what you're saying, that's crazy.'

'You could get her in. You said you wanted to help us. Now's your chance.'

'Yes, I suppose I could get her in. But. It's just...' Ariella wondered if her willingness to help prisoners was just an act. Granted, she got her out of the factory work, then again, that was to give her heavier duties. Was she really on their side?

'Just what? Look, can you help her or not?'

'Ariella, the orchestra...after the Sonderkommandos, they've got the next highest rate for suicides.'

'That won't affect Ester. You've seen what she's like, she's full of hope. The lighter duties could surely save her life.'

'Ariella, they play for the arrival of prisoners and–'

'And what?'

'They play while others march to the showers, you know.' She bowed her head in sorrow.

The showers. The words stung in Ariella's ears. She had learned what the showers meant for the majority of people. 'The gas chambers you mean. Marched to their death,' Ariella spat the words out at Jana as though it were her fault the Nazis were gradually eradicating Jews and anyone else considered unfit for society.

In the barracks, the inmates frequently talked about stories spreading through the camp. The Sonderkommandos who worked in the crematoriums were kept in separate barracks to prevent other inmates from knowing what was really happening. But, as in any prison, information had a way of filtering through.

Ariella thought about the many people who were marched for de-lousing, uncertain as to what de-lousing actually meant for them. She imagined their trembling, naked bodies inside those dark shower rooms, and their innocent eyes gazing hopefully at the spigots, but instead of water flowing, many were to hear the trickling of Zyklon B pellets pattering against the pipes. Terror struck, they would probably cling to their loved ones. Tear stained faces and agony cries as they tasted their last pure air before gas permeated their lungs and choked them to death.

Ariella grasped her throat without realising. Many times she had wondered when it would be her turn. She sprang back from her nightmare and turned her thoughts to Ester again. The orchestra wasn't an option.

'No, you're right, Jana. If Ester played music while inmates marched to their death everybody would hate her, they would beat her up and I wouldn't be in the same barracks to protect her.'

'Wait a minute,' Jana said. Her face lit up, 'only the orchestra will be in the barracks with her, she'll be safe, Ariella.'

'What? Are you sure there's nobody else in the barracks?'

'Positive. And better accommodation. Even more food.' Jana looked hopeful.

Ariella glanced at Ester who was lagging behind. She struggled to keep pace with Sarah, every footstep looked like a real effort. Something had to be done soon or she too, would end up in the showers.

'Well? What do you think? Jana awaited Ariella's decision. A decision to release Ester into her care. Intuition told her Ester would be safe with Jana. Her gut feelings had been accurate up and until now, but could she really trust an Auschwitz guard?

CHAPTER 39

At four thirty the next morning, Ariella and Sarah scrambled outside to join the others for roll call. Then Eva marched them all off to work.

Ariella couldn't stop thinking about Ester. Was she really being sent to work in the orchestra? Her stomach was in a tight knot, so tight, she struggled to eat her bread roll and even the smell of the disgusting coffee was making her nauseous.

She scanned the surrounding barracks, searching for her friend. They marched past the Kanada warehouse. There was a whole new language in the camp. Kanada symbolised wealth to the prisoners. Ariella had learned it was an expression prisoners used when viewing a valuable and fine gift. The saying derived from the time when Polish emigrants were sending gifts home from Canada. In the concentration camp, prisoners who worked in the Kanada sorting section, sifted through their fellow inmates' possessions and anything valuable was shipped back to Germany.

From the open door, Ariella could see piles of jewellery confiscated from the prisoners.

'They're leaving us with nothing,' she said to a woman who marched alongside her.

'Huh, that's nothing,' she said, like a child trying to get one up on her.

'What do you mean?'

'I heard they take prisoners eye-glasses. They even use workers to remove gold fillings from those who've been gassed.' The coldness in her voice was frightening, as if this had become a natural way of life.

'Surely not?' Ariella turned away, stomach retching and glanced heavenward, hoping that somebody somewhere had spared the life of her friend.

At last they reached the camp entrance where the girls' orchestra picked up its speed for the approaching workers. Ariella scanned the group, looking for Ester. She was nowhere to be seen. Ariella's heart raced. Her morning bread was climbing back up her throat. What had she done? Jana was nothing more than another deceitful Kraut.

She searched among the faces. Finally, she spotted the delicate frame of Ester Kolleck. She sighed with relief. Jana Bach, the Austrian guard could be trusted after all.

Eva marched them outside the camp past the orchestra. Ester never looked up, she focused on her music sheets and tapped her foot in time with the beat. Ariella smiled and paraded on with the others to work on the roads.

The sun was burning hot and made it even harder for the labourers to maintain their duties. The sweat trickled down Ariella's back. Women dropped one after the after. Their exhausted, weak bodies battered against the ground creating a flurry of dust into the air. Guards frequently ordered inmates to carry the dead to the crematorium. Ariella thumped her heavy pick into the ground, thinking, dreaming of an escape from the nightmare. There was no way out.

She forced her thoughts onto Nadette. While the hot sun beat down on her back, she was imagining herself lying somewhere exotic, soaking up the sun's rays, and sipping a cool drink with her lover. It was hard to keep focus with so much anger and hatred flooding her thoughts. How the Nazis were treating them, and especially how Kaarl had separated her from Nadette in the first place. She gripped the shaft of that pick, and promised herself that one day, she would squeeze the life out of Kaarl Bergmann – an opportunity that was soon to be presented to her.

A Nazi truck load of soldiers screeched outside the camp. Instantly the orchestra picked up its tempo again for the arriving prisoners. A few men, already dressed in prison stripes, were hauled out from the truck. They wore a pink, inverted triangle on their armband.

'Careful, Ariella. Keep in line,' Jana said and strolled past her. She was keeping an eye on the marching women who were far from replete after watery, turnip soup for lunch.

'Jana,' Ariella called after her and urged her over. 'Who are they?' She nodded to the new arrivals.

'Pink triangles. Homosexuals,' she said.

'Pink?'

'Sure. Pink's a colour men like to wear. So they give them pink triangles for their affection for the same sex.'

'Where are they taking them?'

'Down there.' She was pointing to a red-bricked building, further down the camp. 'It's a Puffkommando, you know.'

'It's a brothel?' Ariella struggled to believe Jana's words.

'Yes. They've got them in several camps. That one there,' she said, 'it's Herr Bergmann's. He set it up to rehabilitate homosexuals, and of course, to service his SS guards.'

'Bergmann?' Ariella felt giddy. Surely not? The homosexual men descended from the truck and a uniformed Nazi shoved them into order. The hairs stood on the back of Ariella's neck, tingles ran down her arms. 'Kaarl Bergmann,' she said and gritted her teeth. 'There is a God.'

'You know him? Gruppenführer-SS Bergmann?'

'Oh, yes I do. He murdered my father and sent us here. And I want revenge.'

Ariella stepped out from the marching women and dropped the heavy pick to the ground. She glared at Kaarl, like a hawk, never to take its' eye off its kill, and stomped towards him. She reached for the sleeve of her uniform and unravelled the cotton to release a coarsely-crafted knife. Weapon gripped tight, Ariella broke into a sprint.

'Yeah, you go, girl,' Sarah cried.

'Stop it, Sarah, get back in line,' Jana shouted at her. She bolted after Ariella and grabbed her back. Ariella shoved Jana aside. Nothing would stop her. The adrenalin was flowing fast, thrusting her forward to seek her long awaited revenge.

'Ariella, no. Think about Nadette.'

'I am thinking about Nadette.'

'What's wrong with you?' she roared. 'Nadette's probably doing her best to survive to be with you and all you can think about is how to get yourself killed.'

Ariella slowed down then stopped. She stared ahead, letting Jana's words slowly sink in. She had no idea where Nadette was, or indeed if she was still alive. But she knew that Jana was right, Nadette would do everything in her power to be with her. She had to hold on to that.

Ariella threw down her knife and kicked some soil over it, burying her chance at revenge. She rushed back into line and picked up the pace of the marching women.

Although Jana had helped her to see sense, Ariella had to work hard to simmer down each time she looked at Kaarl. He marched his prisoners along past the orchestra. Ariella soon realised the danger Ester was in. It wasn't likely that he would recognise Ester, especially with the state of her. Nevertheless, she couldn't take a chance.

Ariella whistled with her dirty fingers shoved into her mouth. It was useless. The girls in the orchestra were terrified to raise their heads at any time let alone when an SS Gruppenführer passed by. They swiped their bows across their strings keeping time with the conductor. Ariella waved and tried to signal. It was no use, she couldn't catch Ester's attention.

Ester's head wobbled in time with her playing. Her eyes were on her music sheet. She was engrossed in her performance and oblivious to everything else. Ester was completely unaware that the man who had arrested them was standing right in front of her, admiring the new orchestra.

Where was Jana when she needed her? She was plodding alongside the marching row of construction workers, away at the other end from Ariella. Ariella ran her hand over her stubbly hair, trying to come up with a solution to distract Kaarl away from Ester.

Sarah was next to Ariella, her pick held over her shoulder. She looked lost in a dream world and hadn't noticed Ariella's panic.

'Help me,' Ariella grabbed Sarah's arm.

'What? What's going on?' she looked as though she was trying to focus after her dream state.

'Help me, Sarah. Quick. Do something.' She nodded over to Kaarl.

'Hey back off, Ariella. You coward. You should've knifed him when you had the chance.'

'Yeah, then where would I be? Look no time for that. If he recognises Ester or me we'll be gassed. You going to help me or what?'

Sarah glanced over to Kaarl then pushed Ariella to the ground and jumped on top of her. The marching women crashed into each other and forced them to come to a halt. Eva, the short guard ran up to them. She reached for her baton and crashed it down across Sarah's back. Ariella flinched, she could feel every thud for her. Eva manoeuvred herself in between them, searching for ways to reach Ariella too. The strikes were hard and stung against her face. Ariella put her hands up defensively to block her blows but most importantly, she was shielding her identity from Kaarl who was now standing over them. He laughed and swung in a kick for the hell of it.

'Right. Move on, men,' Kaarl ordered his pink triangle group. The men marched on and followed the leader.

Ariella lay on the ground, Sarah and Eva piled on top. Sarah winked down at her and pretended to punch her in the ribs. Kaarl wiped his forehead in the blistering heat and plodded ahead. One stray prisoner lingered behind. He was tall and balding on top with no hair worth shaving.

'Move it, Otto,' Kaarl shouted.

He actually referred to him by name, he must've known him. Ariella wouldn't be surprised if Kaarl had imprisoned one of his own friends. After all, he had no hesitation when it came to arresting his own fiancée.

CHAPTER 40

January 1944

The icy cold winter took its toll on the women prisoners in Ravensbrück concentration camp. Many dropped dead, exhausted and half-starved and no resilience to the bitter, chilling weather. Frost bite numbed the flesh of the survivors. Snow fell relentlessly, and the boulder-laden cart still had to be hauled up and down the camp roads. I wondered how much more punishment we could handle.

Pounds of flesh shed from our fragile bodies. Gabriele looked scrawny. Her freckly face was drawn and her cheeks were sunken in. Even her auburn hair looked limp, but not lifeless. The head lice fed on those of us who still had long hair.

My long hair was probably all that remained to confirm my identity as a woman; I had lost all shape. I was determined to keep going, aching for the day when I was free to find Ariella.

A guard blew a whistle in the background, 'Stop. A-Socials get in rank.'

We didn't have to be told twice. The cart-handle clattered to the ground and the boulders bounced off its side. The skeletal army formed rows; our black triangles stood out against the white snow.

Somebody shoved me on the back. I spun round to see what was going on.

'Get in that row.' It was another inmate snarling at me. After almost a year of imprisonment alongside bullying inmates, I had learned a few tactics. I pushed into her chest, forcing her to stumble backwards.

'Get lost. You get in that row.'

The whistle blew again. The guard watched us squabbling women. 'I said, get in line, now.'

I stood to attention in the back row alongside Gabriele. The bullying inmate had manoeuvred herself into the row in front.

We were up to our ankles in snow. The blizzard had picked up. White, furious flakes raged from the heavens, we were well under attack.

'What's going on?' I asked Gabriele, 'Can you see anything?'

Gabriele stared at the ground, as if she couldn't care less.

I looked out past the rows of women to see what was happening at the front of the ranks but swiftly jerked back in. Kaarl Bergmann, full of self-importance, strutted towards our group alongside one of his minions.

'Oh my God.'

'What is it?' Gabriele asked.

'Kaarl.'

'Lucky you. Probably here to get you out,' Gabriele said and bowed her head once again.

And to go back to Kaarl would be better than this? I dreaded the thought.

Kaarl and the SS man sauntered in through the ranks and inspected the women.

'I understand the work is really hard here,' Kaarl said. His smile was fake and so was his sympathetic voice, 'and the accommodation, not so good, huh?'

He stopped right at me. I dipped my head, clenched my trembling hands against my mouth. He lowered his voice, tilted my chin and ran his cold finger down my cheek. 'It's cold here,' he said. 'Warm, hot bath back home, hmmm?'

I flinched at his evil paw on my face. He smirked and paraded on through the women. The thought of that bath was tempting but to be back with Kaarl in that abusive relationship turned my stomach. But maybe, I could find a way to escape from him, find Ariella?

Kaarl continued to tempt the women.

'There is a better place for some of you,' he said. 'Good food. Good beds. No more heavy work.'

Nobody dared to look up at him. He came back to Gabriele. She shivered in the cold.

'Warm, comfortable barracks,' he continued. 'We have a sonderbau, a very special building in ten of our concentration camps equipped with all of this for you.' His voice was so calm and soothing I could see why the women would believe him. I knew him only too well. He was lying.

Gabriele raised her head with interest. Kaarl walked away from her, striding through the lines with his hands behind his back, clasping his leather gloves. He marched to the front of the ranks and turned to face us. He tilted to look under the rim of his cap and scanned the group for interested women.

Only a few heads were raised.

Kaarl continued with his speech, luring the women into his trap. 'You will be required to service your fellow detainees who mistakenly think they are homosexual. Or, entertain the camp guards. And some of you will provide a service to your fellow prisoners who pay from their own wages in the factories. And better still, you will be paid.' Kaarl smiled proudly, as though he had made an offer the women couldn't refuse. I could understand why it sounded so appealing to some, considering the harsh conditions we were subjected to every day. And many women had already experienced prostitution as a means of survival. But this was different. I could feel it. Kaarl wasn't telling the whole story.

'Easy enough,' Gabriele said, her pupils dilating with interest at Kaarl's proposal, clearly taken in by the illusion.

'What? Are you mad?'

Gabriele shrugged.

'After only six months, you will be released,' Kaarl continued. 'I need ten volunteers, ten who have not had their hair shaved.'

Three women, renowned prostitutes, including Gabriele rushed forward. Panda strutted out front to join them.

Kaarl pouted his lips and studied Panda. He sniggered and walked around her. He twisted her frizzy hair round his fingers then ran his thumb along her pointed chin. He moved in closer to her, scrutinizing her deep, dark eyes and ran his thumb slowly around the black circles formed underneath. 'Somebody was having a laugh leaving you with your long hair. You're no use. Too ugly,' he said. 'Get back in line.'

Panda's face fell. I actually thought she was going to burst into tears as she hurried back into rank.

'No. Wait,' Kaarl shouted. He rubbed his chin as though trying to think of some usefulness for the unattractive inmate. 'On second thoughts, you'll do. We've got some fat, worthless guards that might prick up with a cheap service. We'll put you in, half price,' Kaarl said and roared with laughter. He waved the dejected Panda back into line.

Kaarl strutted among the freezing women, looked them up and down. 'I need ten volunteers.' Kaarl's voice was toughening.

No one else was taken in by his deceitfulness. He walked back through the lines. His face was hard, his lips tight. 'I will select if there are no volunteers.'

A woman in front of Kaarl stepped forward. Kaarl smirked at her, nodded his approval then walked on. He picked a tall woman. She walked out to the front to join the others. She kept her head down, thumb in front of her mouth, no doubt, terror struck, wondering what next.

'You,' Kaarl continued to pick random women who timidly walked to the front. He stopped when he came back to me. 'What's it to be, Nadette? Had enough here?'

Who was I trying to kid? There was no way I could get to Ariella if I went home with him. I'd be kept under permanent lock down. No, I had only one chance.

At last I understood why the Jehovah's Witnesses wouldn't take up the chance to be free from the Ravensbrück nightmare. All they had to do was give up their beliefs and walk away from their faith. And now, I had a choice. All I had to do was tell Kaarl I would go home with him and I too, could walk out of Ravensbrück... And walk away from Ariella.

I looked into his eyes, 'I'd rather serve the rest of my sentence here.'

He leaned right into my face. His breath was stinking of stale alcohol and cigarette smoke. He spoke through clenched teeth like a ventriloquist trying not to move his lips. 'You don't understand. You don't get to leave me.' He pointed his finger right into my face. 'Join the others at the front, now.'

I gasped and looked up at him. He couldn't do that to me. He wouldn't send me to a brothel. Would he?

There was so much I wanted to say to him. But I daren't. I bit down on my lip, bowed my head and timidly ran out past him to join the selected women and squeezed in between Gabriele and Panda.

Kaarl paraded up and down, inspecting the ten women. He flipped his wrist over, palm up and pointed his finger at the first woman. 'Buchenwald,' he said. He moved to the next woman, 'Mauthausen.'

'What's he doing?' I whispered out the side of my mouth to Gabriele.

'Names of concentration camps. We're being sent to the camp brothels.'

'Auschwitz... Dachau... Sachsenhausen... Buchenwald... Dachau...' Kaarl grinned as though he was enjoying himself, allocating our brothels. He reached Gabriele and Panda, both sent to Auschwitz.

At last he came to me. Kaarl's eyes widened. He grabbed me by the throat and shoved his forehead right down into mine. 'You will be rehabilitated and you will want me.' He pressed so hard against my brow, I'm sure he left an imprint. He jerked back, swiftly released his grasp, 'Mauthausen camp brothel,' he said and stared at me. With a swipe of his shovel hand, he tossed me aside and walked away and called out his orders to the lower ranked SS man who shadowed his every step, 'March them off.'

The selected women were marched inside to be primped up. We were ordered to wear stylish dresses and handed make-up to enhance our appearance. Reluctantly I complied. Gabriele was overjoyed at the treatment, 'Struck it lucky here, Nadette,' she said and with a beaming smile she applied foundation, covering her red freckles and her ashen face.

'Lucky? Are you crazy?'

'Anything to get away from here, Nadette.'

The SS man returned and ordered us to stand in a row. He called another SS guard into the room who sauntered along the line of prepared women and looked us up and down. I bit down on my lip, dreading what was to come.

The guard stood in front of a young girl with long, blonde hair. Her make-up coarsely applied. She stood trembling with both fists clenched in front of her mouth.

'You,' he said and pointed his index finger to the timid, young girl. He spun his hand and slowly curled his finger back and forth, beckoning her to follow him into a nearby room.

My stomach turned over; sick at the thought of the young girl being tested out before we headed off to our assigned brothels.

We piled into a truck outside the camp gates. An armed guard climbed in with us. Gabriele, Panda and I were seated together. I stared at the truck's floor and chewed frantically on my bottom lip.

'I've got to swap camps,' I said and jumped to my feet with the obvious answer to my problem. 'I've got to get to Auschwitz. Ariella's there.'

'What are you nuts?' Gabriele said. 'She's probably dead.'

'I don't think so, I don't feel it.'

'What's this?' Panda frowned, she had never heard me mention Ariella before.

'It's nothing,' I said and glared at Gabriele, willing her to shut her mouth. Panda had never given me anymore trouble since that night we came to blows. Nevertheless, I didn't really know her and I certainly didn't trust her.

'So what if she knows,' Gabriele said. She clearly had more to worry about than the love life between two women. 'You're crazy, Nadette,' she said, 'you'll never find her. Go where Kaarl sent you. At least you know he'll come get you out. Never get out of Auschwitz,' she added and bowed her head as though accepting her own fate.

'You got a woman in Auschwitz?' Panda's face twisted with curiosity. 'What a sister? Friend? Or... a lover?' She sat back in the truck, head against the tarpaulin and forced a laugh. 'Ha, who would've thought? Nadette. A lesbian.'

'Back off, Panda,' I said.

'Hey. No big deal,' she said, hands up defensively. 'Just surprised, that's all. But hey, that's good.' She nodded her head and rolled out her bottom lip. 'Yeah, that's good. Good that you got somebody to hang onto. But Auschwitz, Nadette? Gab's right. Not much chance she's alive.'

'She's alive,' I said with confidence.

'And who's this, Kaarl, fella?' Panda asked. Her pointed chin stuck out. 'Can he get you out?'

'It's her fiancé. He sent her to Mauthausen. He'll come back for her. Nadette's determined to get herself in Auschwitz though,' Gabriele said, pulled a face and twirled her finger at the side of her head.

'Don't do it, Nadette,' Panda said. 'You got a chance to survive these camps, take it. Not much chance your girl's alive in Auschwitz.'

I sat and stared at the floor, adopting my previous thinking stance.

CHAPTER 41

The guard pulled up the tarpaulin from the back of the truck and pointed a torch inside. 'Prisoners for Auschwitz, out, now,' he said.

'Get that torch out my face,' I said and shielded my eyes from the beam pointing right at me.

'Don't antagonise them, Nadette,' Gabriele said and jumped to her feet, ready to obey orders.

Gabriele, Panda and another couple of women, were all that remained with me in the truck. All the others had already been dropped off at their allocated concentration camps. Panda stood up alongside Gabriele ready to dismount. One more woman reluctantly got up from her seat.

Now was my chance if I wanted to get into Auschwitz. I stood up and pushed the other woman back onto the wooden bench and quickly took her place. I was expecting a fight but the woman was so worn and weary she sat back down and stared ahead. She had a glazed look in her eyes, didn't seem to care where she was being sent.

The soldier reached into the truck to grab us one by one and haul us down onto the thick snow. Only a flutter of flakes still trickled from the sky leaving dandruff speckles on the guard's shoulders.

'Move it. Quick,' he said to me. I pulled away from his clutches and climbed down by myself.

'Okay, okay. I'm coming.'

He pushed me towards the massive camp gates.

As soon as we stepped inside Auschwitz, female guards, similarly dressed to the Ravensbrück women, ran towards us. The soldier pulled the iron gates closed and trapped us within the camp.

A girl's orchestra, lined up at the camp entrance, started playing as we marched into the grounds. Immediately I thought of Ariella and scanned the gaunt faces.

'Ariella? Ariella? Does anyone know Ariella Ish-Shalom?' The musicians kept playing, keeping their heads bowed, probably too afraid to look up.

The guards were nearing us. I had to find out about Ariella. I threw myself amongst the orchestra, causing a disturbance to their playing.

'Ariella Ish-Shalom, is she here? Ester Kolleck then, does anyone know Ariella or Ester?' One of the musicians looked up. She seemed to recognise Ester's name. Before I could ask her anymore questions, a heavy guard with cropped hair and wrestlers arms dived in after me and pulled me out from the crowd. I tried to shove her off but she was so strong.

'What do you think you're doing?' she roared with an incredibly deep voice. 'Get away from them.' She grabbed me, trailed me backwards away from the orchestra. She threw me so hard I fell, my hands sunk deep into the chilling snow. I scrambled to my feet and hurried alongside Gabriele and Panda on the march to our new accommodation.

We marched through the camp in the darkness, passed by rows and rows of dismal wooden barracks. It certainly wasn't an improvement from Ravensbrück. The snow was gathering momentum again making it increasingly more difficult to see where we were going. The thick, mesmerizing flakes blurred my vision, I had no idea what was ahead.

At last we reached our destination. The guard shoved the three of us inside the red-bricked building. A bit different from the wooden barracks and the warmth inside was a definite bonus.

Female guards patrolled the corridors. We were marched past several incredibly small, single rooms on each side, each with a heavily stained mattress on the floor. I felt quite nauseous at the smell of sex and body odour reeking from the cells.

Some of the doors were already closed and sexual grunting echoed from the mini cells. A voyeur in SS uniform peered through a small spy hole on one of the cell doors. He laughed heartily then turned to eye the new arrivals.

'Hey Berta, what you got here?' he said to the cropped haired guard who marched us along.

'Just newly in from Ravensbrück. Be ready shortly,' she said and spun us around for inspection. He was salivating at the mouth as he inspected my breasts. I forced my shoulders back, held my head high and strutted on past him. I really was feeling the strength from Ariella's necklace.

We plodded on down the corridor to more cells horizontally across the back of the building. Berta pulled out a bunch of keys, jingled them noisily and searched for the appropriate one to unlock the door to our new abode.

Oh no, another tiny cell. Get over it Nadette. You survived the punishment cells, you can deal with this. I took deep breaths.

One by one, Berta shoved us into the same cell.

The room was small. Plaster crumbled from the dirty walls. A three-tier bunk bed took up most of the floor space. Two beds were already taken. The single toilet and wash-hand basin were a luxury for the five occupants. The small barred window was decorated with floral curtains to give the room a homely appearance. The window was open a fraction but made little difference to clear the smell of unkempt bodies that lingered in the air.

I was drawn to the beds and the battered women who occupied them. A woman lay slumped on the middle bunk. She was pale, emaciated and stared ahead with a dead gaze. If it wasn't for the slight flicker from her eyelids, I would've sworn she had passed away.

The woman on the bottom bunk didn't look much healthier. Her back was to me and the vertebrae of her spine stuck out from under her prison dress. Her long, dark hair hung in waves, covering her face. She lay there groaning.

'Oh, my God,' that dark, wavy hair. 'Ariella,' I shouted and ran towards her. She dangled her scrawny arm over the bedside and revealed her armband. It was a red triangle. Not a Jew then. Nevertheless, I turned her around in hope. She had dark brown eyes like Ariella. I was disappointed, yet relieved at the same time. Her face did look familiar though. I couldn't place it at the time.

'What you doing?' Gabriele said. She stood with Panda at the entrance to the cell. 'Get back before you catch something,' she said, and sniffed as though the air was polluted with germs.

'She needs my help,' I said and walked to the wash-hand basin to soak a rag for the woman's forehead. 'She's burning with fever.'

Gabriele's eyes looked like they were going to pop out of her head. 'Get me out this disease-ridden joint,' she said to the stout guard.

'Nope,' Berta said, 'you're all on my watch, keeping you together.'

'I'm not staying in here,' Panda said and backed out of the cell door.

'You'll go where I say.' The stout guard pushed Panda inside the cell. 'I said I'm keeping you lot together.'

'Well move the three of us then,' Gabriele said.

'I'm not going anywhere. I'm staying here.' I couldn't leave that poor woman in the state she was in. I turned to her, 'It's all right. I'm a Doctor.' Not like that made any difference in the concentration camps. I had no medicine and no way of nursing this poor woman back to health. Perhaps my reassuring words could alleviate some of her anxiety though. The woman half smiled and breathed a deep sigh.

'Are you mad?' Gabriele said. 'Come on, let's get outta here. She could be contagious.'

'I'm not leaving her,' I said, 'or her,' indicating the near corpse in the bed above.

'Get me outta here,' Gabriele grabbed the guard's cape and clutched tight in desperation for her help.

'Calm down, Gabriele,' I said. 'It's probably excessive abuse and exhaustion, you won't get it,' I lowered my voice, 'from her.'

'There you are then,' Berta said. She sniggered, 'the Doctor has spoken.'

Gabriele was pushed aside and the cell door clanked shut. A dim light from the corridor shone through the small barred opening on the cell door. Panda scrambled up to the vacant top bunk whilst Gabriele stood at the door and stared at her new inmates. Eventually she climbed up beside Panda, lay top to toe and pulled the blanket over her head as though protecting herself from the diseased prisoners.

I dampened the forehead of the woman who resembled Ariella and stroked her hair to ease her suffering. She drifted off to sleep. My mind wandered off, thinking about Ariella. I removed my necklace to study its beauty and squeezed it tight. I fell back, exhausted against the feverish woman and closed my eyes, the tension in my hand released.

Dawn was breaking and we were still in the cell, a change from the early morning, four-thirty roll call. Was this a good sign I wondered. Berta, the guard entered with a small urn of coffee and a basket of rolls.

Room service? What was this place?

I rose from the bed to take the mouth-watering food from Berta. She looked at me, seemed to study my face before handing me our lavish meal. She had nice, small features and dazzling green eyes. If it wasn't for that cropped hair and excessive weight, she could be really quite pretty.

Berta slammed the door shut; Gabriele and Panda dived off the bed and snatched the food from my hand. Their bread was devoured in seconds. I carried mine over to the feverish woman's bedside. Her temperature had gone down slightly. Together we ravished our morsels of bread and enjoyed the sweet smell of coffee, the taste was something else.

There was no sound from the woman in the middle bunk. I reached up and felt for her carotid pulse. Not even a ripple. I pulled the blanket up over her head, shook my head at Gabriele and Panda, sharing the news of my discovery.

Panda clenched her fist and turned away. Gabriele puffed out an uncaring sigh. The concentration camps were destroying everybody's emotions but I'm sure there was more to it than that with Gabriele.

'She's dead, isn't she?' It was the woman with the fever. 'Nobody survives this place. The SS are liars. They promised us better conditions. Said we would be released after six months. It's a lie,' she said. She was sobbing uncontrollably now. I held her close trying to calm her down. 'She's been here nearly a year, now look at her. Nobody survives.'

'Sshh, calm down.' The woman was frantic. I rocked her in my arms, 'It's okay. You'll be out of here soon I'm sure.' I stared over her shoulder and bit on my lip.

Gradually she stopped sobbing. 'What's your name?' I asked. She had a small round face; a face I'm sure I had seen before.

'Ingrid. Ingrid Schreiner,' she said in a soft, Berlin accent. 'They sent me here because I'm a lesbian. They send in ten men or more every day, trying to cure me.' I frowned curiously at her red triangle. I couldn't understand why hers was red and mine was black considering we were in for the same crime. She must've seen me staring at her armband. 'Oh, that,' she said. 'Political reasons. They said I spoke out against the Führer. I did no such thing. It's not an offence to be a lesbian. They just hate it. They find another excuse.'

It dawned on me where I knew her from. 'You're Otto Schreiner's wife,' I said. Ingrid looked surprised and sat back, studying my face. 'Nadette Eichmann. You don't know me. I was there the day they arrested you and Otto.'

'Oh Otto,' she said and dipped her head in sadness. 'God knows what they did to him and his lover, Anton.'

'Anton's dead, I'm afraid. I saw them in the Alex. Otto's friend, Kaarl Bergmann, shot Anton and took Otto to a concentration camp.'

'Oh no,' she covered her mouth, 'poor Anton. And Otto?'

'I don't know. That's the last I heard.'

'The SS get it bad in the camps. Homosexuals. They hate them.'

I tried to lighten up the conversation. 'So how did you two meet?'

She smiled slightly. 'We were in a gay bar before they were all closed down. I was with my girlfriend and Otto was with Anton. We just got talking. Him being in the SS, he seemed to know the Nazi plans and feared for us all. We ended up getting married for security. I was sure we were safe and so was Otto. He was friends with that SS Leader, Kaarl, who didn't know about us, but Otto felt sure he would be protected if it ever came out.' She bowed her head. 'How wrong could he be?' I gave a sympathetic squeeze of Ingrid's hand. I was too ashamed to tell her Kaarl had been my fiancé.

'Nadette thinks she can find her Jewish girlfriend in the camp,' Gabriele said. She sniggered and returned to her bunk.

Ingrid looked up at me, her eyebrows squeezed together. 'You too?' she asked. I nodded my head. 'We're never in with the other prisoners and Jews are never allowed in here. You won't find her,' she said and grabbed hold of my dress.

'Tried to tell her that. She'll be dead anyway,' Gabriele said with such coldness.

That was it. The final blow. I jumped off the bed and snarled up at Gabriele, 'You don't know that. 'What the hell made you so cold hearted?'

Gabriele sat upright, hand on her hip. 'Years on the street darlin', that's what. Tossed out after my step-father raped me when I was fourteen years old. My mother was too pissed to care.' She jumped down from the bunk. 'Fuck them. I got my own ways to survive.'

How I wished I could retract my words. 'I'm sorry, Gabriele, that's none of my business,' I edged towards her and squeezed her arm.

She shoved me off, 'Damn right. It's none of your business.' She paced the room.

'Ha, at least you chose to go into prostitution,' Panda said. 'My mother forced me. When she couldn't make enough off her own back, she brought fellas around for me. I was only twelve. Fifteen years ago. Screwed them for every penny I thought I was worth.'

My stomach churned, appalled at the heart breaking stories of these two women.

'You got it easy with that Nazi boyfriend of yours,' Gabriele said.

Easy? Raped repeatedly since that first time in the basement when Kaarl wore his shiny, new SS uniform.

I wandered over to the tiny barred window and stared at the snow melting down the glass, facing those memories I had worked so hard to block. A key slipped in the lock of the cell door bringing me back from my nightmare, not realising I was about to face another.

Berta, the guard entered with a clipboard.

'Eichmann, Feurst, Becker.' She read the names from the clipboard. I had never heard Panda's real name, she was being called too. 'Prostitutes, come with me.'

'What? I'm not a prostitute.'

Berta looked at me and sniggered. She handed me the board to see for myself. There it was typed in bold: "Nadette Eichmann Code 998 - Prostitute. Reason for Internment – Lesbian relationship with Jew".

Berta snatched the board back from my hand and dictated, 'You are a lesbian,' she said and spat on the floor with disgust. 'You must be rehabilitated.'

'No. I won't go.' I backed off into the room.

'Suit yourself,' she said and walked over and dragged Ingrid from her bed. 'She can take your men,' Berta said, 'then after that, she can take her own.'

'Berta, no. Please. No. You'll kill me,' Ingrid dragged her heels. She turned to me, 'Please, Nadette, I couldn't take it.'

The guard squeezed Ingrid's scrawny arm and stared into my eyes, 'Well?' How could that evil cow put me in such a position? Ingrid's weary body could never survive that amount of abuse. Besides, they would get to me eventually. I took Ingrid's arm and guided her back to her bed.

Berta marched us out of the cell and along the corridor to the working cells. My legs were buckling under me.

Some more women were in front of us, heads bowed, shoulders hunched and shuffled along the corridor. Each of them shoved into separate cells. Queues of SS men waited outside each room. They chatted and laughed, discussed what they expected from their whores. On the other side of the corridor, men in striped uniform lined up, all wearing the pink triangle. There was no laughter or chatter among them.

'Isn't that Kaarl?' Gabriele said. I looked down the pink triangle line. Right at the bottom, shoving them all into order, was Kaarl Bergmann.

'Oh my God.' I had to hide. He didn't know I was in Auschwitz. He walked up past the line of men, inspecting them. I cowered in behind Berta and thanked God she was broad enough to shield me.

'Feurst, homosexuals are yours,' Berta said.

Gabriele swaggered towards the appointed cell. The door was open and a stained mattress awaited her on the wooden floor. Berta shoved the base of her palm right into Gabriele's back.

'You're the professional,' Berta said, 'see if you can convert them.'

Gabriele scowled at Berta then swaggered nonchalantly into the working cell in front of Kaarl. She looked him up and down, smiling, teasing him. I don't think she realised she wasn't quite the beauty she was when she was first imprisoned. Her face was gaunt with sunken cheeks and her eyes lay deep inside their sockets surrounded by black circles, not unlike Panda's.

Kaarl smirked at her, watched her swagger into the cell. He didn't seem to notice me hiding behind Berta. He patted the first man in the queue on the back. 'Show you how it's done,' he said. He walked into the cell with Gabriele and closed the door without turning around. My jaw dropped.

Panda was next. 'Half-price for ugliness.' Berta snorted and screwed up her face to examine the features of the chosen prostitute. 'The SS Leader's having a laugh here,' she said scrutinizing the sheet with Panda's details. 'It's alright,' she said, 'you'll be paid the same as the rest.'

Paid? A mere pittance to buy extra food.

Berta pushed Panda into a cell where a short, fat, unkempt SS guard waited with keen eyes and a slobbering grin.

She grabbed hold of me and shoved me along the corridor. 'Move it. These men don't have all day to wait for you,' she said and led me to the row of SS who queued outside the next cell.

My stomach was in a knot but I wouldn't show it. I straightened myself up, held my head high, drew Berta a look of disgust and walked into the cell. The SS men whistled and cheered and shoved the first man ahead. His eyes practically popped out, eager to get started. Berta smirked and led him in. He reached for his zip under his overhanging belly.

'Can't be hard, lying on your back all day,' Berta called out before she closed the door.

Inside the room, the fat SS man stood in front me and grinned. I froze to the spot. He placed his hands on my shoulders, guided me towards the mattress, grabbed my face and bent forward to kiss me. His hand was stinking of urine. Beads of sweat danced around his upper lip. His breath smelled like a sewer. My stomach retched, vomit bubbled up my throat and sprayed all over his SS uniform.

He jumped back and scrambled for a hanky to wipe himself down. He glared at me, teeth clenched. He unbuttoned his tunic with great haste, threw it on the floor then lunged at me. He thrust me onto my back on that foul smelling mattress, pulled my dress up and yanked my underwear off. I tried to shove him off. I was so weak and unable to move under his heavy weight. I reached inside my dress to grab my necklace, praying it would give me strength to see this ordeal through. It wasn't there. Where was it? I scrambled around my clothing. Nothing. I felt all around the side of the mattress, feeling all around the floor. Nothing. I had lost Ariella's necklace. I welled up with tears and lay there numb as the monster pounded his fat flesh against me.

When he was done, he stood up and booted me in the ribs, calling me as many trashy names he could think of. I pushed my dress down, rolled onto my side and cowered into the foetal position. How I wished I was still in the womb, protected by my mother from this horrible world we were living in.

The door screeched open, the SS man was leaving. For a moment I felt relief, until I heard the footsteps of another entering.

'She's all yours, mate,' the fat man said on the way out.

I turned around to see what was happening. Another obese, SS man entered, his eyes lit up, as though desperate for his turn when he saw me lying in wait. He didn't waste any time, he dived on me and tore at my clothing. His dark, greasy hair dangled down onto my face as he slobbered his wet lips over my cheeks and licked me like a lion with his captured prey. His unshaven chin rubbed against me, stinging my face. I tried to shove him off. He slapped me so hard across the face, he burst my lip. The blood trickled between my teeth. I could only pray it would be over soon.

It was ages later before the SS queue finally dispersed. Satiated men marched out of my cell, ready to commence work. I lay there, motionless. I was exhausted and externally and internally bruised. I had been lying there for some time and Berta hadn't come back for me. At last I heard a key in the door. I scrambled to my feet. My legs were so weak I could barely stand let alone walk.

The door swung open and Berta entered. 'Another stray here,' she said, 'he's only just off duty. See that you treat him well, Eichmann.' Berta shoved an SS man into the cell.

'No. No more. Please,' I could only mumble the words out.

He walked towards me with an evil grin on his face and pulled his zip down. I backed off, hands in the air, pleaded with him, begged him to stop but he shoved me so hard I lost my balance and fell back onto the stinking mattress. I rolled over onto my side to try and escape his clutches.

'No. Leave me alone.'

He bent down behind me and wrapped my hair around his knuckles and pressed something cold and hard against my temple. From the corner of my eye, I saw it was a gun.

'What's it to be?' he said and rammed his pistol against my head. 'Your choice.'

I had never been so tempted in my life to give in and let him blow my brain to pieces. I lay there contemplating my decision. I had to keep going for Ariella. I had to find her. I had to survive. I took a deep breath, squeezed my fists tight, clenched my teeth and rolled over to stare into the face of my predator. I had a strange feeling, an eerie feeling, someone was watching us through the spy hole.

When Berta eventually came back for me, she had to drag me along the corridor, my legs simply failed me. She shoved me back into our sleeping cell, I landed face down on the floor. My eyes were so swollen after so many beatings I could barely find my way around the cell. Every inch of me ached, it was a struggle to drag myself to the bunk.

At least I had a bed now. The corpse had been removed but the air was still rancid from the smell of death. They must have left that poor woman lying there all day and night before the guards finally decided to take her away.

Ingrid lay on her bunk with her clothes all ripped. She must've been subjected to another round of abuse. Gabriele slumped on the top bunk, staring ahead in silence. Her face was bruised and her cheek was ripped, blood oozed from the gash.

The door clanked open again. Berta entered with Panda, shoved her beaten body onto the hard floor and slammed the door shut. I was beaten badly and any movement caused me severe pain but I crawled down from that bunk and hobbled across the floor, aiming for my enemy.

'You thief,' I cried and lunged at Panda.

'What the-'

'You stole my necklace. You won't get away with it.'

'I never touched it. I swear,' Panda's dark eyes were wide. She stared at me. 'Honest, Nadette. It wasn't me.'

She looked genuine. I let go and moved away from her. Gabriele was still motionless on the top bunk. Outside the door, a chuckling Berta peered in through the bars.

'Get lost. You freak.' I shouted.

Berta laughed louder then booted the door before storming off.

A while later, Berta returned with some food. I was salivating at the aroma. It was only watery soup with a few slices of potato and turnip mixed through but it tasted divine. I slurped and sipped the hot fluid past my swollen lips, desperate for some nourishment then lay back and passed out.

I couldn't have been asleep for long when I heard the key rattle in the cell door. Darkness had descended upon us again. The room was lit up by the faint corridor light and a sliver of creepy moonlight from the window. My head felt so heavy, I struggled to sit up to see what was going on.

Berta swaggered in with her clipboard again. 'Ingrid Schreiner,' she called then smirked as she looked over to me, 'and Nadette Eichmann.'

'No. No more.' I huddled into a ball and pulled as far away from her as I possibly could. Ingrid robotically rose from the bed, stared straight ahead and marched to the door.

Berta laughed at me, reached up, dragged me from the bunk and trailed me to the ground. I battered against the wooden floor, my ribs took full force. Berta grabbed me by the hair and hauled me onto my feet.

'Filthy lesbians,' she snarled. 'It's an abomination.'

'An abomination?' I said. 'You don't know the meaning of the word.'

'The bible says homosexuality is wrong. It's an abomination,' Berta said with authority in her voice.

'And what about prostitutes? Do you think that's acceptable in the bible? Do you really know your scripture, Berta?'

'Of course I do. Leviticus 18:22, if a man lies with another man, it's an abomination.' Berta was determined to rattle off the facts about homosexuality. I was ready for her and her preaching. The bible had caused me enough pain over the years about my sexuality and I had studied it well.

'Abomination at that time, meant unclean. Leviticus 11:12 said it was also unclean to eat any type of creatures that live in the water that don't have fins or scales.' I gestured to Berta's fat body. 'Do you obey that one, Berta, when you study the menu for shellfish?'

Berta was jittery and stuttering, searching her memory for biblical verse. 'Leviticus 20:13, if a man has sexual relations with another man, they both shall be put to death.'

'Leviticus also says the same thing about a child who disobeys his parents. I don't think we interpret that scripture literally, do we Berta? And what about Mark 10:1-12, the passages that forbid divorce? Where does that leave you Berta? We all know about you. We've heard all about your wrecked marriage.' I continued to ramble on with my bible quotes. 'And Deuteronomy 22:21, if a woman is not a virgin on her wedding night, she shall be stoned to death by the men of her city outside her father's house. Do you think that's right, Berta? Do you think we still carry out that punishment? The bible is written and interpreted by mortal man. The interpretations are a reflection of the time in which they lived. We've moved on since then. Anyway we're not in here for biblical reasons. Hitler hates homosexuals simply because we won't reproduce to increase his Master Race. Women are nothing more than Nazi baby-making machines. He hasn't sent us here for punishment. He sent us here for rehabilitation until we are prepared to reproduce more blue-eyed Germans.'

Berta was flapping. 'No, no it's a sin.' Her hands were shaking as she reached out and grabbed my arm. 'You will burn in hell.'

'Hell?' I cried. 'And what do you call this? We're living in hell in here.'

'What are you two on about?' Gabriele sat up on her bunk and rubbed her eyes as though disturbed from precious sleep. 'You quoting scripture? What has God got to do with all of this?'

'Don't you start about God,' Berta said.

'What do you know about God?' Gabriele said, 'He doesn't give a shit about any of us. I was brought up a Catholic and believed in Him for years and look where it got me. You're off your head Berta going on about the Bible like that. There is no God. We can only count on ourselves to survive.'

'You're wrong, Feurst. The Bible is right.'

There are so many versions of the bible, Berta, they can't all be right,' I said. 'God loves us, all of us. You don't need your Bible to know that.'

'No. The Christian bible is right and homosexuality is wrong. Our Führer says lesbians can be rehabilitated. Now move, Eichmann. You must be rehabilitated.'

I elbowed Berta in the ribs. She grabbed my arm and pulled it up my back and ran me out of the door.

I knew I would pay for that.

CHAPTER 42

Ariella and Sarah lay in bed, top to toe, sharing the same bottom bunk with two others. Everybody huddled in together for heat. The thin blankets were useless in the freezing cold barracks. They were all enjoying a free meal from Sarah's imagination. Sarah had told Ariella about all the fancy meals she used to cook for her husband. Ariella thought about skinny Ruben; either Sarah's cooking was awful or she kept most for herself. Nevertheless, her descriptions were good and helped satiate the hunger of so many starving women. She had often told them every detail of cooking a three-course meal and Ariella actually felt full at the thought of it.

'This is daft, Ariella,' Sarah said, sick of the pretence. 'You don't really believe it makes you feel full up when I tell you about my recipes, do you? I just tell you 'cause I love cooking and it keeps my mind occupied in this shit hole.'

'No, Sarah, it's good for us. Keep going,' one of the bed sharer's said.

'Yeah, there's got to be something in it. Let's face it, if bedridden people can imagine themselves doing exercises, and their muscles actually develop without moving an inch, surely imagining your delicious dinners can keep us feeling full?' Ariella said.

Sarah sat up with interest, back against the wall, 'Is that right? Okay then, where was I?'

By the time she finished running through the ingredients of a three course dinner, describing the beautiful aroma of a cooked sirloin steak, the group were drooling at the mouth, smacking their lips as though they could actually taste her fancy feast.

The women cuddled in, smiling, and closed their eyes ready for sleep as if they had just been told a lovely bed-time story.

Ariella and Sarah still sat up talking, their conversation swiftly brought to a halt when the barracks' door swung open. Their Kapo entered wearing a long, army coat. It hung loosely on her and the piece of string tied around its middle emphasised the fact that it was at least three sizes too big for her, a gift from a male guard perhaps. The coat together with her Kapo armband around it seemed to give her that sense of superiority and inflated her ego. She was only in her early twenties yet she paraded around their barracks giving out orders to elderly women and smacked a whip at them if they didn't comply.

'Everybody in bed, now,' the Kapo roared.

'Who does she think she is?' Sarah said. 'She's a Jew, she's one of us. An ugly one maybe, but she's still one of us.'

The Kapo did have a strange face, Ariella had to agree. She had large popping eyes which stuck out like ping-pong balls beyond her skeletal features. Her nose splattered across her face from one cheek to the other and a rubbery bottom lip stuck out every time she spoke.

'She's just trying to keep herself away from the gas chambers by working for the Nazis,' Ariella said.

'Maybe for a while,' Sarah said, 'they'll get to the Kapos too, eventually. Anyway she's got no right to treat us like that. And the way she prances about in that coat, reporting us, telling Eva if we don't obey her orders, that Kapo needs sorting out. Her and Eva.'

'Lie down you two, get to sleep,' the Kapo said and whacked their bed with her trusty whip.

'Beat it, Kapo.'

'What did you say?' the Kapo turned and stuck her ugly face down to the bottom bunk where Sarah lay.

'You heard. What's the matter with you? You're supposed to be one of us.'

'I've a job to do. I've got children to see to when I get outta here and none of you are gonna ruin that for me.'

'You don't honestly believe you're gonna get out? Just 'cause you wear that fancy hat and armband doesn't grant you freedom. They're just using Kapos to make the guards jobs easier, you daft cow. When they're finished with you, you're a gonner too.'

'You're wrong, Sarah. I'm getting out and I'll collect my children on the way,' she said and walked on past them.

'What do you mean collect your kids?' Sarah shouted after her.

'They took them into a different part of the camp when we arrived. If I do my job right, I'll get them back when I leave,' she said and paraded on down past the row of beds, checking the other women were asleep.

'Are you mad, Kapo,' Sarah cried after her, 'They're dead. Most kids are automatically gassed when they arrive. They're no use for the workforce.'

Ariella cringed at Sarah's angry words, brutal to the Kapo's ears. She charged back up to their bunk and rammed the handle of her whip into Sarah's throat. Her golf-ball eyes bulged even further. 'Don't you ever say that about my children again. They're alive. They're alive!'

Sarah lay back, stared into Kapo's bulging eyes. Her own eyes were popping wide, her face flushed at the lack of air passing through her wind-pipe. At last the

Kapo let go, strutted down the line of women and scanned their beds as though daring them to goad her.

Sarah leaned forward to whisper to Ariella. 'She's been eating again. Her face is all greasy.' She licked her lips as if she was thinking about the Kapo's tasty food.

'I want to know where she's getting it,' Ariella whispered. 'Kapos are only entitled to some extra rations, nothing like the amount she keeps eating.'

'What do you suggest?'

'Let's follow her and find out.'

'No, we could get caught.' Sarah said.

'Not if we're careful. Besides, she's supposed to be here to watch us. We'll wait till she's done her rounds of the barracks then slip out behind her.'

When the Kapo left their hut, Ariella tapped Sarah's leg to wake her. She'd nodded off.

'C'mon lets go,' Ariella said and tiptoed across the concrete floor. The door creaked open, they stepped out to the darkness and crunched their feet into the bitter cold snow.

'Sshh. Not a sound,' Ariella whispered to Sarah as they crept all the way through the Auschwitz camp in the darkness, their feet sinking into the thick, glistening snow, their backs fastened tight against the wooden huts to avoid the sweeping light beams. Soldiers patrolled their guard towers, their guns to the ready for any prisoner crazy enough to leave their allocated quarters. Guards roamed the grounds, their fiercely trained Alsatian dogs ready to pounce on enemy flesh.

Ariella and Sarah pushed on, arms spread out, and eased along the barracks wall. At the end of the hut, Ariella peered out and scanned the area for guards, and the mysterious Kapo. She was nowhere to be seen but there was a repetitive thumping noise nearby. Every sound was magnified in the eerie silence coating the concentration camp.

'Look, over there,' whispered Sarah. She pointed out to two dark figures standing between two huts. It was impossible to make out who they were but obvious they were having sex.

'I bet that's her, linking with the enemy,' Sarah said. 'I'll kill her.' She stepped forward, ready to run at her.

Ariella grabbed her back. 'What're you doing, Sarah? You're going to get us killed. We don't even know if that's her. C'mon creep closer. Slowly.'

They ran across to the next barracks. Ariella spied round the corner on the two love-making shadows. He had spiked hair and a scar down his face and was dressed in long boots and grey uniform. He was definitely an SS guard. Ariella couldn't make out who she was at first. He had pulled her head into his chest.

Sarah pushed Ariella aside. 'What's going on? Let me see.'

'What the...' Sarah said and peered closer. 'Ha, would you look at that.'
'What? Who is it?'
'I'm surprised the ugly cow could get a man. She probably paid him.'
Ariella poked her head out, trying to see the Kapo.
'Eva!'
'Let's snitch on her,' Sarah said.
'Who're we going to tell? Another guard? Do you think they'll believe us?'
'Yeah, you're right. And they'd probably send us straight to be gassed to silence us.'
'C'mon, let's get back in before she sees us. We'll get the Kapo tomorrow night,' Ariella said and tugged on Sarah's arm.

The next night, the Kapo came back to their barracks with obvious food residue again.
'I'm not giving up till I catch her,' Sarah said. 'I don't know which one I hate the most, the Kapo or Evil Eva.'
'We'll get her tonight. As soon as she leaves we'll tail her right away, we won't give her a second's head start.'
They didn't. They jumped straight off the bunk the moment the barracks' door was closed and ran after her, careful not to make a sound.
The Kapo was nimble and darted between the barracks, right, left, right... as if she was trying to lose the scent from anyone who dared to track her.
'Hold on. Wait,' Sarah said, puffing and holding onto the side of the barracks. 'She's like a lab rat darting around a maze in search of its precious food.'
'C'mon hurry up, we're going to lose her,' Ariella said and grabbed Sarah's arm.
She panted for breath as they trailed the vermin. It was no wonder they couldn't find her, the Kapo was right behind a red-bricked building, standing up against the back wall along with a man.
'It's Kaarl Bergmann's brothel,' Ariella said and gritted her teeth. She climbed up to peer in the window. Loud screams came from inside the block. 'What the hell are they doing to those poor women in there?' Ariella said.
'Get down before we get caught. You had your chance at getting Bergmann and blew it,' Sarah said. 'You'll never get him now.'
Ariella wasn't so sure about that.
Sarah grabbed her arm. 'C'mon let's get closer, see who that Kapo's with.'
It didn't take them long to work out who he was, an SS guard, the same one they had seen the night before. It would appear the Kapo was bartering with Eva's boyfriend. A quick fumble for a half-eaten potato. Her coat swung open. Small compartments lined the inside, each one stuffed with scraps of food.

'What's the matter with that man? Do you think he's got an attraction for ugly women?' Sarah said.

Ariella's mind was elsewhere. 'This is information we can use,' Ariella said, 'but first, I'm going to see Ester.'

'No way, Ariella. It's miles away. We won't get back in time.'

'C'mon we've come this far, and she's busy,' Ariella said, nodding to the Kapo.

CHAPTER 43

The camp light swooped towards Ariella and Sarah. They darted in between two sets of huts and waited till it passed before they made a run through the thick snow to get to the orchestra barracks.

The women lay sleeping, each bed accommodating two girls, sometimes only one to a bed. The barracks had its very own toilet for the fifty odd women. There was even a wooden floor, probably to protect their instruments from damp and cold. What price they had to pay for luxury though; they played marching music for hours on end and cheerful music to entertain the SS. And worst of all, the orchestra fell under attack from their comrades for strumming their instruments as prisoners marched to their death. It's no wonder their suicide rate was so high.

Ariella tiptoed around the surviving inmates and searched for Ester.

'Ariella.' The whisper came from the opposite side of the room. 'Oh thank goodness you're alive,' Ariella's dear friend said. She sat up with welcoming arms and waited for Ariella to run to her.

'What are you doing here?' she said, 'If they catch you they'll send you for punishment.'

'I had to see you.'

After a warm hug, Ariella pulled back to study her face. She was pale and gaunt and dark bags gathered under eyes.

'I'm alright, I'm alright,' she said in reply to Ariella's worried expression. 'The guard has been kind to me. I've been allowed to stay in bed for late night arrivals, give me a chance to get my strength back for the morning shifts.'

Ester swung her legs around to stand up. The moment her feet hit the cold floor, she started coughing. Her cough was much worse. Ariella rubbed her back to help her to settle to avoid disturbing the others. It was too late, some of the women aroused and grunted at her to shut up.

A young girl popped her head out from the blanket in Ester's bed.

'Sshh, it's okay, Bessie,' Ester said, 'lie down, get some rest.'

The young girl stared at Ariella and Sarah standing around her bed, her eyes wide, thin lips trembling.

'This is Bessie,' Ester said.

She was a child of no more than fifteen. Bessie huddled in against Ester as though waiting for her to hold her in a secure mother's embrace. Ester obliged. She was in her element, nurturing her longed for child. She rocked Bessie back and forth whilst the young girl lay with her head against Ester's chest.

'Isn't she beautiful?' Ester said. 'She's on her own. Her parents were quite poorly when they arrived from Theresienstadt Ghetto. The SS took them away with the elderly and other sick people. Probably took them to hospital to get them better again. Hmmm, isn't that right, Bessie?' Ester said and nursed the young girl. She held her close as if she was holding an infant in her arms and snuggled her face in against Bessie's neck, like a mother revelling in the smell of her baby's young skin. 'There wasn't enough food to go around in the ghetto,' Ester continued, 'they just need to feed your parents up a bit and they'll be okay, hmmm, Bessie?' Ester said. She smiled and smoothed back Bessie's cropped hair.

Sarah frowned at Ester's delusion and stepped forward, 'Ester they're-'

'No,' Ariella said and yanked Sarah's arm to silence her before she ruined the young girl's hope. Bessie was pale and thin. Her bony arms lay tight around Ester. She looked like she was struggling to hold onto life as it was.

Between Ester and Bessie, Ariella didn't know who was in the most danger from being marked as useless. She knew exactly what she had to do.

CHAPTER 44

The Kapo strutted in the next night, slapped the beds, ordered the women to get to sleep. She whacked Ariella and Sarah's bunk on the way past. Sarah was ready for her this time. She pounced out of bed and grabbed the Kapo by the neck, pressed her thumb against her windpipe.

'We know what you're up to. You're caught,' Sarah said.

'You get your hands off me right now or I'll call the guard.'

'Yeah, you go right ahead and tell her what you've been doing.'

'What're you talking about?'

'You know what we're talking about, Kapo,' Ariella said and jealously ripped her warm, winter coat open. The secret food storage areas were revealed, each one empty.

'You better get us some extra food,' Sarah said.

Ariella's stomach turned. She grabbed Sarah's arm and pulled her away from the Kapo, 'Look, Sarah, I can't do this.' She didn't want food from a guard, especially not in the way the Kapo was getting it.

Ariella looked into the Kapo's bulging eyes, 'Just back off Kapo, stop thrashing the women in the barracks, or else,' Ariella said.

'Or else what?' said the bold Kapo.

Ariella pounced on her this time. 'We'll tell Eva what you've been up to with her boyfriend, that's what.'

The Kapo jerked back, frowned and glared with those bulging eyes. 'How do you-'

'What? Know Eva's got a man?' Ariella interrupted. 'Never you mind.' Ariella shoved her palm into the Kapo's face, forcing her neck backwards.

'You just back off from now on,' Ariella said.

'And get me extra food,' Sarah said. She looked at Ariella for her decision.

'And some for me,' Ariella said. She dipped her head, not a proud moment but what else could she do?

CHAPTER 45

The Kapo wasn't any trouble the next night. She never slapped their beds or ordered them about. In fact she was very calm with all the women in the barracks. When she sneaked out for her secret meeting, Sarah glared at her to remind her of their understanding. Ariella looked away, her stomach all knotted, sick at the thought of her participation. She lay down and waited but was overcome by exhaustion and dozed off.

It must have been early hours in the morning when Ariella heard Sarah creep back in to the bottom of their bunk. Her feet were freezing from the chilling, cold.

'Where have you been?'

Sarah sat up in bed, shivering and delving into a piece of bread. A few delicious moans, she enjoyed every bite. Her eyes were on Ariella the whole time she chewed.

'You get that from that Kapo?'

Sarah turned her hand over and stared at the bread before she grudgingly offered Ariella a piece. Her mouth was drooling at the sweet smell of newly cooked dough. Ariella snatched the bread from her palm. It was white and crumbly with a crusty edge. She was salivating and desperate to take a bite.

'I can't do this. I've never been so tempted, but I can't do it.' Ariella couldn't stand the thought of that guard using the Kapo for a few scraps of food and then for her to take the miserable ration away from her. Ariella held onto the bread, sniffing the warm dough and rubbed it between her fingertips.

'You going to do this every night then?' Ariella asked.

'Every night she sees that guard, yeah, why not?'

'It's criminal, Sarah. You're making yourself as bad as she is.'

'Who cares? Survival, Ariella. Survival. And it's not for you, is it?'

Ariella hesitated one last time.

'You want it or not?'

Ariella shoved the bread into her apron pocket and bolted for the door.

'You'll never make it. It's nearly time for morning appell,' Sarah said.

'I have to. Ester needs me.'

CHAPTER 46

Ester and Bessie seemed to benefit from the few scraps of food that Ariella carried in at every opportunity. Ariella never told Ester about her sordid arrangement with the Kapo. She couldn't. Ester would never accept it. Instead, she told her she had a good guard who helped her out. That was the kind of story Ester would believe, that there was still some goodness in people. Ariella wasn't so sure.

One night, straight after work, the Kapo walked into the barracks, sneaking bites of a hot potato smeared in melting margarine. Sarah detected the greasy smell straight away and ambushed her.

'You'll have scoffed yours already then?' Sarah said, swiped the potato from her hand and left only a fragment tucked between the Kapo's fingers.

The Kapo retreated back out the door, probably to dig into her secret supply inside her coat.

Sarah had the hot potato right in front of her lips, mouth open ready to bite when another inmate snatched it from her hand. She looked more dependent on the extra ration than Sarah was.

'Give me it,' Sarah said and tried to snatch the food back.

'Get lost, fatso. You don't need it,' said the potato thief.

Fatso? Was she seeing double?

Sarah dived on her. The noise of them scrapping around the concrete floor startled the other women. As soon as they realised it was food, hot food, they pounced upon Sarah and the prisoner who stole the potato from her. Punches were flying, women's cropped hair was grabbed and foul language filtered through the air as the starving prisoners violently fought for a few morsels of food.

Ariella sat back on her bunk, stared, watching how the Nazis had so easily turned these women into savages. They were playing right into their hands.

The barracks' door flew open. The winter's breeze blew in. Eva at the entrance, laughing at the women humiliating themselves as they rolled around the floor in search of the Kapo's hard-earned scraps.

'Enough,' she shouted. The food was too precious. The brawl went on. 'I said, enough.' She marched towards the women, boots thumped the concrete, her rubber truncheon battered against her palm.

It took a few shouts and a few whacks from Eva's baton before the group finally dispersed and everybody retreated to their bunk.

The door opened again and the Kapo crept in, shaking the snow off her shoes. Eva spun round. 'Where have you been?'

'J-just checking the barracks,' the Kapo said and wiped her mouth.

'You've been eating?'

'No, ma'am, no.'

'Liar.'

Eva gave her a backhand slap across the face.

'You tell me where this extra food is coming from, now. Or this whole barracks gets punished.'

There was an outburst of shouting from the women. They ordered her to tell the guard where she was getting the food. Sarah glared at the Kapo, willed her to shut her mouth. Ariella bowed her head, her conscience killing her.

'Somebody better tell me where this food is coming from or you're all out for roll call. And you know I'll keep you there for as many hours as it takes to find out.'

To be forced to stand to attention for hours after a day's heavy labour was not something to look forward to. Many women had collapsed and died on the spot before and nobody dared to help them.

The women kept shouting at the Kapo, begging her to tell Eva where the food was coming from. Ariella fidgeted on the edge of the bed. The Kapo clammed up, her eyes shifted between Eva and the angry women.

'Right. Outside, now. Every one of you,' Eva gave the dreaded order. Sarah took another blow to the back of her head.

Ariella stood up. She had to do something. Before she could open her mouth, Sarah ran at Eva, her hands wide and fingers spread, ready to wrap them around her neck.

'You evil bitch,' Sarah said and grabbed hold of Eva.

Eva reached for her whistle. She blasted several blows on her alarm until Sarah was surrounded by a pile of guards and ready to be carted off. 'I'll tell you where the food's coming from. The Kapo's got a man. Your man. You know the SS guard with the spiked hair and the scar across his face?' Sarah said, loving every minute, tearing at Eva's heart.

Eva's eyes widened, she blushed.

'He brings her food in exchange for favours, know what I mean?' Sarah winked at Eva, antagonising her further.

Eva's lip twitched. Her face turned grey, her breathing noticeably faster.

'What? You liar,' Kapo said and backed off, seeing the look on Eva's face.

'Get them out of here. Punishment cells, now,' she roared. And Sarah and the Kapo were dragged off by the hefty guards.

CHAPTER 47

It was days before Sarah and the Kapo were back on the road construction. They were so badly beaten in the punishment cells, blood wept from their open wounds across their backs.

Eva made it her point to parade in front of the two women and whacked them with her baton at every opportunity, accusing them of not working hard enough. Sarah was robust and determined to survive and seek revenge on the evil guard, whereas the Kapo looked fragile and struggled to keep up with her new heavy workloads. And as for Ariella, all she could think about was getting to Ester's barracks. She looked weaker and struggled to hold herself up in the orchestra.

It wasn't so easy to get out of the barracks at night with the newly appointed Kapo. Nevertheless, they managed it. A few distractions from some trustworthy inmates and they were off.

They were gathered round Ester's bed when suddenly there was a thud in the background. The outside door swung open and battered against the wall. Ariella and Sarah dived to the ground and rolled under Ester's bed. Heavy boots thundered against the wooden floor, a guard was coming in their direction.

'What's going on in here? You can't hide, you know,' said the soft, familiar voice.

Ariella peered out from under the bed, scanned the guard's broad body. Jana Bach towered over them.

'Jana. It's you,' Ariella said and heaved a sigh.

'I've been assigned to these barracks,' Jana said. 'What are you doing here? If Eva catches you, it's the showers, for sure, you know.'

'Not if I got my hands on her first,' Sarah said and clambered out from under the bed. 'I'd wring her scrawny, little neck,' she demonstrated her strangle hold with her chubby fingers.

'Sarah you mustn't talk like that,' Ester piped up from the bed.

'What you on about?' Sarah said. 'Can't you see what's going on here? That evil cow hates us and is going to make sure she destroys us, if we don't get to her first.'

'No, Sarah. You mustn't–'

'Ester,' Sarah interrupted her, 'she beats me a hundred times a day. I'm just biding my time to nail her.'

'Revenge is not the answer, Sarah. You'll make yourself as bad as she is,' Ester said. 'I'll bet she's just fighting back because somebody beat her.'

'Never. That scrawny little shit was born that way.'

'I don't think so, Sarah,' Jana joined in with the debate. 'I've heard stories about her. The guards talk, you know. And I think you're right, Ester. Eva was picked on since she was a child. She was always shorter than everyone else and the butt of everybody's jokes. She was always in fights at school.'

'And let's face it, she's not exactly the prettiest either,' Ariella said, 'with that furry face of hers and those ugly pock-marks. Suppose they picked on her for that too.'

'Ariella. You sound as if you actually feel sorry for her.'

'No, Sarah,' Ester interrupted, 'Ariella's just saying that perhaps she wasn't born evil.'

'That's right,' Jana said, 'I heard that Eva purposely came to Poland from her home Town in Hamburg to join the camp guards. That way she could gain authority and take her spite out on innocent prisoners.'

'She definitely enjoys beating us,' Sarah said. 'Who cares whether she practised evil from birth or not. She's wicked now and determined to bring us down, all of us, Ester. She's got to be stopped.'

'And how do you plan to stop her?' Ester said, her nervous coughing started up again.

'I'm going to kill her,' Sarah said, pressed her finger against her head and imitated the click of a trigger.

'Enough,' Jana said then lowered her voice, 'you're frightening Bessie.'

Ester pulled the trembling girl in closer and patted her back.

'So how come you're not like the other guards?' Sarah asked. 'Why did you join?'

Jana dipped her head and mumbled, 'I just want to do what I can to help.'

'Why?' Sarah frowned. 'There must be loads of other jobs you could do to help others, why a prison guard?'

Jana fidgeted and walked out of earshot from Ester and the young girl. Ariella and Sarah followed her. Ester stayed put and cradled Bessie in her arms.

'My mother was sick for years, you know. She was a cripple. She lost the power of her legs and then her arms until eventually she couldn't speak.' The tears were welling in Jana's eyes. 'I had no choice but to trust the Doctors,' she continued, 'they took her to a hospital and told me she would be well cared for.' Jana shook her head and covered her mouth with a trembling hand. She struggled to finish her story.

Ariella compassionately touched her arm. 'Did she die in hospital?'

'Within a few days of being taken in, the Doctor sent me a letter saying she had died of pneumonia.' Jana took a deep breath and looked straight at Ariella, her demeanour had changed. Her eyes were narrow slits. 'I didn't believe it. I had heard about other people who received letters about relatives who had died of pneumonia, especially in the concentration camps. Nobody believed them. I joined the camp guards to see what I could find out.'

'And what did you find out?' Ariella asked.

'Pneumonia usually meant gassed to death. Invalids, my mother included, didn't even reach the hospital. They murdered her in a mobile gassing van using its exhaust fumes.' She dipped her head. 'And I sent her there.'

'It's not your fault,' Ariella said and squeezed Jana's arm, 'You weren't to know what they were going to do.'

Jana's fists were clenched. A solitary tear trickled down her cheek.

'So you hate the Nazis then?' Sarah said. 'You want to kill one too?'

'No. Absolutely not. I don't believe in revenge, you know. They will answer to God. I'm in here now to see what I can do to help others, somehow, lessen their burden,' she sighed, 'somehow, make up for what I didn't do for my mother.'

'You're crazy, Jana. The Nazis murdered your mother. And you don't want revenge? They took my parents and Ruben's to a ghetto, years ago. They'll be dead by now. They were elderly and struggled with the food rations and the quality of life we had in Frankfurt, what chance would they have in a ghetto?' Sarah's face twisted with rage, her dirty teeth, in desperate need of a toothbrush, crunched together. Foul fumes reeked from her mouth, 'No, I want revenge all right.'

'It's not the answer, Sarah,' Jana said. 'Stay focused on survival. Hang on for Ruben.'

Sarah looked up. 'Hey you could find out if he's still alive?'

'And my family too,' Ester called out from the background. She had eased herself away from the sleeping Bessie and walked towards them.

'I don't think I want to know about my mother,' Ariella said and stared at the floor. 'Think I already know the answer to that one.'

'It's too dangerous. It's not my job to go into the records room.'

'Oh come on now, Jana,' Ariella said, 'thought you were in here to help others?'

'I am,' Jana said. She fidgeted, rubbing her hands together, 'I can't do that.'

'Course you can,' Ariella said. 'I'll come with you.'

'It's just not that easy, you know.' She tapped the tips of her fingers against the bedpost and drummed out a rapid beat. Perspiration formed on her forehead.

'You can do it, Jana. We'll go tomorrow night. Got to get back to the barracks now. It will soon be roll call.'

'Mama?' It was Bessie. She sat up in bed.

'I'm coming, honey,' Ester said.

Ariella smiled at Ester. At least something good had come out of this nightmare.

CHAPTER 48

The next night, Ariella and Sarah crept into the orchestra barracks again. Ester paced the floor, waiting for them to arrive. She was shaking, trembling fists squeezed tight against her mouth. Not a good sign. Ariella ran to her, put her arm around her shoulder.

'What is it? What's wrong?'

'It's Bessie,' she said, her voice breaking up, 'they took her tonight. Said she wasn't good enough for the orchestra. They put her in the barracks over there.' She nodded, indicating to the wooden hut parallel to hers. 'She's not fit for heavy construction,' Ester said, 'the work will kill her.'

Ariella held Ester tight in her arms and tried to comfort her but she knew Bessie was weak and Ester was right, the young girl was sure to die soon.

Ester's chest crackled. She sounded a lot worse than the night before. Ariella rubbed her back whilst she coughed and expectorated into a rag. It was riddled with splashes of blood. Ariella gasped at the sight.

'I'm alright, I'm alright,' Ester said and shoved Ariella aside.

She wasn't alright. Far from it. Her face was paler than ever and that blood, that wasn't a good sign at all.

The barracks' door flew open. Ariella grabbed Ester and Sarah and hid behind a three-tier bunk bed.

'It's alright,' whispered Jana, 'It's only me.'

They walked out to greet their Austrian buddy.

'Keep quiet,' she said, 'there's a group of guards marching up this way. I'm not sure where they're heading.'

Ariella rushed over to the window, held tight against the wall, eased onto her tiptoes and glanced sideways to peer out. The long boots and skirts headed in their direction. Ariella's heart thumped. She signalled for Ester and Sarah to hide under the blanket on Ester's bed. Jana moved up to Ariella.

'Find out where they're going,' Ariella said. Jana's mouth gaped. She stared at Ariella. 'Go.' She waved her towards the door.

Jana rushed out to meet the approaching guards. Ariella could hear her soft, Austrian accent talking to her fellow comrades. She couldn't hear all the words, only one that mattered. De-lousing. A whole barracks load was being sent for de-lousing.

At that time of night? It could only mean one thing. Whose barracks was it? Which one was being evacuated?

There was no way Ariella was leaving Ester alone. She ran to Ester and Sarah, put her arms around them and they all huddled together in a circle.

CHAPTER 49

Jana hurried in, breathless, 'It's the next barracks.' She clutched her chest, gasping for air. 'Everyone. All of them. To be sent for de-lousing. I knew it,' she said. 'They were all weak and on their last legs, you know.'

Ariella sighed, relieved that it wasn't them. And instantly felt guilty. Then she remembered Bessie and glanced over to Ester. It was as if she had read her thoughts.

'It's okay, Ariella,' she said and smiled. With an odd calmness to her voice, she said, 'don't look so worried, she's only going for a shower.'

Ariella frowned. Ester didn't really believe that? Or maybe she just needed to.

They rushed to the window, peered out and watched the matchstick women form into rows and huddle together. Bessie was with an older woman who walked just as poorly as the young girl. The old woman put her arm around Bessie and held her head close in against her chest telling her that her worries would soon be washed away. Terror was written across everybody's faces as they marched off, puffing their last small streams of air into the frosty night as they took their last steps towards the fake showers.

Ariella pulled back from the window, stomach churning. She felt nauseous at her helplessness and slammed her hand against the wooden wall.

'Ariella, stop that,' Ester shouted. 'You're only going to hurt yourself, and that won't do you any good.'

'Those Nazis!'

'Let's do something then,' Sarah said. 'Let's get them.'

'There's nothing we can do,' Ariella said, paced about the room and swept her hand over her cropped hair.

'Let's just try to survive for our families.' Ester said. 'Please don't cause any trouble.'

'Your family's dead, Ester,' Sarah roared. 'And so is mine.'

'You don't know that for sure,' Ester said. 'Jana, you said you were going to try and find out.'

'No, not now it's too dangerous, Ester. There are too many guards around with all that going on out there,' Jana said.

'No, wait,' Ariella said and stopped abruptly. 'Tonight would be ideal. It's horrible what's going on out there, but don't you see,' she said and grabbed Jana's hands, 'it's the ideal diversion.'

'No, Ariella, they'll see us,' Jana said.

'No they won't. Even the guards in the towers will be focused on the next batch of dead Jews. Come on, let's go.'

Ariella and Jana crept round to the records room. They were ankle deep in snow. Jana's legs were protected by her long boots, but the frost was chilling Ariella to the bone. She shivered and fumbled with the hairpin to pick the lock on the door to the records room whilst Jana scanned the grounds for onlookers.

'That's it, come on,' Ariella said. 'You go search the files, I'll stay here, keep look out.'

'No, you go,' she said and took a step back.

'Look, you have to do it,' Ariella said, 'I've no idea what I'm looking for. You've at least seen some records before. Go. Quick. I'll watch out.'

Jana's wide shoulders hunched as she crept inside. She flashed her torch light around the room full of filing cabinets. The metal drawers screeched as they dragged along the ridges. Jana pulled the files out, musty records, yellowing at the edges, files that had been in there for a long, long time. One by one, she searched for the truth on their missing families.

Ariella scanned the camp, ducking down every few minutes when the search light swooped past them.

'C'mon.' Hurry up,' she whispered into the office.

Jana frantically scribbled notes. A few more drawers scraped open. The torch light went out. Jana rushed towards the door, pulled it closed and clicked the lock back into place. They hurried back to the orchestra barracks.

Ester had begged Jana to search through the records for her family's whereabouts. She felt certain they were in Auschwitz.

'Please, Jana, check again for me,' Ester begged her, unable to comprehend the news.

'Your parents, Ester,' Jana explained again, 'I'm sorry. They were selected to the left on arrival,' Jana said then turned to Ariella. Her face was sombre and she bit on her lip as if not wanting to be the bearer of bad news.

Ariella only had her mother left. The Nazis took her years ago. She felt she already knew in her heart where she was and wasn't sure that she wanted Jana to confirm her suspicion.

'Ariella, I'm afraid your mother-'

'The same.' She finished her sentence, turned away and swallowed hard. It wasn't tears she was choking down, it was burning rage. She stomped about the barracks, kicking anything in sight.

'Calm down, Ariella. They'll all be fine, 'Ester said. She was breathing fast, coughing and spluttering up blood into her ragged hanky. Her mouth quivered as she forced a smile past her blood stained lips.

'Ester, they're dead. All of them,' Ariella barked at her. 'Don't you understand? Those selected to the left went straight to the gas chambers.'

'Of course the records don't actually say they were gassed,' Jana said.

'No, the Nazis are too clever for that. The death certificates are filled in with fake diseases,' Ariella said.

'No, no. It's not true,' Ester mumbled. She was frantic, sat on her bunk, rocked back and forth and covered her ears.

'They're dead,' Sarah shouted. 'And so are my parents. And Ruben's probably dead too. They're all gone. Gone.'

'I don't know about Ruben, Sarah. I couldn't find out anymore. We just have to hope,' Jana said.

'Hope?' Sarah said. 'Ruben was full of hope. He even got a symbol of hope, a dove tattooed on his arm. Fat lot of good it did him.'

'Just hold on to that, Sarah, he might still be alive,' Ariella said. 'But Ester you've got to face facts. Jana saw the records. Your parents are dead.'

'Ariella's right, Ester,' Jana's voice was soothing as she pulled back Ester's hands from her ears. 'And your brothers are gone too I'm afraid.'

'No. Absolutely not possible.' Ester jumped to her feet and paced the barracks. 'They're strong, young boys. You said so too, Ariella. Remember?'

Ariella remembered only too well that night the boys were arrested, late back for curfew, and how she had tried to convince Ester that the boys would be okay.

'It was the full barracks, emptied, sent to the showers, just like Bessie's,' Jana said.

'What?' Ariella said. 'That's impossible, they were fit and healthy. Why would the Nazis destroy their healthy workforce?'

'Who knows,' Jana said and shook her head, 'maybe they wanted to make room for new prisoners arriving.'

'No, I won't hear it. It's not true. They're alive, they're alive, all of them.' Ester sobbed and continued to pace the room. She was becoming quite breathless. Her energy resources, draining low. Ariella walked over to her and tried to comfort her. All she wanted was to take her pain away. What could she do?

'You're probably right, Ester. It's all been a huge mistake. Come on, get some rest,' she said and led her back to her bunk.

CHAPTER 50

Several days had passed since that night Jana delivered that dreadful news. Ester never asked Jana to check the records again. She talked frequently about her reunion with her family when she got out, refused to face the reality that she would never see them all again.

Ariella smiled, watching the courageous efforts still from her dear friend as she struggled to play the violin on a snowy winter's night. She was weak and struggled to stand, yet she tried so hard to run the bow gracefully across the violin strings. Her feeble body looked so fragile, Ariella didn't think Ester could take much more.

Fortunately, Ariella was now working close by and could keep an eye on her. Some road construction workers had been re-assigned duties. They were now on the new railway track running inside the Auschwitz camp gates.

'Don't suppose you've heard what this track's for?' Ariella asked a woman next to her who had just slammed a sledgehammer down on a bolt.

'For the Jews,' she said. She screwed up her face, looking at Ariella as if she ought to know.

'What do you mean?'

'The Nazis are planning to railroad the Jews straight to their death. This railway will run straight to the crematorium.' She spoke in a flat voice as if she was speaking in a foreign language and didn't really understand what she was saying.

Sarah's jaw dropped. She battered her heavy pick into the ground as though she was plunging it into the face of Evil Eva.

'What?' Ariella threw the sledgehammer down, 'I can't do this.'

'Pick it up. Quick,' Sarah said and furtively checked all around her. 'Eva, she'll beat you.'

Kapo was working alongside her. Her eyes darted back and forth, as though dreading another whack from the short guard. Every day the Kapo was beat up by Eva who was determined to have her revenge since the Kapo stole her boyfriend. Kapo bowed her head, ignored her and shovelled up dirt, keeping pace with the working women.

'I don't bloody care about Eva. I'm not helping them to railroad our race into the gas chambers,' Ariella said.

'You'll be in there with them if you don't work. Don't be a fool. You've got somebody waiting for you, haven't you?' Sarah said.

Ariella paused for a moment, thinking about Nadette. She picked up the tool and resumed the arduous task of laying a Nazi railway line straight to the gas chambers.

Heavy snow tumbled down on the workers and lay thick on the ground. It was virtually impossible trying to see where the track should be laid. And the darkness presented its own problems but the guards refused to let them give in for the day.

'Faster, Jew.' It was the short guard who marched up and whacked Ariella with her baton.

Ariella spun around to retaliate but Eva had already moved onto her next victim. Eva swiped her baton across the troublesome Kapo who ruined her love life. Kapo couldn't take much more, her body was frail; her legs were weak and struggled to support her weight. Eva wouldn't give in until the former Kapo was finished.

She walked along, thumped Sarah across her face, forcing her to fall backwards. Sarah scrambled to her feet, itching to grab her nemesis but another inmate in the line grabbed her and held her back. It was a matter of time until Sarah snapped.

A screeching sound in the background caught their attention. It was from the orchestra. Somebody was struggling to play their instrument. Ariella jerked back and forth, trying to see Ester. She was the one struggling. Ester could barely stand up let alone play for the arrival of a returning workforce. She was so frail and in such poor health, only her inner reserves kept her going.

Jana walked in front of Ariella and blocked her view of Ester. 'She'll be okay. They'll be finishing soon, you know. She'll get some food,' Jana said, trying to stop Ariella from worrying. 'She'll get some rest then.'

'Hope you're right,' Ariella said, not at all convinced Ester was safe. She heaved her sledgehammer up, back to work and Jana walked on to inspect the work line.

The terrible screeching from a violin's bow scraped down its' strings. Ester's legs had buckled under her. She collided into the group and forced the orchestra to come to a standstill.

Ariella downed tools, ready to run to Ester's aid. Eva rushed up in front of her and forced her baton under her chin. 'Where do you think you're going?'

'It's Ester, I have to help her.'

'No chance. Get on with your work.'

Ariella clenched her fist. 'Get out my way, Eva.'

'Touch me and it's punishment cells for you.' She rammed her ugly face in against Ariella's, breathing repulsive fumes. Ariella turned away, nauseous at the dragon's breath.

Ester lay on the ground. The other musicians played on, too afraid to help her.

Ariella grabbed the baton pressing against her wind pipe and forced it away from under her chin. With a backhand swipe, she pushed Eva aside. Eva stumbled and fell to the ground leaving a clear path for Ariella to sprint over to Ester's aid.

'I'll kill you,' Eva roared after her.

Ariella bolted across the camp, pushed in amongst the orchestra and interrupted their play. At last she reached Ester and crouched down beside her. She dragged the frail woman across her legs and wrapped her safely in her arms. Ariella's tears still would not come.

'Hang on, Ester. Damn it. Those Nazi-'

'No. You mustn't,' Ester said and grabbed hold of Ariella's dress. She was determined to see her let go of her hatred. Ariella was grabbed by the shoulders. Eva dragged her away from her dear friend. Ariella reached up, grabbed Eva's arms and with all the strength she had left, she hauled Eva over her shoulders and punched into her ribs.

Jana and Sarah rushed over towards them. Ariella grabbed a rock and swung her arm back to smash it into Eva's face.

'Kill her,' Sarah roared. Her eyes popped wide and she had a horrible, evil grin. Jana shoved Sarah back. Eva cowered down pathetically, her hands up to protect her face. Jana towered over them and slowly shook her head, willing Ariella not to do it.

A voice in the background, 'Ariella, you're just as bad if you do it.' It was Ester fighting for the strength to save her lifelong friend from becoming a murderer. The crumbling rock shook in Ariella's trembling hand. She stared at the evil midget, debating whether or not to smash the ugly face to a pulp.

It took a few seconds before she finally realised the heinous crime she was about to commit. She rammed the rock into the snowy ground next to Eva's head and rushed over to Ester.

'Stop fighting them,' Ester begged. 'You must survive.' Her brown eyes were glazing over.

'What for? There's no point-'

'You must have hope, Ariella. Without it, there's nothing.' Ester fell back in her arms. Her eyes rolled, she was barely conscious.

'Somebody help me. Get over here.'

Two guards rushed over and ordered some inmates to carry Ester off. She was incredibly weak but at least she was still alive.

'Hang on, Ester,' Ariella called after her, willing her to survive. Ester smiled back courageously. The inmates carried Ester off with ease, she was lighter than a floating feather. Ariella's skin and bone friend was ushered into the hospital barracks.

'Get her.' It was Eva. She had scrambled to her feet and was ordering the guards to grab Ariella. She was soon ambushed and dragged away from behind, her feet left deep grooves in the snow, like another rail track, all the way to the punishment cells.

CHAPTER 51

Autumn 1944

The rain poured down and the wind howled. Glorious shades of autumnal reds, greens and yellows dropped from the deciduous trees. No matter what their colour, they could hang on no longer and drifted to the ground. There was only a few stragglers, the strong and the robust still hanging on. A group of women were selected to sweep up the fallen, shovel them into wheelbarrows and cart them off to another growing pile to be burnt.

The remaining women in the camp scurried through the mud puddles, stripped naked and forced to run past the Nazi Doctors in their white coats. Another Selection Process was taking place. A group of women in front of Ariella, one by one, selected to the left, unfit for work, and marched off to meet their maker. Most of the gaunt faces looked tired and weary. They walked off without a murmur, almost as if they were relieved it was soon to be over. Others cried in desperation and begged for their lives to be spared.

Ariella was weak and badly battered after her episode in the punishment cells and struggled to keep pace with the other women. Somehow she passed the inspection and was pushed to the right; selected to live.

Sarah came up behind her. She also looked weak and worn out. Her loss of weight was more visible in her nakedness; her bony ribcage stuck out.

'I don't know why I even try to survive these selections,' Sarah said.'

'I know what you mean.'

'Hey you never know, maybe the Sonderkommandos plan will work,' Sarah said. 'Put an end to all this.'

'I hope that's not just a rumour,' Ariella said, 'I hope they really do have a plan. Do you think it's true about the Sonderkommandos? Their duties I mean? Do you really think they strip the clothes from the prisoners and send them into the fake showers?'

'It's true alright, Ariella. The Sonderkommandos got the worst job of all. I've heard they've even had to send in their families and friends to get gassed and had to listen to their dying screams. Then they got to remove the bodies and burn them in the Nazis' ovens.'

'It just sounds so awful. I can't believe it.'

'Of course you don't believe it. That's why the Sonderkommandos don't last long. The Nazis gas the workers there and select a new bunch from the transports. Stops us finding out what's really going on. But information like that has got a way of getting out.'

'And you think the next lot of Sonderkommandos know it's their turn to be gassed?'

'So I've heard. But not if they manage to blow up the crematoriums first.'

'Don't know, Sarah, even if it is true, the women from the armaments factory are supposed to smuggle explosives into the camp. How the hell are they going to manage that?'

'Sure hope they manage it soon. Look at Kapo. She's never going to pass the inspection.'

The former Kapo hobbled in behind Ariella. Her face was ashen. Her golf ball eyes protruded beyond the sagging black circles formed underneath. Eva's repetitive beatings had taken its toll on the Kapo, making her sorry for ever having interfered with the guard's love life. In a desperate attempt to pass the inspection, Kapo had coloured her cheeks with droplets of blood from a finger prick, mimicking a healthy glow. She looked far from well.

'Left,' the SS Doctor said. He sat behind a wooden table, dressed in a white overcoat and a stethoscope dangled from his neck.

'What? No. I'm healthy, sir, please?' Kapo protested.

'Left. Now.'

'Sir, please, I can work.'

The SS Doctor curled his finger, ordering a guard to come forward. 'Take her away,' he said to the smirking Eva.

Eva gloated as she marched towards Kapo and dragged her away. Kapo continued to protest, 'My children, sir. I have children, they need me.'

'Move it. Bet you're sorry you screwed my boyfriend now?' Eva smirked into Kapo's face.

'I'm sorry, Eva, I was just hungry. He gave me food.'

'He was mine,' Eva roared into her face. 'And now he's gone because of you.'

'Eva, I'm sorry, I'm sorry, help me please. My children-'

'Your children are dead. And you will be too shortly,' she said and laughed viciously.

Kapo wriggled to break free. It was no use. She was soon surrounded by guards and ushered off with the other naked women who had been selected to the left.

Ariella turned away, couldn't watch anymore. She yanked her dress from the pile of clothes and squeezed it tight letting all her anger rush into the fabric before she slipped it over her head. The cotton brushed the ridges across her back; the flogging had left her covered in scars.

'We're all going to die in this hell,' Sarah said and watched the Kapo being hauled away.

'Don't give up hope, Sarah. It's all we've got.' Ariella thought about Ester's words of encouragement. 'Picture yourself snuggling up to Ruben at home on the couch, that's what I do with Nadette.'

'Well, well, well, Ish-Shalom,' Eva said. The short guard crept up behind them. Ariella wondered what she'd heard. She padded around them, battered her baton repeatedly against her hand. They ignored her and continued to dress. Eva was persistent. She grabbed Ariella's short hair and yanked her head to the side.

'Always knew there was something queer about you,' she said. Ariella tingled with rage, but refused to let her antagonise her anymore.

'Back off, Eva,' Sarah said.

'Move away, Jew.' Eva bared her teeth at Sarah. 'Got news for you, fatso,' Eva continued. Ariella frowned in confusion, there wasn't a bit of fat left on Sarah, the only swollen lumps were muscles on her arms. 'Your precious Ruben's dead,' Eva said and chuckled.

Sarah glared. 'Liar,' she roared.

Eva grinned and forced an evil laugh, 'I was coming to deliver the good news when I got caught up in that racket.' She signalled towards Kapo and the others marching off. 'And then there was this interesting conversation,' she said. She smirked, her eyes shifted between Ariella and Sarah. 'Your husband's barracks was emptied this morning.' Eva looked up at Sarah, 'They were all taken and gassed.' She hissed the words out.

'She's lying, Sarah,' Ariella said. 'She's trying to antagonise you, give her another excuse to beat you.'

'Believe that if you like. I know your husband. Been watching him. Short, skinny, weak man,' Eva said and sneered. 'He had a dove tattooed on his arm. Sound familiar, Jew?'

Sarah ran at her. Eva swiped her across the face with her baton. She stumbled, fell to the ground and cupped her hands over her nose to catch the blood.

Eva grabbed Ariella's arm to drag her away. 'You're coming with me, lesbian. Got something special for you.'

Ariella resisted, tried to push past her to reach Sarah. It was no use. Eva signalled for the assistance of another guard.

'Unnatural fornication,' Eva said, 'special treatment for you, Ish-Shalom. Let the Doctor's experiment. That's if you survive my punishment first.'

Ariella thought about Ester's words and refused to retaliate, hanging onto the hope that Nadette was still alive. She was dragged across the camp grounds. Sarah, on the other hand, looked like she had had enough of Evil Eva. She stood, grinding her teeth and thumped her blood-stained fist against her palm. Ariella could only shake her head and mouth words, begging her not to do anything stupid.

Suddenly there was an almighty bang in the distance. Smoke poured from one of the crematoriums, a different kind of smoke from the usual. The building was on fire and engulfed in glorious red and yellow flames.

'Yes,' Ariella whispered. The Sonderkommandos' plan had worked.

The camp crawled with guards, they flooded towards the explosion. Ariella was eager to know how well their plan had worked. Perhaps the gas chambers had all been blown up and the Kapo had been saved from her de-lousing shower. Ariella tingled, this time with excitement. She wished all the success in the world for her comrades.

Eva wasn't interested in assisting the guards to control the rebellion. She was too focused in trailing Ariella to the punishment cells.

Ariella was dragged once again into the familiar torture block where a woman lay strapped to the unforgettable flogging table.

At last they tossed her into a small cell. Her head dropped and her feet dragged. She would be lucky if she made it through the night. The brutal guards walked towards Ariella, stretched their fingers and cracked their knuckles.

'She's mine,' Eva said and brushed the two guards aside. The guards didn't look too perturbed. They smirked and stomped out.

Eva and her co-worker dragged Ariella towards the table. She had an evil grin and wide eyes; madness was staring out of her now.

'C'mon, c'mon,' Eva mumbled, tightened the straps and secured Ariella to the flogging bench.

'Don't do it, Eva,' Ariella said.

She cackled like a witch dancing around her cauldron. The other guard stood in front of Ariella, held her arms out while Eva fastened the straps around her wrists.

'You can go,' Eva told her comrade.

'What?'

'Go. I'll take it from here.'

'What you going to do, Eva?' the guard said with a worried look.

'Just go. Now. Get out of here. Go and see what's going on at the crematoriums. They need all the guards up there.'

Ariella stared, begging the guard not to leave her with the mad woman. Eva gave her an appreciative slap on the back as she hurried out of the building.

She walked around and crouched down in front of Ariella, slapped the leather whip against her hand. 'Just you and me now, lesbian,' Eva said. 'Do you still think you can survive for your girlfriend?'

'Don't do it, Eva, I'm really not worth it.'

She drew back the whip in front of Ariella in slow motion. Her eyes were gawking wide. Then with slow, deliberate steps, she walked around behind Ariella.

'No, Eva.' The whip cracked down across Ariella's back and pounded against her already scarred flesh. Ariella flinched with every stroke but still, the tears would not come.

The flogging seemed to last for hours. It was as though Eva had stopped to rest every so often and then started again. Ariella drifted in and out of consciousness. In the background, the door creaked open. She eased around to see who was entering. She dreaded the thought of another guard coming to take over. Instead it was a prisoner in striped uniform, tiptoeing along the concrete floor. Sarah, with a rock in hand, ready to batter Eva. The evil guard spun around as she approached. She grappled for her whistle. Sarah lunged at her and yanked it from her neck. She swiped the rock across the side of Eva's head and knocked her unconscious.

By the time she came around, Sarah had the evil guard strapped onto the table. Ariella was heaped against the wall, trying to focus.

'The Sonderkommandos' plan didn't work, Ariella,' Sarah said and tightened Eva's straps. 'They only managed to blow up one of the crematoriums, the others are still operational. At least they killed three guards.'

'And the Sonderkommandos?'

'Murdered,' Sarah said. 'And the women who smuggled the explosives are being tortured.'

Ariella gave a sigh of despair. Then she remembered the last selection. 'The Kapo?'

'Still in the queue for gassing. And it was her fault,' she said. She whacked the leather whip against her hand in front of Eva's face. Then ripped the guard's blouse apart, her naked back exposed. Sarah raised the whip high in the air ready to lash out on her archenemy.

'Sarah. No please. I beg you,' Eva was frantic and wriggled to get free. 'I'm sorry. I'll go easy from now on. I'll get you extra rations. Please. Anything.'

'Too late,' Sarah said and gave a last yank on the straps. She placed the whip against Eva's bare back before she began.

Eva flinched. 'You'll never get away with it, Jew,' she said. Sarah punched and gagged her then raised the whip high in the air, ready to deliver her first blow.

Ariella scrambled to her feet and dived in front of Eva. 'No, Sarah, stop. Don't do it.'

'What's got into you? Move aside.' She eased Ariella away from the table. Ariella moved in again and grabbed Sarah's hand with the whip.

'Look, she's not worth it,' Ariella pleaded with Sarah.

Sarah's arm trembled. Her knuckles white, firmly clasped around the whip. 'Move, Ariella,' she said, 'or you can go in there.' She nodded to the pitch black cells where many were forgotten about, left to die.

Ariella's heart leapt, surely she wouldn't put her in there? Ariella took a deep breath and dived over Eva's body.

'I'm not going to let you, you're not evil.'

'Ariella, I warned you.' She dragged her to the darkened cells.

'No, Sarah, no please.' She shoved her in and slammed the door shut and locked the door.

Ariella shouted out but her shrieks were drowned out by the noise coming from the flogging table. Eva's screams were muffled past the rag in her mouth but the loud whacks from Sarah's weapon were overpowering and made Ariella flinch every time it came crashing down on Eva's back. She lay flat on the floor, squeezed her trembling hands tight against her ears. The cracking against Eva's skin could not be shut out.

After a while the screams stopped. The whacking continued. Ariella scrambled to her knees, following the light from a narrow hole in the wooden door surround. She could only see Sarah from the waist down. She was still at the flogging table. Ariella dug her nails in deep and gouged at the hole till she could see her face. Sarah laughed hysterically. She was like a lunatic who had just escaped from a mental institution. Eva was flat out, dead. Sarah continued to flog the lifeless body.

The door to the punishment building swung open. A group of guards rushed inside and ambushed Sarah.

'You'll hang for this,' a guard said.

Sarah stared at them, chuckled and licked Eva's blood from her fingers before they dragged her away. There was no resistance whatsoever.

The guards flicked the light switch on the way out. The building was in complete darkness, not even a flicker of light through the tiny gap that Ariella had gouged from the door surround.

The outside door blew open, swung back and forth and creaked in the dead of the night. A ghostly chill crept in and a burning glow lit up the entire room. The sun was going down.

Ariella slid down the wall. Madness, madness. The whole place. Everything, evil. She could hold on no more. It's over, Nadette. It's over.

CHAPTER 52

Survival was becoming more and more difficult in the brothel. Berta seemed to enjoy rattling her key in our cell door, coming to fetch us for the awaiting queues. Rows of men waited outside the working cells for us whores to service them. The SS guards waited for me daily.

'C'mon, Nadette,' they called. They got hold of my name from Berta and often asked for me, special request.

Hour after hour, I lay on my back, rigid and numb to each performance. Ariella was the one name that continuously pulsed through my mind with each pounding.

After every session in the brothel, I was exhausted and ripped apart a little bit more. By the end of the day, ten or more contented SS men left my working cell. I was dragged back and dumped into the sleeping quarters alongside the others.

Ingrid was poorly and feverish. I comforted her as best as I could but as usual, with no medicine, there was not a lot I could do for her. She had been subjected to the same daily abuse, helping to satisfy the SS guards.

Panda and Gabriele on the other hand, were used by both the SS and homosexual men. Panda's skin was gradually breaking out in sores. Small lesions appeared along her hairline and foul smelling puss trickled out. She pulled her blonde, springy hair forward in an effort to disguise her disease. I was sure it could only be sexually transmitted; nevertheless, it was extremely difficult for me to exercise my duty of care. I furiously scrubbed at my hands after my feeble attempt to clean her wounds.

Gabriele wasn't much better. The SS guards seemed to recognise her from the Berlin brothel and were out to get her for infecting one of their comrades. She received a terrible beating from the SS every time she entered the working cell.

The pink triangles however, wouldn't lay a finger on her; in fact they refused to touch her in any way. That's when Kaarl joined in with the performance. He insisted that the homosexual men harden up. He demonstrated to them how the lesser species should be treated. To exhibit his requirements, Kaarl usually beat Gabriele, raped her repeatedly and then handed her over for effeminate men to treat her in the same way. Gabriele was bruised, battered and cut with wounds so deep, she should've had stitches. I bandaged her up with parts from our ripped dresses. Blood seeped from the crude bandages. It was without a doubt Gabriele received the worst punishments and was becoming weaker and weaker. She was struggling to survive our darkest days.

Kaarl still didn't know I was in there. Could I help Gabriele and the others if I told him? It didn't look like I was ever going to see Ariella again anyway.

CHAPTER 53

Kaarl hadn't appeared. What good would it do letting him know I was in Auschwitz anyway? Who was I trying to kid? He wouldn't show any more compassion for Gabriele and the others than he had for me. All I could do was hang on and wait for my day to be released, or better still, find a plan to get to Ariella.

Daily I hoped for an opportunity. Was this my chance today?

In a small fenced off area, the prostituted women, padded around in a circle like rodents on a rat wheel, going nowhere. Faces showed no emotion, prisoners stared at the ground, treaded through the scattered leaves. We swished our feet along the same path in the circle we had formed. Gabriele and Panda marched in front of me. Ingrid hurried in behind, struggling to keep pace. Her legs were collapsing under her.

Within no time at all, Ingrid collapsed in a heap. I rushed in behind her and lifted her head from the dirty leaves. I felt for her pulse. Dead. Gabriele helped me lift her aside away from the monotonous marching. The others continued to tread the circle. Not a single woman raised her head.

'This is hell,' Gabriele said. She was incredibly weak, her face, hardly recognisable with all the cuts and bruises. She was near to tears. 'Even in a Berlin brothel we only had a few men a day. We're never going to get out. I can't take anymore beatings. We're going to die in here too.'

'Calm down, Gabriele. One day this will all be over. There's a better life out there... for all of us,' I assured her.

Gabriele shook her head, stared down at the dead Ingrid, 'We're never going to get out. Never.'

A strange rumbling sound distracted me. Two female inmates hauled a garbage cart along through the leafy ground outside the fence. They were wearing a yellow star.

'Hoy, prostitutes,' they shouted over and threw empty food cans at the parading women. 'Easy for you, with your lying down job.'

Insults from fellow prisoners; that was all we needed. My immediate reaction was to ignore them but then I had quick thought. 'Ariella,' I mumbled and rushed towards the fence. Gabriele grabbed my arm and pulled me back.

'No. They'll attack you,' she said.

'Don't go near them, Nadette,' Panda whispered and paraded past, still plodding around the same circle.

'They might know something.'

'You're crazy. They're not going to tell you anything, they hate us,' Gabriele said.

She was right but I had to take the chance. I lifted her hand off my arm. She shrugged her scrawny shoulders, leaving me to face the lions on my own.

'I need to find someone,' I said, approaching the fence with caution.

'Beat it, whore,' one of them said as she struggled on, hauling the heavy cart full of stinking rubbish.

'No. Wait. Please. I need your help.'

'Get out here and do some real work,' the woman said and threw some empty food cans at me.

I ran and shook the fence, 'You think I want to be in here?'

They rushed towards me and grabbed hold of my dress through the fence and yanked me closer. One of them wrapped her scrawny hand around my throat. I struggled to breathe.

'Nazi lover,' they shouted and spat in my face. I tried to wriggle free but it was impossible. I could feel the blood rushing to my face, I gasped for air. Of all the torture I had survived in the camp, and here I was, having the life strangled out of me by fellow inmates. I wasn't going to die. Not now. Not today. I grabbed her arm, eased it from my throat and backed away from their clutches.

'Time's up,' Berta shouted and threw the brothel door open. The garbage cart clattered away before the guard stepped outside.

I walked in behind the robotic women who strolled back inside past the stern guard. Berta grabbed my arm and ran me indoors.

'Get cleaned up,' she said, 'you're wanted in the office.' Oh no, what now?

CHAPTER 54

I stripped off to wash myself at the tiny wash hand basin in our room. I had that eerie feeling again as if someone was watching me. I spun around fast and stared at the cell door. And there she was, Berta peering in through the bars on the door, ogling my partially naked body.

Berta jerked back, trying to hide at the side of the door. Ah ha. I smiled in sheer delight.

Berta clanked the keys in the cell and threw the door open. 'Okay, enough,' she said.

'Time to come out, eh, Berta?' I said and took my time to pull on my dress. I ran my hands across my breasts, smoothing over the creases, all the while I stayed focused on Berta, smiling at her.

'Where do you want me, Berta?' I said in my sexiest voice, eyeing her up and down on the way out the door.

'In the office. Now,' Berta said, red-faced and pulled me out of the cell.

We walked along the corridor. A few stray SS men stood outside various working cells, waiting to be serviced. A group of women were being marched along in front. One by one, they disappeared into rooms on either side of the corridor. Mattresses awaited them.

Heavy footsteps marched closer. I glanced past the remaining women to see who was entering the brothel now. I gasped and jumped back in. Kaarl walked towards us. He stopped to nosey in through a working cell's spy hole. He let out a roar and ordered a guard to unlock the door then stormed inside, left the door swinging open behind him.

The office was across the corridor from the cell that Kaarl had just entered. Berta knocked on the door.

C'mon, c'mon, open, open. I nibbled along the edges of my dirty finger nails.

'Enter,' at last a voice from inside called out.

Thank God.

Berta led me into the room. There was a wooden desk and a comfy looking, leather chair on the far side and rows of filing cabinets. A fat SS man with a rotund, beer belly, walked out from a small kitchen area, biting strips of meat from a chicken leg. He swept his black, greasy hair from his face.

'Sit, sit, please, both of you,' he said and indicated to the two plastic seats by the door. 'I'll be back in a minute,' he said and hobbled out of the office.

The door was left wide open. I sat nearest the entrance. 'Don't get any bright ideas,' Berta said. I was more interested in watching to see what Kaarl was up to.

Kaarl towered over a pink triangle prisoner who sat with his back against the wall alongside a prostituted woman. The man was battered and bruised and his prison uniform hung on him. I edged forward, I was sure I recognised him.

'What's going on?' Kaarl demanded.

'Kaarl. We were just talking.'

'You're not here to talk, Otto,' Kaarl booted him in the ribs.

'Kaarl, we go back a long way, why are you doing this to me?' Otto looked tired and haggard. He feebly tried to raise his arms to defend himself.

'Will you never learn?' Kaarl said. 'We cannot have homosexual men in Germany and especially not in the SS.' He continued to beat up his best friend.

The fat SS man returned to the office and swung the door shut behind him. He carried a pile of bandages. His creased tunic was unbuttoned at the neck and a button had popped at his beer belly. He was still munching away, his jaws sweeping wide, as though enjoying every bite. I licked my lips, humiliating myself and drooled over the smell of the hot food.

Berta elbowed me in the ribs then dragged me to my feet. 'The prisoner you requested, sir,' she said, clicked her heels and tipped her head.

'Ah, the Doctor,' the fat man said. He waved the chicken leg to the side to dismiss Berta. He took one last bite before he launched the remnants in the waste paper bin. He hobbled towards the leather seat and removed his army boot.

'Come closer, please. Bring your seat,' he said, smiled and curled his fingers towards his palm, beckoning me over. 'It's my blisters,' he grimaced as though in agony, 'they're killing me.'

Was he serious?

I shook my head in disgust.

'Pathetic,' he admitted, 'I know. But I'm no hero,' he drew his trembling hand across his mouth, wiped away the chicken grease and drew his hand down the front of his shabby tunic. He limped towards me, bare foot, and dragged a plastic seat over to the desk, then pulled back the comfy, leather chair and begged me to take his seat.

'Please,' he said and gestured with a trembling hand. I took the seat and enjoyed my moment of comfort. He held out his shaking hand and offered me the bandage, 'Please?' he begged. I heaved a sigh, swiped the dressing from his hand and kneeled down to take a look at his blistered feet.

'There's a medicine cabinet if you need anything else,' he said and pointed to the box on the wall. I walked across to rummage the cupboard and picked up the iodine for his sores. A tiny capsule hid in at the back. I recognised it instantly. It was a fragile, glass ampoule, coated in brown rubber to prevent accidental breakage; its contents, a concentrated solution of potassium cyanide, to be crushed between the teeth to release the fast acting poison. Typical the pathetic SS man kept it in his cabinet and not on his person.

I headed back with the iodine but not before discreetly shoving his cyanide pill into my dress pocket. He bent over me as I tended to his feet. I could feel his warm, chicken breath on my neck. I splattered the stingy solution over his sores and wrapped the bandage as fast as I could around his ankles and finished with a very tight knot. I sprung to my feet.

'Sorry, sorry,' he said and shoved his boot back on. 'That's not what...' He raised his hands and backed off. 'You look familiar, that's all. Have I seen you somewhere before?'

'Brothel?' I said, hand on hip.

He jumped to his feet and thumped his fist on the wooden desk. 'No. I'm not here for sex.' He dragged a filing cabinet drawer open, 'I'm a records man.'

'A records man?' I smiled at the SS leader.

He frowned at me as though still trying to place me. His eyes widened. 'Ah,' he said, 'I know, Kaarl Bergmann. 'You're his, his wife?'

'Was his fiancée,' I said and studied his face. He didn't look at all familiar to me.

'We met at a party. Remember?' he said. He smiled as though we were long, lost friends. I racked my brain, shook my head and shrugged. 'Kaarl had just been promoted in the Gestapo,' he said. 'It was a celebration party, remember? I'm Eric Hagen. He scowled as though recalling events of that night. He swiftly buttoned up his tunic, 'Kaarl told me off for being a slob.'

'Ah,' I said with a slow nod. I held my throat, remembering that night when Kaarl tried to throttle me and this shabby soldier, the weak man, refused to come to my aid. He was the one who begged Kaarl not to send him to work in Auschwitz.

'What the hell are you doing in here?'

'What do you think?' I said.

He jolted back at my coarseness.

'Kaarl sent me for rehabilitation.'

Eric frowned.

I'm in love with a Jew... a female Jew,' I stared at him arrogantly and waited for his reaction.

'And he sent you to a brothel?' He shook his head and walked off in disgust. 'Kaarl can be real horrible,' he said. 'I've known him since the Hitler Youth. He was just as evil then. He bullied all the boys, anybody who was weaker than him. He tormented me all the time, still does.' Eric paced the room, wringing his hands as though recalling painful memories. He pulled out a steel cigarette-case from his tunic pocket. 'Wouldn't believe we're the same rank,' he said and inhaled deeply, trying to calm down. 'He thinks I'm a weak German because I don't control people like he does.' His hand flapped about, polluting the air with his cigarette smoke. 'It's just a job to me. I've got a wife. And two teenage sons sent out to fight in this damn war.'

I touched his arm and smiled. He exhaled the smoke from the side of his mouth then patted my hand. 'I'm no fighter,' he said and pointed to the open drawer of the filing cabinet, 'that's all I know. That's all I'm good at. Paperwork,' he swept his hand carelessly over the files. 'It's all I've ever been good at.'

'You handle prisoners' records?' I asked.

'Yes. Prostitutes. Why?'

'You can access other records?'

'Maybe. Why?'

'I was just wondering,' I bit on my lip. 'Maybe, maybe you could check something for me?' I blurted it out.

He frowned. Then as if just realising, 'Oh no,' he said and crossed his hands back and forth.

'Ariella Ish-Shalom, my Jewish lover. Kaarl had her sent here nearly two years ago. Help me, please?'

'No way,' he said. His hand was shaking as he drew in a long drag from his cigarette. 'I could get into trouble,' he said in a child's voice and stormed away from me and paced the room again.

Into trouble? I clenched my teeth in a silent scream then ran at him, spun him around and clutched his arms tight. 'I just need to know if she's alive. Or her friend even, Ester Kolleck. Somebody from the orchestra recognised her name. Just check the records, damn it.'

'No,' he cried and covered his ears. 'I told you, I'm no hero.'

'I've noticed,' I shouted.

He cowered down, covered his head with his trembling hands. I felt sorry for him. I eased his hands back down. He stood with timid posture and puffed repeatedly on his cigarette.

'Help me. Please?' I whispered.

There was a voice in the corridor. Shouting. Eric flinched and ran to the door and eased it open a fraction to peer out.

'It's Kaarl,' he whispered and called me over to see. Kaarl was dragging Otto out from the working cell.

'Where are you taking me, Kaarl?' Otto said with desperation in his voice.

'You must be castrated. We will do whatever it takes to rehabilitate you,' Kaarl said.

He signalled to a nearby guard, ordered him to send in more men to the woman in the cell. The woman's face fell, she slumped forward.

Kaarl strutted along the corridor. Otto tottered behind and glanced in my direction. I held my breath. When he saw the state of me and my tattered clothing, he shook his head in sorrow then toddled along after Kaarl.

Eric ran to the opened window. I followed.

Kaarl marched across the leafy courtyard with a firm grasp of Otto's arm. Otto's hands were tied behind his back. His legs wobbled, he struggled to keep up with Kaarl.

'Don't do this,' Otto said.

'I'll make a man of you yet.'

'Like your father?' Otto said.

Kaarl stopped abruptly. 'What's my father got to do with this?'

'You knew didn't you? You just didn't want to see it.'

'Knew what? My father was a good man,' Kaarl said. 'A well respected SS Leader. Died for his Führer and country.'

'And a homosexual,' Otto said.

Kaarl grabbed Otto's prison uniform. 'Don't you disparage my father's good name. He idolised my mother.'

'He had affairs, Kaarl. Your mother knew but refused to accept it. Why do you think she pushed you to be the man of the house?'

'Liar.' Kaarl swiped Otto across the face, knocked him to the ground. 'My father hated homosexuals.'

'No, Kaarl. It was your mother who hated homosexuals. Her hatred has rubbed off on you. It wasn't your father's fault. It's the way we are.'

'Silence. I won't hear another word.' He grabbed Otto and fiercely chained him to a nearby punishment pole.

'Oh no,' Eric said. I've heard about other homosexuals who got this, but not Otto. Kaarl won't do it to Otto.'

'Do what?' I asked.

Too late, Kaarl signalled to two guards with ferocious Alsatian dogs. 'Let the dogs finish him,' he said.

Kaarl marched off, fixing his cap as though he couldn't care less but the look of hurt on his colour-drained face said otherwise.

The sound of the snarling dogs tearing at Otto's body was enough for me. I pulled back from the window and clutched my retching stomach. Eric's jaw hung open, frozen to the spot, he stared out the window in disbelief. His hand trembled, reaching for his cigarettes.

'You better go,' he said, took a quick puff on the cigarette, 'I'll call the guard.'

CHAPTER 55

Berta marched me along the corridor and shoved me back into our cell. It didn't take the guards long to fill Ingrid's empty bed. A new inmate had already arrived. A young girl, about sixteen sat with her head down, trembling fists in front of her mouth. Her long, blonde hair drooped over her face; she rocked back and forth on the bunk.

'Hello,' I said, approaching her with caution. 'I'm Nadette. What's your name, honey?' I crouched down in front of her and swept her hair back from her face. Her sad, blue eyes stared past me. She had a tiny pug nose and a round, plump face. She looked remarkably healthy in comparison to us skeletons. She clearly hadn't been in camp for long.

'It's Trudi. She won't talk,' Gabriele shouted down from the top bunk. She sat up, 'Berta said she was transferred in from Ravensbrück. Her parents were caught hiding Jews in their attic. They were all shot. The Jews, Trudi's mother and father, all dead. She was the only one to survive... and we know why.'

I looked at the pretty face and bit on my lip, dreading her future in the brothel. I sat beside her on the bed, put my arm around her and pulled her in close.

Berta soon rattled the keys outside the door and fumbled with the lock as though in a deliberate attempt to frighten us. She walked in with her clipboard in hand. Trudi was ordered to the working cells.

The young girl rose from the bunk, Berta took her by the hand like a mother leading her sleepy child to her bed. After she left the cell, I hugged myself tightly and rocked back and forth, nursing my internal agony.

Hours later, Berta brought Trudi back into the cell. Berta laughed and shoved her inside. Trudi's matted hair fell across her bruised and swollen face. Blood trickled down her legs. I ran and guided the young girl to her bed. She struggled to sit. I lay her on her back and cleaned her up, wiped the blood from her face, from her beaten body and from her legs. I gradually worked out the knots from her long hair. She flinched with every stroke of the brush. There were tears, floods of them, flowing down my face.

Trudi lay curled in a ball unable to sleep. I stroked her hair and whispered false promises, 'Sshh, Trudi, it won't be long till we get out of here. It'll all be over soon.' Trudi sucked on her thumb.

Darkness was falling. The moon was covered by black clouds. The corridor's dim light flickered in through the bars on the door. I hoped there would be no more calls for the night.

A short while later and Berta rattled her keys again. I begged her not to take the young girl.

'She must be punished,' she said. 'Those are the rules.'

'Berta, please. She's just a child.'

'Wasn't a child when she was hiding Jews was she? Now get out my way. I've got a job to do.'

That was the pattern for weeks. Trudi was taken away, returned and I cleaned her up. The whole time she was in there, she never spoke a word. Each night she stood by the window, staring out at the darkened sky as though silently communicating with her dead parents. Her fingernails scratched back and forth in a repetitive motion, sinking into the window sill and chipping away fragments from the plaster. She was like a caged animal determined to dig her way to freedom.

'Stop that, will you? My blood's running cold here,' Panda said.

'Leave her alone,' I shouted. 'C'mon honey, let's get you back to bed,' I said and led Trudi away from her disturbing ritual.

But Trudi continued. As soon as Berta brought her back to the cell in the evenings, Trudi resumed her stance at the window and gouged at the plaster. I continually picked up the chunks that fell from the wall and threw them out past the tiny opening in the window. But the chunks were getting bigger, harder to hide.

'Trudi, you must stop this,' I begged. 'If Berta sees this, we're all for it. The window's secured in there. It won't budge. It's not the way out. C'mon, angel let's get you cleaned up,' I said and led her to her bed once again.

I placed her on her back and was about to pull the thin blanket up to tuck her in when I noticed a small bump on her belly. It wasn't big; in fact it was only noticeable because her body was losing its shape. She was almost as skinny as the rest of us now. I ran my hand across, feeling, pressing, diagnosing. She was pregnant.

Gabriele watched. 'Going to have to do something, Nadette. She can't have a baby in here. You're going to have to get rid of it for her.'

'No. I couldn't possibly. I'm a Doctor, I'm supposed to preserve life not take it.'

'She'll never make it to term anyway,' Panda said, 'the Nazi's will kill it and her too. You got to do something.'

I slept in beside Trudi that night, held her close, prayed and begged for a solution to her problem.

Berta rattled the door open. 'Get up, lazy whores. Got some early birds in, just finished the night shift.'

I ran at her and grabbed her arm, 'Berta, you've got to help Trudi.'

'How many times have I to tell you? She's here for punishment.' She pushed me aside and grabbed Trudi's arm.

'Berta, please, she's pregnant,' I blurted it out before I really thought it through.

Berta stopped in her tracks and stared at the bump. 'Come with me,' she said.

'Where are you taking her?' I called after her through the bars on the door.

'Hospital,' Berta replied and gave a filthy laugh. Somehow I didn't think she was going to get the help she needed.

A few days later, Trudi returned. The bump was gone. She immediately curled up on her bed while Gabriele, Panda and I were sent to the working cells.

By the time we came back, Trudi was lying in a blood bath. Her slashed arm dangled over the side of the bed. A chunk of plaster, coarsely sharpened to a point, lay on the floor next to her.

'Trudi, no,' I shouted and ran and pressed my hands over her wounded arms.

'How did she manage that?' Panda said.

'She's been working that plaster and we didn't even see it,' Gabriele said. For once she actually sounded shocked.

'What's going on in there? Let me see.' Berta pushed her way past Panda and Gabriele. Her jaw dropped when she saw me hold the dead girl in my arms.

CHAPTER 56

The sun shone in through the window, brightening up the room. Trudi had been removed and no new prisoner had arrived to take her place. Berta continued to march in with the clipboard, enjoying that Gabriele, Panda and I had to split the workload between us.

'Eichmann. Office. Now,' she ordered.

My heart skipped a beat. Eric. Did he have news on Ariella?

'Ah, Nadette,' he said and slammed the door, shutting Berta out. 'Please, take a seat.' His thumb and index finger were tight against his mouth as he took the last drag from a cigarette.

I edged onto the plastic seat, watched him parade around the room and waited for his news.

'I need your help again, Nadette,' he said and stubbed out his cigarette. 'I jammed my thumb in that filing cabinet.' His face was distorted as though in severe pain. 'And look, it's all black. I can hardly bend it,' he said and tried to wiggle his fat thumb.

I frowned at him. I had had enough. I rose from my seat and beckoned him to show me his wound. I grabbed his thumb and squeezed as hard as I could, my teeth clenched as tight as my fist. He roared and tried to pull back but I held on.

'What's the matter with you,' I said. 'Have you seen what's going on in this camp? And you're worried about a fucking bruised thumb.' I let go and thrust his hand away from me, 'You make me sick.'

Eric looked flabbergasted. He backed off, nursing his throbbing thumb. 'Have you gone mad?' he asked.

'Yes, I suppose as a matter of fact I have. This place is making me fucking mad. You're making me fucking mad. Have you even bothered to check the records I asked you about?'

'It's not that simple. I only have prostitute records in here. The other files are in another building. Another clerk handles them.'

Eric reached for a fresh cigarette. He dropped the steel case and the cigarettes rolled across the floor. He scrambled about trying to grab them. One rolled towards me. I slammed my foot down on top of it, missing Eric's fingers by inches. He looked up, slowly, and bit down on his lip. I glared down at him and shifted my gaze towards the filing cabinets.

CHAPTER 57

'Dead? She can't be,' I said to Eric.

'I'm sorry, Nadette.' He through the file down on the desk. 'Here, see for yourself.'

I flipped through the pages of the Nazi document confirming Ariella's death. 'It must be a mistake. Ariella must be alive. She's not dead I'm telling you.' I squeezed his arms and shook him.

'We do not make mistakes. I saw it, you saw it, Ariella Ish-Shalom. I'm sorry. I truly am sorry.'

Eric paced about, wringing his hands. His head down in sympathy.

All that time, all that time. All that abuse. Hanging on for her. Hanging on for Ariella and she was dead. Dead. I felt drained of all energy, my legs wouldn't hold me up anymore. I dropped to my knees, clutched my stomach, until I could no longer hold in the agony. 'Noooo!' I thumped my fists against the wooden floor and burst the sides of my hands. My heart throbbed, ached with excruciating pain, as if at any minute it would burst and explode a river of blood through every orifice. I rolled over into a ball, covered my head with my bleeding hands and wept and wept and wept.

Eric awkwardly patted my head, 'I-I'll try to find the other one. Kolleck, Ester Kolleck wasn't it?'

CHAPTER 58

'Ariella died,' Jana said. 'Remember, Ester?' she said, she was furtively checking the room. The orchestra barracks looked confusing to her. She didn't recognise any faces and they didn't seem to recognise hers. 'Prisoners change duties all the time, you know,' Jana said. 'Sent wherever they're told.'

'You should be in hospital,' Jana said, 'but it's much too dangerous now.'

There wasn't an ounce of her body that didn't ache. She was very weak and delirious.

'I brought you here, Ester, remember?' She didn't remember. Her heart ached and she felt so alone. She didn't understand why.

Jana handed her some hot, dirty water, said it was coffee. The foul taste slid over her throat, warming her up. She told her to eat the black piece of bread that she shoved into her hand. She obeyed but didn't feel any better for it.

The rest of the women rushed into line, stormed the exit. They were laden with musical instruments. Jana dumped a violin and a bow into her arms.

'You must play, Ester,' she said. She wasn't sure she knew how. 'You must find the strength to keep going.' She wasn't sure she knew how to do that either.

They marched in rows towards their station. Jana marched at her side, watched her every move, making sure she didn't collapse. Her legs were buckling under her.

'Keep going, keep going,' Jana whispered. She obeyed, picked up her pace and marched in time with the others.

They stopped outside the shower room and began to play something upbeat. She couldn't remember what it was, but somehow her bow slid across the strings with little effort and produced fine chords.

A group of prisoners tramped towards them. A guard marched them in time. 'You must go for de-lousing,' the guard called out to the gloomy faced women.

'Don't tap your feet, Ester,' Jana said. She was keeping time with their march. One woman lunged at her and spat in her face. She couldn't understand why.

Jana hauled the woman off. 'They're going to the showers, Ester,' she said. A blank expression. Nothing registered.

'They're going to get gassed,' a woman in the orchestra said. 'What's the matter with you?'

'What?' She threw the violin down.

'Pick it up,' the woman next to her said, 'or you'll go too.'

Jana ran at her, thrust the violin into her hands before any other guards noticed. 'Play, for God's sake, play, or all this has been for nothing. Do you understand?'

She stared into Jana's eyes and finally nodded her head.

CHAPTER 59

It was the last night they were to spend in the orchestra barracks. Jana's inside information was right enough, the orchestra members were being transported to Bergen-Belsen. There was no orchestra required there and no special privileges. All musical instruments were to be left behind.

The building was in total darkness, the only sounds were from the snoring inmates and the groans and agony cries from those who were starving, frozen, beaten and with their spirits broken. Their retired musical instruments lay beside their beds as though worn out and relieved to have played their last concerto.

The door creaked open. The camp's swooping lights shone inside the barracks. An SS man timidly poked his head inside. His tunic lay open at the neck and his beer belly hung over his trousers. He twirled his cap in his hand leaving a greasy wave of hair to flop over his face. He tramped carefully indoors, avoiding creaking floorboards. It was as though he was trying not to awake the sleeping inmates.

A few inmates stirred, sat up to see who was entering and lay back down, trembling arms tight around each other. They watched his every move.

'Ester Kolleck?' he said, 'Is there an Ester Kolleck in here?'

A few more sleeping inmates stirred. One woman sat up, rubbed her sleepy eyes and tried to focus.

'Ester Kolleck? Are you Ester Kolleck?' The woman timidly shook her head and lay back down and ducked under her blanket. He tutted and walked to the bottom end of the barracks and stopped.

'I wish to speak to Ester Kolleck,' he said. His voice was louder. 'Is she here?' he asked. 'You have nothing to fear.' Nobody answered. He tried again, 'I have information on Nadette Eichmann for Ester Kolleck. One last time, is she here?'

She was tempted but cowered down under the blanket. He took one last look around. Nobody moved. He sighed and hurried towards the door.

'Wait.'

He stopped abruptly and spun around to peer into her face. 'I'm... I'm Ester,' she said and gasped for breath as she tried to sit up. 'I'm Ester Kolleck.'

He removed his cap, crouched down and swept his dark, greasy hair away from his forehead. Compassion was written across his face as he scanned her battered body. He moved in closer to whisper. He was stinking of cigarette smoke. 'You are a friend of Nadette Eichmann?' he asked. She looked at him hesitantly. 'It's alright,' he said. 'My name is Eric Hagen. I met Nadette. She's alive. She's here in Auschwitz... in the special building.' He bowed his head, as though ashamed.

'The... the brothel? What she's–'

'I'm afraid so,' he said and reached for her hand. His fingers were covered with smelly, food grease. 'But she's alive, Ester.'

She gritted her teeth and clenched her fist. She wanted to get up and punch something or somebody but the anger was using up all her energy. She had to calm down. She ran her hand over her cropped hair, clasped the back of her neck and took long, deep breaths.

'She sent me to find you,' Eric said, 'and your friend Ariella,' he dipped his head again, 'but I'm afraid she's dead.'

His compassion seemed real. She slid her hand over the top of his and gently squeezed. 'I'm, I'm Ariella,' she said. 'Ester is dead.'

He slowly raised his head and glanced at her hand positioned over his, then stared into her eyes with a puzzled look on his face.

'Someone helped me,' she said. 'A good woman.'

'Who? How? Your file says you're dead.'

'I know. I was in the punishment cells for ages. I had been severely beaten by a guard.' She closed her eyes and shook her head, recalling that terrible night when Eva beat her up. 'Another inmate crept into the barracks and stopped her from killing me.'

'Who? How did she manage that? What happened to her?' Eric threw questions faster than she could answer.

'Her name was Sarah. A good woman. Pushed too far I'm afraid. She flogged the evil guard to death and suffered the consequences.'

Eric shook his head as though ashamed at the work of his people. 'But how did you get out?'

'I was sure I was going to die. I was in agony and given only scraps of food for goodness knows how long. Another guard, a good guard, came and got me out. My legs wouldn't hold me. I was so weak she had to drag me from the darkness. And after so long without light, the pain was torture.'

'How did she manage to get you out? Where did she take you?'

'Another guard helped her to carry me out from the punishment cells. It was the middle of the night. The camp was in darkness and very few guards around. She brought me here to the orchestra barracks. To take Ester's place.' She closed her eyes and rubbed her forehead, remembering her dear friend.

'And what happened to Ester? How did you manage to trade places?'

'The guards carried me inside the barracks. One of them, my friend,' she smiled as she thought about Jana and remembered how she wouldn't trust her in the beginning, 'she brought out a file. Ester Kolleck's file and told me I must trade places with her. I was confused and delirious and struggled to focus on the documents. I couldn't understand what she was saying to me. She told me Ester had died in hospital. I couldn't take it in. All I could think about was getting to Ester to save her. My mind was drawing blanks, forgetting how weak and ill Ester had been before she collapsed and was carried off to hospital.'

She struggled to sit up to talk to Eric, gasped for breaths in between sentences. But she had to tell him. He had put himself in jeopardy to find her and report back to Nadette. The least she could do was tell him the truth.

'Why change records though?' he asked.

'I had been working on the railway. There's no way I could continue with the heavy labour but apart from that, the guards there knew about me.' She paused for Eric's reaction. 'They knew about my sexuality. I was to be sent for special treatment.'

'Special treatment.' He shook his head. 'You're lucky you didn't go there. The Doctors carry out experiments on prisoners. Not many survive their evil operations.' He paused, sadness in his eyes and stared at the ground. 'How on earth did you find the strength to keep going?'

'At first I didn't really know what I was doing. I was confused. The guard placed a violin in my hands and told me I must play to survive. I wasn't even sure I knew how to play. I didn't know why I had to survive. I just kept going, doing what I was told. She told me she had been assigned to the orchestra and would look out for me.'

Eric pulled back and lifted her Jewish hand away from his. 'The guard's name?' he said, 'the woman who helped you?' She frowned at the sudden change in his demeanour and stared at him without uttering a word on Jana's identity. He rose from the bed and placed his cap back on. 'Guard,' he shouted.

She tried to scramble to her feet but her feeble body wouldn't hold her up.

She fell back onto the bed. Jana rushed in. 'Sir?' She clicked her heels to attention.

'Is this the guard?' he asked.

She glanced up at Jana and never spoke a word. Jana stared ahead, her chest visibly rose up and down.

'Did you help this woman?' Eric asked her. She signalled to Jana to deny it. Eric reached out and squeezed Jana's shoulder, 'It's alright,' he said, 'you can tell me. You can trust me.'

'Yes, sir,' Jana said. 'I helped her.'

He patted her on the shoulder and smiled as though acknowledging her heroism. 'I need you to take her to the hospital-'

'But, sir,' Jana interrupted. 'What if they find out who she really is? She'll be selected for special treatment.'

'Oh, yes of course. Homosexuals.' Eric chewed on his lip. 'Right. Eh, let me think. You go with her,' he said to Jana. 'I want you to go with her, keep her safe. Won't be for long, the Russians are not too far off. Make sure she's properly cared for... under my orders,' he said and straightened his cap.

CHAPTER 60

Gabriele and Panda were ordered out of the room. Berta dragged them along for another session in the working cells. I lay on my bunk, knees pulled up, once again into the foetal position and rolled Eric's cyanide pill between my fingers. I had burst a hole in the mattress that day I stole it from his medicine cabinet and tucked it inside. Kept it for emergencies.

I stared out of the window, watched the early morning sunrise. Its' faint golden glow suggested a hint of warmth.

Footsteps thumped along the corridor, approached our cell. I didn't even flinch, remained focused on the sunrise. I was going nowhere today. If I lay still, I was sure to have a gun put to my head. If not, there was the kill-pill.

Whoever was outside shuffled about, the door never opened. Something was dropped in through the bars and tumbled to the wooden floor. The footsteps scurried away. I slid the cyanide capsule back in its safe place and dragged myself off the bed to find a piece of paper addressed to me. What the hell? Where did this come from? I unfolded it and gasped when I read the contents. It was a message from Eric with good news of Ariella. I ran over to the window, clutched the bars, stared out at the glorious sunshine and screamed at the top of my voice, 'Yes!'

Footsteps approached the cell again. This time the key clinked in the door. Berta marched back in with Gabriele and Panda.

'What you shouting about?' Berta said and walked over to see what I was looking at outside. I smirked and sauntered away from the window and discreetly shoved the note into my pocket. She looked me up and down as though looking for something suspicious. 'Move it,' she said. She grabbed my arm and pulled me towards the door, 'Got men waiting for you.' I shrugged her off and swayed my hips from side to side and swaggered out of the cell, trying to conceal my beaming grin. Gabriele and Panda came in past me, they frowned at my strange behaviour.

Berta and I marched along the corridor to the working cells. A line of men awaited me. A fat SS man at the top of the queue grinned. My stomach turned. I reached into my pocket to remind me of my good news. There was nothing but a hole in my dress. The paper was gone. Frantically I padded myself down, searching for the precious note. Nothing. I scanned the corridor behind me. It was bare. I was dizzy and felt so sick that I had to cover mouth.

'Make you sick, do I?' the fat SS man said. He was reeking of sweat. He grabbed me by the hair and ran me into the cell and threw me onto the disgusting mattress.

By the time I got back to the room, Gabriele and Panda were flat out on their bunks, exhausted after another session in the working cells.

The piece of paper was nowhere to be seen. Neither of the two worn out women mentioned it and neither did I. My only hope was that it had been swept aside and binned somewhere. Gabriele and Panda looked weak and fatigued and ready to give up, my good news would've been too painful for either of them. They had nobody, no husband and no family waiting for them. They only had themselves to think about.

CHAPTER 61

January 1945

The weeks dragged past. Christmas had been and gone. It meant nothing to us except more drunken SS men and their comrades had visited the brothel, celebrated, popped champagne and brought in the New Year with a bang.

Gabriele, Panda and I still shared the same cell. No further women were thrown in along with us. I hadn't heard anymore from Eric. I stared out of the window and prayed that Ariella was still alive. The snow battered against the glass and piled up thick on the window ledge. The wind howled in through the cracks in the wooden window frame. A fierce storm swept across the camp. Prisoners battled against the powerful white sheet, restricting them as they scurried across the courtyard attending to their duties. Many women collapsed under the strain. The chilling winter was claiming the lives of so many. And it wasn't over yet.

Some women were trailed through the snow to the gallows. They looked as though they had been tortured.

The key turned in the lock behind me. Berta came in.

'Who are those women, Berta?' I asked her and pointed out of the window.

'That's the idiots who smuggled explosives from the armaments factory. Tried to help the Sonderkommandos blow up the crematoriums,' Berta said. She sniggered and peered out past me. 'It's all their fault we were never able to use one of the gas chambers after that.' She scrunched her eyes and stared out at the women. 'Those stupid women never talked. Wouldn't give up the others.'

I stood up straight with admiration, stared at the brave women and felt the tears well in my eyes. How I wished I had their courage.

Berta stepped back from the window and pulled her clipboard up in front of her nose. She didn't need that board. She knew our names. She seemed to have a sordid pleasure in reading from the list and to grin every single time she called out a name.

'Gabriele Feurst. Move it, whore. And you, Becker. Come with me.'

Gabriele lay on her bunk. She was so very weak and stared ahead with a blank expression. She was extremely thin and had been battered over and over. Her face was all lacerations. The pretty red-head I had first met back in the Alexanderplatz prison had been completely destroyed. Her cheek bones stuck out past a mass of bruises and her reddish-brown hair was thin and falling out. She climbed down from the bunk, her frail legs shook as she tried to find her balance. Berta grabbed her and ran her towards the door.

'Move it,' she said, 'and you too, Becker,'

Panda climbed down from her bunk, her crusted hands clung on tight. Her body was diseased and withered. Panda was barely recognisable, her face and torso covered in scabs now.

I felt so helpless watching my two friends, I could only stare and fear for their lives. Gabriele was not far from death and Panda urgently needed medical attention. She was polluted with disease, nobody wanted her. It would take a miracle to save either of the two women's lives.

I clung onto the bars on the cell door and watched Berta drag Gabriele and Panda along the corridor. A queue of pink triangles waited, solemn faced outside a working cell. Kaarl marched up the corridor past the men and stopped in front of Berta.

'This woman claims she has something to tell you, sir,' Berta said. She stood between her two prostitutes.

'Well. Get on with it,' Kaarl said and looked between Gabriele and Panda.

Both women kept their heads down as though in shame. Nobody uttered a word.

'What is it? Do you think I've got all day to stand here and look at you pathetic whores?'

'She said she found a piece of paper this morning, sir. Said it was tucked in between the floorboards, wouldn't tell me what was on it, sir, but said you would be interested.' Berta's voice was quivering. She stood to attention, head held high, as though seeking the approval of the SS Leader.

Oh my God. I felt the energy drain from me and slowly slid down the cell door, but I still clung to the bars, refusing to let go. The voices continued in the corridor but the words were inaudible. I had to get up. I had to know what was going to happen.

'Come with me,' Kaarl said and marched Panda down the corridor. 'Put her in a cell,' he said and ordered Berta to take Gabriele into a nearby working room. Berta obliged and shoved a pink triangle, homosexual man in with Gabriele.

Panda followed Kaarl down the corridor. She shuffled behind him, head bowed down and clutched her flaky hands around her diseased body.

Anger rushed through me, poured into the bars through my tightly squeezed hands. I stood there, helpless, and watched the enemy march off to furnish Kaarl with information on my Ariella. Pins and needles finally forced me to let go and drop to the floor. My stomach was twisted in knots. To come this far. And now this. I felt breathless, gasped for air, rolled over and clutched my aching belly until there were loud, painful sobs.

'Shut up in there,' Berta said. She still paraded the corridor.

The wound was too much, uncontrollable sobs. Berta stormed along the corridor and battered on the cell door. 'Shut up. Shut up, I said.' She hammered and kicked on the door like a mad woman, desperate to silence my screams.

'Leave me alone.'

'There will be no howling in here,' she said and jingled her keys and forced the lock open. She burst into the cell and glared at me, her rubber baton in hand.

She swung her baton, I didn't even care. I waited for the blow, but it never came. Before Berta could lash out with her weapon, she spun around to stare down the corridor. Heavy footsteps thumped across the wooden floor. Berta rushed out and quickly locked me in.

'I sent that scab to be jagged.' It was Kaarl's voice.

Oh no. I remembered what happened in Ravensbrück when a diseased woman came back from the brothel. I felt a stabbing pain in my heart, almost as if I had been given the phenol injection myself.

'Where is she?' Kaarl said.

I was still sitting on the floor, quickly dug my heels in, shuffled backwards and manoeuvred myself away from the approaching voices.

'In here, sir.' I heard Berta, the snake, tell Kaarl my whereabouts.

She rattled her keys once more, but the creaking of the lock opening was further away. I crept across the floor on hands and knees and drew myself up to peer out through the bars on the door.

Kaarl entered the working cell where Gabriele had been tossed. He left the door wide open. The man in the striped suit with pink triangle was ordered out. Berta disappeared with the prisoner along the corridor and out of the building. Presumably she was taking him back to his work station.

'Get up, you lazy whore,' Kaarl said. I imagined poor Gabriele lying practically unconscious on that stinking mattress. There was a dull thud and a long painful moan from Gabriele. I cringed feeling her pain. I just knew he was kicking her. 'Get up. I expect a good performance for these men.'

'No more,' Gabriele's weak voice cried.

There was scuffling inside the cell.

'Sit,' Kaarl ordered Gabriele. 'Straighten yourself up. I want these men sorted out. Get rid of their notion of homosexuality.'

'No,' Gabriele said.

'What did you say?'

Footsteps raced across the floor, he must've ran at her. A few hard smacks told me he was beating Gabriele. 'You'll do as I say.'

'Am takin' no more.'

He slapped and slapped her. A tearing sound of clothing. He was going to rape her. I squeezed the bars tight and bit down on my lip, forced myself not to shout out after him.

'The piece of paper,' Gabriele mumbled, 'I got something to tell you.'

My heart missed a beat.

'Oh yeah? What's so important about this paper?' Kaarl said. He laughed and continued to rip at her clothes.

'I know about Nadette,' Gabriele cried out.

Oh no. And all this time I was blaming Panda.

I listened closer at the door, willed her not to let me down.

The scuffle stopped. Kaarl paid attention. 'What? How do you know Nadette? I sent her to Mauthausen.'

I bit on my thumb nail, stared heavenward, prayed that she wouldn't tell and listened carefully for her reply. Nothing.

Kaarl smacked her again. 'You know nothing,' he said.

Gabriele hissed a reply, 'She's not in Mauthausen and she's still got her lover.'

Oh my God. Why get me this far and then this? I slid down the door, disgusted at my saviour.

'What? No. She will not disappoint me.' I heard him roar at Gabriele and thump into her feeble body. 'What do you know about Nadette and that fucking Jew?'

I held onto the bars again and dragged myself up, forced myself to stand. I had to know how much she was going to tell him.

'Get me outta here first,' Gabriele demanded.

'Don't you barter with me.' Another whack.

'Am dead anyway if I'm here any longer,' Gabriele said. 'You'll never find the Jew. She's under a different name. It's too late, the Russians are coming. If you want her now, then get me out.'

'Aagghh,' Kaarl let out one of his roars.

Kaarl came out from the cell and paced the corridor, rubbed his chin and pouted those thick his lips. Gabriele had him like a cornered rat, forced him to make a decision. He ordered the awaiting queue of homosexual men to about turn and instructed a guard to march them out of the building. He went back into the working cell and was about to close the door.

'Herr Bergmann, Herr Bergmann, sir.' A young soldier ran along the corridor. The cell door swung open and Kaarl popped his head out. 'Herr Bergmann, you're wanted urgently, sir, Herr Himmler wants to see you.'

Kaarl wanted on some other business. That was a relief. He'd be back though. But when?

Berta and another guard dragged Gabriele along the corridor. Her legs wouldn't carry her. Her face was dripping with blood. I ran at her when she arrived back in the cell. 'What have you done?' I said and pulled her from the guards.

'Leave me alone,' she mumbled. Her legs buckled under her, she collapsed against me. I slid to the ground and held her on my lap.

'Why, Gabriele? Why?'

She lay there, motionless, her features hardly recognisable passed the gushing blood. I wanted to grab her by the shoulders and shake her. I wanted to slap some sense into her. How could I? Only a monster could beat her in the state she was in. I looked at her frail, beaten body and wiped away the blood from her face. Her eyes were blackened and swollen where Kaarl had punched her. Her neck had deep, red marks, Kaarl's fingerprints pressed into her throat. I recognised those prints only too well.

I eased her to the floor and dampened a cloth at the wash-hand basin. With slow delicate strokes, I wiped over her blood stained face and cradled the sad, broken woman in my arms. The smell of Kaarl's aftershave reeked from her clothing. Terror tightened my throat and perspiration trickled down my back. I took a few deep breaths, trying to remain calm.

'What makes you so sure he'll let you go free?' I asked.

'I'll tell him nothing until I'm on the other side of that gate. I just got to get out then I can get back to a Berlin brothel where I'll be safe.'

'Gabriele you can do much better than that. You've got to stop hating yourself. All that abuse when you were growing up, it's not your fault. You were just a child.' Tears were in my eyes. 'We are not to blame,' I stared over her shoulder and let my own words sink in.

Gabriele looked at me with mouth hanging open then bowed her head and burst into tears. I held her in my arms, rocked her back and forth and gave her as much love as I possibly could in those few minutes of comfort.

CHAPTER 62

It had been about two weeks and Kaarl still hadn't been back. Perhaps Himmler had sent him elsewhere. Or maybe he had been killed in a bomb explosion. I could only hope.

I stared out past the bars on the window at the magnificent sun rising against the white sky. Snow still lay thick on the ground, the winter sun attempted to melt the hardened surface. If I wasn't trapped in a brothel, I would swear we were wakening up to a glorious day.

Guards blew on whistles, rounded up prisoners and formed them into hundreds of ranks. Rows of worn out, malnourished inmates evacuated their barracks and swarmed the courtyard. They were marched towards the exit through the slushy snow. A clear path towards the way out was becoming apparent.

'Looks like we're being evacuated,' I said to Gabriele. 'You don't have to tell Kaarl anything. We're getting out.'

Gabriele sat on the bunk, head down and her legs dangling over the side. She fidgeted with her hands.

The key rattled in the lock. Berta burst into the room. 'Feurst, Get ready. I'll be back in half an hour. It's your lucky day.' Gabriele climbed down from the bunk and stared at the floor without uttering a word.

'Where are they taking us?' I asked Berta.

'The camp's being evacuated. Everybody must march to camps in the West away from the Russians. They're getting nearer,' Berta said. 'She's being released.' She nodded to Gabriele who paced the floor, wringing her hands. 'For some reason, Herr Bergmann wants her out. You'll be marched to another camp with that lot out there.'

'You don't need to go now,' I whispered to Gabriele. 'You don't need to tell him anything.' I grabbed hold of her, begged her. 'The camp's being emptied. We'll march side by side. Get out the brothel together, Gabriele.'

'It's a death march, Eichmann,' Berta said, 'about 35 miles to Wodzislaw. Long days, long nights, trudging through deep snow. Stop and you're shot.' She laughed and continued, 'They don't expect many to make it to the other side. Do you think she can cope with that, Eichmann?' Berta slammed the door shut.

'I'll never make it,' Gabriele said. 'This is my only chance.' She sat on the edge of the bed, eagerly waiting for Berta to return. I paced the room and then stopped abruptly. A solution. Why hadn't I thought of it before?

'I've got some spare bread I'll give you for the journey,' I said and wandered over to my bed. The cyanide pill was discreetly removed from its hiding place in the mattress.

Gabriele sat with her head down. I snapped the capsule and emptied its contents into a tin cup.

'Here, some water,' I said and handed her the cup and a treasured piece of bread. 'Eat it now, give you some strength.'

She reached out, trusting her cell mate and grabbed the cup. What was I doing? What was I thinking about? This wasn't me. I quickly faked a stumble, knocked the cup from her hand and spilled the lethal liquid over the floor. Gabriele grabbed the bread and shoved it into her mouth before I could change my mind.

The key in the lock again. Berta returned. 'Let's go, Feurst.'

Gabriele rose to her feet and proceeded towards the door with Berta. I rushed after her, grabbed her hand and hauled her back into the cell. Berta swiped her strong arm against my chest and knocked me backwards to the floor. She trailed Gabriele out of the cell before I could get back up and quickly locked the door. I ran at the bars, clung on and begged Gabriele to reconsider. She kept her head down. All I could think about was Ariella and what Kaarl was going to do to her. I felt washed out, depleted of all energy, lightheaded and woozy. I clasped hold of the bars, trying to stop myself from passing out.

'Gabriele, please don't do this,' I struggled to speak. 'I thought you were my friend?'

At last she turned to face me, 'We do what we got to do to survive, right?'

She hurried away down the corridor then stopped abruptly. She reached into her pocket and pulled something out and snapped her hand shut as though hiding it from Berta. She shoved Berta aside and rushed back towards me.

Gabriele took my hand in hers and dropped a gold chain into my palm. It was my necklace, Ariella's necklace. I stared at the jewel then back to Gabriele, 'You?'

'Might as well have this back. It's brought me nothing but bad luck since I stole it.'

I stared at the precious gift. Then it dawned on me, it wasn't gifted to her. Is that why she was struggling to survive the darkest days? The story of the necklace couldn't be true – could it?

Gabriele looked at me and for the first time, I didn't see coldness. I saw true remorse. 'I'm sorry,' she said. And I knew she meant it, for everything.

I slid down the door, still clutching the bars and listened to Gabriele march along the corridor. She wasn't going to get out. I knew that. Kaarl would get the information he needed from her and then plant a bullet in her brain.

I squeezed tight on the necklace, closed my eyes and tried to draw strength from its power. Was I going mad, believing in the heirloom? Believing in its history?

CHAPTER 63

It seemed like an eternity, that short while I sat behind the door, my heart aching, my head swimming, thinking of ways to reach Ariella.

Footsteps thumped along the corridor. I used all the strength I had left to pull myself up.

Berta grabbed the bars, poked her smug face through and gloated in at me. I was ready to reach out and throttle her but I had a better idea.

'Oh, Berta,' I said and frowned in sympathy, staring at her swollen, weather-beaten hands, 'you're hurting,' I said, rubbed over the hacks and stared into her eyes. I forced a smile.

'What the...' Berta said, jerking her hand away. Only a fraction. I reached out again. She was blushing. Her breathing was fast as though tingling at my touch, wanting more. Her tense hand gradually relaxed and opened into mine. I caressed it, massaged the swelling and looked into her eyes, 'I can ease your suffering.'

Berta was transfixed. She was glowing, 'Take my pain away?' She wasn't asking. She was begging.

I touched Berta's arm, stroked it with delicate finger-tips, and stared into her eyes. 'Yes, Berta. Open up,' I said and glanced towards the door.

Berta fumbled with the keys. She dropped them from her shaking hands, they clattered to the ground. At last, she threw the cell door open and charged into the room. I forced a broad smile and reached out for Berta's hand and pulled her towards me. Her breathing was loud and fast, panting heavily. I wrapped my arms around her broad body and snuggled into her neck. Her wrestler's arms held me tight. She clumsily patted my hair, like a child learning to stroke a puppy for the first time. 'Oh, Nadette. This is so wrong.'

I pulled back to look into Berta's eyes and forced a smile again, 'No, Berta, it's natural.' I kissed her softly across her cheeks, down her face and onto her lips. I nestled into her neck again with soft kisses, barely touching her skin. Berta swooned in ecstasy and let herself be guided to the bed. I unbuttoned her cape, it tumbled to the floor. I reached for her uniform and unfastened the buttons. Berta's clumsy, shaking hands assisted. I guided her to the bottom bunk and climbed on top of her. Her chest was heaving. Her mouth gaped wide, she stared up at me, waiting for my next move. I lowered myself down closer. She moaned, feeling my warmth press against her. I closed my eyes as my mouth met hers. She groaned moving her lips in motion against mine.

I curled my fingers in towards my palm, jolted back from her slobbery lips and with a swift uppercut to Berta's chin, I knocked her out.

'Sorry for that, Berta,' I said. I meant it. Without wasting anymore time, I removed Berta's uniform.

CHAPTER 64

The corridor was empty. Cell doors swung back and forth. A whistling breeze hurled in past the open door to the abandoned brothel. Every working cell, deserted. Worn out mattresses lay redundant, relieved of duty, glad to see their last customer and their last sperm donations. The smell of unwanted sex lingered in the air and the agony screams from raped women haunted the cells, leaving an unforgettable scar on the memory of anyone who passed through the doors.

Eric's office was still functional. He sat behind his desk, filtering through piles of documents when I barged into his space. He looked shocked when he saw me in that ridiculous, ill-fitting uniform.

'Sorry,' he said, when I begged for his help one more time. 'There's nothing I can do.'

'Sorry? That's it?' Hands on my hips. 'You must be able to do something?'

He paced up and down, dragging on a cigarette. 'No. Can't do it,' he said with a slight tremor in his voice. 'Kaarl, he'll, he'll come after me,' he said and ran his hand through his greasy hair.

'If Kaarl gets to Ariella first he'll kill her.' My nose was inches from his.

'No. I've done enough,' he said and continued to pace the floor.

I took a deep breath, walked towards him and touched his arm. 'We're all scared, Eric.' He raised his shaking hand up to wave me away. 'You're a strong man, Eric,' I said to bolster his ego. He smirked. He could see through my lie. 'You are, Eric. Ariella's safe because of you.' At least that part was true.

'Hmmm for now,' he said. He seemed much more relaxed and walked across the floor and stubbed out the cigarette. 'You know what will happen if they catch you?'

I smiled, threw the guard's cape around my shoulders before he could change his mind. 'What about Berta?' My concern was genuine.

'Hmmm. Don't worry about her. I'll let her out later. Send her on the march.'

We stepped outside the brothel. I placed the guard's cap on to complete the hideous outfit and walked onto the main ground.

'Get in line. Quick,' guards screamed and shouted at the inmates who poured onto the snowy courtyard. Swarms of matchstick bodies flooded the grounds, slipping and sliding in the deep snow as they rushed to join their allocated lines.

The Auschwitz gates were wide open. Armed SS men surrounded the hundreds of prisoners who marched away from the horrors of the concentration camp to unknown territory. The prisoners looked sad and gloomy as though daring not to hope for a better life.

Eric and I marched past the shouting guards and scurrying inmates. Anxiety tightened my windpipe making it hard to breathe, let alone talk. I could only force a high-pitched squeak when I spoke to Eric. 'Useless Jews,' I said and forced a laugh, 'better to leave them here. Let them starve to death.'

Eric bit on his lip. He was scanning the camp, as if he expected to get caught when we passed clusters of soldiers on our way to the hospital. I spun around and glared at him.

'Yes, yes,' he said, 'I agree.'

On the far side of the courtyard, I was sure I saw Kaarl shove his way through the crowds. Prisoners rushed out from a nearby barracks, Kaarl was engulfed in the swarm.

I stayed focused on the hospital sign while Eric and I marched across the courtyard and chatted away like camp comrades.

When we entered the hospital we stopped dead on our tracks and scanned the room. The windows were all barred but there was no other means of security. The guards had abandoned the diseased and withering women who occupied rows of beds.

A cast iron stove in the centre emitted very little heat. I rubbed my shivering hands together and watch streams of my hot breath diffuse through the stinking air. The combined stench of urine, vomit, faeces and death dominated the surroundings making it impossible not to gag.

'Use this,' Eric said and pulled a handkerchief from his pocket. I covered my nose to mask the odours.

We walked past the patients and searched for Ariella. Women groaned, crouched in a ball and clutched their stomachs, starvation pain was horrendous. Others were battered and bruised, ring cuts on their faces and torsos. Some women nursed open, infected wounds, others lay stitched up and moaned in agony. Nazi Doctors had probably performed experimental operations.

My eyes filled as I walked among the near dead. To most of them, death would be a blessing. I scanned the beds in hope and prayed that Ariella was alive but not in this state of despair.

Eric stopped and bent over a patient and reached out to take her hand in his. She was motionless and her eyes stared wide. Eric shook his head in sorrow, her limp hand slid from his clutches and dangled over the side. He pulled the thin blanket over her head.

I walked up and placed a comforting hand on his shoulder. In the bed next to the dead woman, a prisoner's eyelids flickered, tried to focus on us. Her hair was cropped short, her face was drawn in and her eyes were sunken deep beneath black rings. She looked no different to any other corpse in the hospital. I hurried on to the next bed to search through the almost identical skeletons. Something made me stop. I spun back to the frail woman. Her brown eyes were open, she blinked over and over and stared at me. Oh my God. I realised who it was. She didn't recognise me. She closed her eyes tight and raised her feeble hands up to shield her face as though anticipating another beating. I clasped my hand across my chest, remembering I was standing in that ferocious guard's uniform. I bent down over her and eased her hands back from her face, 'Ariella. It's okay, it's me,' I whispered.

She let me guide her hands away and blinked repeatedly, still trying to focus. My heart was breaking looking at the state of her. Warm tears slid down the side of my face, I leaned in closer to hold her, careful not to squeeze her delicate, bony frame. My necklace, Ariella's necklace dangled down across her face. She gasped, reached out to grab it and tried to push herself up. 'Nadette?'

'Yes, it's me, angel. Sshh, don't try to talk. Save your strength.'

She wrapped her feeble arms around me and burst into tears. I had never heard her cry so hard, in fact, I had never heard her cry at all. I held her close in my arms. Her shoulders shook, she wept hard and heavy sobs. I rubbed her back and patted her, she was like an inconsolable baby with severe inner pain that no one could understand.

At last, I pulled away and eased her back down to rest. 'Sshh, baby. It's okay,' I said. 'What have they done to you?' I said and gritted my teeth. She gaped up at me, eyeing my angry face and ugly uniform. She was probably wondering the same thing.

The hospital door swung open and battered against the wall. An eerie breeze howled in. Kaarl Bergmann stepped inside, his long, army coat drooped over his shoulders. He swaggered from side to side, paraded through the passageways and scanned the faces of the diseased women. 'Ish-Shalom. Ariella Ish-Shalom,' he shouted. 'I know you're in here.'

We were up at the top end of the building. He didn't seem to notice us at first. I froze, terrified to move an inch. Eric appeared out of the shadows and walked towards him, 'C-C'mon Kaarl, take it easy,' Eric said. His hands were up in surrender.

Kaarl elbowed Eric in the ribs. 'Move. Useless slob.'

Eric fell to the floor and lay doubled up, winded and gasped for breath.

Kaarl slowed his pace when he approached me. He frowned in confusion. 'Nadette? What the...' he said and pointed to guard's uniform. He stared at me, long and hard, examining my scrawny face.

He covered his mouth, sadness in his eyes, as though he regretted sending me to a concentration camp brothel. He tilted his head to the side in sympathy, turned his palm up and edged his fingers softly under my chin. A tear ran down his face. He quickly turned away to wipe it.

Kaarl's sympathy was short lived. He straightened his shoulders, head back and looked under the rim of his all-important cap. 'I followed orders,' he said, as though convincing himself he did the right thing. He reached for his holster and brought out a black Luger. I took a step backwards and spread out my trembling arms to shield Ariella.

'Come on, let's go home,' he said and moved towards the bed, 'we'll finish her off and forget about this whole episode.'

The adrenalin rushed. I clenched my fists, tightened my arms as strong as I could manage and leaned right back against the bed to protect Ariella. 'No!'

Kaarl's lip twitched and his eyes grew wider. He ran at me and grabbed my arm, 'You're coming with me.'

I yanked my arm back and finally mustered the strength to tell him, 'I don't want you, I want Ariella.'

He stepped back, stared at me as though I had lost my mind. 'What is this... nonsense?' he said and wafted his hand in the air at Ariella. 'Have you not been rehabilitated yet?'

'We can't be converted, Kaarl. It's the way we are.'

He grabbed my arm, squeezed his fingernails tight into my skin. 'Come with me.' He paused and tilted his head to look at me. 'You love me.' His sad eyes lingered, waiting for my response. Years of boiling rage bubbled up inside me. I lifted his arm and shoved him away.

'I never loved you,' I said. 'I stayed with you because I was too afraid to leave you... back then.'

Kaarl let out one of his roars, lunged at me and shoved me away from the bedside. His powerful hands were enough to knock me off my feet. I stumbled, bumped my head off the wooden bedpost and slid to the floor. I tried to scramble to my feet but my head was throbbing and I was seeing double.

Kaarl pointed his gun at Ariella and I couldn't get up. Eric seemed to appear from nowhere and dived on Kaarl from behind. He grabbed Kaarl's wrist and forced the Luger to go flying onto the bed. Kaarl elbowed Eric in the ribs then punched into his fat beer-belly until he was forced to the ground, gasping for breath. He turned and dived on Ariella's throat and squeezed his thick fingers around her tiny neck. 'Die!' he shouted, his face contorted with rage as he proceeded to try and strangle the last remaining breath from Ariella.

I crawled along the floor, tried to stand up but I was too dizzy. Ariella tried to push Kaarl off, she was too weak. She glanced at Eric, begging him to help her. Eric looked dazed as well. He managed to regain control of his breathing, staggered to his feet and hobbled around the other side of the bed. Eric grabbed Kaarl's fingers and tried to prise them from Ariella's throat. Kaarl's grip was too tight and Ariella was losing consciousness.

I caught sight of my baton across the floor, crawled onto my knees, scrambled to reach it and forced myself to my feet. The room was spinning, somehow I managed to focus and swing the baton and smacked it as hard as I could across the back of Kaarl's neck. He fell backwards and crashed his skull on the concrete floor.

Ariella clutched her throat, panting for air. Eric threw his clumsy arms around her shoulders to comfort her.

Kaarl lay on the ground, dazed. I threw the baton across the hard floor and ran at him. His army coat lay open, his groin exposed. I raised my foot high in the air, still wearing my heavy guard's boots. 'Since I was fifteen years old. No more.' I stamped between his legs.

He lay curled in a ball, clasped his genitals and groaned in agony.

Something caught my eye. It was Kaarl's Luger tucked in at the bottom of Ariella's bed. I walked over and grabbed the gun.

Kaarl tried to focus through his obvious pain. His all-important cap lay on the ground beside him.

I walked across the concrete floor towards the whimpering Kaarl. I towered over him, stared into his evil eyes then booted his cap with full force and knocked it high into the air.

I needed both hands to hold the heavy pistol and raise the barrel up to look down its sights. With one eye closed, I pointed the gun with dead aim at the centre of his forehead.

Kaarl's hands were up in front of his face. He peeked through a gap in his fingers. 'N-No, Nadette. Please don't do it.'

I gloated, loved every minute, watching him plead for his life. I had no mercy. I had had enough. My fingers curled in slow motion, squeezing the trigger. But a hand reached over the top of mine. It was Ariella. She had managed to scramble to her feet and crept up behind me. 'Nadette,' she said softly, 'you're not like him.'

I was focused on my enemy, head tilted to the side, one eye still shut, still aiming the gun at his head. 'He'll keep coming back.'

'You'll never be free of him this way,' Ariella said.

Eric edged around the bed. 'It's over, Nadette,' he said. 'The Russians are on their way. We'll lock him up, let them deal with him. Come on, Nadette, put the gun down.'

Ariella curled her hand around the gun's barrel and tried to ease it away. I yanked the gun back and knocked her hand aside.

'Look, it's over, Nadette, we can have a future,' Ariella said.

I wouldn't budge.

'Come on, girl.' She stared into my face, begged me, 'Let it go. You're not one of them,' she said.

Her words were like an electric shock shuddering through me. What had I become? I wasn't like him or any of the evil surrounding us. The Luger still pointed at my prisoner. Kaarl lay on the floor, still clutching his groin. I stared at the pistol, turned my hand to loosen the grip and let the gun lie slack in my palm until it slid from my fingers. Ariella grabbed it and threw it onto the bed. I snapped the ferocious cape from my shoulders and dropped it to the floor and wrapped my arms around Ariella.

She snuggled into my neck, her short, dark hair brushed against my face. I nuzzled against her skin. Despite her sorry state, I could still smell my Ariella.

All of a sudden, she drew back, gasped and stared past my shoulder. I pulled back from her trembling body and spun around. Kaarl had scrambled to his feet. His face twisted in a jealous rage. He reached inside his long, army coat and pulled out a spare pistol and pointed it straight at us. 'My war isn't over,' he said.

The gunshot rattled through the hospital barracks and stirred the sleeping patients. A few sat up, others cowered under the blankets.

Ariella gasped. Her eyes closed. Her body, limp in my arms.

'Ariella. Ariella. Please. Noooo.' I eased her down to the ground and studied her face, her head, her body, checking for wounds, checking for blood. Nothing. I patted her face, 'Ariella. Ariella. Wake up.' Her eyes slowly opened, I pulled her into my arms and squeezed her tight. 'Oh thank God. Thank God you're okay.'

Kaarl landed on the floor, clutching the bullet wound to his shoulder. His pistol lay on the ground. Eric stood above Kaarl, gloated over him and held a smoking gun.

'You're the one who is a disgrace to the German people,' Eric said, the same as Kaarl had once told him. He shoved his gun back into its holster and stood up straight and tidied his uniform before carefully placing his cap back on. Then Eric turned to see that we were alright.

Kaarl crawled onto his hands and knees and slithered across the floor like a creeping panther sneaking towards its victim. His eyes never left mine as he stretched and curled his fingers, inching towards that spare pistol. Then with a quick swipe of his paw, he clasped his gun and spun around to shoot me.

I dived onto the bed and snatched the black Luger and without further hesitation, I pointed the gun at Kaarl and squeezed the trigger. He was lying flat out on the concrete floor, his piercing blue eyes staring ahead. The hand that held the gun, fell back, palm open and his weapon tumbled to the floor. A stream of blood trickled from his mouth. His other hand fell away and exposed a blood spattered, gunshot wound to his stomach.

CODE 998 PRISONER

The hospital door swung open again. A guard rushed in, probably in response to the gunfire. It was Jana. Why was she still in the camp?

CHAPTER 65

'Jana, why are you still here? I thought you would be on the march?' Eric asked.

'I managed to get out of it. I came back to see what I could do. Looks like matters are under control here,' she said and nodded to the dead Kaarl.

'Nadette Eichmann,' I said and shook her hand. 'I can't thank you enough for helping Ariella.'

Jana looked me up and down, sadness in her eyes, 'Wish I could've done something for you.'

'You can,' Eric said. 'Help me dispose of this garbage.'

They grabbed Kaarl's body and dumped it on the ground alongside the other decaying dead. I stood over him, stared at my tormentor and dusted my hands together before throwing his cap on top of his rotten corpse.

'C'mon lets go,' Eric said and grabbed my arm. 'Turn away from him.'

We walked away and headed back among the dying patients.

'They're all being left here, not fit for the march,' Eric said. 'Will you be okay till the Russians arrive? There's no saying when they'll get here.'

I walked over to Ariella. She lay back on the bed, resting. She needed strength to survive those remaining dark days in the concentration camp hospital. I fastened the precious jewel back around her neck. Well, you never know.

'We'll be okay,' I said. 'I'm not leaving her side.'

Eric pulled some chocolate from his pocket and handed it to me. I was drooling, imagining I could smell the sugary delight. 'It's all I have,' he said with a guilty expression. 'Forgive me, please, but I think we should flee. C'mon, Jana,' he said.

I touched his shoulder and smiled warmly at him. 'You're a good man, Eric.' I meant it.

Eric stood with his head down, biting his lip, 'You don't understand…' he raised his head, scanned the room, 'I played a part in this.'

'Eric, we're alive because of you. And you, Jana. People will know,' I said and looked at them both and smiled.

'I would just like to say goodbye to Ariella,' Jana said. Ariella stirred and squeezed Jana's hand. She couldn't thank her enough for everything she had done to help her. Jana bent over and kissed her gently on the forehead before giving her a farewell hug.

I threw my arms around Eric's neck and squeezed him tight. He patted my back and eased himself away. He reached over to a vacant bed and grabbed a blanket and slipped it around my shoulders.

'Stay warm,' he said and smiled. I knew what he meant.

CHAPTER 66

Berlin, summer 1945

Berlin was in ruins. Buildings were demolished. Years of architectural beauty, reduced to rubble. The population greatly diminished. Millions of innocent people perished, murdered through the evil that crept across the land, infecting and polluting the minds of many.

Still, the sun came up. The bright glowing fire lit up the sky, brightening the remaining buildings that had survived the bomb blasts before Germany capitulated. The glowing sun radiated warmth across the faces of the survivors, bringing a hope for a brighter future to the despondent residents of Berlin.

The sun shone through our small apartment window. I was hot, perspiration soaking my dress. I walked across the bare floorboards to open a window. For just a moment, I studied the bar-free, glass panes before pushing the window open to a beautiful day.

Ariella sunk into our battered, leather sofa. Her arms dropped across the back, her necklace dangled and sparkled in the sunlight. The colour was restored to her face and her body was regaining its shape, even her dark hair looked healthy and strong.

'I don't understand why they all could be so full of hatred,' Ariella said.

I walked back from the window and picked up my black triangle, brought back from the camp. 'You'd be surprised how easily people are brainwashed with other's beliefs,' I said and stared at the black symbol, 'and how people can actually be taught to hate anyone who's different.'

'But mass murder? Experiments? Prostitution?'

I rubbed the triangle between my fingers, remembering the insult of us all being labelled and suffering the designated punishment for our category distinction.

'The hatred is indoctrinated, Ariella,' I said without tearing my eyes away from the black fabric between my fingertips. 'They actually believe they're doing the world a favour by getting rid of anybody they think is of lesser value than themselves.' I turned my attention to Ariella. 'People can change though,' I said.

'And we must, all of us,' Ariella said. 'Lessons must be learned from the millions who have suffered. We must somehow re-educate others to stop their hatred and teach them to accept that we are all different in some way or another.'

I reached out and squeezed her hand. A warm glow spread across my heart just touching her skin. I sat the triangle down beside her. 'We can only live in hope, Ariella.'

'It's all there is,' Ariella said, reminding me of Ester's last words to her, 'and we can start with this,' she picked up the black triangle, sparked a match, set fire to the fabric and left it to fizzle out in a glass ashtray.

I leaned in against her and kissed her gently. The crumbling remains of the black triangle disintegrated, and a thin puff of hatred dispersed into the air.

EPILOGUE

Homosexuality between men remained a criminal offence in Germany until 1969 when the Law was liberalized. Many men served the remainder of their sentence in prison after enduring the horrors of the concentration camps.

Paragraph 175 of the German Criminal Code was not completely repealed until 1994.

In 1985 homosexuals were finally recognised as victims of Nazis but did not receive any compensation until the new millennium.

Brothel women on the other hand, despite suffering severe physical and mental damage, did not receive recognition from the German State as victims of sex slavery and NONE OF THEM received compensation for their ordeal.

This book is therefore dedicated to these women as a belated recognition of their suffering. And in their memory, a donation from every new copy of this book purchased will be sent to the NSPCC, helping to prevent sex trafficking.

SOURCES OF REFERENCE

There were many years of research to ensure the accuracy of detail in this novel and it would take almost another book to list the references. I have therefore condensed the list to some of the main sources which provided me with much information on this seldom discussed topic.

***

A very dear friend, and Holocaust survivor, Dorrith M Sim, talked to me on a regular basis about her childhood in Nazi Germany. She was sent to Scotland on the Kinder transport by her parents who later sadly died in Auschwitz. Dorrith published a children's book, *In My Pocket* (All Books for Children, 1996). Sadly Dorrith passed away but not without living a full and well-spared life. Dorrith gave me the sense of feeling for a Jew living in such fear.

Another Holocaust survivor, Johanna-Ruth Dobschiner, whom I met many years ago, talked about her escape from the Nazis and losing her family to the concentration camp horrors. Johanna published, *Selected to Live* (Lowe and Brydon, Norfolk, 1969). Johanna provided me with information on what life was like for a Jew in hiding.

Corrie Ten Boom, another Holocaust survivor who wrote *The Hiding Place* (Hodder and Stoughton and Christian Literature Crusade, 1972). Corrie's story gave me an insight into the appalling conditions of the Ravensbrück concentration camp. Corrie tells the story of her imprisonment along with her sister for helping Jews. Initially I wanted Ester in my story to be Ariella's sister but the pain was too hard to imagine.

An Italian, Jewish journalist, Liana Millu, was arrested in 1944 and deported to Auschwitz-Birkenau. She wrote the book, *Smoke Over Birkenau* (Northwestern University Press, 1986). Liana's heartbreaking story about Jews and other inmates whom she worked alongside, helped me to understand the backbreaking duties of the workforce and the overcrowded, disease ridden sleeping quarters in Birkenau. As well as this, Liana's book first brought the Puffkommando to my attention which I realise was in Auschwitz I, but for the sake of my story line, I created an identical fictional one in Auschwitz Birkenau.

The Blessed Abyss (Wayne State University Press, Detroit, Michigan, 48201., 2000) written by Nanda Herbermann, a religious German who resisted Nazism. Her memoir provided much information on the inside of the Alexanderplatz prison in Berlin and in the prostitutes block in Ravensbrück concentration camp.

Days of Masquerade, Life Stories of Lesbians During the Third Reich (Columbia University Press, 1996) by Claudia Schoppmann. Despite the fact that lesbians were excluded from Paragraph 175 of the German Criminal Code, these interviews confirm that they were persecuted and forced into hiding, marriage or sent to concentration camps.

As well as many more books, numerous World War II documentaries also helped me to understand the movement of the Nazis and the Allies which helped me to create an accurate timeline of events.

The Internet, of course, was an invaluable tool which confirmed details on my existing findings. There were hundreds of websites searched to give me a true account of life in Berlin during that era, the treatment in the concentration camps, as well as contact details for people in Germany who were also researching this topic.

The white flag system mentioned in this book is based on the work of Doctor Eugene Lazowski, a hero who saved the lives of thousands of Jews.

The incident with the bucket and the Alsatian dogs is in memory of an eighteen year old victim who sadly is remembered only by the name of 'Jo'.

The heroic women who smuggled gunpowder from the munitions factory for the Sonderkommandos revolt, and despite their torture, never gave up the identity of their comrades, were Regina Safirsztain, Ala Gertner, Roza Robota and Ester Wajcblum.

Printed in Great Britain
by Amazon